FALLEN
ANGELS

ALSO BY CONNIE DIAL

Internal Affairs
The Broken Blue Line

FALLEN ANGELS

CONNIE DIAL

The Permanent Press
Sag Harbor, NY 11963

For information, address:
  The Permanent Press
  4170 Noyac Road
  Sag Harbor, NY 11963
  www.thepermanentpress.com

Library of Congress Cataloging-in-Publication Data

Dial, Connie–
    Fallen angels / Connie Dial.
        p. cm.
    ISBN 978-1-57962-274-9
        1. Police—California—Los Angeles—Fiction. 2. Los Angeles
    (Calif.)—Fiction. I. Title.

PS3604.I126F35 2012
813'.6—dc23   2011051392

Printed in the United States of America.

To Paula and Patricia Milazzo

ONE

Captain Josie Corsino stood near the open door and studied the dead girl's face. She'd seen plenty of corpses during her twenty-one years with the Los Angeles Police Department, but still thought it was odd the way each victim had such a unique expression—fear, surprise, anger, resignation—but this was new: the dead girl was smiling.

What dying people thought or saw in the last few seconds before vacant stares signaled cognitive life had gone forever was something that always fascinated Josie. Despite all the claims by those Sunday morning television evangelists, she knew there was really only one way to find out. She wasn't that curious.

The victim looked young, maybe early teens, but a premature beauty with thick blond hair, perfect skin and a well-developed figure flaunted in tight designer jeans and a spandex halter top. At the moment, the girl smelled like sour milk and was unattractively sprawled on the couch in this living room with a bloody gaping hole in her right temple and her brains splattered all over the wallpaper. A chrome-plated semi-automatic handgun lay on the floor between a leather ottoman and her lifeless fingers.

"Recognize her, Captain?" A uniformed sergeant asked from the doorway. It was three A.M. and Josie was having trouble recognizing the sergeant. She looked at his name tag, Richards.

"You work Hollywood, Sergeant Richards?" She thought she knew most of her patrol guys even though they transferred in and out every month—the chief's clever shell game designed to fool the public into thinking there were lots of cops on the streets as he shifted warm bodies from division to division riding the crime waves.

"No ma'am, Rampart, but it was quiet tonight so I rolled on the call. I know this place."

She nodded at him and thought, cops, we're all alike . . . little kids chasing fire trucks and sirens. The Hollywood Hills party house. Josie knew it too. Her vice and narcotics detectives had conducted more than a dozen investigations at this house for high-priced prostitution and drug parties.

The lab squints and a few detectives had gathered in the kitchen waiting for the coroner. Lieutenant Tony Ibarra looked up when she entered.

"You recognize her?" Ibarra asked.

"No, but I guess I'm the only one who doesn't," she said.

"Hillary Dennis," Ibarra said, looking surprised by her ignorance when she shrugged. "She's one of those up and coming kiddie movie stars, making millions between drug and alcohol binges."

"Sorry," Josie said. She didn't follow Hollywood gossip and only watched classic black and white movies on television. "It's late; I'm tired. Tell me again why you need me here."

"Headline stuff," Ibarra said, giving her the "duh" look.

"A teenager's suicide?"

"Who said it was a suicide? It's a homicide, and she's a movie star."

"I saw the gun near her body . . . you got the shooter?" Josie never understood why Ibarra couldn't just tell her the whole story instead of feeding it to her piecemeal and forcing her to ask endless questions to get information he knew she needed. He was a middle-aged man but behaved like an old querulous woman. His promotion to lieutenant came late in his career and he never seemed entirely comfortable in the position, but that didn't stop him from stepping up, taking charge and making terrible decisions. He was shorter than Josie and she felt he always tried to stand anywhere but next to her. With his small stature, lean body and tendency to mumble, Ibarra seemed to fade into the background when she was anywhere in the room. His parents were

Cuban, and his one valuable asset to her division was his ability to speak fluent Spanish.

"Don't know. It was a party, but the cockroaches scattered. We caught the stupid one, but he claims he's just the caretaker and doesn't know who else was here. We'll test his hands for gunshot residue, but I don't think he did it," Ibarra said.

Josie slid her slender frame onto the bench in the breakfast nook without asking Ibarra why he thought the caretaker wasn't involved. She was done with him and started checking out the room. It was a gourmet kitchen with a huge granite-top island, sub-zero refrigerator, and two professional stoves. She loved to cook and felt a touch of envy. Her kitchen was 1950's vintage, big but designed by Betty Crocker or some other ancient woman of that era. Somebody put a lot of money into this place since the last time she saw it. Thinking about the kitchen was a nice distraction. She hated dealing with Ibarra, but for now he was in charge of all her detectives. His people knew their jobs, but he insisted on sticking his nose in their business, making things more complicated than they needed to be. She would talk to Red Behan later when she got to her office at Hollywood station. He was the homicide investigators' immediate supervisor who usually managed to get things done despite Ibarra's oversight.

"Who's living here, now?" she asked. "Is this still a party rental?"

"Nope, according to the caretaker some big-deal downtown attorney bought it the end of last year. He's in New York on business."

The caffeine deprivation headache was drilling like a jackhammer in Josie's brain. She would call press relations and have them prepare something for the media. The hordes would eventually discover the identity of the victim. Ibarra should've handled it, but he wouldn't or couldn't. It was easier for him to dump his responsibilities on her, so he could continue playing detective.

"Did you notify the bureau?" she asked but knew the answer.

"Not yet."

Josie said she would make the notifications and take care of the media. She knew Ibarra was delegating up, but everything would get done right if she did it. She'd been stuck with him since she took command of Hollywood division less than a year ago, but had learned to work around his incompetence. She was too busy to do his job, but it was especially important now to make him look good. The captain at Wilshire division wanted a detective commanding officer who spoke Spanish. Josie knew he'd try to steal the bilingual Ibarra if she could make him seem halfway competent. It was a difficult task, and Ibarra wasn't helping.

HOLLYWOOD STATION was nearly empty when Josie arrived. She'd left Ibarra at the crime scene gossiping with a busty neighbor who looked like somebody who used to be famous . . . skeletally skinny and surgically altered. Josie waved at the graveyard shift watch commander who looked irritated that the captain would dare show up on his watch. If Josie came in this early, it usually meant she wanted to talk to him or look over his shoulder to see what he actually did for his paycheck. Josie knew Lieutenant Howard Owens worked in the middle of the night to avoid her. She'd inherited him as well as Ibarra from her predecessor. She gave him a hard time because he was lazy and had made it known he didn't like having a female boss. Eventually she'd have to deal with Owens, but kept prodding him hoping he'd either get better or retire. The rest of her lieutenants had proven to be topnotch, but Ibarra and Owens were useless and a constant source of irritation.

Owens should have retired years ago, but the money was too good. This guy was a prime example of why she hated DROP, the city's deferred retirement plan. It was another bureaucratic Ponzi scheme designed to make the department look bigger, with a lot of dead weight kept afloat with the promise of more money after retirement.

He was in her office before she could close the door.

"What's up, Howard?" she asked, feigning interest.

"Somebody's gonna have to deal with all the calls we're getting on this homicide. I haven't got time to babysit every reporter who needs a thirty-second sound bite. I got real work to do . . ."

"Give them to me," she said, interrupting him. "I'll handle the press, and why don't you ask a day watch supervisor to have his team relieve your guys at the crime scene before they go up to roll call so you can all go home on time?" Josie crossed her arms and waited. Owens was a big man, taller than her, and she was nearly six feet. He had thinning blond hair that never looked combed and a receding chin that disappeared into his flabby neck. He seemed to enjoy complaining, and she'd just taken away his reason to whine. His pink face flushed; he mumbled something and walked away. Kill the turd with kindness, she thought, loving her job at moments like this. Howard Owens was a guy who'd made Josie's life miserable many years ago when she was a young uniformed officer, one of the few females in patrol, and he was her training officer. She'd promoted faster than him and knew he expected her to retaliate for his prior asinine behavior. She never had any desire to get even because she figured her success really irritated him and that was the best revenge.

In less than an hour, Josie had made all the notifications and had press relations handling the calls. She found a full pot of fresh coffee in the detective's squad room and felt her headache dissipating as she drank from an almost clean oversized mug. Detective Red Behan was at his desk scribbling on a yellow pad. He was tall and lanky, a redheaded Ichabod Crane who looked as if he'd slept in his jeans and short-sleeved blue plaid shirt. His fourth wife had thrown him out of the house a few weeks ago, so he probably had. His unruly red hair needed combing and his puffy eyes were an indication that he had spent a good part of the night drinking, again. He was in his forties, but was one of those boyish guys who would never look or act his age, but lately, Josie worried her friend seemed a bit frayed around the edges.

She sat at the desk next to his and waited until he finished writing. He had a new computer but preferred writing everything in longhand first.

"Morning, boss," he said, not looking up. "Did my fearless leader get you out of bed for this mess?" he asked. Josie realized she probably looked like a train wreck, too. Ibarra's phone call woke her from a restless sleep. She didn't bother to shower or brush her teeth, and dressed in the jeans and sweater she'd thrown on a chair next to her bed late last night. She and Jake had stayed up arguing about their son again. David wasn't the only subject they disagreed on lately, but he'd become the favorite.

Eventually, she'd take a shower at the station and change into her uniform. Before driving from her house to Hollywood, she managed to brush and twist her long black hair into something resembling a messy French twist. Makeup wasn't anything she needed or ever wore. Nature had blessed her with thick eyelashes and a clear olive complexion, but over all, she figured the best description of her appearance this morning was chaos.

"Tell me important stuff," Josie said. She knew the big redhead didn't like long stories either.

"Miss underage, never-gonna-see-eighteen movie star goes to a party, gets shot in the head by unknown assailant and dies. Nobody saw or heard anything, and it looks like there's no prints on the gun." He stopped and looked at his watch. "As of 0630 hours, detectives are baffled." He glanced up at her and grinned. "There's nothing important to tell yet."

Josie stretched her long legs and pulled herself up. "Thanks," she said. "That's what I figured."

"Happy to help, boss," he said to her back.

"Asshole," she mumbled and heard him chuckling as she walked away. Red Behan was one of the good guys. He couldn't be politically correct even if she threatened him. He said what he thought, and Josie always went out of her way to protect him because he was as loyal to her as an old hound dog and the best detective in Hollywood. Ten years ago, when she was a detective, they worked and drank together. These days he consumed enough alcohol for both of them, and she preferred to do her drinking alone, but they remained friends.

When Josie got back to the captain's office, her adjutant was watching her television. The local news station was showing pictures of the party house surrounded by yards of yellow crime scene tape. Reporters were interviewing neighbors, gardeners, any live body they could find in the neighborhood. A studio photo of Hillary Dennis in an evening gown was set in a corner of the screen, as an Asian woman questioned the pool cleaner from next door. Josie was grateful there was no sign of Ibarra.

Josie turned off the television and sat on the couch across from her desk. She had slept on this couch for more nights than she could remember, and it was tempting to stretch out now and sleep for a couple of hours. Jake had accused her of pretending to have call-outs so she could sleep here instead of in their bed. Sometimes, he was right.

"You okay?" the adjutant asked, sitting in the chair behind her desk. Sergeant Bobby Jones was a young stocky black man with an easygoing manner, a smooth, youthful face and big brown intelligent eyes. He liked to talk and was smart, but she wasn't in the mood this morning.

"Call West bureau and find out what time I can brief the chief on this Dennis thing. I'm going up to roll call." She got up and left him in her office. Josie hadn't been to roll call for a few weeks, and she knew the uniformed patrol officers liked to have her there so they could find out what was going on in their division, especially on mornings like this. Besides, a few minutes with them always left her energized.

Half an hour later, she had answered every question she could about the morning's events and made a mental list of all the officers' complaints, including those problems she couldn't solve. It was important to make contact because their lives were tied to her. She had a son, but was ashamed to admit she never worried about him as much as she worried about these young men and women. They might die doing what she asked them to do every day. A few had. David was . . . David wasn't likely to expose himself to danger for anyone, especially his mother.

Behan was waiting in her office when she got back. He was sitting on her couch shuffling through a pile of photos.

"You've got a visitor," he said without looking up. "Mrs. Joyce Dennis, Hillary's mommy, is waiting in Ibarra's office. She wants to talk to you."

Josie groaned. "What for? I can't tell her anything more than you or Ibarra."

"I mentioned that, but she thinks talking to you will inspire us to solve her little girl's murder."

"What are those?" Josie asked, attempting to see the pictures Behan kept mixing up.

"Shots of the killer, according to Mrs. Dennis," he said, handing her one of the photos. "Looks like it was taken at a club. Quality's not good. It was printed on one of those cheap digital printers." He pointed at a tattooed young man with a shaved head standing beside a somber, glassy-eyed Hillary Dennis. She was wearing a rhinestone-studded tank top, silk shorts, and knee-high white leather boots. "Mom says this handsome guy threatened Hillary yesterday morning, swore he would blow her brains out."

"Does he have a name?" Josie asked.

"Cory Goldman."

"Any relation to . . ."

"His son," Behan answered before she could finish. "The honorable Los Angeles City Councilman Eli Goldman's first born."

TWO

Every decision Josie made as the commanding officer of the Hollywood station was potentially explosive in a city full of unmarked special-interest landmines. The chief of police, police commission, her bureau, the diverse community, the ACLU, the officers and their union—all their needs and demands kept in perfect balance like a juggler spinning plates. Josie thrived on the work. Her marriage might be in a tailspin and her son a complete mystery to her, but she knew she was good at her job.

She went to the locker room, took a shower, put on her uniform, and invited Mrs. Dennis to step into her office. The woman wasn't what Josie had expected, not the hardcore, stage-mother type. Mrs. Dennis was old and ordinary with sparse grey hair and an off-the-rack, faded brown matronly dress. Apparently, Hillary hadn't shared any of her considerable wealth with her mother.

Mrs. Dennis explained that Hillary, the youngest of her five children, had been spotted by a talent agent four years ago at the L.A. County Museum of Art when she was thirteen. The agent got her a bit part in a B-movie where Hillary's sultry Lolita look caught on. Bigger parts and more money followed.

"She hasn't listened to me since she was sixteen," Mrs. Dennis said. "There was so much money. Shoulda had a firm hand, but they let her run wild. All they wanted was money . . . stole my little girl from me, got her killed."

"Was she an emancipated minor?" Josie asked. Mrs. Dennis stared blankly at her. "Did the court let her live on her own?"

The older woman nodded. "Too young," she mumbled and her eyes narrowed. "Her agent's a whore . . . she's a evil bitch."

"Detective Behan's very good, Mrs. Dennis," Josie said, a little taken aback by the prudish-looking woman's profanity.

"I want that boy arrested."

"If detective . . ."

"I don't care about no goddamn detective," she said interrupting Josie. Her eyes were filled with hate. "I want that devil's spawn and that whore to pay for what they did to my baby."

She was shouting now. The adjutant got up from his desk in the outer office and came to the doorway, but Josie waved him away. She sat on the couch beside the older woman and touched her hand. The gesture seemed to jolt Mrs. Dennis back to the present.

"I know God's gonna punish them to burn in hell for what they done, but I need some peace of mind," Mrs. Dennis whined, looking up at the ceiling and squeezing Josie's hand.

She blushed as if she had revealed too much, stood, thanked Josie for her time and left. As soon as the door to the lobby closed, Jones was out of his chair and back in the captain's office.

"Scary old woman," he said.

"Her kid's dead. That'll make you scary." Josie had never worked juvenile or family crimes, but even she recognized a dysfunctional family. Hillary might've had good reason to find a life away from her mother.

"Bureau called. 'Not So' wants to see you as soon as you're available," the adjutant said, grinning.

"I told you not to call him that," Josie said, trying to sound serious. She wasn't fond of Deputy Chief Eric Bright and knew the officers had given him the nickname 'Not So,' but she insisted they at least respect the man's rank. Police officers were intuitive and quick to label. They didn't trust a leader who lacked experience or failed to demonstrate he or she could make sound decisions. They had decided Deputy Chief Bright fit that description.

Josie wondered if she was the only commanding officer who worried what her officers said about her in the locker rooms or in the privacy of their patrol cars. She knew command wasn't a popularity contest, but she needed their respect and understood in this volatile police world how little it took—a misspoken word, a moment of indecision—to lose their esteem forever.

It was nearly noon, but Josie called the bureau and was told Bright was eating lunch at his desk today. She drove across the Westside to the Wilshire area where West bureau was located. The prospect of dealing with Bright today wasn't pleasant, but it had to be done. As one of West bureau's four division captains, Josie had to report to Deputy Chief Bright every day. Josie thought he ran West bureau like a preschool. She didn't need or want his assistance or constant input. She knew how to run Hollywood, and her stats confirmed she did a good job, but Bright insisted she report daily on every routine activity. With a high profile homicide, Josie knew the deputy chief's interference would become intolerable.

The bureau had newer offices adjacent to the Wilshire police station. Unlike Josie, the Wilshire captain spent as much time as possible hanging around the bureau. He and Bright had lunch together several times a week. Josie was certain if she could make Ibarra appear competent, the Wilshire captain would steal him, and the bureau would bless the deal. Josie would pretend to be outraged, but she already had transfer papers in her desk for a highly respected, talented lieutenant who wanted to move to Hollywood detectives as soon as Ibarra was gone.

Bright's adjutant Art Perry was a tall, handsome sergeant who looked better in uniform than anyone Josie had ever seen. She didn't know how successful he'd been as a field supervisor, but she didn't like him. He was smug, condescending and often acted as if he were speaking for himself rather than his boss, the first cardinal sin of adjutants.

"Morning, Art," she said, walking past him into Eric Bright's office. The sergeant mumbled something.

The chief's office was smaller than Josie's at Hollywood. It had room for a desk and a few nearly empty bookshelves. The primary reason she never wanted to promote higher than captain was beautifully demonstrated in this office. Any rank above captain had nothing important to do except create meaningless projects and audits, or find other ways to annoy cops with real jobs.

"Here's all we have on the Hillary Dennis homicide and a copy of the press release," Josie said, placing a folder on his nearly empty desk as she sat on the only other chair.

"Sergeant Perry," Bright shouted to his adjutant. Perry popped into the doorway. "Get the daily logs for Hollywood," he said, ignoring Josie. She was about the same age as Chief Bright, but Josie had to admit he looked younger. He had a passion for exercise and weight training and spent a good part of his day at the Police Academy gym. He was shorter than her but wore shoes with lifts to appear taller. He couldn't compensate, however, for a lack of command presence—that strong personality and inner strength signaling to everyone you're in charge.

"You need anything else?" Josie asked, wanting to get out of there as quickly as possible.

"I finished your performance rating report," Bright said. "But my secretary isn't done typing it, so you'll have to come back."

"No problem," Josie said, but they both knew it was an inconvenience.

"So, give me a briefing on this Dennis case."

"There's nothing more than what's in the report, Eric," Josie said, pointing at the folder. She noticed him cringe a little when she used his first name instead of chief, but they were alone and she didn't see how it could be disrespectful. They'd known each other most of their careers. They weren't friends, but at that moment formality seemed stupid.

"I don't have time to go through that."

Josie almost laughed. How could someone who had nothing to do, not have time. She recited the morning's events, regurgitating every detail from memory including the contents of the press release.

"I want you to notify me before you talk to the councilman's son or pick him up."

"Okay," Josie said and almost asked why, but she knew. Councilman Goldman was Bright's friend and mentor in city politics.

Their kids went to the same school and their families lived in the same neighborhood. "Anything else?"

"I'm not going to sign the commendation for your detectives in the bowling alley murder."

"Why?" Josie asked, trying to stay calm. She had written the commendation for two of Behan's detectives who'd worked three days without sleep to arrest the killer of a young business owner. It was extraordinary police work. A bureau commendation would have given them the recognition they deserved.

"It was, of course, a good investigation." Bright hesitated and added, "but really doesn't rise to the level of a bureau commendation."

"You're joking," Josie said, sarcastically. "What level is that?"

"It's difficult to explain, but I know it when I see it." There was the slightest nervous break in his voice. He wasn't comfortable being challenged.

She wanted to argue but didn't. It was a waste of time trying to change Bright's mind. The man had no sense of proportion. He lived within artificial boundaries and rules he'd created because he could. It would be more productive to find another way to honor the detectives.

"Fine," she said, standing. "Let me know when you want me to come back."

She didn't ask if Bright had anything else to discuss. She didn't care, and wanted to leave before she made her usual mistake of saying what she was thinking. Eric Bright was her boss, and Josie knew she had to work with him. Her only hope was that the chief of police, with his penchant for playing command staff musical chairs, would shift Deputy Chief Bright somewhere away from Hollywood and out of her life.

Bright's adjutant was talking with the secretary and didn't bother to acknowledge Josie when she left. She knew Sergeant Perry was the kind of guy that, if he worked for her, would be falling all over himself kissing her butt, trying to impress her. She couldn't affect his career at the moment, so he felt comfortable being rude.

Josie fought traffic on her way back to Hollywood station. Before she turned off LaBrea onto Sunset Boulevard, she caught a glimpse of Red's city car parked behind the Gables restaurant and bar, but kept driving. Drinking on duty was a major transgression, but Behan would never be stupid enough to allow her to smell alcohol on his breath or do anything that would prove he'd been drinking. He was old school and followed the code, "never make the boss clean up your mess." Besides, he did some of his most creative thinking leaning on the Gables' bar.

The traffic wasn't getting better, so she took a circuitous route back to the office in an attempt to clear her mind after the annoying meeting at the bureau. She worked her way up to Hollywood Boulevard where she parked in front of the Roosevelt Hotel, and got out when she spotted two footbeat officers struggling with a belligerent drunk. After a brief scuffle, they got him safely handcuffed and sitting on the curb. A dose of police action, even this routine stuff, always brought some balance to her life. After a taste of reality, she was ready to go back to the paperwork and deal with all the administrative bullshit.

She walked into the Hollywood division lobby less than two hours after leaving the bureau, and was surprised to see Councilman Goldman and Chief Bright standing at the front counter. It was an unannounced visit by a boss who rarely set foot inside her station. Josie figured Goldman wanted to meet with her and had dragged Bright along for support.

Although it would've only delayed the inevitable, Josie regretted her last-minute decision not to use the back entrance as soon as she saw them. Now Bright was standing in front of the security door that led to the captain's office, waiting for the uniformed desk officer to buzz it open. The deputy chief wasn't in uniform and never wore his identification card so the young probationary officer ignored him. Josie knew it would never occur to her boss that not every officer in the department knew who he was, so she leaned over the desk and hit the buzzer to unlock the door, allowing him to enter.

"Deputy Chief," Josie whispered to the young man behind the desk. He blushed and was embarrassed, but that was okay. Even if it wasn't his fault, she wanted to keep him on his toes until he knew what he was doing. When baby cops relaxed, they got killed.

She followed Bright and the councilman into her office. Goldman was quiet and serious. He sat on the couch and waited for the deputy chief to begin the conversation.

"You know why we're here," Bright said, perusing the photos on her office wall. They weren't the usual management décor, no certificates and college degrees, although Josie had plenty of those in a box at home. Her walls were covered with pictures of the different enforcement units she'd worked, and her favorite autographed photo was of LAPD's last civil service chief of police in his class-A uniform. All the police chiefs after him—including the current one—had been political appointments, so displaying his image was a quiet act of rebellion, mostly because it annoyed Bright.

"I've got a pretty good idea," Josie said, glancing at the councilman.

"My boy had nothing to do with that business this morning," Goldman said.

Josie noticed he wouldn't make eye contact with her.

"Nevertheless, he's a potential witness, possibly a suspect, and we'll have to talk to him," she said, pretending not to notice Bright's frown.

"I won't have him dragged in here like a common criminal," Goldman said. His tone raised up a few octaves. He was a tall man, but sickly pale and thin with long frizzy grey hair, a throwback to the "Sixties." His council voting record made it clear he didn't like the police department, and "more oversight" was his mantra, but he seemed to realize he wasn't in any position to make demands in this situation and his conciliatory voice kicked in. "I understand you have a job to do. My son will of course cooperate, but I'd prefer that my lawyer escort him in."

Josie knew she'd have to be careful. Goldman seldom said what he meant and never did anything that might interfere with his political future, but he could be ruthless if he considered someone his enemy or couldn't get his way. There was no right or wrong in his world; getting what he wanted was all that mattered.

"Detective Behan will call and set up an interview," Josie said. "He'll be discreet."

Bright planted himself behind Josie's desk and leaned back in her comfortable leather chair. "I'm thinking the detectives should go to your house, Eli, and avoid having your son come to a police station," he said, looking pleased. "With all the studios around here the news media watches this station like a hawk."

"I'll leave that up to Detective Behan," she said, with a thin smile. Bright wouldn't agree, but he wouldn't challenge her either. He didn't like public confrontations, but based on past experience he'd find another way to get Josie to do what he wanted. She had grown up with two older brothers and didn't back down easily when she thought she was right. Josie knew that little personality trait really annoyed the deputy chief, because he saw any disagreement as defying his authority.

"I warned Cory hanging around with that crowd would get him in trouble," Goldman mumbled to no one in particular.

"What crowd is that?" she asked, relieved to change the subject.

The councilman looked confused as if he hadn't intended to say what he'd been thinking.

"You know," Goldman said, shrugging.

"No, don't think I do," Josie persisted. "Who are you talking about?"

Bright got up and moved toward the door.

"He and his so-called friends party all night, drink too much. I wouldn't be surprised if there's some drugs involved. He swears he doesn't use anything now, but he's got no ambition, no real job . . . no future, plays on that damn computer all day . . . wasted talent." Goldman's voice trailed off. He slid off the couch with a groan. "I'm tired of worrying about him. I've got a city to run and he's twenty-two years old. It's about time my son grew up."

When they left, she watched the two men walk toward the back door, whispering like a couple of delinquents who just escaped the principal's office unscathed. They passed two uniformed officers coming the other way, but didn't bother to acknowledge their greetings. One of the officers waited a few seconds and then dropped to his knees and bowed, touching the floor with both hands several times. A couple of clerks and the secretaries in the administrative office laughed. When Bright turned around to see what was so funny, the officer pretended to be looking under a desk for something.

"You two get in here," Josie ordered, and watched while Officer Donnie Fricke got off his knees. He grinned at her, and his partner Frank Butler shook his head and followed Fricke into the captain's office. Fricke was a twelve-year veteran who was one of her most productive patrol officers, but he couldn't manage to stay out of trouble. His partner Frank Butler was younger and a good policeman who was slowly evolving into another Fricke. One of their frustrated sergeants had coined the term "Fricked up" for when things went wrong with them, which was frequently.

Fricke was a human bloodhound for finding bad guys and narcotics. As Hollywood's only "hype car," he and Butler were responsible for catching heroin addicts. They averaged thirty arrests a month and had become a legend on the seedier streets of Hollywood. The addicts referred to the two officers as Batman and Robin, and not only feared but respected them. Josie wasn't certain the two men always played strictly by the rules, but she never got complaints from citizens and even arrestees gave them grudging respect. Fricke's problems developed because he was fearless, always putting himself in the middle of everything and reacting immediately if not properly. He had one gear, forward, but more often than not he did the right thing or at least tried to. Butler was quiet and steady and would work twenty-four hours straight if Josie let him. A former marine, Butler was big and muscular but rarely swore or raised his voice, and had the patience of Job with his partner.

"Get in here," Josie said again as they slipped past her.

Fricke pretended to be contrite, grinning as he sat in the chair in front of her desk.

"You know Officer Butler told me to do that, ma'am, or I never woulda done it," Fricke said. Frank Butler shook his head. He'd given up a long time ago trying to straighten out his partner's stories and lies.

"You hear about this Hillary Dennis homicide?" Josie asked, ignoring Fricke.

"Yeah, Red asked us to squeeze a couple a snitches," Fricke said. "Excuse me, Detective Behan asked us," he added, correcting himself. Josie had chided Fricke in the past for ignoring rank, but she knew it didn't mean anything to him. Everybody was his equal except her. She was always 'captain or ma'am.' Any rank above or below her didn't exist in his world. "Everybody says she was strictly a party girl, liked booze and rich old men."

"What about this Goldman kid?" she asked.

Fricke whistled and rolled his eyes back.

"The guy's freaky. Got that whole Gothic thing going with the black outfits all tattooed and pierced up, head shaved," Fricke said. "But he's into boys."

"Pedophile?"

Butler shook his head and said, "No, ma'am, big boys, occasionally girls. I checked his rap sheet, nothing but the three 'd's'— disorderly, drunk and drugs."

"What's Detective Behan think?" Josie knew as soon as she asked she should've saved that question for Behan.

"He ain't saying," Fricke said.

She chatted with the two officers for a few more minutes. Fricke was brutally honest, and after twelve years on the force remained in the lowest rank of police officer, insisting he didn't care as long as "he could keep putting assholes in jail." Josie always wondered why she liked this man so much considering all his imperfections, and finally decided it was because in a lot of ways he was her twenty years ago without the survival instincts.

"We're gonna shake some bushes out there tonight, Cap', and see what we can get for Red," Fricke said on his way out. Butler silently tagged along, staring at the floor until he was in the hall-way where he playfully slapped Fricke on the back of his head.

Her intercom buzzed. It was Behan.

"Wanna sit in on the Goldman interview at 1800?" he asked.

"Where's it going to be?"

"Here, where else would it be?"

"Chief Bright didn't talk to you?"

"The chief and me don't converse much. What's up?"

"Nothing, I'll let you know if I can stay."

For a moment, she thought maybe Bright had a change of heart and wouldn't try to manipulate the interview of Councilman Goldman's son, but Josie knew better, and it didn't take long to find out what he had in mind.

Half an hour later, Bright called her and said he was giving the Hillary Dennis investigation to Robbery Homicide division. He reasoned that RHD was better able to handle the high profile case, and he didn't want to burden Hollywood's detectives with "the time-consuming, politically challenging investigation."

"Great," Josie said, and to her surprise actually meant it. She knew the bureau and the chief of police couldn't keep themselves from interfering in this case. They would drive her and her detectives crazy, and then blame them when it all fell apart. Behan wouldn't like it, but she knew giving this can of worms to RHD would save her and her people a lot of heartburn.

Later that day, Behan, always the loyal soldier, sat quietly with Josie in her office as she transferred what evidence and interviews they had to the RHD detectives. Behan meticulously recited every aspect of the investigation before handing over the homicide book. As they were leaving, the RHD detectives mentioned they would interview Cory Goldman at his father's house that evening. She and Red exchanged a quick smirk before wishing them good luck.

"Those poor slobs don't have a teenage boy's chance at Never-land," Behan said, when they were alone again.

"Better them than you," Josie said.

"Still, this thing has possibilities."

"Such as?" she asked.

"How do you shoot the prettiest girl in a room full of people and nobody sees it or hears anything? There's no trace of drugs or alcohol anywhere near her but she doesn't struggle with the killer, who probably shoots her from no more than a foot away while she's smiling at him, then drops the gun and walks away. That kind of stuff piques my Irish curiosity."

"You interviewed everybody who was there?"

"According to the caretaker, there were about half a dozen people. We've ID'd them, but the interesting ones are her agent, a filmmaker, and two aspiring actresses, aka porn stars."

"Whose party was it?"

Behan grunted. "That's the twist. Nobody knows. They all got one of those text message twitter things, or whatever the hell they call them, about a party that day. When they get to the Hollywood Hills house the door's unlocked. They raid the liquor cabinet and the fridge . . . like magic they got a party."

"Did any of them remember Goldman's kid being there?"

"Nope. I got our computer geek trying to back-track on the message, but it's a dead end. Maybe RHD will have better luck," Behan said and rolled his eyes back. Neither one of them believed the downtown detectives were as good as Behan and his people.

"Guess it's not our problem anymore," Josie said, but didn't like the way that sounded. There was something offensive about finding a dead body in her division and then asking RHD to track down the killer. It was a little like bringing in the snooty neighbors to clean your toilets.

"If you don't mind, I'm gonna let Fricke do his thing for a few nights. He's got some good snitches. Whatever he digs up we can pass on to RHD."

Josie didn't mind. Actually, she was curious to see what Fricke and his partner could uncover. Hollywood was crawling with snitches. Prostitutes, addicts, parolees, they all quickly learned the secret of Fricke's get-out-of-jail-free card—give up a bigger fish and swim away to be caught again another day.

Any other night, she might've stayed a few hours to see if anything turned up, but now the murder investigation was somebody else's headache, and she was tired. It was nearly eight P.M. and rush-hour traffic should have cleared. She called home hoping Jake was there. Maybe he wanted to go out to dinner, some place noisy where they couldn't argue and then get to bed early. David answered the phone.

"You're home," Josie said, instinctively. Her son rarely spent any time at home these days. He had a part-time job at a thrift store and slept in a shabby one-room apartment above a friend's garage. He was a twenty-two-year-old artist and musician. Two completely impractical professions Josie thought, but she had to admit he was talented if unsuccessful.

"Big surprise, you're not."

Smartass, Josie thought, but said, "I'm on my way; is your dad there?"

"No, there's another big surprise."

"Has he called?" She wasn't going to play this guilt game. He was a big boy now, too old to be crying about his neglected childhood. Maybe she hadn't been the perfect mother, but hell's bells, she hadn't beaten or starved him either. He had more than most kids and was old enough to get on with his life.

"What's the story on Hillary Dennis? Did she kill herself?"

"Did your dad call?"

"He'll be here in twenty minutes. Did she?"

"It's not my investigation. You want to stay for dinner?" The last thing she wanted was to talk about Hillary Dennis. She knew he'd stay. The only time David got a good meal was when she or his father cooked it or paid for it.

It took half an hour to drive from Hollywood to Pasadena. She loved the house she and Jake had purchased sixteen years ago on a shaded street within walking distance of Old Town Pasadena. The homes here were anywhere from fifty to a hundred years old. They were multi-story and sat back on the properties. Theirs was a white, three-story craftsman with a screened-in front porch. Jake's Porsche was in the driveway parked next to her son's piece-of-junk Jeep Wrangler convertible, leaving no room for her city car. She was annoyed and almost called to have David move his car, but instead parked in the street. The department wanted command officers to park their city cars in the garage for a lot of good reasons, but she wasn't in the mood to deal with her son's infantile pouting if he had to come out and move his car.

David was in the family room watching a Dodger play-off game and drinking a beer he must've brought with him, because she and Jake only had wine and a few bottles of hard liquor at home. He waved at her, but didn't stop staring at the television screen. She walked behind him and kissed him on top of his head, felt his soft brown hair rub against her cheek. He was a grown man, but she couldn't touch him without feeling as protective as she had the day the doctor placed him in her arms for the first time.

"You need a haircut," she said, gently tugging on his stubby ponytail. He was wearing the same worn Levi's he wore everyday, and she worried he was too thin. "Where's your father?"

"Kitchen," he said, pointing over his head.

She threw her briefcase and coat on the recliner and went upstairs, unbuckling her gun belt to slide off the holster with her .45 semi-auto before she reached their third-floor bedroom. Home was the only place she didn't wear her gun. If she was too dressed up to wear it on her belt, Josie carried it in her purse. Whether it was the Philharmonic, a baseball game or shopping for groceries, the gun went with her. Having been a cop for so many years and having dealt with the horrors one human being could inflict on another, Josie vowed she was never going to be a victim or let anyone she loved be a crime statistic, not without a hellacious battle.

She put the gun on a nightstand near her side of the bed. Jake hated seeing it there, but she kept telling him if a burglar tried to break in, he'd be very grateful after she saved them from getting murdered in their sleep. Jake thought that scenario was pretty funny and unlikely since earthquakes couldn't wake her. He'd moved the telephone to her side of the bed because she got so many calls from her station in the middle of the night, but she rarely heard the ringing unless he shook her. They'd been married nearly twenty-three years, and sometimes she wondered why the man put up with her three-ring-circus career, and lately worried maybe he was wondering the same thing.

As a deputy district attorney with a passion for the law, Jake seemed to be her perfect life partner. They both worked hard and disliked criminals, but she suspected in the last few years he wanted a real wife who wasn't too tired to cook and keep house, and would spend more time with him. Their sex life was fine, that wasn't the problem; but she was afraid the occasional intense intimacy only made him crave more. They were growing distant, but neither of them wanted to talk about it, so they rarely talked about anything and pretended nothing was wrong.

Jake was in the kitchen with his shirtsleeves rolled up making marinara sauce and pasta.

"You hungry?" he asked, and when he turned she saw his apron was covered with several large red stains.

"You have to kill the meatballs?"

Jake laughed. She was crazy about his laugh. It always made her smile. He was ten years older than her. His hair was grey but still thick like his father's, while David's hair was already thinning. Wrong gene selection. Jake came from Sicilian ancestry and had the dark skin and ebony eyes of all the Corsino men. A six-footer, he was bigger than most of his family, but David was both taller than his father and ten pounds skinnier.

"I dropped the first can of tomato sauce. Luckily most of it hit my apron. You done for the night?"

"Keep your fingers crossed," she said, and told him about the Hillary Dennis homicide. She explained how the investigation had been taken from her detectives and given to RHD, and she could see the relief on his face.

"They're transferring me downtown next week," he said, putting the lid back on the sauce pot. "Wanna whip up some garlic bread?" he asked, making room on the already crowded tile counter.

"How can they do that? I thought you were next in line to take over Santa Monica."

"So did I, but the D.A. says he needs to put me in the Central division snake pit, again. Caseload's huge, and he's got too many baby lizards. Most of them can't figure out how to find the right court, let alone prosecute a case."

She felt bad for him. In Santa Monica he'd had a lighter caseload and a better class of clientele. Jake liked getting home early, playing tennis and sitting in their second floor den drinking his Napa Pinot. His hours and workload were about to change drastically. If it were Josie, she'd have welcomed the change, but they were different that way.

"Maybe it's just temporary," she said, thinking that was a pretty lame consolation, but in a way the adjustment wasn't all bad. He'd be working so late he'd never notice her hours, and stop complaining about how much time she spent at the office.

"It is temporary. I'm retiring at the end of the month."

She stopped slicing bread and stared at him. It wasn't often she had difficulty finding the right words, but this was one of those rare moments. "When did you make that decision?" she asked after several seconds of tense silence.

"Right after the D.A. made his."

"Can we afford your retirement?" She heard the testiness in her voice, but it really wasn't about the money. Didn't she get a say in something as big as this that affected both their lives?

"I'm going into private practice with Bob Steiner's firm."

"Defending rapists and murderers?" she asked and thought, this just keeps getting better. Steiner had a reputation as a high-priced sleazy ambulance chaser.

"Defending people accused of crimes. I'll make more money and work fewer hours."

She slid the baking sheet with the garlic bread into the oven and asked, "Can you really do that after you've been prosecuting dirtbags for the last twenty years."

"For fewer hours and a couple hundred grand a year, yeah, I think I can do that."

"We make enough money."

He didn't respond and poured the sauce over the pasta. He'd made up his mind, and when Jake made up his mind the discussion was over.

The aroma of sautéed garlic and onions filled the dining room as Josie set dishes and silverware on the table. She opened a bottle of Chianti, took a wineglass from the china hutch, poured herself a full glass and took a long drink. David came into the room and watched her finish that glass and fill it again.

"He told you," David said, smirking.

"Sit down, dinner's ready," she ordered, as she smelled bread burning in the kitchen.

The garlic bread was ruined, but the pasta, Italian sausage and salad were good. Josie ate and drank too much and didn't revisit the subject of Jake's retirement. They weren't connecting anymore. He didn't need or want her input for important decisions, but had no problem telling her how much he loved and wanted her in those wonderfully sweaty romantic moments while they made love. It was frustrating and confusing.

David was in a good mood. Josie wasn't. The day's events mixed with wine had snowballed into a gigantic headache. Losing the Dennis case was just the teaser. Jake's revelation on top of her son's practiced sarcasm shifting into high gear was almost enough to send her back to the couch in her Hollywood office. Her son was a talented pianist who knew his mother wanted him to play with a reputable orchestra, so he was bragging about joining forces with a blues guitarist and lining up a couple of jobs that gave him a lot of exposure but no money or future. One of his drawings had sold at a local art show for almost a hundred dollars, so he boasted he wouldn't be borrowing as much cash from her or Jake for a few weeks.

She stared at her husband, hoping he might start a discussion on his decision to retire, but it didn't happen. She knew if she brought it up he'd dodge any meaningful conversation. He sat quietly or talked to David about his music. Josie must've tuned out her son because she felt him touch her hand, and when she glanced up he was looking at her.

"I asked what the story was on Hillary Dennis." David said, as he finished the last of the Chianti. "Did she kill herself?"

"You knew who she was?" Josie asked. Was she really the only person in town who'd never heard of this woman? Why did he care if some underage stranger killed herself?

"Sure, her name's always in the news. She's one screwed-up kid." David paused only a second before adding, "And Cory dated her for a while."

"Cory? Cory Goldman?"

"Yeah."

"How do you know him?" Now Josie was paying attention.

David shook his head trying to remember. "We met years ago, at one of the clubs. We've got a bunch of mutual friends, and he likes my music."

"Did he ask you to pump me for information?"

"You make it sound sinister, Mom. He liked Hillary and was curious if the drugs finally got her."

"How close a friend is he?" Josie was becoming sober in a hurry. Anxiety always produced that effect. She didn't like where this conversation was going, and her motherly instincts warned her there was danger ahead for her six-foot-four-inch baby.

THREE

W eary from a stressful day and lack of sleep, Josie made a pot of coffee in an attempt to clear her head. It was going to be a long night. She'd pushed Jake's job situation to the bottom of her priority stack, and he seemed to sense his comments were unwelcome. After a weak attempt to interject his thoughts, Jake faded into a shadowy presence, picking up empty plates and making familiar kitchen cleaning noises. He managed to keep out of their way in another part of the house while Josie and David stayed up until after midnight drinking coffee at the kitchen table and talking about David's association with Cory Goldman and the murder victim.

Josie wanted to believe her son was telling the truth about a casual and infrequent relationship, but she was a skeptic and suspicious by nature. David swore theirs wasn't a close friendship; he liked Cory but hadn't seen him for days before the councilman's son called him that afternoon. Josie's gentle but persuasive badgering eventually forced David to admit Cory knew he was a suspect in Hillary's murder and had asked David to find out what he could from his mother.

"I refused to do that," David said. "But I'm still curious. Cory's screwed up, but I don't believe he could kill anyone, especially Hillary."

"Why especially Hillary?"

"He dumped her, then changed his door locks and phone numbers to get away from her and her crazy mother."

"Mrs. Dennis says Cory threatened to kill Hillary yesterday."

"She's lying. Mrs. Dennis hates Cory . . . the way he dresses and the tattoos and the . . ." David hesitated.

"Drugs?" Josie finished his sentence instinctively knowing that had to be what he was trying not to say. Josie had made it clear his entire life she had no tolerance for drug users.

"It wasn't that way. Hillary was hardcore. Cory only used a little meth and grass."

Josie stared at him. "What do you consider hardcore?"

"Needles, 'H.'"

"Heroin . . . I didn't see any tracks on her. Where'd she shoot up?"

"Don't know, but she did."

She made a mental note to tell Red in the morning. The wine had done its magic, and despite the caffeine and growing concern, Josie was finally tired enough to sleep. She got up and kissed David on the cheek.

"Stay here tonight," she said. "Your father'll make you breakfast."

She shut off all the lights and checked the doors. By the time she climbed the stairs, she noticed the light was out in David's old room and she could hear him snoring.

She'd consumed enough wine to be grateful the watch commander hadn't called her that night, but wasn't so wasted she didn't notice Jake never came to bed. When she got up early the next morning, she looked out the bedroom window and saw his Porsche was gone and her city car was parked in the driveway in its place. Her son's Jeep was still there.

Josie took a shower and dressed in a black pantsuit and white silk blouse instead of her jeans. She needed to drop her uniforms off at the cleaners. She put the .45 in her briefcase and wore a smaller 9mm Beretta under her suit jacket. There was a coffee shop near the cleaners where she could get her caffeine fix and something disgustingly unhealthy for breakfast. She peeked in David's bedroom. He was still sleeping. There was an empty feeling in the pit of her stomach as she watched him for a few seconds. It wasn't hunger.

By the time Josie arrived at Hollywood station, the coffee was gone, crumbs and powdered sugar covered her lap, and she was on a caffeine-sugar high and primed to start her day.

Lieutenant Ibarra informed her Behan was in the middle of the Dennis autopsy at the morgue, so she called him on his cell phone and told him what David had disclosed about the victim's drug use.

"Do I need to interview your kid?" Behan asked.

"We'll talk when you get back," she said and hung up. Stupid question, she thought. Of course he would, but she didn't like it. Knowing Behan, she figured he asked just to annoy her.

"Hey, Captain," Donnie Fricke said, leaning into her office from the doorway. "Got a minute?"

"Come in," she said, relaxing. At last, a touch of controlled insanity.

Officer Fricke came in without Frank Butler trailing a step behind him.

"Where's your partner?"

"I got here early. Figured I'd let him sleep in. Me and Frankie, we turned over a lot a rocks last night."

"How many arrests you make?" she asked. Josie loved the way Fricke talked. He sounded like a Chicago gangster, but was born and raised in L.A.'s San Fernando Valley. She was a little uneasy about the way he made his own work schedule. She'd been lenient with him because of the special detail and his incredible productivity, but she was about to assign an immediate supervisor to his narcotics car. He and Butler were supposed to report to the lieutenant watch commander at night, but Fricke had a habit of frequently coming to work early or late depending on his target for the night.

"It was a slow night, Cap'. We only hooked up six."

They both knew that number was an incredible amount of work for two officers, but Fricke had perfected an assembly-line process for booking heroin addicts.

"You solve the Dennis murder, yet?"

Now Fricke laughed. "No, ma'am, but we got this snitch that says she knows where Hillary copped her drugs."

"You tell Behan?"

"Ain't seen him this morning. Want us to drop her name on the guys at RHD."

"Give it to Behan, let him deal with downtown," she said. "What did you promise her?"

Fricke glanced at the floor and said, "Fifty, but we don't gotta sweat it. The dope guys got a package on her. They'll front the money."

He lingered in her office for half an hour. Fricke knew all the gossip in the division and couldn't keep anything to himself. She listened, and in some cases was surprised by the actions of a few officers she thought she knew better. It shouldn't have surprised her. Most cops were very intelligent with a highly developed sense of mischief. They could get themselves into some jaw-dropping adventures all in the name of fun. She figured their high jinks were a kind of pressure release valve, and tried to stay out of it unless their actions harmed someone or affected their work. Josie knew Fricke told her everything because he trusted her not to overreact. She listened to Fricke because the things she couldn't do anything about he kept to himself.

Fricke was barely out of the office when Sergeant Jones stepped in and said, "Chief Bright called. He wants you back at the bureau when you get a chance."

Josie felt a pain between her eyes as if she'd just swallowed a big chunk of ice. She had better things to do than bounce back and forth between the bureau and Hollywood station just to give 'Not So' something to occupy his time.

"Call his adjutant and set something up for tomorrow morning. I'll stop by on my way to the office."

The adjutant was leaving, but moved aside to let Behan enter. The big redhead didn't acknowledge him and dropped wearily onto the chair in front of Josie's desk. He pulled a yellow legal notepad out of his briefcase and put it on his lap.

"Coffee?" Josie asked, grabbing her cup and waving it at the detective. Behan shook his head and thumbed through several pages in the notepad. She filled her cup from a pot in the admin office and came back.

"When's that guy gonna get a real job?" Behan asked, not looking up.

"What guy?" she asked.

"Your adjutant."

"He's only been here four months. What's wrong with him?" she asked.

"Too salty for a sergeant with one hash mark."

"Five years is a lot these days, Red," she said, closing the door.

"Still too cocky . . . needs to get knocked on his ass a few times."

Josie recognized the crankiness that came when Behan had more alcohol than sleep, and opted to change the subject.

"RHD object to you sitting in on the post?"

"I trained both those guys. Besides they're pissed off; they don't want this loser case any more than you do. They said their boss is trying to find a way to give it back."

"Find anything interesting?"

"Won't know much until the labs come back, but she was shot at close range, probably with the nine millimeter we recovered near the body. No ballistics yet, and no residue on her hands. Gun's stolen, six months ago in a burglary on Yucca, from the Palms— that dirtbag apartment building Fricke's always rousting."

"Any marks?"

"Your kid had it right. They found fresh puncture wounds on her feet and in the groin area. Looks like she might've tried the needle once or twice in her arm, too."

"Until she got smart enough to hide it." Josie had worked narcotics for a lot of years and knew how ingenious heroin addicts could be.

Behan flipped through the yellow notepad, searching for anything he might've missed. She watched him and thought he looked more haggard and stressed-out than usual. He shifted his big frame trying to get comfortable, and his hands trembled slightly as he slipped the notepad back into his briefcase.

"RHD figures we dumped this stinker on them," he said, rubbing his eyes. "I explained how that decision got made in the rarified air staff guys breathe, not by us lowly worker bees."

"I want you to talk to Fricke's snitch before we give her up to RHD."

Behan said, "I already told him to bring her to me as soon as he digs her up again. Wanna listen in?"

"Maybe, but first I'm taking you to breakfast."

"I ate."

"When?"

"I don't know. I had a hamburger."

"When?"

"Yesterday, I guess; I'm not hungry," he said, irritated with her interrogation.

"Either we eat or you go home. You look like hammered shit."

They argued another ten minutes about where to eat, and finally Josie told him they were going to Murray's, a hole-in-the-wall coffee shop on Santa Monica Boulevard that had the best breakfast in the city. It was owned by a retired boxer from England and his gay son. Sammy, the ex-boxer, was in his late seventies and had a touch of dementia. He was a great cook, but sometimes you got your meal twice.

It was an off-hour so they found one of the four tables empty. Josie loved the food, but hated the environment. The place was stuck on a corner surrounded by the film industry's dreary post-production houses where homeless bums fought teenage male prostitutes for standing room. The graffiti was crafted by mindless taggers, not rival gangs, but it looked just as ugly. Occasionally, some of the street people would wander inside, and Sammy would feed them. If they smelled too bad, he made them take their food to the plastic tables outside.

On other days, she'd see an actor or some other celebrity sitting at the counter devouring one of Sammy's omelets. Today, she spotted Councilwoman Susan Fletcher who, like Eli Goldman, represented sections of Hollywood. She was sitting at the far end of the counter with one of her community organizer aides. Fletcher was grossly overweight and balanced precariously on a wobbly stool. Josie glanced down and pretended not to notice her. She actually liked Fletcher, but wasn't in the mood to talk politics.

The smell of sautéed onions must've affected Behan. He ordered a sausage and cheese omelet, hash browns, sourdough toast, and a side of pancakes. Josie drank coffee and watched him, wondering what Red ate when he was hungry. By the time he wiped his plate with the last piece of toast and drank half a pot of coffee, the color had returned to his face and his hands were steady. He sat back and opened a notch on his belt.

Josie wanted to ask Behan what was happening to him, but knew he wouldn't tell her. His life was a mess, but he was too proud to whine about it.

"Thanks," he said, finally. "Guess I needed that."

She smiled but didn't ask the question she was aching to spring on him: What the hell's wrong with you? Unfortunately, before he could open that door or volunteer any personal information, Councilwoman Fletcher was off her stool and hovering over their table.

"Captain Corsino," Fletcher said, and held out her chubby hand to Josie. "Thanks, Sammy," she bellowed, waving her other hand at the cook standing across the room. The old guy ignored her and slipped into the back room. Fletcher was probably in her forties, but had an old lady appearance with her henna-colored hair cut just below her ears and curled under at the ends, and her dark matronly business suit.

"Councilwoman," Josie said, smiling. "Detective Behan, my homicide supervisor," she added, pointing at Behan.

Fletcher reached down and grabbed the detective's hand. "Pleasure to meet you," she said. "How's the Dennis investigation going?" she asked, and pulled an empty chair from the table behind them. She moved it beside Behan and settled her considerable bulk without an invitation. Her preppie-looking aide, who never did get an introduction, stood, clipboard in hand, leaning against the counter. "I know Eli Goldman is terrified his son might be involved," Fletcher said. She tried to sound concerned, but Josie caught just the slightest trace of a smile cross the woman's plump face.

Before her election, Fletcher was a vocal left-wing liberal; but during her first year on the council, she'd proven to be one of Josie's strongest supporters . . . most of the time. It wasn't friendship, but Josie and the councilwoman had a solid and respectful working relationship.

"It's not my investigation anymore," Behan said.

Fletcher turned to Josie. "Why not? I thought the girl died in Hollywood."

"Deputy Chief Bright gave the case to RHD," Behan said, before Josie could think of an answer that would offer her boss some protection. She didn't like Bright, but generally felt an obligation to shield the rank above her.

Josie glared at Behan. She knew what he was doing. It was common knowledge Eli Goldman and Fletcher didn't get along. They never fought in public, but behind the scenes there were rumors of threats and backstabbing recriminations. Behan was a master at pushing people's buttons. He had to know Fletcher would suspect Goldman's hand in the investigation's abrupt transfer to RHD, a move which meant greater oversight and control by the chief of police, who also happened to be Eli Goldman's good friend.

The aide whispered something in Fletcher's ear; she nodded, and he faded back to the counter.

"I've got a meeting," Fletcher said, grunting as she used everything within reach to get herself back on her feet. "I am not pleased with this. It doesn't pass the smell test." She turned to leave, stopped, came back and challenged Josie. "Did you agree with the decision to pass this investigation to RHD?" she asked, her eyes narrowing.

Damn you, Behan, Josie thought, and said, "Actually, I wasn't given a vote or I would've kept it."

They were gone, the councilwoman and her Sancho Panza on a mission to the civic center to hack down a few political windmills in the City of the Angels.

After several seconds of painful silence, Behan put his hand over his mouth and said, "Oops."

"I should've let you starve to death," Josie whispered.

"Come on, I want the case back; you want it back; RHD wants to give it back, so everybody's happy."

"Everybody except that deputy chief guy who can transfer my ass to Jail division for the rest of my career."

"They're not gonna know it was you."

"It wasn't me," Josie said, tossing twenty dollars on the table. "It was my big-mouthed, conniving D-III." She actually wasn't all that angry, which surprised her. There would be some questions, but she hadn't initiated anything. Councilwoman Fletcher would do all the dirty work, ask embarrassing questions and make accusations until the chief either gave in and returned the investigation to Hollywood, or got angry and went after the culprit who'd talked to Fletcher. It was a crap shoot, but Josie knew the chief of police was too smart to make Susan Fletcher an enemy.

It didn't take long to find out. Behan was driving them back to Hollywood station when Josie got a message on her Blackberry from Bright's adjutant to go code-three, emergency speed, to West bureau. If she were in a more charitable mood, Josie might've had Behan drop her at the station, and she would've gone alone, but somehow it seemed appropriate that he face the firing squad with her.

"Are you okay?" she asked after several minutes of watching Behan drive too slowly without a word of conversation.

"I hate the bureau."

"You know what I mean. Something's going on with you. Can I help?"

"You can stop asking me if I'm okay."

"I'm not going to do that. What else?"

"Pay my alimony and child support."

"Why do you keep marrying these women? Why don't you just live with them like everybody else? That way when you break up you don't have to support them and their kids for the rest of your life. She takes the wide-screen TV; you get the dog, and it's over."

"I'm Irish Catholic. That's what we do."

"You need money?"

"Yeah, but not from you. Don't worry about it. I got a plan."

Now Josie was worried. "Am I gonna start getting reports of some big, grumpy, red-headed bank robber?"

"Better. I know this very rich, very old widow who's about to become the next Mrs. Phillip Behan."

Josie slumped back in the passenger seat and stared out the window. The man was hopeless. She was grateful they'd reached the bureau before she got details about the bride or the pending marriage. Behan straightened his tie as he got out of the car and looked somewhat presentable. He always seemed to patch his life together when he was married or had decided to get married again.

They walked past Sergeant Perry and the secretary and into Bright's office. The chief was reading and didn't bother to acknowledge them until he finished. When Bright saw them standing on either side of the only other chair in the room, he shouted for Perry to bring in another one. The adjutant responded immediately, arranged the furniture so everyone faced the chief and left. Josie pictured Perry kissing Bright's ass and twirling out of the room. She smiled at the mental image.

"Something funny, Captain?" Bright asked her. He wasn't pleased.

"No," Josie said, trying not to look at Behan. "Guess I'm just in a good mood."

"Enjoy it. It won't last," Bright said.

"Why's that?" Josie asked as innocently as she could.

"You're getting the Dennis investigation back."

"I thought RHD had it," she said, giving Behan a look that warned him not to say a word. This was her show.

"The chief wants your people to handle it."

Josie turned toward Behan and asked, "How's your workload?"

Before Behan could respond, Bright said, "This isn't negotiable. It's yours." He was visibly irritated.

"We'll pick up the homicide book and start today," Josie said with a forced smile.

Bright reached into the side desk drawer, handed a large binder to Behan and said, "Just remember, I'm really in charge of this investigation. I want to be informed on every move you make. I don't want any blunders on this one."

Josie could feel herself blushing and knew it was frustration. She knew better than to let anything Bright said bother her, but this did. The man knew nothing about criminal investigations. He was a careerist who hadn't worked at anything for years except his next promotion, and he certainly didn't know how to manage a homicide case. She didn't say anything but heard Behan, always the loyal soldier, respond.

"Yes sir."

"Anything else?" Josie asked, standing.

"Rating report," he said, removing a folder from his desk drawer, then immediately tossed it back. "Just remembered, I can't do that now . . . got to leave early. Have Sandy put you on my calendar for early tomorrow morning," he said to Josie.

She nodded and left his office, stopped at the secretary's desk and got penciled in for the next morning. Behan was chatting with one of the young record clerks, but Josie wanted to leave and said she'd wait for him by the car. She could feel the anger and disappointment simmering inside her, and it wasn't just the investigation. Josie never expected or wanted to promote higher than area captain, but she wanted a fair evaluation of her work. She'd labored too hard to have someone like 'Not So' assess her performance.

She leaned against Behan's vehicle. The fresh air and a light breeze cleared her head. Maybe she was making too much of something that really wasn't all that important. If the rating wasn't fair, she'd fight it. She gazed at the black and white patrol cars returning to the division's parking lot one by one until they were lined up by the back door of Wilshire station. It was a change of watch. The returning officers cleaned out their cars, joked or shared information with the men and women who would work the P.M. watch, some of the dodgiest hours to patrol L.A.'s streets. Josie always marveled at how nonchalant and relaxed they could be about such a dangerous job. She liked watching them; it put the world back into perspective.

Being in a patrol car had been one of the most enjoyable times she'd had during her career. She missed the simplicity of driving out of the station every night with her partner and looking for trouble, police work in its purest form—every day different, every radio call possibly the most important event in another person's life or the last precious moments of your own. Patrol was sporadic doses of adrenaline or boredom frequently mixed with mind-numbing fear. A person got tested, courage and ability measured every day. Maybe that's what really bothered Josie about Bright. By all accounts, he'd failed the test but still got rewarded.

Behan had them back at Hollywood station by late afternoon. He'd stopped talking about the rich widow and was thinking about the Dennis homicide again. Josie had flipped through the pages of the binder as Behan drove, and was disappointed to discover the RHD detectives had already interviewed Cory Goldman at his home with his father and an attorney present. The interview had revealed no new information and basically Cory repeated the same scenario David had given her the night before. He claimed he wasn't at the party and hadn't seen Hillary for weeks, and was in fact trying to avoid her and her crazy mother. Cory described Hillary's mother as a "religious crackpot" who had driven Hillary from her house with her constant ravings. There was a recent photo of the young man. He could've been handsome, but had pierced both ears and one nostril, shaved his head and had extensive tattoos on his neck and arms. It was difficult for Josie to believe this guy and her David were friends. In a lot of ways her son was conservative by today's standards. He hadn't done anything that caused permanent damage to his body and dressed like a flower child.

"So, what's your game plan," Josie asked Behan as they entered the back door of Hollywood station.

"Interview Fricke's snitch and the other wits from the party," he said, taking the binder from her.

"Captain, Red, where you been?" Fricke shouted at them from down the corridor near the division's jail. "We been waiting." He grinned and pointed at the closest holding cell.

Behan ordered Fricke to take the snitch back to the detectives' interview room, and he'd be there in a few minutes. He waited until they were in her office, then asked Josie how she wanted to handle the investigation.

"The same way you handle all your investigations . . . ignore Ibarra and pester me," Josie said.

"You know Bright will talk to Ibarra, and the little kiss-ass is gonna wanna run everything I do by the bureau first."

They were standing just inside her office. Josie gently pushed the door closed with her foot.

"We'll do what Chief Bright told us to do," she said. "He's the boss and it's his investigation now, but everything goes through me first, same as always. Ibarra's your boss. I'll make him the official liaison between Hollywood and the bureau," she said, thinking that would keep him preoccupied and out of everybody's hair.

"What a fucking disaster," Behan said.

"Do the best you can. You'll make it work like you always do." She tried to sound positive, but knew with Bright's oversight and Ibarra's ineptitude the case was destined to become a fucking mess, just like Behan said.

Behan reached for the door when the adjutant knocked from the other side, then pushed it open almost hitting the big detective.

"Sorry," Sergeant Jones said, moving his stocky frame away from Behan. "Thought you'd want to know. Footbeat called in a dead body in an alley off the boulevard."

"Homeless?" Josie asked. She knew street people were always overdosing and dying in those alleys off Hollywood Boulevard.

"Nope," he said, shaking his head. "She had ID. It's Misty Skylar."

"Fuck." Behan mumbled.

"Another movie star?" Josie asked. She'd have to start using some of those AMC gift cards gathering dust in her desk.

"Hillary's agent," Behan said on his way out. He told Fricke to put his snitch back in the holding cell while he tracked down a team of detectives to send to the alley.

"You want to go out there with me?" he asked Josie, who'd followed him back to the homicide table. She had a stack of work waiting on her desk and wasn't interested until Behan reminded her that Misty Skylar had been at the Hollywood Hills party house with Hillary the night she was killed. It was too much of a coincidence even for the Hollywood crowd.

Lieutenant Ibarra was already on the scene when they arrived and was interviewing a pretty older woman in a revealing waitress uniform. The dead body had been discovered outside the back door of the bar where the waitress worked. Yellow police tape sealed the only entrance to the alley, and two uniformed officers stood in front of that flimsy barrier to keep curious pedestrians and the media from trampling the crime scene.

Josie couldn't see the body until she passed the dumpster. Misty Skylar was propped against the wall between the dumpster and a pile of trash. She was wearing an expensive-looking black strapless cocktail dress, her legs stretched out and crossed at the ankles, and her arms folded against her chest. Her feet were bare but clean. Her head was back as if she was staring at the stars, though her star-gazing days were definitely over.

Josie moved around the body, careful not to touch or step on anything, and glanced at the face. The eyes were swollen shut and blood was caked under the victim's nose and both ears. The spot where Misty's mouth should have been was a black hole. The flesh around it burned or shredded. The wall behind her was covered with blood, pieces of cartilage, teeth and brain matter. A high-caliber explosion had gone off in the woman's mouth.

"Too much blood and debris above her head," Behan said, examining the gruesome mosaic on the wall. "She wasn't in that position when the gun discharged in her mouth."

"The body was staged," Josie said and asked, "How old is she?" Misty had a young woman's figure, but Josie noticed that the skin on the arms wasn't firm and the manicured hands had a few age spots.

"Fifty-four," Behan said.

"Found the shoes and her purse with ID and money in the dumpster," Ibarra said, leaving the waitress with one of Behan's detectives. "Megan's a pretty good wit," he added pointing at the waitress. "She remembers Skylar was in the bar last night, but barely drank anything."

"Was she alone?" Josie asked.

"No, she was with some guy, but Megan didn't get a good look at him. They left around midnight with another guy she can't ID either."

"Who does that belong to?" Josie asked, pointing at a large box with a dirty blanket thrown over the top, tucked in a corner at the back of the alley. She guessed from his blank expression Ibarra didn't have any idea what she was talking about, so she added, "Looks like some homeless person is sleeping there, probably gets handouts from the bar. Does this Megan know who it is?"

Ibarra looked confused. "I don't know. We'll have to ask her."

She wanted to say something like, "No shit?" but didn't. Officers and detectives were milling around and always listening. Josie wouldn't undermine her lieutenant. Though most of his subordinates didn't have a high opinion of Ibarra, she wouldn't contribute to his poor reputation while he worked for her.

An hour and a half later, Behan left his detectives in the alley and drove Josie back to the station.

"What do you think?" she asked, as he merged into heavy traffic on the boulevard.

"Ibarra's an idiot."

"About the homicide."

"Somebody stuck a very big gun in her mouth and blew her brains out and then arranged her body like she was lounging at home watching TV. It wasn't a robbery. Her cash and credit cards were in the trash and that diamond ring on her finger looks real, so I've pretty much eliminated the homeless guy as a good suspect unless he's just a sicko who enjoys killing." He was quiet a few seconds and then asked, "Don't you think it's odd the killer shot her in the mouth?"

"Why, is there a better place to shoot her?"

"It looks like somebody got her out of the bar to kill her. So, why risk her screaming for help or fighting. Why not shoot her in the back of the head?"

"Maybe the killer needed to talk to her first."

"Maybe," he said.

"You interview the waitress?"

"She knows the bum as Mitch, says she slips him a bottle of beer once a night. The footbeat cops say they've booked him a couple of times. He's a drunk and his real name is Roy Mitchell," Behan said.

"Did she see him last night?"

"Nope, hasn't seen him since the night before last."

"That doesn't bode well for Mr. Mitch."

Josie returned half a dozen phone calls and cut her stack of papers down to a manageable number before Behan was ready to interview Fricke's snitch.

She sat in the room adjacent to the interview room and could see and hear everything on a video feed. Sara Jean Dupont or "Mouse" as she was known on the street was a short, skinny woman with little studs piercing her nose and near her right eyebrow. Tattoos decorated both arms and her right leg had a vine-like tattoo from her ankle to the top of her cut-off Levi's. Her long hair was dyed blond.

She waited patiently with her legs crossed until Behan entered the room. As soon as he sat across the table from her, Mouse smiled, and Josie thought she might've been a very attractive girl without all the permanent bodywork.

After the preliminary information was put on record, Behan got to the substantive questions. Mouse claimed she had encountered Hillary Dennis at the Oasis Club in Hollywood and had introduced the movie star to a guy she knew only as Little Joe, an unemployed musician and part-time pimp, who dealt a little heroin on the side. She claimed Hillary kept pestering her until she agreed to introduce her to the dealer.

"Like I told Officer Fricke, Hilly don't come round much the last few weeks, so I figure she got connected somewheres else," Mouse said. She spoke barely above a whisper and very slow.

"Did Hillary have problems with Little Joe or anyone you know about?" Behan asked.

"Hilly pays up front, so I don't believe so. . . ." Mouse hesitated as if she were remembering something and deciding whether or not she should speak. She looked around the room. "Is anybody besides you hearing me?"

"No, absolutely not," Behan lied.

Josie turned up the volume. She could barely understand the little woman.

"She told me once . . . there was this Hollywood cop that hassled her some when he catched her coming outta the Palms. She weren't worried. She had the junk hid up her pussy but he give her a hard time."

"Did he know who she was?"

"Oh yeah, he messed with her a couple a times. She says they got to some kinda understanding. If you know what I mean," she said, almost whispering, and winked at Behan.

"Did she say who the cop was or mention anything else about him?"

"No," Mouse said.

Behan looked up at the hidden camera and mouthed the word, "Fuck."

Josie turned down the volume, sat back and knew it was always foolish to think things couldn't get worse.

FOUR

Without dates and times, it was nearly impossible to find out which cop had stopped Hillary Dennis. To make things even more difficult, Mouse didn't know if the officer was in uniform or plainclothes, and it was impossible to know if he was a real or fake police officer or if Mouse was making up the whole thing. The list of possible suspects had to include Donnie Fricke since the Palms was his favorite and frequent target, but Josie wasn't ready to believe Fricke would or could do what Mouse described.

Behan was willing to keep an open mind and although he liked Fricke, told Josie he'd seen better cops do worse and anything was possible. Just the idea one of her officers might be involved in a homicide left Josie feeling sick.

She went back to her office but couldn't concentrate on routine tasks. She threw a stack of unsigned papers in her desk drawer and locked it. It was only seven P.M. but there weren't any community meetings on her calendar tonight so she was done. An early dinner, a long luxurious bath and a good night's sleep were the only plans she had until Jake called. The phone rang just as she was about to leave. He wanted to meet at a little bar in Old Town Pasadena. From the sound of his voice he'd been there a while.

The prospect of sitting in a bar with her husband—who hadn't been home all night and had fortified his courage with alcohol—wasn't appealing, but Josie knew they had to talk. Jake was a good man, but he wasn't content with his life and was making hers miserable too. She was already feeling so shitty it was probably the perfect time to do this. Why ruin a good day.

The Carriage Inn was on a one-way street, three long blocks from their house. It was in a refurbished brick building with a copper-plated oversized door and green shuttered windows. It had a hand-carved mahogany bar with a black marble surface scratched and stained from nearly fifty years of service. Jake enjoyed drinking there. Although the place was small, dark, and barely surviving on a handful of locals, Josie didn't mind—it was the perfect place for a family dispute.

Parking space was nearly nonexistent in that part of Old Town, so she decided to leave her car at home and walk to the bar. The Porsche was in the driveway, so Jake was on foot too. The late summer evenings were getting cooler. It would be a pleasant walk, a way to release some of the tension that had been building all day. She changed into a nice pair of jeans, her comfortable boots, a clean shirt and jacket to cover her .45. Maybe this wasn't such a terrible idea.

Josie found her husband in one of the tight straight-backed wooden booths. The bartender Stu, an older man with close-cropped, dyed black hair and a large diamond stud in his left ear, was talking to two skinny young women, the only other patrons. Stu waved at Josie, and she nodded at the bottle of red wine he held up. Jake had his suit jacket folded on the seat beside him and was sipping something that looked like scotch.

"You came," he said, smiling with a confused half-grin that meant he probably didn't remember exactly why he'd called her.

"Are we celebrating something?" she asked, sliding into the booth across from him. "Like you coming home," she added barely above a whisper.

"Are you happy?" he asked, after a long silence, ignoring or missing her sarcasm.

"Mostly, how about you?"

"I don't think so."

He said it so casually Josie didn't know how to respond. She suddenly had a strong desire to go home. Something bad was about to happen.

The bartender brought Jake another drink and put a large goblet of red wine in front of her. She didn't ask what it was, took a big swallow and then sat back and waited. He stared at his fresh drink but didn't touch it. His hair needed combing, and he hadn't shaved. There were a few tiny red spots on his right sleeve. Spaghetti sauce, she thought. So, he hadn't changed his clothes since yesterday.

"What's going on with you?" she asked. "If you wanna work with Bob Steiner then quit the D.A. and do it," and just stop pissing and moaning about it, she thought.

He glanced up at her. "You don't care?"

"Of course I care, Jake, but you made the decision, so what's the problem?"

"I'm not happy."

Josie exhaled and leaned on the table. She loved her husband. Usually, he made her happy, at times angry, but at this particular moment he was really annoying her.

"Why?" she asked, attempting to control that touch of sarcasm she'd been told slipped into her voice when they argued.

"Maybe I need a change," he said, not looking at her.

"Because?" she asked, in a tone she usually reserved for one of her denser police probationers.

"I don't know how to explain . . . it's a feeling, a big empty space in my gut. You know I really care for you and David, but something's not right with my life. I don't want to hurt you . . . it's not your fault. It's me, my problem."

He was slurring his words a little and trying to organize his unruly thoughts, but she immediately picked up on the phrase "care for you" instead of love you.

Finally, when she couldn't listen to the illogical rambling anymore, she interrupted and said, "It's not that difficult; just tell me what's bothering you."

"I'm not happy," he repeated as if she didn't get it the first time.

"With me," she said, firmly. One of them had to say it.

"No, no," he protested. "You're a great wife and mother. . . ."

"Bullshit," she interrupted. "I'm never home. I hardly ever cook or clean. We can't enjoy a movie or dinner without my lieutenant calling me about a dead body or officer-involved shooting. David's a mess. He's practically raised himself . . . badly." She stopped. He wasn't disagreeing with her. "This is my job. We've lived this way for twenty-two years. I haven't changed. I still love you." She knew she should shut up now, but couldn't stop herself from saying it. "Be man enough to tell me if you don't feel the same way."

He straightened his back just slightly, and she knew she'd hit the testosterone target dead center. Working around mostly men for so many years, she'd discovered the one certain way to get a guy's attention was to question his manhood.

"I need some time by myself."

Josie finished the glass of wine. "I'm tired," she said. She wasn't, but wanted to go home. If they were going to have a real conversation, she needed him sober enough to figure out what he wanted to say and then remember he said it. Also, it was important to look in his eyes, but he was carefully avoiding that. Jake wasn't a good liar. They both knew it. She figured that's why he wasn't telling her anything. A lie wouldn't work, and the truth might hurt. In her experience, the statement "I need some time by myself" was a euphemism for, "I want to try somebody else. If it doesn't work out, I'll be back." She got up to leave, and he didn't move to stop her.

It was a difficult walk back to the house. A few blocks seemed like miles, and the San Gabriel Valley had turned cold. There were people on the street—distracting activity around her. She checked her Blackberry. No messages.

As Josie walked up the sidewalk toward the house, it was dark—but she could see there were two cars in her driveway. The city car was parked safely in the garage. She got closer and could make out David's jeep beside the Porsche. Her first thought was wondering why David had been home more in the last two days than in the last two months, and immediately she felt guilty. A mother should be happy to see her son and she was, but David's companionship frequently came not only with his dirty laundry but with conditions.

When he was a boy, David was closer to her, but as he got older Jake was his confidant and mentor. She was never certain what was going on in her son's life—what was real, or what he wanted her to believe so she wouldn't ask too many prying questions. She was a cop and maybe not as gullible as Jake or most of the other mothers, but lately she was resigned to ignoring his deceptions, knowing inevitably the truth would surface. Otherwise, she feared their relationship might become a series of nasty interrogations. Tonight she wasn't certain she could play his games. Her nerves were already on overload.

She found him rummaging in the refrigerator. When she said "Hi" he straightened up and hit his head on the top shelf.

"You alright," she said, trying to touch the back of his neck. "Kind of jumpy, aren't you?"

He moved away. "I'm fine. You scared me. I didn't expect you home."

"Where did you expect me?"

"With Dad. What happened?" He pulled the butter dish out and closed the refrigerator door.

Great, she thought. They've already talked about it. Well, she wasn't going to discuss her marriage problems with her son.

"You staying? Want me to make you something to eat?"

"What happened with Dad?" David asked again, taking a loaf of bread from the counter.

She sat at the breakfast table and watched him. He buttered four slices and started devouring the bread. Josie always marveled at how much food her son could consume and never gain a pound. Obviously, he got his metabolism from her. He was skinny but ate enough to keep three people alive.

"I'm guessing you already know," she said with a tight smile.

"Male menopause."

"Possibly." She watched him butter and eat his fifth slice of bread. "I can make you a steak or heat up some soup. You don't have to eat like a prisoner."

"I told him he was a shit if he left you."

"He's . . . confused," she said, not wanting to have this conversation.

"You don't quit on people you're supposed to love."

Who is this guy, she thought staring at her son, this tall, good-looking young man who was coming to her defense. At times, she wasn't certain David even liked her anymore, but here he was on one of the weirder nights of her life taking her side, defending her instead of his father.

"Thanks," she said. "Don't worry about it. We'll work things out. You wanna stay tonight?"

"Can't," he said, standing, brushing crumbs off his Levi's, and leaving a mess on the table.

Josie couldn't explain why, but the question popped into her mind, so she asked, "Did you know Misty Skylar?"

"She's my agent. How do you know her?"

Josie rubbed her temples. It was the wrong answer. "I met her in an alley this afternoon. She's dead."

The color faded from David's face. He pulled out the chair and sat. "I don't believe it," he whispered. "What the hell's going on?"

"How long have you had an agent?" Her son's proximity to two murder victims was pushing things way beyond coincidence.

"Cory introduced us a few weeks ago. She caught my set and liked the sound. We signed with her that night and that's the only time I've ever spoken to her."

"Did you know she was Hillary's agent?"

"No . . . well, maybe yes. I don't know. What difference does that make?"

He was upset and becoming emotional. Josie didn't like what she was seeing. Supposedly, he hardly knew the dead woman, but he was behaving as if he'd lost a close friend.

She'd been a cop long enough to know when someone, even if he was her son, wasn't responding the way he should.

But almost as quickly as David's distress appeared, it vanished. He got up and walked around her to the door.

"Is it okay if I tell Cory?" he asked, before leaving. "So he doesn't hear it on the news or the street."

Josie didn't care. She was more concerned about her son's odd behavior and his connection to these people.

"Can I make a suggestion? Actually, it's more than a suggestion," she said before he could get away. He stopped and shrugged. She said in her captain voice, "Stay away from Cory Goldman until this investigation is over."

"Sorry, Mom, not gonna happen, I'm not Dad. I don't quit on people," he responded and was gone before she could object.

Josie cleaned up the kitchen and sat alone in the den. She turned down the lights and poured herself a full glass of wine, the last of a really good Cabernet she had started a few nights ago. She flipped the switch on the CD player, and the disc was one of Jake's, a Glen Miller big band classic, good drinking music.

She finished the wine, stretched out on the couch and closed her eyes. Her intention was to relax and try not to panic about the avalanche of events coming perilously close to smothering her family.

FIVE

She woke up on the couch at five A.M. with a stiff neck and
a headache. When she went upstairs to take a shower, Josie
noticed that Jake's bedroom closet was nearly empty. All of his
favorite suits and shoes and his workout bag were gone. Somehow
he'd managed to pack his belongings and get out without her
knowing when or how it happened. The big surprise this morning
was that his departure didn't devastate as much as sadden her.
He'd left the closet door open probably to be certain she'd realize
he was gone. She closed it.

The hot shower fixed her neck and coffee cleared her head.
Josie needed to work. Running her division was the one thing that
kept her sane. She was always in control there and knew how to
make things happen.

It was so early she beat most of the rush-hour traffic and made
good time driving to Hollywood. She got off the 101 Freeway at
Cahuenga and made the quick jog onto Wilcox. She stopped at
the light on Yucca, and was pleased to see the street was fairly
clean with no sign of the homeless encampments that occasionally
popped up during the night. The faded blue wall of the Palms
was visible to her right. When the light turned green, she made a
turn in that direction. She hadn't been to this location for a while
and was curious to see if the infamous Palms had changed. The
three-story building with the painted-over graffiti, chipped stucco
and peeling wood trim looked exactly like it did fifteen years ago
when she'd worked the Narcotics division. The front yard was
cement with a couple of untrimmed ugly bushes in a patch of dirt

near the front door. A brick planter with dead flowers and thriving weeds was under the first floor windows.

There were several loose bricks in the planter where dime dealers kept their stash. Everyone knew that was where they hid the plastic baggies, but they still did it and always got arrested. This was where Hillary allegedly bought her drugs, an unlikely hangout for the rich movie star but an easy place to score. Josie knew Fricke thought of the Palms as an easy mark for catching heroin users. It wasn't inconceivable that the two could've crossed paths here.

It was quiet now. When the sun came up, most drug dealers and users were just getting to bed. She drove around the block toward the station and had to admit arresting criminals was a lot more satisfying than some of the things she was expected to do as a captain, but she figured an important function of her job was insulating her officers from all the noise and official nonsense that blew down and around them. Until somebody proved to her that Fricke was involved in this mess she was determined to protect him.

Behan was waiting in her office when she arrived. He appeared rested and wore a clean shirt and dress pants.

Josie guessed the widow had agreed to be his next bride, so she asked, "Did you and the unfortunate woman set a date?"

"Vegas, this weekend."

"Do you even have any pension left to give this person after the divorce?"

"She's never gonna divorce me. I've learned my lesson. I'll treat her like a queen, and she'll support me for the rest of my life."

"There's a name for men who do that," Josie said, opening her wardrobe closet and taking a clean uniform out of the plastic bag.

"Bad news; Mouse is gone," Behan said, ignoring her comment.

"Gone as in left town, or she's dead kind of gone?"

"Don't know. Her stuff's not in her room at the Palms."

"Did Fricke work last night?" Josie asked, feeling a little guilty for thinking what she was thinking.

"Yeah, but he and his partner had a ton of arrests. They were tied up all night. I'm guessing she got cold feet and split."

"Maybe," Josie said. She was still preoccupied thinking about her son's proximity to both murder victims, but she didn't want to say anything to Behan. Eventually, he'd interview David, and all of that would come out. It made her uneasy to discuss her son's involvement because she didn't want Behan to think he had to treat David any differently than any other witness; but then she knew she'd be really annoyed if he didn't. It was complicated.

"My guys are gonna do another interview with the two porn stars that were at Hillary's going-away-permanently party . . . see if they can remember anything about anything." Behan looked embarrassed and hesitated a few seconds before asking, "You got time to go up to that party house with me today?"

She was fighting the wire hanger, attempting to pin the silver captain bars on the collar of her uniform. "Why can't Ibarra go?" she asked, knowing Behan did everything he could to stay away from his lieutenant, but she was too busy to keep filling in for her subordinate.

"The owner's back and he's pissed about the pieces of movie star brain all over his expensive wall. He's some rich, big-shot attorney and the mayor's bud. Chief Bright wants me to go up there and smooth his feathers which ain't exactly my area of expertise, and I know it's not Ibarra's."

"I've got to be at a Rotary Lunch in about half an hour . . . 1400 hours okay?"

"Perfect, thanks boss," Behan said with a big relieved grin.

"Get out. I've got to change."

He bounced off the couch and for the first time in months, the big redhead looked completely sober. Maybe wedding the widow wasn't such a bad plan, Josie thought, but knew this was how it always started with Behan's marriages—euphoria followed by a slow but inevitable descent into alcoholic misery. For his sake, she hoped this time it would be different.

The monthly Rotary Lunch was always held in an expensive restaurant off Hollywood Boulevard. Josie wasn't a member, but usually got invited by one of the business people in the city.

She exchanged greetings with a number of the small business owners and with Harry Walsh, the head deputy city attorney assigned to the Hollywood court. Harry was a sharp, philosophical lawyer who could quote Plato and Justice Scalia with equal authority. Josie got along with him because he hated criminals as much as she did, and unlike a lot of city attorneys actually tried to find ways to put bad guys in jail.

"How's Donnie Fricke?" Harry asked when they were alone. He made no secret of the fact he admired Fricke's dedication and willingness to work closely with his office. He looked away when he asked the question. She couldn't explain why, but the guy always seemed a bit intimidated by her. They laughed and joked together, but Harry always held back a little. He was younger than her, but his hair was thinning and he wore dark-rimmed glasses that made him look older and a lot shyer than he was.

"He's okay; why'd you ask?"

"I had to kick back some of his reports. I thought he might've been upset."

"Hasn't mentioned it," she said. "What was wrong with the reports?"

He shook his head and said, "No big deal; they were starting to sound a little too boiler plate."

She laughed. "Under-the-influence symptoms don't change much from one heroin addict to another."

"I know," he said, nervously. "We fixed the problem. I worried something might be wrong. He's usually so careful. . . ."

Harry didn't finish his thought and found them a couple of places at a table in the corner far enough away from the podium and those service club rituals that always preceded the lunch. When the president banged his gavel for everyone to be seated for lunch, there was one open place beside her at their table. Councilman Eli Goldman pulled out the chair and sat down as he asked, "Is this taken?"

Everyone but Josie immediately welcomed him. She smiled and knew what his first words would be before he opened his mouth.

"How's the Dennis investigation going?" he asked, whispering and leaning toward her.

"It's still early," she said.

"I understand there's a second killing that may be related," he said. Her expression must've revealed her displeasure because he quickly added, "Chief Bright has kept me in the loop on this one. I told him to let me know if there's anything the council can do . . . you know, like reward money or anything like that."

"Thank you, I appreciate that," Josie said, calmly, but inside she was fuming. Cory Goldman, their primary suspect, could go to his father and find out everything her detectives were doing. What a stupid way to do police work. At that moment, she decided Behan was about to get her new directive on not sharing any pertinent information with the bureau.

Goldman didn't pursue the conversation about the homicides. Instead, he chatted with Harry. The councilman had been invited to the lunch to give a city commendation to one of the social service organizations that assisted the homeless in Hollywood; and as soon as the paper with the city seal changed hands he was out of the room.

Josie wasn't far behind him, and noticed that Goldman had been intercepted on the sidewalk by a tall good-looking man with grey hair and a great tan. She didn't recognize the man and hadn't seen him in the restaurant. The two men shook hands but appeared to be arguing about something. Harry Walsh was standing in front of the entrance with her waiting for the valet parking attendant to return with his car. He was saying something to Josie, but she was more interested in the sidewalk conversation.

"You know him?" she asked Harry, nodding in their direction.

"With Goldman?" Harry asked and hesitated just a moment, squinting to make out the other man's features. "Peter Lange; he's an entertainment lawyer. I think he practices in New York."

"Let me take a shot in the dark. Did he just buy a house in the Hollywood Hills?"

"I don't know. Why?"

She shook her head. "It's nothing. I'll tell you later." Harry's car arrived; they shook hands, and he was gone. When she looked up, Goldman was nowhere in sight, and Lange was getting into a black limo that had pulled to the curb. Josie watched until the limo eased into traffic.

When Josie got back to the station, Behan confirmed Peter Lange was the new owner of the Hollywood Hills party house. Detectives had verified his alibi and established he was in New York on the day Hillary was murdered. He had no idea who had commandeered his new home for the deadly gathering, didn't know Hillary Dennis or any of the other guests, and had given no one permission to be there. The caretaker had been hired by the real estate agency. Lange had never met him until he arrived the day after the killing, whereupon he immediately fired the man and hired another caretaker the same day.

"How does he know Goldman?" Josie asked.

"Lange's a big political contributor. His MO is to move in and start laying down cash to anybody that can help him, including the mayor."

"Actually, his house is in Susie Fletcher's section of Holly-wood," Josie said, recalling the crazy gerrymandered districts in the city established more for political expediency than logic or convenience.

"He bought an office building on Sunset. That's Goldman's domain, but I'm sure Fletcher got her tribute too."

She knew Behan was probably right. That's how politics worked in L.A. Money had the loudest voice in public policy decisions.

Despite some last minute crises around the station, she and Behan managed to get to the party house on time. Josie was surprised how much better it looked in the daylight. The outside was freshly painted, and a new six-foot wall with an electronic gate surrounded the place. She pressed the buzzer and looked up at a security camera on the roof of the garage. The gate opened, and Peter Lange was standing on the step by the open front door.

None of these hill houses had much of a front yard, but the view of the canyon was spectacular. Josie noticed the small courtyard area inside the wall had recently been paved with Spanish tiles and looked great.

Lange was cordial and gave her a long, firm handshake. He had a dark complexion and brown eyes. She thought he looked more Mediterranean than his name would indicate. Living with Jake all those years, she'd met hordes of her husband's Italian relatives, and Peter Lange could easily have been one of them. He invited them inside.

There was no trace of the gruesome murder scene in the large front room. A new black leather couch had replaced the bloody one, and the wall had been scrubbed and painted sage green. Josie noticed all the furniture was new, and included contemporary glass-topped tables and recessed lighting. The space had a more masculine look now. It wasn't her taste, but was very well done.

Lange sat on the couch beside her; she could smell his cologne. It was spicy, almost a fresh-cut wood scent, and she was about to ask what it was before remembering she might not have anyone to give it to.

"I want to apologize for dragging you out here. I know you're both busy," Lange said after they declined anything to drink. "You can understand how disturbing it would be to have something like this happen in your home."

"I see you've added some security," Josie said.

"It was either that or sell the place," he said, but those words didn't fit the man. Josie couldn't picture him as the sort of guy who'd run from trouble. Actually, she thought something didn't feel right about him. He was trying too hard to be nice.

"Do you have a new address or phone number for the former caretaker?" Behan asked.

"Sorry no, I just wanted him out of here. Despite his denials I can't believe he didn't help arrange the whole party thing."

"Is there anything we can do for you?" Josie asked, beginning to wonder why he wanted them there.

"I need to know who did this and why they picked my house. I saw you today at the Rotary," he said, as an afterthought. For some reason, Josie blushed as if she'd been caught doing something bad.

He continued, "I confronted Goldman there because I believe his son is involved, but you saw how he reacted. He denied Cory knew anything. I don't believe that. Do you?"

"We haven't eliminated him as a suspect," Behan said. "But there's really nothing that puts him in your house that night."

"I know," Lange said, running his fingers through his thick hair. "But it's frustrating. I want you to know I'm willing to do whatever's necessary to help solve this terrible thing. I didn't know the girl, but no one deserves to die like that."

"Thank you. We appreciate your offer," Josie said, not having a clue about what he thought he could do. In her suspicious mind, she wondered if he was attempting to redirect her attention away from the odd confrontation she'd seen between him and Goldman that afternoon.

"Do you represent specific entertainers?" Behan asked, changing the subject.

"Yes, but not actors, mostly musicians."

"Anyone on the West Coast?"

"Of course," Lange said. "I have a number of clients here."

"Any reason one of your clients might think he or she could borrow your home for the night?" Behan asked.

Lange folded his arms and exhaled. "Surely you don't believe I'm involved in this business except to the extent that someone broke into my home," he said.

Lange turned toward Josie. She didn't want to answer for Behan, but her detective wasn't responding so she didn't have much choice.

"Absolutely not," she said, thinking that's what he expected to hear. She believed he was as much a suspect as anyone else, but had no intention of telling him that. "We appreciate your offer of assistance, and of course we'll keep you informed about anything that concerns you or your property."

"Thank you," he said and seemed to relax. "I appreciate that. What happened here was shocking. I want to stay in L.A. and keep my businesses here, but like I told the mayor, my decision depends on how this investigation is handled."

After the veiled threat, he offered to show them around the property. Josie wasn't interested. She'd had enough of Peter Lange, but Behan jumped at the invitation. The house was approximately three thousand square feet and every room was professionally decorated. She thought Behan would start drooling when they arrived in the game room where a full-sized pool table and bar were prominently displayed. From there, French doors led to the backyard which featured a small lap pool and a huge canyon view.

When the tour was over, Lange escorted them to the front gate.

"Is Corsino your married name?" he asked, before she could get into Behan's car. She nodded, and he said, "Too bad, I thought we might be paisans."

"Change your name?" she asked.

"My dad Giovanni Langella became Johnny Lange at Ellis Island."

"Pastore was my maiden name, but my dad split when I was a kid and on my mom's side they were all hard-drinking Irish."

"Buono," Lange said, laughing and hugging her. "Sorry," he said stepping back almost as quickly. "For a second there I forgot you were a cop."

She looked down at her uniform. "I can see how you'd make that mistake."

Peter Lange stood by his front gate and watched as they drove away.

"I'd say you smoothed his feathers," Behan said, grinning and looking intently at the road. "How're your feathers doing there, boss?"

SIX

There were two events Josie had promised to attend that evening. The first was a homeowners' association meeting at a residence in the Hills where she assured a group of about fifty, mostly older, wealthy men and women that there wasn't a crazed serial killer skulking in their backyards, waiting in the heavy undergrowth until they closed their eyes so he could butcher them in their sleep. She didn't know that for a fact, but believed it was a logical deduction from the known facts in the Dennis murder.

The meeting was down the street from Lange's home, but he didn't attend. His neighbors were grateful Josie came and thanked her profusely for the meager information she'd provided about the case. They had as many questions about Lange as they had about the murder in his house, wanting to know what he did for a living and describing all the strange-looking characters he entertained almost every night. Josie didn't have any answers, but she learned from the old woman who lived next door that a police cruiser had been routinely making nightly visits before the murder.

Josie drank a respectable amount of coffee and ate too many cookies before leaving. She was sorry she had another meeting that night because she was enjoying their company and probably would've stayed longer. As she got older, she was finding successful old people were fascinating, and eventually one of them always opened an expensive bottle of wine which made bullshitting sessions a lot more enjoyable. Unfortunately, many of them were easily frightened. They didn't seem to fear death as much as departing the world at a time when they had so much of life figured out.

Her misgivings about leaving the Hills were reinforced as soon as she arrived at the second meeting. A group of Hollywood nightclub owners had asked to get together with her about the manner in which her vice unit was enforcing ordinances in their establishments. They felt the detectives were being too heavy-handed. So that night Josie invited ten of them to come to Hollywood station and talk about it.

It was ten P.M., the middle of the work day for these people, and the roll call room would be empty until the next patrol watch started in about an hour and a half. Josie intentionally scheduled the meeting with built-in time restrictions in a space where the seats weren't all that comfortable. She didn't want the gathering transforming into a bitch session. If there were real problems, the owners would be forced to address those first. Besides, she didn't want to stay up all night listening to these guys complain when she had no intention of reining in her vice officers.

Harry Walsh had agreed to attend, and when Josie arrived at the roll call room he was already there along with most of the owners. She knew the deputy city attorney could explain most of the convoluted ordinances better than she could, and the two of them generally made a good team.

"Thanks for staying up so late," she said, cornering Harry behind the rows of wooden chairs.

"Did you invite Vince Milano?" he asked, nervously stroking his thinning hair.

"He's got the biggest club in Hollywood with the biggest problems."

"I know, but he's such a sleazebag," Harry whispered.

Josie laughed. That was harsh language for the mild-mannered attorney.

"That's the world we work in, Harry. Frankly, this whole thing was Milano's idea. He wants me to give him the bottom-line ground rules."

"Why, so he can keep ignoring them? You know Avanti's is where most of the underage drinking goes on. That's where Hillary Dennis and her crowd hung out."

Josie hadn't heard that. "How do you know?"

"Citations come through my office. They're licensed with the city, too."

"If they're that bad, why are they still open?" she asked, and when Harry smirked, she added, "Never mind." The clubs were a rich source of tax and fee revenue for the city. Their owners contributed generously to political campaigns and pet projects.

Minutes later, Josie joined Harry behind the desk on a raised platform where the watch commander usually sat. She looked out at the odd collection of owners, and for the first time noticed Peter Lange sitting beside Vince Milano in the second row. That explained Lange's absence from the neighborhood meeting.

Milano was short and stocky. He wore an expensive dark suit, but looked very uncomfortable squeezed into the tight space between his bolted seat and the immoveable roll call table. Otherwise, he and Lange could've been a couple of affluent bankers. The rest of the owners were a mix of cheap suits and casual work clothes.

When Josie finished her opening remarks, the only female popped up and complained that the frequent bar checks by vice detectives were chasing away her customers. Harry politely interrupted and recounted the exact number of checks, which weren't excessive, and noted how many of them had produced numerous violations in her club. The barrage of complaints continued for a few minutes until Milano shouted down his colleagues.

"This is stupid," he said to no one in particular when the room was quiet. "We need some kind of checklist of the most frequent violations so we can police ourselves. Then when the officers come, we'll be in compliance."

Josie stared at him for a few seconds . . . the voice of reason. Where did that come from? When Lange reached over and jotted something on Milano's notes, and they exchanged whispers, she surmised the lawyer had coached him.

"I'll have my detectives put something together for you," she said, glancing at Peter Lange whose expression displayed just a trace of satisfaction. He had prepared his client well.

"I also figured we might put some kinda warning in the clubs about the danger of these kids drinking and using drugs," Milano said in his most serious, concerned citizen voice. He tried to straighten his suit, but it was pushed tight against his substantial belly and the table and wouldn't move.

Josie jotted down a note to herself to check with Behan if the pictures he had of Hillary and Cory Goldman were taken at Avanti's. She knew Milano's gesture was primarily intended to placate her and take pressure off his establishment, but it wasn't a bad idea.

The discussion continued until the first morning-watch uniformed officer opened the door. He peeked in and closed it as soon as he realized the room was being used. Everyone got the hint and the meeting was over. Josie thanked them and promised to have the list of the most frequently violated ordinances available in a few days. Milano volunteered to have the "don't drink and don't use drugs" sign designed. He agreed to show it to Josie before printing and posting it in all the clubs.

Peter Lange waited until most of the owners were gone before approaching Josie and Harry in the hallway outside the roll call room.

"Thanks for your help," she said, smiling at Lange.

"Actually, it was Vince's idea. Maybe I helped organize his thoughts," Lange said.

"How long have you worked for Milano?" Harry asked.

"Not long," Lange said, still looking at Josie. "He's smarter than most of them and knows he can't continue to flaunt the law or he'll lose his business. I think you'll find he's a strong ally."

"What does he expect in return?" Harry asked, forcing a smile, but Josie knew he was dead serious. Harry believed most of the nightclubs were fronts for organized crime. She didn't think she agreed, but trusted Harry's instincts enough to keep an open mind.

Lange was unfazed. "He wants to make money. Cops in Avanti's all the time is bad for business. Are you guys done for the night?"

"I hope so," Josie said.

"Can I buy both of you a drink across the street?" Lange asked. "That restaurant has a decent bar."

Harry and Josie exchanged a look that said, "Is this guy serious?"

"I'm too tired to drink. Think I'll just go home, but thanks," Josie said.

"Me too," Harry chimed in, already moving in the direction of the stairs.

If Lange was disappointed he didn't show it. He thanked Josie for her hospitality, apologized for missing the community meeting, and followed Harry down the stairs and out the back door.

Josie couldn't believe how much she wanted that drink, but knew it wasn't going to happen. Lange was handsome and trying to be charming. He was openly flirting with her, and although she was in a sort of marriage limbo, she wasn't going to play in the muck. Not only was he Vince Milano's lawyer, but despite his efforts to hide it she sensed a coldhearted meanness in the man.

She changed out of her uniform and into her jeans and sweater and drove to Pasadena. There weren't any cars in her driveway as she approached the house and none of the lights were on inside. Jake and David were doing whatever it was they did without her. She parked in the garage, closed the door, and stood in the driveway. The neighborhood was dead quiet.

The whole day had been packed with other people's problems. She was tired, but this was her time, and she didn't want to spend it alone in that house. She threw her keys in her purse and slung the strap over her shoulder. The weight of the semi-auto almost made her take the weapon out and hide it under the driver's seat of the city car, but she decided it wouldn't do much good under there if she needed it on her stroll to the Carriage Inn and back.

It was midnight. Two good hours left for sipping wine and people-watching at the bar before she had to come back to an empty house.

The Inn was respectably crowded, but she found several empty booths in the back. The waitress who looked to be barely twenty-one took her order and brought her wine and a basket of small cheese-filled puffs. Josie tried one. Garlic and onions were mixed into the mild cheese. The little hors d'oeuvres made the wine taste so much better. She'd nearly finished her second glass of Cabernet and the tasty appetizer when she spotted her son standing at the bar. He was at least a head taller than everyone else who clustered there, trying to catch the lone bartender's attention. Josie was about to slide out of the booth and surprise him when she noticed he wasn't alone. Sitting on the stool beside David was a skinny young man with a shaved head. He was wearing a sleeveless t-shirt revealing a variety of tattoos covering his arms and neck. Both ears were pierced with diamond studs. Hoping David didn't have too many friends who looked like that, she guessed his companion was Cory Goldman. Her first reaction was disappointment. She knew her kid hardly ever listened to her, but still hoped he was smart enough to heed a sensible warning and stay away from the councilman's son.

Her second reaction was curiosity about Cory Goldman. She wondered what this strange-looking kid was all about. It didn't take long to find out. When the crowd thinned, David, sitting with his back leaning against the bar, noticed Josie. She smiled, and he waved at her. He slapped Cory on the arm and must've told him to follow, because they both came to her booth carrying their drinks. David bent over and kissed her on the cheek.

"Mom, this is Cory," he said, and slid into the seat across from her. He moved over for his friend to get in.

Cory hesitated and seemed uncomfortable. "Maybe this isn't such a good idea," he said, standing near the table.

"It's fine. Get in," Josie ordered, thinking it was a great opportunity. If the wine hadn't muddled her brain too much, she might actually get some idea of what this kid was about.

"Thanks," Cory mumbled, but couldn't conceal the fact that he would rather be anywhere but in that booth.

"What are you two doing in my part of the world? I thought Hollywood was more to your taste," she said, looking at Cory.

"The house was dark; I thought you'd be asleep," David said.

"Nope, just got home . . . had a meeting with some of the club owners. You guys spend any time in Avanti's?"

"Sure," David said. "That's the hottest place on the west side."

Cory glanced down at the table. He nervously rubbed a black spider tattooed on the back of his hand and scratched at his left arm.

"You know Vince Milano?" she asked.

"Who's he?" David asked.

Cory stared into his drink.

"You know him, Cory?" she asked, tilting her head a little in an attempt to make eye contact.

"He owns Avanti's," Cory said, in a tone that asked 'how stupid can you be?' but he didn't volunteer more information.

"Are you a musician, too?" she asked.

"No," he said, finally looking at her. His eyes were big blue empty pools with that impenetrable gaze usually reserved for con men or serial killers.

"What do you do?" she asked him, and was tempted to add 'besides lying around all day getting high,' but didn't. Her David was a smart young man. She couldn't understand why he'd waste his time with this loser.

"Nothing much," Cory said, clearly not enjoying himself.

"He's a terrific artist," David said.

"How would you know," Cory shot back. He appeared to be angry at the compliment.

"Don't have to be Picasso to recognize good stuff," David said, unfazed.

"You're not so bad yourself," Josie said, looking at David. She didn't know why, but felt compelled to defend her son's talent.

Cory gulped down the remainder of his drink and mumbled, "I gotta split." Without another word the young man was out of the booth and gone.

"Don't think he likes me," Josie said when she and her son were alone.

"Actually, he told me he's pretty impressed with you being a police captain and all. It's me he's pissed at."

"Really," she said and sat back. She'd used one of those words that made people either tell you everything or change the subject. She was too tired to be clever.

David parroted her. "Really," he said, his voice dripping sarcasm. He was definitely her kid. "Doesn't get it when somebody's trying to help. The guy's a mess."

"I guessed as much," she said.

"His dad's a jerk; mom's gone; he's got zero self-esteem and a shit-pot full of talent he has no idea how to use. That's why Hillary glommed on to him. He's so insecure he'd do anything she said."

"Thought he dumped her."

"He did, but not before she did serious damage. He's still confused by all that."

"Enough to kill her."

David shook his head. "He'd kill himself first. That's why I won't walk out on him."

"How good an artist is he?" she asked. "As good as you?"

"Hundred times better. His dad sent him to some art school in Italy when he was in high school. They thought he was the second coming of Michelangelo, but as soon as he started getting some attention he ran away. His dad hired a private detective who found him snorting coke, living on the streets in Venice, and dragged him home."

"I know you feel sorry for him, but don't let Cory drag you into something you can't handle."

David sighed and got up wearily. "Don't know why I try. In a million years, somebody like you couldn't understand a guy like Cory." He gently hugged her, said "night, Mom" and was gone.

Within seconds of his departure, the bar lights flashed. Josie left half a glass of wine on the table and stepped outside to a welcome blast of cold air that splashed against her face, reviving her long enough to make the short walk home.

No cars in the driveway. She went inside the house and turned on all the downstairs lights. Dark rooms depressed her. The words 'somebody like you' kept replaying in her mind. Who did David

• 74 •

think she was, Josie wondered. Her biggest fear was David wasn't somebody like her.

She went upstairs and fell into bed. She'd intended to get up in a few minutes, put on her nightgown and brush her teeth. None of that happened. Josie woke at seven A.M., fully rested, still wearing her jeans with her purse tucked under her arm.

After a few minutes of lounging in bed, she got up and took a shower. It felt great, but she couldn't stop thinking about her son's comment. Following the tirades of his teenage years, she should've been way beyond feeling hurt over anything he said, but at his age he should know better. It bothered Josie that he was willing to forgive Cory just about anything, but wouldn't cut her any slack.

Downstairs all the lights were still on from last night. She went from room to room switching them off. She'd already decided to send all the utility bills to Jake as soon as she got an address for him. Keeping the lights on was the least he could do until he found himself.

She wanted to talk with Behan but knew she'd better stop at the bureau first. Her appointment to review her rating with Bright was at nine. The handsome Sergeant Perry wasn't at his desk, but Bright's secretary greeted her with an invitation to sit in the conference room where there was a fresh pot of coffee and muffins. Josie found a clean coffee mug and filled it. She rummaged through the muffins and found a big blueberry one that she'd half-finished when Bright walked in.

"Morning, Chief," she said, before stuffing another large chunk of muffin in her mouth.

"How do you stay so thin eating like that?" he asked, looking disgusted. She knew he ran a couple of miles every morning, but still had a respectable potbelly.

"Nervous energy, it burns calories."

He put a red folder in front of her. "I'll give you a few minutes to review this," Bright said, moving toward the door. "Then we'll discuss it."

As soon as he left, Josie opened the folder and started reading. Overall, it wasn't a bad rating. It wasn't great either, and noted several areas that needed improvement such as working with the bureau. In so many words, the rating said she wasn't satisfactorily promoting the department's goals. She closed the folder, sat back and waited for his return.

A few months ago, Bright had made the mistake of putting together a binder on the crime stats, overtime hours, response times, filing rates, etc., comparing his four West bureau divisions. Hollywood had excelled in every category.

As soon as Bright sat down, Josie started quoting the report. She asked him to explain what he based his evaluation on if these numbers were correct. He didn't know.

"We believe you're too close to the officers," he said weakly, concentrating on twisting a paper clip.

"Who's we, and what does that mean?" she asked.

"You're too lenient with discipline."

She demanded he produce a single case where she hadn't given the appropriate penalty for misconduct. He couldn't.

Josie confronted him on every item that wasn't rated correctly or high enough, and he backed down. It was obvious to her that he couldn't defend it. Finally, after nearly an hour, he took the evaluation from her hands and shoved it back into the folder.

"This needs work. My secretary will call you when it's ready," he said, clearly irritated, and left her in the conference room. He'd lost the battle and wasn't happy.

She filled a Styrofoam cup with coffee and took another muffin. Bright's secretary smiled at her when she came out of the conference room.

"Have a nice day, Captain," the secretary said, with a broad smile.

Josie grinned and said, "I am."

———

SHE ENTERED the back door of Hollywood station and went directly to Behan's desk. They discussed Lange's association with Vince Milano and agreed the attorney now seemed more interesting than he had appeared at first. Josie was telling him about the neighbor's statement about the police car at Lange's house and her chance meeting with Cory Goldman in Pasadena, when Lieutenant Ibarra sauntered across the room.

"I've got a meeting with Chief Bright," he said, standing behind Behan and attempting to read paperwork on the big detective's desk. "Anything new for the briefing?"

Ibarra considered himself a ladies' man, and Josie could smell his heavy cologne or aftershave from the other side of the desk. His shirt was tailored and fit his slender frame like a latex glove. She had to admit he was a friendly, usually likeable guy, but she needed a better manager. If he knew how to do his job, she could put up with his little idiosyncrasies.

"Can't find the bum living behind the bar and Fricke's snitch has disappeared," Behan said. "Bright's heard everything else at least twice."

"That's something," Ibarra said and asked, "What about the councilman's kid, nothing new on him?"

"No," Josie said before Behan could respond. At the right time, she would tell Bright about her son's connection to Cory Goldman. That revelation wasn't something she'd entrust to Ibarra. Besides, she wasn't certain what David's role was in all of this other than his friendship with the councilman's son. She was beginning to think she might never understand her son's world, where young adults didn't plan their lives beyond the moment. She knew her son wasn't like that, but for some reason he didn't reject those people either.

"You haven't told the bureau about your kid," Behan said, when Ibarra had returned to his office.

"Have you interviewed David?"

"He's coming in this afternoon. I'm not expecting much."

"Don't tell me about it. Just do what you've got to do."

Josie got up. She would talk to Bright tomorrow. At least now she could tell her boss that David had known both victims, but he'd been interviewed like any other witness. To demonstrate her determination not to interfere, Josie would tell Bright he'd have to get details of David's interview from Ibarra or Behan to prevent a conflict of interest since she would have heard none of it.

Josie was annoyed. She hated being on the defensive, but her son's actions had put her in a bad position, possibly tainted her reputation. She wouldn't believe he'd intended to hurt her, but nevertheless, here she was having to explain his flaky lifestyle.

THE CHIEF of police had scheduled a meeting for all department captains that afternoon at the Police Administration Building downtown. He was a numbers guy and was happy as long as crime was going down. Josie firmly believed the police department had very little to do with crime trends. However, she'd been a manager in the LAPD long enough to know if you wanted to survive, you played the game, so she regurgitated her stats and claimed victory over the evildoers in Hollywood.

She left the police building and drove away from downtown L.A. in heavy rush-hour traffic thinking there were so many important things she could've been doing with that time.

By the time she got off the freeway, it was dark. She drove straight down Cahuenga and past the police station. She'd scheduled a meeting with Councilwoman Fletcher for Monday morning and wanted some firsthand information about the needle exchange center on Santa Monica Boulevard. Fletcher was reluctant to support her, but the needle exchange had become a spawning ground for drug-induced crime in that area, and Josie wanted it shut down. Burglaries and car break-ins were rampant, and Fricke complained conditions were getting worse. Josie figured as long as she was out, she'd see if it was as bad as he said.

According to her officers, employees at the exchange were handing out bundles of needles to anyone who asked. They were supposed to take a dirty needle and give a clean one in return. Some customers were given ten or twenty needles, and they turned around and sold those needles to addicts who were either afraid or too lazy to go to the exchange, or too stupid to realize they could get one for nothing.

The center was situated in an RV parked on an empty lot on Santa Monica Boulevard near Western. A light was on inside and a couple of dozen shady-looking characters were scattered around the lot. Josie parked a block away and watched. A street-light was directly over the vehicle, and two tripods with floodlights had been placed near the RV door. There was plenty of activity in the parking lot, but no one approached the vehicle. After half an hour, a woman wearing a white oversized lab coat came out of the RV and stood on the top step. She lit a cigarette and leaned against a flimsy railing. With her binoculars, Josie could identify the woman's familiar symptoms—slow deliberate movements, droopy eyelids, scratching her arms and face, the head nodding. It would be difficult for Josie not to recognize a full-blown heroin addict after all her years as a dope cop. This wasn't what she'd expected to see, but it would do and should help get this place closed down. She tried to see the name tag on the lab coat, but it was covered by folds of material. She memorized the woman's description: thin, bad complexion, stringy brown hair, black-rimmed glasses, and average height. Normally, she would've had a narcotics detective arrest her for being under the influence, but the political ramifications would be horrendous. Council-woman Fletcher had decreed the needle exchange off-limits for law enforcement. Any arrests within a block of the RV would be heavily criticized. Josie was savvy enough to pick her fights. There might come a time when she would be willing to fight that battle, but not yet.

She started the car and was about to back up when someone else came out of the RV. She quickly put the car in park and picked up the binoculars again. It was a smaller woman who maneuvered around the mellow addict and stepped down to the parking lot. Josie immediately recognized the vine tattoo that ran from her ankle to the top of her very short shorts. Mouse carried a brown paper bag that she stuffed into her purse as she scampered across the parking lot, and was out of sight before Josie could pick up her radio. She finally managed to get Fricke on the air and asked him to meet her several blocks from the needle exchange in a Starbucks parking lot.

Josie had barely arrived when the black and white police vehicle pulled in beside her car. She explained what she'd seen at the needle exchange, but cautioned Fricke and his partner not to stake out the center, explaining she didn't want to deal with the repercussions if they made an arrest anywhere near it.

"Mouse is back in the area. I want you to take some time and find out what she's up to. Maybe she'll take you to Little Joe," she said, as they stood near her car drinking the coffee she bought. "My guess is that paper bag was full of syringes."

"Makes a few bucks, supports her habit," Fricke said. "Hypes sell anything that ain't nailed down."

Donnie Fricke wasn't his usual animated self tonight, and his partner kicked at the police car's back tire while staring out over the boulevard. They looked like a married couple that just had a fight, but were obliged to put on a good face for the relatives. Josie knew having the right partner was more critical than being married to the right person. Partners depended on each other to stay alive, and if they weren't clicking it was a recipe for a "Fricke-up" of the worst kind.

"You guys okay?" she asked.

"You know, ma'am, this guy's like a rock around my neck," Fricke said with a forced grin. "Gotta carry him all night. It's a burden."

Frank Butler didn't react, but behaved as if he hadn't heard the remark and remained focused on the street. Fricke was joking as usual, but Butler wasn't responding the way he normally did.

"I'm thinking of splitting you two up," Josie said, trying to sound serious and getting the expected reaction.

"What!" they shouted in unison. Frank straightened up and stood beside Fricke. He definitely heard that. They both moved closer to her, agitated and clearly unnerved.

"Just kidding," Josie said, raising her hands and backing away. "What are you fighting about?"

"Nothing, it wasn't nothing, ma'am," Fricke mumbled, still shaken by the prospect of losing his partner. It wasn't easy for Fricke to find someone who'd work with him every night. He was intense, and his big personality seemed to wear on everyone except Josie and Butler.

"I want the squad to grow, train more hype cops, and get a full-time sergeant so we can make more arrests and cover longer hours. Knucklehead here thinks it's fine the way it is, thinks we're the only guys in the world that can do this the right way," Frank said. "It's too much. I'm tired. We need help."

He crossed his arms and stared at Fricke. Josie was stunned. She'd never heard Butler say more than a couple of words, or challenge Fricke, but she knew he had a valid point since she'd been contemplating doing what he was suggesting for several weeks. Judging by the number of arrests they made, there was enough work for a squad and supervisor.

Josie wondered why Fricke objected to the help . . . enough to fight with his partner. Maybe he didn't. She worried his real objection was answering to a supervisor. Fricke pretty much did what he wanted now. The constant scrutiny of a sergeant would definitely cramp his style.

"Knucklehead?" Fricke asked, with a hurt expression. "I ain't the one that lost my car keys tonight."

Josie left them outside the coffee shop arguing in their usual way, and knew everything was back to normal between them. She admired and trusted Fricke, but realized with some sadness she wasn't as concerned about locating Mouse as she was nervous about those bad vibes growing around one of her officers.

SEVEN

Criminals didn't take days off, so weekends, holidays, kids' birthdays, and special occasions meant business as usual for most cops. Sometimes they got lucky and were given the time off, but Josie had never counted on it. She went to the office every day. Her staff didn't come in on the weekends, but it was quiet so she usually got caught up on a week's worth of paperwork. The bureau rarely worked on weekends, meaning there were no annoying phone calls or worthless trips to the Wilshire offices.

The adjutant's desk was clean, which meant Bobby Jones had dumped everything back on hers. Her adjutant was a good worker. Josie didn't understand why Behan disliked the guy so much, but chalked it up to the veteran detective's irritable disposition.

She'd almost forgotten Behan was in Las Vegas getting married this weekend. Josie couldn't wait to see the bride. She pictured this cranky white-haired old woman with a cane, stuffing stale wedding cake into the big grouchy redhead's mouth. The image was so bizarre she forced herself to stop thinking about it.

Most of the paperwork was finished and stacked on her secretary's desk or shifted to her computer before noon. Josie straightened up her office and went upstairs to see if her vice lieutenant was working. The office was empty except for Lieutenant Marge Bailey, hunched over a computer keyboard arranging an assortment of booking photos on the monitor.

Marge supervised the biggest vice unit in the city with a major portion of her efforts and personnel dedicated to prostitution enforcement. Hollywood had more than its share of working ladies who'd come to tinseltown by the truckload looking for fame and fortune, and when they got hungry enough settled for a dime bag and the price of a room.

This lieutenant seemed to be the most unlikely person to run an operation as unwieldy and gritty as this one. Marge was beauty-queen gorgeous, tall, with a swimsuit-model figure and long, naturally blond hair. She was in her thirties but looked twenty, and became something of a legend in undercover vice lore as a young officer when she dressed as a hooker and tried to catch unsuspecting johns on Sunset Boulevard. This gorgeous blond stopped traffic for hours and drew an unruly crowd of admirers, causing a mini-riot. But, anyone who mistook her for anything but a dead serious cop was in for an eye-opening experience. She was an expert shot, studied martial arts and swore like a longshoreman. Josie considered her a friend, probably the only female friend she had in the department.

"What's up?" Marge said, still fixated on her keyboard.

"You busy?"

"Fuck, yes."

"Good. Want to hear about your meeting last night?"

Marge groaned and finally looked up. "No, but I guess since you took mercy and let me celebrate my birthday away from Vince Milano, I should pretend to care. Did he ask about me?" She grinned and turned off the computer.

"He was a perfect gentleman and your name never came up."

"Did he hit on you?" Marge asked and laughed when Josie grimaced. "Why not? You're tall, dark and beautiful."

"I'm also over thirteen years old which in his world is ancient."

"What'd he want?"

Josie told her what happened at the meeting and everything she had learned about Peter Lange. The prospect of creating a cheat sheet for the club owners to obey the law didn't appeal to Marge but she agreed to do it.

"Have you and Behan compared notes on this Hillary Dennis homicide?" Josie asked. With the murder happening in Lange's house and his connection to Vince Milano, she wanted Marge's resources involved.

"Kind of."

"What's that mean?"

"I asked if I could help and he told me to fuck off . . . in so many words."

"What's Avanti's like?" Josie changed the subject. She'd deal with Behan when he returned.

"Basically, an old warehouse cesspool, but a very enticing, well-decorated septic tank. The music's too loud; it's too dark; crowd's too young . . . got everything from alcohol to drugs and unprotected sex in dark corners. Your typical Vince Milano dive. We're checking a couple of clubs tonight. Want to go with us? See for yourself."

"How often are your people in there?"

"At least a couple times a week," Marge said and sat back. "Wait, is that dirtbag complaining about us, again?"

"Actually no, he was one of the few that didn't, but I was wondering if you might have citations that could tell us who Hillary went clubbing with. Do you remember seeing her at Avanti's?"

"Probably not, but we can do a run on citations and FI's."

Josie knew the field interview cards were probably more valuable since officers really didn't need a violation of law to make one. Sometimes it was just a suspicion, an intuitive nagging that made them jot down the information that put a particular person in a place at a certain time. On numerous occasions those FI's identified a suspect when all other means had failed.

Josie wasn't crazy about spending her Saturday night club-hopping, but it wasn't as if she had anything else to do, so she agreed to tag along for a few hours.

"I'll talk to Behan on Monday," Josie said. "He's got to work with you."

"Thanks, I love sharing my day with Mr. Sunshine."

"He's getting married today. He should be pleasant for a few months."

"He's divorced again?"

"Hope so," Josie said. "Wanna get something to eat when you're done here?"

"No mad dash to get home . . . Is hubby out of town?" Marge asked.

"Don't exactly know where he is. But I'm not in the mood to talk about it."

Marge got up quickly and covered the computer. She was wearing tight Levi's and a belt equipped with a brown leather holster containing a small .45 semi-auto. She took a long leather jacket from another chair and slipped it on to cover the gun, her badge and a small handcuff case on her belt.

"Let's go across the street and get a glass of wine," Marge said, gently pushing Josie toward the door. "I gotta hear all about this."

They walked across Sunset to Nora's, an upscale restaurant with a dingy bar that had great chili fries and a decent selection of beer and wine. After several minutes of insisting she didn't want to talk about her marriage, Josie told her friend everything.

"Do you want him back?" Marge asked when Josie finished.

Josie hesitated, but not because she didn't know the answer. She wanted Jake back, but was determined not to sound pathetic.

"We'll see," she said.

They were both hungry and ate large hamburgers and a couple of orders of chili fries washed down with glasses of Pinot. Marge didn't give advice or pretend to understand what Josie was feeling. She allowed Josie to talk and share her thoughts because they were both old enough to know this wasn't an intellectual problem that could be fixed with counseling or rational thinking. She listened, and at the right time changed the subject.

"You kill 'Not So' yet?" Marge asked, raising an eyebrow as she sipped her wine.

"You always know how to make me feel better."

"Bastard needs to die."

"No, he needs to irritate somebody else. I kind of feel sorry for him," Josie said and wondered if she really meant that or if it was the wine talking.

"Why? He's evil."

"No," Josie said, trying to sound serious. "You've got to be smart to be evil . . . he's just nasty."

"That's our bureau, 'Not So' Bright and Art Perry . . . Nasty and Sneaky, two of the original department dwarfs."

They nearly finished a bottle of wine while identifying the other five dwarfs—Jerky, Shaky, Slimy, Nerdy, and Dopey—within the department's higher ranks. Josie realized this was the first hurts-to-breathe laugh she'd had in a long time. It revived her spirits. The wine, however, made her tired, and she excused herself after a couple of hours to take a nap on her office couch before the vice unit started its trek through the clubs.

Traffic in the administrative area was Saturday afternoon light. Most cops knew these office workers took weekends off, so one or two of the uniformed officers would use the empty desks to write reports or make personal calls in a quiet place. Josie closed the door to her office and turned off the lights. There wasn't a window in the building, so the room darkened immediately. She lay down on the couch but couldn't sleep. Her thoughts were a mix of David and Jake, mostly Jake. She wondered how he was doing on his own. He'd seemed pretty pathetic the last time she saw him with his wrinkled suit and sauce-stained shirt. For days, she'd resisted the temptation to call his cell phone or leave a text message. It would be easier to talk to him in person, but she finally turned on the light and took her Blackberry out of her jacket. "Hi, hope you're ok, love J," was all she sent. That was enough. She curled up on the couch and fell asleep.

The pounding on her door woke her about three hours later.

"Ma'am, Lieutenant Bailey says it's time for roll call," a female voice shouted from the other side of the door.

"I'm coming," she yelled back, surprised at not feeling any ill-effects from the lunchtime wine fest. Actually, it was the best sleep she'd had in days, and she was completely refreshed. She checked her Blackberry, no messages.

On her way to roll call, Josie stopped in the locker room, washed her face, combed her hair and was ready to enjoy the night's activities.

Marge organized about thirty officers to work the task force. They gathered in the roll call room and waited for their assignments. She'd borrowed six uniformed officers from patrol and Fricke and his partner had offered to assist. Josie knew the two hype officers frequently worked with vice since they shared a number of the same clientele.

Fricke stopped Josie as she entered the roll call room and explained that he and Frank hadn't been able to locate Mouse, but would continue to look for her. He seemed distracted and excused himself after a few seconds. She watched him jostle for space on the back row bench, leaning against Butler until his partner was pressed against the wall. Their behavior and banter was normal again . . . as normal as they got, but Fricke wasn't as chatty with her tonight as he usually was.

The other vice officers were in plainclothes, and were assigned to mingle among the crowds in the different clubs to spot violations. Josie sat in the back of the room and watched Marge go over the game plan for the evening. That night, they'd inspect six of the biggest night clubs in Hollywood. The plainclothes officers would go in groups of five to each of the locations. When Marge and the uniformed officers arrived they would start writing the citations and/or making arrests. It was a concise and simple plan. Marge understood the secret to a good strategy—don't have too many moving parts because nothing ever goes according to plan; and when it turns to shit you've got to have confidence that you've picked the best people who can improvise and get the job done anyway. Some supervisors never understood that basic rule and were constantly frustrated.

"You can ride with me, Captain," Marge said, after she'd dismissed the officers. "Nothing's gonna happen till I get there."

"Where's Avanti's on your list?" Josie asked.

"I figured we'd stop there close to the end, give them time to work themselves into a fucking frenzy of violations," Marge said, grinning. "But, we can't wait too long. Sometimes word gets out we're working, and they clean up their shit before we get there."

Their first stop was the club belonging to the woman who objected to the frequent vice checks. Her doorman, an overweight Samoan-looking young man in a polyester Hawaiian shirt, groaned when he saw Marge.

"Man, don't you guys got nowhere else to go?" he whined, as they moved past him into the barely lit lobby.

The owner immediately appeared. She was ready to do battle until she noticed Josie standing next to Marge.

"Captain Corsino," she said, sweetly. "I'm so pleased to see you. You've never been in my club. Let me show you around."

Josie thanked her but instead asked the woman to join them as they did their working tour of the club. One by one the undercover officers stepped up to Marge and listed at least a dozen violations of everything from underage drinking to indecent exposure on the dance floor. The owner became very quiet and apologetic. She promised to have a meeting with her manager in the morning.

"I can't believe how fucking civil she was," Marge said, as she and Josie left the club. "That was bitchin' sweet. Usually she's motherfucking and threatening us with lawsuits all the way to our cars."

"I have that effect on people. It's difficult to make a complaint if the person you're supposed to complain to is standing there watching it happen."

"Work with us every night. Look at all the paperwork you'd avoid."

"Don't I wish?"

Marge laughed. "Everybody knows you're a frustrated street cop. Sneak out, make a few arrests, bust a few heads. It'll feel good."

Josie looked around to be certain none of the officers was close enough to hear. "Then who'd be there to keep Nasty and Sneaky off your back?"

They followed the same routine in three more clubs. When it was close to one A.M., Marge announced it was time to descend on Avanti's. Josie had only seen Vince Milano's club in the daylight. It was a drab warehouse. Tonight with the loud pounding music and a rainbow of neon lights, the place had been transformed into a gaudy warehouse. Hundreds of young adults milled around the front of the building where there was a huge lighted fountain; others stood in line waiting to get inside.

From the sidewalk, Josie felt the amplified music shake the ground like a rolling earthquake. Now she understood why David's hearing was so bad. Before she and Marge could reach the door, Vince Milano was in front of them. He was several inches shorter than Josie had remembered, and with his substantial tummy and spindly legs, he resembled a cartoon tycoon in an expensive three-piece suit. His dyed dark hair was thinning, and he combed it over just enough to cover a tiny bald spot.

Milano, like all the previous club owners, was surprised to see Josie with the vice officers. He was nervous and obsequious, and couldn't stop admiring everything about her. Finally, Josie explained it wasn't a social visit and stepped aside to let Marge enlighten the little man about the reason for their call. His smile faded, but he remained cordial and led the way inside his club.

They were met by the undercover officers who detailed a number of violations and started writing the citations. The club was dark with flashes of light that gave it an eerie, broken film projector look. A gigantic disco ball hung from the ceiling and caught the light rays, sprinkling them over the dance floor like colorful confetti. While Marge talked with Milano and his man-ager, Josie wandered around the cavernous room. A number of the patrons looked to be in their teens, not old enough to drive. She wondered what sort of parent would allow a kid to come to a place like this, maybe even deliver them to the front door. The young girls' clothes or lack of clothing resembled that worn by Hillary Dennis in her mother's pictures. These kids were celebrity MTV clones with tattoos, body piercing, and hair dyed outrageous colors. She thought if their dance positions didn't produce babies it would be a miracle. Lewd was a mild word for some of their gyrations, and they didn't appear to be the least bit inhibited by the proximity of vice officers.

The pungent odor of marijuana was in the air but she didn't see anyone smoking, which usually meant there was a secluded safe room somewhere in the building designated for that activity and drinking alcohol. Mirrors lined every wall of the room and couples took turns performing simulated sex acts in front of them. Not only was her head throbbing from the noise, but she'd seen enough to close the club.

For a few seconds, the smells, body heat, loud pulsating music, and fractured light flashes made her lightheaded. She stood in place and looked around trying to get her bearings. Several yards away from her, light flickered in a corner reflecting off the mirrors, and during those seconds Josie saw him. Cory Goldman had his back to her but he was easy to recognize in the mirror. He looked up when the light washed over him. He had his arm around a small blond woman. It happened so quickly, Josie couldn't be certain, but she thought the woman might've been Mouse. The light flashed again and they were gone. She pushed through the crowd of gyrating teens to move closer, but it was hopeless. It was too dark and there were too many bodies.

Josie did manage to find the lobby where Marge had relocated with Milano. It was still too loud out there but tolerable. The owner had a fistful of citations and looked distraught. He wiggled from one foot to the other, and tried to explain how all this could be going on under his nose while he designed his DON'T DRINK— DON'T USE DRUGS posters. She took Marge by the arm and pulled her away from Milano, and told her what she'd seen in the club. It was Josie's intention to shut down the place for the remainder of the night, and she wanted the vice officers to find Mouse and the councilman's son.

"There's a few thousand fucked-up, emotionally challenged, wild party animals in here, boss. You sure you wanna chase them

out of the asylum onto the streets before they've had an opportunity to expend all that energy?" Marge said, with that raised
eyebrow.

Josie didn't. "Can your people find Mouse and Cory if I let
this dump stay open? I want a tail on them."

"Sure, describe him. All my guys know Mouse. Unfortunately,
she knows most of us too."

Josie went back and informed Milano how close he'd come to
being shut down; and claimed if it hadn't been for Marge's inter-
vention, she would've chained his doors for at least a week. So,
he'd better get his act together and clean up his club.

Vince Milano was falling all over himself thanking Josie for
not overruling her subordinate and closing Avanti's. He swore he
would personally supervise the enforcement of codes and license
requirements, but he was forever indebted to her. Josie warned
Milano this was his last chance to comply or she'd make certain he
got a stiff fine and lost his club license. He kept trying to kiss her
hand, but Josie insisted they just shake hands and call it a night.
While she was lecturing Milano, Marge huddled with a few of her
vice officers, then sent them back into the club.

By the time they wrapped up business at Avanti's, it was too
late to make the last couple of clubs. Josie was grateful. She was
tired and out of condition for the grind of real police work. There
was a time when she could stay up all night booking suspects,
change her clothes and go to court the next morning. She still
could if she didn't have to run the whole damn division, but that
was another life.

The debriefing was at the twenty-four hour Denny's restaurant
on Sunset. Josie didn't care about a post-game review, but she was
starving. She ordered eggs and pancakes and listened to the young
officers brag about what they'd done that night, as if they were
the first to experience the adrenaline rush of putting themselves in
harm's way. When she thought about it, in a way they were.

They were grateful to her for coming along because they knew
only a few commanding officers ever got involved in operations.

This had been an opportunity to show their captain what they could do, and she let them know they'd done a good job. She finished eating, paid the bill and thanked them again before Marge drove her back to Hollywood station.

"You're such a fucking frustrated street cop," Marge said, shaking her head as Josie got out and walked to her car.

EIGHT

Late Sunday morning, Marge called Josie at home to report her officers had located Mouse and Cory Goldman in the crowd at Avanti's shortly before it closed.

"Did I wake you up, boss?" Marge asked after a few seconds, and added before Josie could answer, "Wish I had more to tell you. They drank and talked at the club, then drove to an apartment building off Melrose."

"Where are they now?" Josie asked, settling into the lounger in her den with the newspaper on her lap. She'd been dead tired when she finally got to bed early that morning, but couldn't sleep; so she got up intending to read the Sunday paper and fell asleep in her chair until the phone rang.

"Still inside a first-floor apartment . . . if you want I'll have my guys watch the little shit birds for a few days and let Behan know if there's anything of interest."

"That's exactly what I want," Josie said. "Now hang up so I can read my Sunday paper in peace."

"Not coming in today?"

"You wore me out last night. Unless there's a call-out, I'll see you Monday."

"Careful you don't become one of those nine-to-five management weenies."

"Careful I don't give your cushy vice job to some deserving lieutenant who isn't such a pain in the ass," Josie said.

"Son of a bitch, I was trying so hard to be good," Marge said before hanging up.

The rest of the day was planned inertia for Josie. She took hours to browse through the L.A. Times with unscheduled naps between the boring news and editorial sections. Shortly before the dinner hour, pleasantly surprised by the lack of any emergency phone calls from the station, she perused the last advertisement and changed out of her pajamas into a pair of shabby cutoff Levi's and sweatshirt.

The house resembled a domestic disaster area badly in need of straightening and cleaning. She picked up a few things from the floor and removed the most visible layers of dust on the furniture before deciding she wanted to cook. It felt strange without Jake and David sharing her space. She could actually do whatever she wanted without getting consensus from the two men in her life. For over twenty years, every choice . . . what, when, and where to eat, what to watch on television, what CD to listen to . . . was a group decision. Suddenly she could decide for herself, and then realized she couldn't remember what she actually liked without at least considering her husband and son.

There was a veal roast, still safely under the expiration date, in the refrigerator. She sharpened her best knife and sliced the veal almost as if she were peeling an apple, and flattened it on the cutting board. It was a technique she'd learned from Jake's Italian mother. She mixed bread crumbs, parsley, parmesan cheese, an assortment of spices, onions, and garlic, sautéed all of it with the pork squeezed from two sausages, then spread the mixture over the veal. Josie rolled the veal like a carpet and tied the reconstructed roast with string. It was big enough for a family of four. She peeled the last two potatoes in the bin, quartered them, put them in a roasting pan with the veal, and poured a glass of the wine she'd been drinking over the whole thing. The oven had been heating so she slid the pan in quickly. She enjoyed cooking but didn't like eating alone. Without giving it much thought, she called Jake's cell phone, and he answered.

"You hungry?" she asked.

"What's up?" he countered, in his best noncommittal tone.

"I'm making veal roast. Want some?"

He cleared his throat and mumbled something Josie couldn't understand.

"I don't wanna sleep with you, dear; I wanna feed you an exquisite meal," she said, getting a little annoyed by his stalling.

"Can I call you right back?"

"No," she said calmly, and hung up. The wonderful smell of the veal cooking in a bath of expensive red wine filled the kitchen, but Josie was losing her appetite. She tried David's number but got his answering machine. Marge was working and Behan was busy getting married so she sat at the breakfast table, drank a little more wine, turned off the stove, and went to bed.

———

DIRTY POTS and cooking utensils covered the countertops, and the kitchen still had the scent of garlic and onions when Josie got up the next morning. She washed the dishes, wiped the oven, and unceremoniously flipped the half-cooked roast into the garbage. She should've felt worse about wasting all that food, but was still too annoyed to worry about it. Her mistake, she'd decided, was calling Jake and expecting him to come home because she'd asked. It was a good lesson. When someone who supposedly loved her could walk away and function without her, the connection was broken. There was no love without respect, so move on she told herself; it's over.

That intellectually sound conclusion got her out of the kitchen, dressed and on her way to work, but she knew rationalizing this stuff wouldn't permanently take care of all those bad feelings she'd buried somewhere in her gut.

When she arrived at the station, the detective squad room was Monday morning busy with forty-eight hour arraignments looming, bulging caseloads, transporting arrestees and witnesses to court, and locating and prepping witnesses. Behan's desk and computer were covered with papers and folders. He was staring at his monitor but looked up when Josie sat in the chair beside him.

"Still married?" she asked.

"This one's a keeper . . . makes me breakfast, doesn't want to work, too old to have kids. It's the perfect marriage."

"Great," Josie said. She knew she sounded grumpy, but didn't care because she figured Behan was the one person who wouldn't make a big deal out of her foul mood. "What's new on the Dennis-Skylar homicides? You talk to Marge about Saturday night?"

He studied her for a second or two as if he were trying to decide how flippant he could be without pissing her off.

"Bad night?" he asked, with just a trace of sarcasm.

"Let's just say there wasn't anybody to make me breakfast." She glanced at the monitor on his desk and saw he was watching a movie she didn't recognize, which wasn't a surprise since it wasn't in black and white and Bogart and Hepburn were nowhere in sight. "Isn't this place entertaining enough for you?" she asked.

He stopped the movie and went back a couple of scenes before starting it again.

"Recognize anybody?"

She did. A very alive Hillary Dennis was lounging on the front porch of a shanty in an image that reminded Josie of a scene from *The Grapes of Wrath*. Hillary had been an incredibly beautiful young woman. On film she appeared to be no older than thirteen or fourteen, but very seductive. She was wearing a faded sundress without underwear, and unbuttoned just enough to keep an R-rating and dodge the kiddie porn label. In this scene, an older man, who Behan told her was Hillary's film father, was pawing at the young girl. It got worse—in every way a terrible movie—but Josie was mesmerized. It was fascinating to watch someone walk and talk, be so vibrant, when just a few days ago she'd witnessed the cold dead flesh.

During the last scene, Behan stopped the DVD.

"See that woman," he said touching the screen. He was pointing at a well-endowed, half-dressed redhead standing in the background, one of Hillary's bumpkin relatives in the movie. It was a non-speaking, strictly eye-candy part. "She's one of the porno stars that was at the party."

"Okay, so what? She's kind of an actress. Isn't she?"

"When we interviewed her she claimed she'd never met Hillary Dennis before the party, and it gets better," he said, stopping the DVD again. He went back to the first few scenes and froze a skuzzy bar scene. It was dark, but sitting at a table in his best *Deliverance* attire—a long-sleeved plaid shirt, baseball cap and torn jeans—was Cory Goldman.

"Hilly, it seems, was a pretty good meal ticket for all her friends and ex-boyfriends. So why would Miss Porno Star say she didn't know her?"

"Good question; I think we'll have to ask her when she's here this afternoon with her lawyer," Behan said, hesitating a second before asking, "Wanna guess who that might be?"

"Peter Lange," she answered without thinking. The slick attorney seemed to be popping up everywhere.

"Right again."

Josie picked up a stack of DVD's from the corner of Behan's desk. She shuffled through a collection of films even Josie recognized as B-movies. Hillary had found her niche as sleazy world-weary jailbait. The teenage ennui dripped from the album art.

"You watch all these?" she asked.

"Me and Vicky."

"Vicky? Is Vicky the new Mrs. Behan?"

"Victoria Kiel Behan."

"Related to those theater chain Kiels?" Josie asked, joking.

"Her recently departed second husband was," he said, enjoying her surprised expression.

Josie laughed. "You're number three. She's number five. You two were made for each other."

"You have no idea." Behan was smug. He looked rested and well-groomed, and Josie was happy for him. "Come to Nora's after work and meet her. We're buying."

You mean she's buying, Josie thought but didn't say anything. He was in good spirits, and she wouldn't spoil it for him.

The end of the DVD was coming up, and Hillary's delinquent character was about to be dragged off by the police for killing her lecherous father. A tall good-looking uniformed policeman cuffed her and led her out of the family shanty. Josie snatched the control from Behan and stopped the movie. She gave it back to him.

"Go back to where they show that policeman's face and freeze it," she ordered.

Behan did what she'd asked, then sat back staring at the screen. "Damn, I've watched this thing twice and never recognized him. That's Art Perry, isn't it?"

"Sergeant Art Perry or his twin brother. Go to the credits."

He scrolled slowly through the credits, and there it was at the bottom—Policeman played by Arthur Perry.

"Ain't that some strange shit? Chief Bright's adjutant in a movie with a murder victim, and he kinda forgets to mention it," Behan said. "Guess I wouldn't be bragging about being in this dog either, but still."

"I got to hear this interview," Josie said. She knew it wasn't nice, but Art Perry was such a pompous ass it would be fun to watch him squirm a little.

"You gonna sit in on the porno queen this afternoon?"

"Maybe I can catch a few minutes. You know she's just going to say she was afraid to admit she knew Hillary." Josie was leaving but had one last thought. "Was this Hillary's last movie?" she asked. She didn't know why but it seemed significant if Art Perry was in her last movie.

"Yeah, it went right to DVD. No big mystery there," Behan said.

Josie knew she had to advise Bright before they dragged his adjutant into the station for an interview. Perry was entitled to get legal representation or call someone from the Police Protective League to deal with the possibility of any internal discipline. She went back to her office, closed the door and called the bureau. Bright was there and listened quietly as Josie described what she and Behan had seen in the movie. She purposely downplayed the interview as routine. Of course, Bright didn't have the same information she had about the possibility a cop might've been involved in Hillary's murder. She'd kept that between Behan and herself. Josie hadn't even told Lieutenant Ibarra.

With Chief Bright talking to Councilman Goldman and now Bright's adjutant appearing in Hillary's film, Josie figured her decision to keep the bureau out of the loop was looking smarter all the time.

"Was Sergeant Perry only in the one movie?" Bright asked when Josie finished telling him about what she'd seen.

"As far as I know, but even so he should've disclosed that information."

"Probably," he said, not sounding too concerned. "But I doubt he's any more involved in all this than your son is."

"Big difference. David admitted immediately he'd had contact with these people," Josie said. She knew she was being defensive, but the man had a talent for provoking her. "Do me a favor, Eric. Don't tell Perry why we want to talk to him. Behan will explain when he gets here."

"Why? Do you suspect him of something?"

Josie shifted in her chair. She was glad this conversation was on the phone because she wasn't a good liar, and Bright would've guessed from her body language she was holding something back.

"No, of course not, but I'd rather have Behan explain it to him."

He agreed, but Josie wouldn't be surprised if Sergeant Perry came to the interview fully prepped by his boss.

⸻

By the time Josie returned from a meeting that afternoon, Behan had finished with the porno star and was interviewing Sergeant Perry. She answered several phone messages and signed some paperwork before sitting in the closet-sized space adjacent to the interrogation room where she could watch Behan question Perry. The two men were alone in the room, no lawyer, no union representative.

The handsome sergeant appeared relaxed and unconcerned. His answers were short and to the point. He said he liked acting and had done several low-budget films as an extra, or brief walk-on parts with an occasional speaking line or two. He didn't have an agent any longer since he was able to get enough work on his own. He didn't know Misty Skylar, and his former agent was selling real estate in New York. Other than on the set, he claimed he never saw Hillary. His part was filmed in half a day, and other than the final take, he'd rehearsed with a stand-in. He asserted that was the only time he'd worked with Hillary and never appeared in any of her other films.

"Why didn't you say something about working with her?" Behan asked.

"Sorry. It was such minimal contact I never thought you'd be interested," Perry answered, trying to sound matter of fact, but Josie picked up a slight break in his voice.

"You know any other cops that had any contact with her or worked in her movies?"

Perry glanced up at the ceiling as if he were trying to recall and then said, "Not that I can remember, but there's tons of cops in the industry. Some of them might've worked with her."

"What do you mean?" Behan asked, shaking his head.

"There's a bunch of us that do bit parts or technical advising, and a lot more of the younger guys do personal security for the bigger honchos. The Hollywood elite all think they need protection from nutty fans or paparazzi."

"How do you get those jobs?"

Perry smirked. "You don't know?"

"Why would I know? And if I did know why would I be asking you?" Behan asked, not attempting to hide his annoyance.

"Howard Owens organizes the whole thing."

"Lieutenant Owens, our morning watch commander?"

"Uh huh," Perry said, nodding.

Josie was leaning on a ledge near the screen and wasn't all that surprised. Owens had time during the night to do whatever he wanted. A competent morning watch lieutenant would've been out in the field observing his people work, but Josie had her loyal spies who told her Lieutenant Owens never left the station. It took him forever to finish projects or rating reports, so he had plenty of time to run his business on the side. She'd given him several poor evaluations and lately had contemplated recommending his demotion, but civil service and the police union protected and insulated him from any meaningful action on her part.

The rest of Behan's questioning failed to reveal much information. After Perry provided a copy of the work permit required by the department, Behan concluded the interview. As soon as Perry was out of the room, Behan made a phone call to the Personnel division and determined that Lieutenant Owens didn't have a work permit.

Josie wanted to confront Owens that night before he started his watch, bring him in her office, ask him about his business, and demand a list of the officers who worked for him as well as a list of his clients.

"What if he denies having any lists or says he doesn't know what the hell Perry's talking about?" Behan asked.

"We could do an administrative search of his locker, but what if he's smart enough to take the stuff home or keep it in his car?" Josie's thoughts were jumbled with too many contingencies.

"He's got to have contact with somebody who sets up the jobs. I'll try to dig up some other cops who got jobs from him. Maybe a couple of my guys can keep an eye on him for a while."

"We don't have anybody good enough to do that." She'd worked a surveillance unit for several years and knew it was more complicated than just following people.

"The new kid on autos made detective from Metro, and Danny Hill on the robbery table worked a few years with the surveillance guys before his back went out. The three of us can watch him a while."

"Let me think about it," she said, and quickly added, "Okay, I thought about it. If we follow him, I'd rather give it to I.A.'s surveillance team. I need you guys here doing your real jobs. By the way, what did the porno queen say?"

Behan shrugged. "You were right. She said she was afraid to admit she knew Hillary. She's acting scared; I don't think she's telling us everything she knows . . . like everybody else I've talked to."

"You think Perry's telling you the truth?"

"Hell no, did you?" Behan asked.

"I don't know," she said, truthfully. "But give a copy of his interview to Ibarra so he can pass it on to Bright."

Because both Hillary and her agent were killed in a similar manner, Josie figured it was a good guess both murders were somehow connected to the movie industry. They worked, partied and were killed in Hollywood. She worried about how many of her officers might be moonlighting, and asked Behan to check work permits for everyone who was assigned to Hollywood division. Without a department work permit, Lieutenant Owens probably used a fictitious business name, so Behan would have to look for any company that employed a lot of LAPD officers.

Within two hours, Behan had an answer. He drove downtown and personally checked the work permits. He called Josie and told her there were a couple dozen Hollywood officers who had work permits for a company name that Behan recognized.

"Carlton Buck's a retired bunco forgery detective who started a P.I. business as soon as he signed his papers. He hires mostly police retirees for mall security, but he's branched out and offers armed bodyguards to rich sheiks, movie stars and a lot of rappers."

"You need to talk to him before you interview Lieutenant Owens," Josie said.

Behan grunted. "Good idea, he's got nothing to fear from the department. As long as we don't threaten to pull the plug on his P.I. ticket, he'll give up Owens like a bad habit."

Josie said she'd talk to him later but got silence on the line.

"There's something else, boss," Behan said finally. His tone was concerned and hesitant.

She mentally braced herself for more bad news.

"Donnie Fricke and Frank Butler are two of Buck's regular employees."

It wasn't good, but it could've been worse. "Aren't most of his guys young cops? They're the ones who usually work off-duty."

"Looks like it, but you gotta remember there's gonna be a few who don't bother with work permits."

"Talk to Buck. We need to know more before we start thinking evil thoughts," she said and hung up.

Josie was sitting at her desk and tossed her pen onto a pile of folders. She hated cops working off-duty. They made good salaries and didn't need to work other jobs. Their quest for the new boat, RV or jet ski that was bigger and better than the next guy's toys was their primary motivation. Young men and women, some without a college education, making more money than they'd ever had in their lives were tempted to live way beyond their means, and they quickly figured out they were a rare sought-after commodity in this dangerous world. They came equipped with the right to carry a deadly weapon. It was a formula for career-ending disaster.

By late afternoon, the station was relatively quiet. Most detectives had gone home or across the street to Nora's restaurant for Behan's post-Vegas celebration. The admin staff had all checked out. Josie sent her adjutant home and was trying to decide if she wanted to make an appearance at Nora's. Behan's marriages were almost becoming an annual event. She could always catch the next one, but knew he'd be hurt and disappointed if she didn't meet his current wife.

"You're not dressed."

The voice startled Josie. She looked up at Marge Bailey peeking around the doorway.

"I'm thinking. It's my job to do a lot of serious thinking. Dressed for what?"

Marge wore her usual jeans, tank top and leather jacket. Her blond hair was in a long French braid.

"We're going to Red's wedding party. I wanna meet the blushing bride," Marge said, grinning.

"Are you and Behan playing nice together now?" Josie asked. She got up and closed the office door. At least, she could get out of her uniform and get ready to go someplace.

"We're buds. He wants my people to stay on Mouse until he's ready to pick her up again."

"She still with Cory Goldman?"

"Nope, he split about an hour ago, but Red told me not to fuck with him and stick with Mouse. He can always find that asshole easy enough."

Josie laughed. She could never reconcile Marge's beautiful face and graceful figure with the language that came out of her mouth.

"Why's that funny?"

"It's not," Josie said. "You are. You look like Princess Di and sound like Al Capone."

"My first husband was a boxer. I was young, sweet and impressionable." She grimaced and under her breath said, "But when he cheated, I kicked his ass."

Josie finished changing her clothes and already knew the rest of that story, so she agreed to go to Nora's. When they arrived, the bar area was packed with detectives and off-duty cops. A few officers in uniform had stopped by and were drinking cokes with their police radios turned on to listen for hot calls. As soon as they spotted Josie, they quickly finished their drinks and made a hasty exit.

The redheaded newlywed was standing at the bar surrounded by coworkers, but Josie didn't see any unfamiliar face who might've been his new wife. She worked her way closer until Behan noticed her. He hugged Josie and Marge and thanked them for coming.

"Where's the little woman?" Marge asked, gulping a beer one of the detectives had passed to her.

"She went someplace quiet to make a phone call. She'll be back," Behan said. He got a glass of red wine for Josie and whispered in her ear, "Thanks, I know how much you hate these things."

A few minutes later, the current Mrs. Behan returned to the bar. Behan had told Josie his wife was over sixty, but it was difficult to believe. The woman was stunning. Her short hair was champagne blond. She had grey eyes and a clear complexion—without wrinkles or age spots. Her figure was terrific, and she wore a silky cream pantsuit that looked elegant and expensive. She was talkative and funny and obviously doted on Behan.

Marge pulled Josie aside. "I hate this damn woman. Nobody should look that fucking good when they're old. It's unnatural."

"Lots of money and good surgeons, the secret to a long and gorgeous life," Josie said, and turned away from the bar just as Chief Bright entered the restaurant. Josie was shocked. The deputy chief never came to any of Hollywood's celebrations, but her surprise didn't last long. Without a glance, he walked past the bar and into the dining area, never bothering to acknowledge any of the Hollywood officers. It was just a scheduling coincidence. A few seconds later, Councilman Goldman entered with Peter Lange and Vince Milano a step or two behind him. A waitress escorted all of them back toward the restaurant.

Voices surrounding Josie became background noise as she stared at the front door wondering who might appear next. Eventually, she maneuvered around the sea of bodies in front of the bar and worked her way back to the foyer where she had a decent view of the dining room. This is damn curious, she thought. The high-powered group sat at a table in the back of the dimly lit room and were laughing and talking like old friends. The restaurant was more upscale than the bar with a better class of clientele, mostly business types in pricey clothes with expense accounts to match. The meeting appeared to be more social than business. Josie was tempted to walk over and say hello, mostly to see their reaction, but decided against it.

"Now there's a what-the-fuck's-that-all-about moment," Marge said, standing behind Josie. "Milano's dirty little paws touch everybody, don't they?"

"Might be nothing," Josie said. "He donates a lot of money to buy stuff for the department."

"Bullshit," Marge said, sarcastically.

Josie took a step back when Lange glanced in their direction. She didn't wait around to see if he noticed her. Instead she pushed Marge back toward the bar.

"I need a drink," Josie said. Once they were back in the crowded bar, she stopped and asked Marge, "I'm not saying I think there's anything going on, but how much info do you have on Milano's businesses?"

"What'd you need?"

"Don't know . . . everything I guess. I want you to take a good look at him and Peter Lange."

"What am I looking for?"

"I don't know."

"Very helpful," Marge said, taking a handful of peanuts from the closest table.

The current Mrs. Behan squeezed through a narrow opening in the wall of detectives and stood between Josie and Marge.

"I wanted to thank you personally for taking time to come, Captain Corsino," Vicky Behan said, touching Josie's arm and getting close enough to be heard.

"My pleasure," Josie said, watching Marge fade into the crowd. "It's good to see Red happy again."

"He's crazy about you. I think you're the only reason he's still sane after all he's been through," Vicky said, with a wry smile. Her teeth were perfect and very white, her voice melodious and soothing—somebody's gorgeous grandma.

Josie wasn't certain how to respond. She didn't know what Behan had been through except his drinking bouts, and she had no idea how to fix that. She made small talk for a while, then excused herself to get another glass of wine. The new Mrs. Behan was a nice lady and Josie liked her, but knew Red Behan had left a trail strewn with nice women who thought they could either live with him or change him. It was just a matter of time, she figured, before number five discovered he wasn't worth the effort.

The crowd was getting noisier and more raucous. She knew it was time for her exit, since the party only got going once the captain left. A commanding officer's presence inhibited most officers, so she'd slip out and let them have their fun without worrying about how she might judge their behavior. Years of experience had taught her self-preservation would keep them from doing anything really stupid.

Outside, the cold fresh air was a welcome change. The streets of Hollywood were never empty or quiet and tonight was no exception. There were fewer tourists on this east side of Sunset, but the bars and restaurants were busy with locals. Most of the more colorful characters were up on Hollywood Boulevard, but Josie spotted familiar street denizens. She was waiting for traffic to clear before crossing the boulevard when she heard someone call her name. She turned and saw Peter Lange coming out of Nora's.

"Captain Corsino, why don't you join us?" he asked when he was within a few yards.

"Actually, I'm pretty tired," she said, rubbing the back of her neck. "I was on my way home, but thanks."

"Too bad; we're trying to design that campaign to educate kids about the dangers of drinking and drugs. We could use your input."

"Looks to me like you've got considerable assistance already," she said, not believing a word he said. "What've you decided so far?"

"Ah, not much," he said, looking slightly perplexed. His confusion confirmed her suspicion that whatever they were discussing had nothing to do with educating kids.

"If we can't pick your brain, can I at least buy you a nightcap?"

"Thanks, but like I said I'm really tired. Maybe another time," she said and crossed the street, leaving him on the curb. When she reached the other side, she glanced back; he shrugged and waved lazily before returning to the restaurant. Peter Lange was a handsome, intelligent, sometimes charming man, and Josie had to admit she was tempted, but she kept imagining this big bright neon sign over his head, flashing "really stupid idea."

THE MIA's were minimal the morning after Behan's post-nuptial celebration. Most detectives were on automatic pilot for getting to the office at seven A.M., but their first item of business was always a big breakfast with lots of black coffee or whatever the concoction was that opened their eyes. By the time Josie arrived, they were at their desks working. She smiled at Behan as she passed the squad room door. He grinned and smugly pointed at his wedding band.

Wow, two whole days and you're still married, she thought, and shook her head believing on occasion her favorite detective was a certifiable dork.

She had about half an hour before Susan Fletcher's appointment, enough time to sit with her adjutant and go over the day's schedule, including an hour meeting with Ibarra and her watch commanders to discuss crime trends. She considered not inviting Ibarra because he usually didn't contribute much, but she needed to keep him busy and out of Behan's hair.

Josie had just finished her first mug of coffee when she heard Councilwoman Fletcher's booming laugh in the lobby. She opened the lobby door to the admin office and Fletcher charged through like a bull elephant and went directly into Josie's office.

The councilwoman was accompanied by the same young man with the clipboard who'd been with her at Murray's. He leaned against the wall as his boss sank into Josie's couch. It would be a miracle, Josie thought, if that woman managed to get up again. Josie tried to convince the young man to sit, but he refused, and Fletcher behaved as if he wasn't there.

Josie dragged a chair over to the couch and sat on the other side of a small wooden coffee table that cost her twenty dollars at a yard sale. It was solid mahogany and looked pretty good after she'd sanded the scratches out and refinished it. She waited while Fletcher searched through her briefcase and produced a small electronic notebook.

"I thought my position was clear on needle exchange. I'll never agree to close that center," Fletcher said, not looking up from the notebook.

A recitation by Josie of all the violations her officers had logged and her personal observations of drug use and indiscriminate distribution of too many syringes didn't sway Fletcher.

Frustrated, Josie finally blurted out, "Allowing that facility to remain open is tacit approval of illicit drug use."

There was no response from Fletcher for a few seconds while she concentrated on the notebook's keyboard, a tiny pad that was no match for the councilwoman's substantial fingers.

"No, it's not," she said, calmly, glancing up. "It's controlling the spread of HIV and hepatitis."

"What do you base that on?" Josie asked and knew her tone was way too pissed-off to achieve a good outcome.

Fletcher gently closed the notebook and smiled at Josie the way someone does when she knows she can't lose the argument. "There are studies. Besides, it's common sense."

"It's a huge source of crime in my division. Look at the crime patterns," Josie said, sliding a copy of a map page with clusters of little red dots across the coffee table toward Fletcher.

"It's my district; a few property crimes are an acceptable trade-off to save lives," Fletcher said, pushing the map away without so much as a glance. "Your officers will have to be more vigilant in that area."

Josie sat back, took a deep breath and blew it out slowly. She wanted to ask what the point was of being vigilant if you weren't allowed to make arrests, but instead requested, "Will you, at least, consider moving the trailer to a more remote, industrial area where these addicts won't be tempted to steal from the neighbors?"

"No, the problem's here. This is where it's needed."

Now they were both quiet. Josie wasn't going to argue any-more because it was clear Fletcher wasn't willing to compromise. Josie would order Fricke and the patrol officers in that area to start making arrests closer to the trailer. When Fletcher found out she'd be irate, but Josie decided it was time to challenge the woman.

"Have you made any progress on the Hillary Dennis murder?" Fletcher asked, stuffing her notebook into the briefcase and giving it to her aide. She yawned, leaned back on the couch and crossed her arms. "Eli Goldman's telling everyone his son's been cleared because there's a serial killer. If that's true, why haven't I heard it from you?" she asked, frowning but not looking at Josie.

"Nobody's been cleared, and two similar killings don't make a serial killer."

Fletcher wiggled closer to the edge. "Good," she said, looking over her shoulder at the preppie clipboard aide who came around, braced his leg against the couch, and tugged on her arm, grimacing and straining until the massive woman was standing. "Have you seen Eli's kid? That's one messed-up boy . . . not the son you'd want in your family album." Fletcher yanked on the back of her dress, freeing it from where it stuck between her legs, and snatched the briefcase from her aide.

The councilwoman kept talking until the door to the lobby closed. Josie didn't accompany her out, but imagined the monologue continuing into the parking lot and all the way back to downtown L.A. She wondered if Fletcher's remark, "not the son you'd want," was meant as a reference to Eli Goldman or a warning to her about David. Either way, Josie agreed.

As soon as she got back, her adjutant was waiting near her desk holding a stack of phone messages.

"That one's from an Internal Affairs guy . . . says he needs to talk to you ASAP, something about the Dennis homicide," he said, pointing to the one on top.

A sergeant in the Special Operations Division of Internal Affairs wanted to meet with her that afternoon about an investigation involving one of her officers, but wouldn't tell her any more until they met.

As usual, Josie's day was slipping away, but she'd managed to get some work done after the councilwoman left. She was returning from a late lunch with Marge when her adjutant warned her he had stashed the I.A. sergeant in her office. He was perusing her wall art and sipping coffee when she entered.

The pale blond man introduced himself and shook her hand. He was tall, overweight, and definitely had been in an office job too long. His grip was damp and flabby. Without asking, he closed her office door and sat in the chair directly in front of her desk.

It might've been nervousness, but he never stopped smiling, an irritating Mona Lisa grin that suggested he knew something she didn't.

"I.A.'s received an anonymous tip that one of your officers is involved in assisting the sale of narcotics at the Palms," he said and added, "and might've had something to do with the Hillary Dennis killing."

"So did we. We're looking into it."

His watery blue eyes widened. "You did? You have an open investigation? I checked; there's no I.A. number." He was wiggling, looked confused and then upset he hadn't surprised her.

"It's part of a homicide investigation . . . unknown officer."

"Oh," he seemed almost relieved. "I've got a name."

Now Josie shifted uncomfortably. "Who?" she asked, annoyed when he'd paused too long.

"Donnie Fricke, he's a . . ."

She interrupted, "I know who he is. Who's the informant and exactly what's the allegation?"

"Anonymous . . . but alleges Fricke and a drug dealer named Little Joe help each other out, and they arranged the Dennis killing."

"Why would Fricke do that?"

"Dennis was having sex with him. She threatened to expose the arrangement to the department unless she got all her drugs gratis."

"So, we've got some unnamed source and nothing else."

"Correct," the sergeant said.

"You're here to tell me the internal surveillance unit is going to follow Fricke."

"Also correct."

"What about his partner Frank Butler?"

"Possible suspect . . . proximity to the subject," he said, reading from his notes.

Josie realized she was so tense her neck and shoulders had begun to ache. She sat back and tried to relax.

"What do you need from me?" she asked.

"Nothing really. We'll coordinate with your homicide detectives so we don't interfere with each other's investigation. Do you have any concerns or reservations about your detective supervisor's ability to keep this confidential?"

"Of course not, but Detective Behan should be the only other person in Hollywood division who knows. You haven't notified the bureau yet, have you?"

"Chief Bright has been briefed."

Great, Josie thought, you might as well put it on the Internet. Fricke was smart and had developed dozens of sources inside and outside the department. If Bright knew, his adjutant and office staff most likely were aware of the I.A. investigation, too. The surveillance would be a waste of time, which Josie thought was a shame because that would've been the best way to find out if Fricke was dirty. She could almost guarantee Fricke would be on his best behavior until I.A. got tired of following him.

She let the man finish his briefing, then directed him back to detectives, knowing Behan would be in her office as soon as the guy left the building. Her detective wasn't fond of I.A., and she was certain this particular I.A. sergeant wouldn't impress the cranky redhead. In less than an hour Behan was standing in front of her desk.

"This is never gonna work," Behan said before she could speak.

"Not with the whole world knowing about it," she said, gesturing for him to sit.

"Fricke's too smart. He'll figure it out before they start. It's a waste of time."

"We need to find this Little Joe. Put everybody you can spare on it; use the narcotics squad. Get him in here before he disappears too," she said. "Better yet, ask Marge Bailey to use her people."

"She's already got some of her guys following Mouse."

"It's all connected. We've got to find him while he's still breathing. I don't want Donnie Fricke taking the fall because we're too inept to catch the real killer."

Behan looked uncomfortable. He ran his hand over his unruly mop of hair.

"I know you like him, but don't be too quick to exonerate Fricke," Behan said, staring at his hands. "I've seen better cops than him do some pretty stupid things."

"I'm not an idiot, Red. You and I both know the difference between someone like Fricke and a bad cop."

"I'm just saying sometimes guys like Fricke stop knowing the difference."

She knew he was right, but hated the idea she could be so wrong about someone she trusted.

"What the fuck is that smell?" Behan shouted, jumping up, covering his mouth and nose with both hands.

Josie stared at him for a few seconds until the odor reached her. A stink worse than decomposing bodies suddenly polluted the air. She heard a chorus of groaning, angry voices from her administrative staff before Behan opened her door, and the full impact of the disgusting stench hit her.

"We opened all the doors and put some fans in the hallway. They're gonna stick him in the showers and give him some clothes from the bin," the uniformed watch commander said, talking through a paper towel covering his nose and mouth.

"What the hell is he?" Behan asked, coughing.

"Some homeless guy. The officers said they picked him up for you . . . Roy something," the lieutenant said, lifting the paper a little to test the air.

Josie left them in the watch commander's office and joined most of the division's personnel in the parking lot. She'd been around a lot of bums, but Roy Mitchell was without a doubt the most wretched-smelling human being who was still breathing. Standing in the clean air, she took several long, deep breaths in an attempt to get the man's body odor out of her nostrils. Her stomach was churning, and she was grateful she hadn't eaten enough to vomit.

Thirty minutes later the faint odor of Roy Mitchell still lingered in the station, but the homeless man was sitting in the interview room with dripping wet clean hair and his leathery skin scrubbed almost clean by the hard antiseptic jail soap. His hands and nails and the tiny crevices in his stubbled face still had traces of caked dirt, but the horrible smell was gone. Josie watched as Behan sat across the table from Mitchell, who readily admitted living in the box in the alley behind the bar where Misty Skylar was killed.

"I seen the lady and two guys come outta the bar," Mitchell said, sucking on his lip as he spoke. Two of his upper teeth were missing, and he had a nervous, annoying habit of drawing his lip into the vacuum.

"Had you seen any of them before?" Behan asked.

"Nope, but nobody 'cept the bar lady hardly never comes out that way. I was tryin' to sleep, but they're yellin' an' I start to crawl outta my box to tell 'em to get the fuck outta my alley when I sees this lady on her knees, an' next thing there's this bang and she falls over . . ."

"Hold on," Behan said, interrupting. "Not so fast. Take your time so you don't skip anything."

Mitchell was getting increasingly anxious as he told his story, tugging at his hair and leaning on the table until he could nearly touch Behan.

"Bad dudes," Mitchell mumbled. He slumped back and scratched his head. Josie and Behan both backed away. Red was probably thinking the same thing she was. The man had head lice. Even the potent jail soap couldn't kill those little critters.

Behan coaxed as many details as he could from the homeless man. Mitchell had seen two men arguing with Misty Skylar. He wasn't always coherent. At first, he couldn't identify them, and then a few minutes later maybe he could and remembered the shooter was a big man, at least a foot taller than Misty. The shooter took the gun from what looked like a shoulder holster under his suit jacket. The men dragged the dead woman from where she died and propped her against the back wall of the bar. They were laughing as they arranged the body and tossed her shoes and purse in the dumpster.

"The big one he spots my box, an' come over where I'm laying. I act dead drunk . . . fucker kicks me in the stomach anyhow . . . hurt real bad, but I don't scream or nothing, don't do nothing."

"He left you there?" Josie asked.

"Yeah, laughs, got a ugly laugh, says I must be dead 'cuz no live man stinks so bad, like a pile a dog shit, he says."

"Can you remember anything about him or the other guy? You see a car or unique jewelry? Did they talk funny, have an accent or anything? Were they black or white?" Behan asked. Josie could hear the frustration in his voice, the need for precious details.

"Both of 'em white dudes, I think. Other one's kinda pretty though, like a big woman, but sounded like a guy," Mitchell said. "The way they talk I kinda figured they might be cops."

He avoided direct eye contact with Behan and nervously rubbed the back of his arm as his lip-sucking accelerated. Clearly, Josie thought, he believed the men were cops, and it was difficult for him to talk about it.

"What do you mean?" Behan asked, looking up at Josie.

"Dunno," he mumbled. "Just kinda figured they was cops, the way you guys move and stuff . . . him having the gun under his coat 'n' all."

Now Mitchell rocked a bit back and forth, his arms crossed tightly against his chest. He was scared, and it had probably taken every remnant of courage he possessed to reveal that last piece of information. Josie didn't know what her detective thought, but she believed the man. Street people had an uncanny talent for knowing the police.

They tried to get the bum's wine-soaked brain to remember more, but it was futile. Roy Mitchell said he hadn't returned to his box in the alley because he was afraid those men would come back and kill him. He hadn't gone to the police station because he was afraid if the killers were cops, other cops would kill him.

"So why talk to us now?" Josie asked.

"I kin see you ain't no badass, lady. There's some . . ." He stopped and rubbed his face with both hands. "No matter," he said relaxing a little.

"If we find you a safe place, will you stay there? We'll need you to identify these guys if we ever catch them," Josie said.

Mitchell wiggled and stood, almost knocking over the chair. "No, can't sleep inside, can't breathe. Jus' let me be . . . can't help no more than what I done."

"If they think you're a witness, those guys might hunt you down and kill you the next time," she said, trying to scare him.

"Gotta find me first," Mitchell said with a toothless grin.

Behan escorted the homeless man back to the jail, where they rummaged through the unclaimed clothes pile and found him a heavy parka and a change of clothes, including a decent pair of boots. Josie watched Mitchell leave the police building with a bundle tucked under his arm. His new wardrobe also included leather gloves and a wool cap. Behan stood on the sidewalk a few moments until Mitchell wandered across Sunset Boulevard, and then he came back into the station shaking his head and stopped near the front counter where Josie was waiting.

"Nobody should live that way," Behan said with a sour expression, and Josie sensed he might've glimpsed one possible outcome of his own life. She also guessed he'd be especially attentive to the new Mrs. Behan that night.

They went back to her office where they could talk in private. Even Josie couldn't deny the growing likelihood that a couple of rogue cops or cop impersonators were operating within the confines of Hollywood division. As soon as Behan left, Josie called Marge Bailey who was in the captain's office in less than a minute.

"How'd you get here so fast . . . you loitering in the hallway?"

"It sounded urgent," Marge said, searching in the bottom drawer of the file cabinet where Josie kept her stash of chocolates. She found a Hershey bar. "Lunch," she said, unwrapping it. "What's up?"

"Close the door," Josie said, and saw a hint of apprehension on Marge's face. "I'm expanding the number of officers on the hype car and giving it to you . . . with another supervisor."

Marge chewed slowly and swallowed the chocolate. She didn't speak but stopped eating and dropped onto the couch.

"It's a joke right?" she asked, after several seconds.

"No, I want them reporting directly to you, start and end of watch."

"If that's what you want, you know I'll do it, but wouldn't it make more sense to give that mess to the narcotics team?"

"I trust you more than narco. Besides, they've got something else to do for Behan."

"Okay," she said. "So, how'd Donnie Fricke fuck up this time?"

"I'll tell you, but only because the bureau knows, which means by now everybody knows." Josie told Marge what the I.A. sergeant had revealed that afternoon about the investigation on Fricke and decided to give her everything Behan had learned from Roy Mitchell and Mouse.

"So we got a couple of bad cops or assholes pretending to be cops," Marge said when Josie had finished. "I'll ride herd on Fricke's ass, no problem. What about Frank Butler?"

"Same," Josie said.

"Too bad, I like him . . . actually offered him a job when he gets tired of cleaning up after Fricke."

Marge said she would coordinate with Behan and the I.A. sergeant on Fricke's surveillance, and continue to keep watch on Mouse who rarely wandered from the Melrose apartment these days.

Behan peeked around the file cabinet but left quickly when he saw Marge was talking to Josie.

"I'm outta here," Marge said, snatching another chocolate bar from the filing cabinet. "I liked Red better when he was fucked-up. He's so goddamn happy lately it's nauseating."

Josie grinned. "Keep in touch."

"Yeah, don't worry 'bout me, boss—you just see if you can come up with a few more ways to fuck up my life," Marge said, saluting as she left.

When Josie got up, she saw Marge had cornered Behan in the outer admin office. They were huddled away from the staff, whispering, but it was a heated discussion. Finally, Marge stomped off and Behan came into Josie's office.

"What was that about?" Josie asked. She didn't understand why two good cops couldn't get along. Their bickering was becoming an irritating distraction.

Behan seemed reluctant to talk about it, but when he realized Josie wasn't going to let it go, he said, "Marge thinks I need to take a closer look at Lange and Milano for the Dennis and Skylar homicides. I got nothing that points to either one of them, but little Miss Potty Mouth's convinced they're dirty. That woman's like a pit bull locked on your balls when she thinks she's right."

"They're probably dirty for lots of things," Josie said. "I can't see how we can connect them to those murders, but I'm not ready to write them off yet either—and I'd still like to know more about both of them. I asked Marge to get some background info." She stood and stretched. Her back and neck were aching from a lack of exercise. Jake had a treadmill and stationary bike in the spare bedroom. She vowed to use them before dinner that night and immediately dismissed the thought. She'd ignored that resolution at least three times a week.

"That wasn't the reason I wanted to see you," Behan said. "I'm going to interview Carlton Buck tonight."

"Who?"

"Buck, the retired sergeant that runs the security firm where half your division works off-duty."

"Before you interview Howard Owens?"

"Like I said, Buck's got nothing to lose. As long as we don't threaten his P.I. ticket, I think he'll cooperate. Howard's got his lieutenant job to protect. Besides, Howard's not working tonight, and I'd like to know more about this arrangement before I confront him."

"Okay, so what's the problem?"

"Because of the personnel thing, I don't want any of my guys involved," he said, and then cleared his throat. "Truth is I'm not sure how many of them are unofficially on Buck's payroll. I could ask that I.A. sergeant to tag along, but I think his tight ass would just complicate everything. I don't think I should do it alone, and Lieutenant Ibarra can't make it. Did you want to come?"

"Where's Ibarra?"

"Don't know . . . took a couple of days off."

Josie felt her face flush. Ibarra hadn't bothered to ask or even notify her that he'd be gone. This was over the line even for him. She told Behan she'd go with him but made no secret of the fact she was angry. The big redhead retreated back to detectives and

Josie told her adjutant to track down Ibarra. She'd been avoiding the situation up to now, but obviously needed to have a serious come-to-Jesus moment with her detective lieutenant.

NINE

I barra called within a few minutes and apologized. He explained how he thought he had notified her in an email about his days off, and claimed he'd left the supervisor on the robbery table in charge of detectives until his return at the end of the week and had expected him to tell her.

"Why not Behan?" Josie asked. They both knew the homicide supervisor usually stepped in when Ibarra was gone.

"I figured he's got enough on his plate," Ibarra said and quickly added, "Look I'm sorry if you didn't get my email, but I'm taking vacation time. It's only a few days." His attitude made it clear he thought she was overreacting. "I'll come back if you really need me."

"No," Josie said, thinking if it were possible she'd rather have him somewhere else most of the time. "Next time tell me face-to-face when you take off, so I don't hear it for the first time from one of your subordinates. We'll discuss this when you get back. Where are you?"

Ibarra stuttered, searching for the right words, and finally said, "I've got some personal stuff I have to take care of."

He apologized again, and she ended the conversation. She was positive if she asked the robbery supervisor, he'd say he didn't know he was in charge until a few minutes before Ibarra called her, and the email she didn't get was never sent. When Ibarra came back from vacation she'd tell him to look for another job. She was done with him and couldn't wait any longer for the Wilshire captain to work up the gumption to steal him.

It was early evening before Behan could arrange a meeting with Carlton Buck. The P.I. invited them to his office on the top floor of a building on Sawtelle Avenue in West L.A. Josie knew from the address it was only a few blocks from the West L.A. police station.

Buck's building was a modern granite and glass structure, six stories high, which covered most of the corner lot where it was located. From the outside, Josie could see the lights were on in the top floor windows, but most of the other offices on the lower floors were dark. There was a sign out front advertising office space for lease, and the large underground parking garage had two cars, both parked near the elevator in spaces marked for Buck, Inc. One of them was a new Porsche Carrera 911 similar to Jake's.

The lobby had a fresh coat of paint and a new carpet smell. The hall was empty when Josie and Behan got off the elevator on the sixth floor. A tasteful bronze plaque with the words "Carlton Buck, Inc." was mounted on the wall between the two elevator doors, and his name was stenciled on the glass doors leading to the receptionist's desk. Behan entered a code Buck had given him earlier into the keypad on the wall near the doors. Once inside, they noticed there was no one at the front desk, and a large room with several cubicles was also unoccupied.

They walked around the empty space and through a hallway with pictures of several downtown and Hollywood locations. Josie thought everything looked expensive and more to a lawyer's taste than a private investigator. Eventually they arrived at a door with Buck's name engraved in the wood. His secretary's desk was empty so Behan knocked on the door.

"Come in," a man's voice shouted from inside.

They entered and were greeted by a well-dressed, stocky bald man with wire-rimmed glasses. When he reached out to shake hands his suit jacket opened a little, and Josie could see he was not only a little overweight but carried a semi-auto handgun. His office was spacious, decorated with mahogany furniture and walnut shelves well-stocked with an assortment of law books and boxed files. His desk was covered with file folders and paperwork, but he had a long glass table in front of the floor to ceiling windows. Josie pulled out a leather chair and sat facing the view which was magnificent—the Century City skyline and, in the distance, the lights of downtown L.A.

Buck invited them to help themselves to an assortment of small crackers and cheese stacked in a tray at the center of the table, and he poured three glasses of sparkling water without asking.

"Sorry I didn't meet you out front," he said, dropping into the chair beside Josie. "I couldn't get a client off the phone. But I figured being cops you'd find your way back here."

"This is pretty impressive," Josie said. "How many employees do you have?"

"In here, about fifty, but there's hundreds in the field."

Behan explained why they had come, and told Buck what Art Perry had said about Hollywood officers working off-duty for him.

Buck was quiet for a few seconds as if he were calculating how much he wanted to reveal, and then said, "Have you talked to Howard Owens? He's my contact man. I get most of my active officers from him."

"Just how's that work?" Behan asked.

"Has Owens done something wrong? I don't want trouble with the department." Buck's demeanor never altered. He didn't look nervous or worried, just curious.

"No," Josie said. "We'd just like to know what your business arrangement is with him."

"That's no problem, but Owens doesn't tell me much, except he's got a list of cops who want to work. He doles out my jobs so everybody gets a chance and one or two of them don't hog all the cash . . . course I know he's got his favorites."

Buck went on to describe how his business provided security guards for stores, banks and other businesses, but those jobs were usually reserved for the LAPD and sheriff retirees who wanted extra cash and could work thirty or forty hours a week. He had a section that provided personal security for movie premieres and for those people who could afford the five-hundred-dollar-an-hour private guard.

"What about supplying extras or guys for bit parts in movies?" Behan asked.

"Not my thing. Owens maybe does that on his own, but it's not something I'm paying for. What's this all about? Did my people do something wrong?"

"Don't know yet," Behan said.

"Do I need a lawyer?" he asked, laying his glasses on the table.

"Up to you, but I'm not accusing you of anything. Now tell me again. Exactly what does Owens do for you?"

Buck didn't answer immediately, maybe considering whether he should continue to talk so freely. After a few seconds he said, "What the hell, Howard recruits the guys to work armed security."

"And you have nothing to do with getting them parts in movies?" Behan asked.

"No, why would I? There's no profit in that for me. My biggest return's in private security. Every bimbo and prima donna in Hollywood wants a clean-cut armed man opening the car door for her or him, or staring down some pimply-faced kid with a Nikon who says he's from TMZ or the *National Enquirer*."

"Has Owens given you a copy of his list of active officers?" Josie asked.

"No, and I don't want it," Buck said quickly. "If he screws up and gives me some psycho cop, I wanna be able to say I don't know nothing about these people. I can fire Owens, and I'm not responsible or liable."

Josie almost laughed. For such a smart guy he was pretty stupid. Any attorney worth his hourly rate would take one look around Buck's office, see deep pockets and push for a nice big settlement as the price for not suing the retired cop out of business. She'd seen the piece of junk SUV that Owens drove. Her lieutenant was barely getting by. Buck's Porsche would be caviar bait for any bottom-feeder with a law degree.

"Great plan," Behan said, sarcastically. "But, you might wanna rethink that one. Can you remember names of any guys you've used for these special security details?"

"Not really."

"Did Hillary Dennis ever use you for protection?" Josie asked.

"I'll have my secretary check in the morning, but I'm almost certain she did a couple of times."

"Would the officers' names who worked her detail be in your paperwork?" Behan asked.

"Don't know, but I can tell you tomorrow."

"While you're at it, check for the name Misty Skylar too," Behan said.

Behan gave him his business card, and Buck promised to call in the morning. Like all retired cops, Buck wanted to know what was going on currently in the department. He asked about a few officers he'd worked with who were still on the job. Although he had little contact any longer with the day-to-day routine of police work, he complained that nothing was being done right, and the job couldn't be as much fun as it was when he was working. Josie never knew a retired cop who thought the department got better after he left. It was a family. No one wanted to believe the family could function as well or be as happy without him.

It took about an hour to break away from Buck's hospitality. The P.I. had a refrigerator full of delicious treats, and Behan could never get enough free food or cop talk. Josie finally insisted they had to leave, saying she had an early meeting in the morning. It was a lie, but the two men weren't showing any signs of tiring and Buck had a seemingly endless supply of food. He walked them to the lobby and kept talking until the elevator doors closed.

"Nice guy," Behan said before they reached the parking level.

"Stuffing your face doesn't make him a nice guy," Josie said, shaking her head. "Tell me you didn't buy that garbage he was selling. I guarantee you he knows every cop that works for him." She'd pegged Carlton Buck as a sleazy little liar.

"It's hard not to like a guy that shares all that good food," Behan said, "but no I don't believe him. Let's face it. He's never gonna admit he's got any list as long as he thinks ignorance keeps him from being sued."

By the time Josie and Behan reached their car, they'd decided with Buck's statement it was time to talk with Howard Owens. It was a chicken-shit charge, but they had enough to charge Owens for working off-duty without a permit, so there really wasn't any reason for him to deny the existence of his list. Behan was certain he could frighten the watch commander into believing he was suspected of complicity in the Hillary Dennis homicide since he employed the officers who might've killed her.

"That's good. Giving up a list of officers' names will seem like a small thing compared to being an accomplice to murder," Josie said. She stopped by the passenger door and watched as Behan removed a small notebook from his jacket pocket and wrote down the license plate numbers on the Porsche and the other car, a silver Lexus, parked in front of the elevator in spaces marked for Buck's business.

"I didn't see anybody else in there did you?" Behan asked.

"No, so what?"

"Maybe nothing, but I always get curious when somebody hides from me," he said, backing out of the parking space. "Wanna grab a shot of something before we hit the freeway?"

It was nearly midnight and Josie was weary, but the thought of going anywhere but her empty house to drink alone sounded good. Years ago, she and Jake frequented a tiny hole-in-the-wall blues club, Jay D's, on Pico Boulevard in West L.A., a few minutes from Buck's office. It was good drinking music and dark enough inside to hide in a back booth and not be bothered or recognized. She didn't like fraternizing with her subordinates, but Behan was more than just another employee.

"Miss Vicky not waiting up for you?" Josie asked, trying not to smile.

"Probably, but I'm thirsty."

"Don't screw up this one, Red. Your pension's not big enough to divide again." Josie was kidding, but Behan didn't seem amused. "Don't tell me you're having problems already."

"No, she's great. I'm a shit."

Josie really didn't want to know but asked anyway. "What'd you do?"

"Married her . . . she deserves a lot better."

"Probably, but it's done, so be a good husband and go home."

"Not yet," he said turning onto Pico. "All that food made me thirsty."

Behan had been to Jay D's on numerous occasions when he worked in the Wilshire area, and he found parking before Josie could convince him it would be better to take her back to Hollywood and go home.

A few patrons were standing by the door talking to an overweight black woman in a shiny red satin dress who took the cover charge from Behan before allowing him and Josie to enter.

Nothing had changed inside since the last time Josie had been here. It was stuffy and smelled like stale beer. The floor was covered with something she hoped were peanut shells. Blue light through a cigarette smoke haze made it nearly impossible to see beyond a few feet. The musicians were between sets, but the glow from the stage helped light the way to two empty stools at the bar. Behan ordered a single malt scotch and a glass of Cabernet for her.

Before the drinks arrived, Josie heard the piano music start behind her on the stage. It was the beginning of a classical piece she'd heard before but couldn't identify. Slowly, the notes distorted to a fractured version of the same piece but definitely had acquired a blues persona. She'd never heard anyone but David play classical music that way, and turned on the stool enough to make out the long thin torso of her son hunched over the keys of the baby grand.

She ignored the bartender when he brought her glass of wine and couldn't stop looking at her son, at first surprised and then disappointed. Behan watched her and followed her stare over his shoulder and back toward the stage.

"Isn't that your kid?" he asked, trying to get her attention. "He's good."

"This is the great job he was bragging about, some filthy dive in the middle of nowhere," Josie said before realizing the bartender was still standing behind her. "Sorry," she said, not wanting to insult the guy who was pouring her drinks, but she was upset. Her kid was too talented for this backroom tinkering.

The room got quiet as soon as the music started. It was a small space. There wasn't any amplification, but the acoustics were great. Every note, every nuance could be clearly heard. She stopped thinking and listened. The performance was flawless. The composer wouldn't have recognized his own creation, Josie thought, but the new blues version was a hit. The crowd applauded spontaneously and often. David's eyes stayed closed as he played; his head turned slightly away from the keys. He'd slipped into that state Josie had observed for so many years when he practiced at home. Nothing around him existed but the sound. He played a dozen variations of the piece until he was done, stood to noisy, sustained applause, and disappeared from the stage as quickly as he'd come.

"You're right," Behan said as soon as David had left. "He's too good for this place."

"It had to be his father," Josie said.

"What?"

"Jake must've arranged for him to play here. He did pro bono work for the owner a few years ago," she said, tapping her fingers on the bar. Josie knew talking to David was a waste of time, but she'd find a way to make Jake get him out of here. She wouldn't have her son wasting his life or talent playing for tips in dingy bars.

"You're not gonna do anything stupid, are you?"

"No, why would you ask that?"

Behan finished the last of his scotch. "I've seen that look before, Corsino. Somebody's in big trouble."

TEN

Thinking about her son's uncertain future contributed to a fretful and less than pleasant night's sleep, but by the next morning Josie had devised a scheme to put David's life back on track with or without his cooperation. She'd talk to Jake and together they'd find enough money to send their son to the best art or music school of his choice, and pay all his expenses if he agreed to find a respectable steady job when he graduated, doing something like teaching where he'd have a steady income. She didn't have much money saved, but they could get a second mortgage on the house. If David refused, they'd cut him off, stop giving him the extra cash he depended on to pay for rent, gas and food.

The only problem she saw with her plan was Jake. Josie wasn't certain he had the heart or will to stop enabling their son's self-indulgence. They were too much alike, her husband and son.

Her intention to devote the day to fixing David's life was derailed as soon as she arrived at Hollywood station. Carlton Buck was waiting in the front lobby.

"Says he's gotta talk to you," the desk officer said, standing in her doorway.

"Send him to Detective Behan," Josie ordered, gently pushing him aside.

The officer returned in a few seconds. "Mr. Buck says he won't give his records to anybody except you."

Behan wandered into Josie's office as the officer was attempting to plead Buck's case.

"No big deal," Behan said. "Buck gives them to you; you give them to me."

"I'm trying to keep the middle person, namely me, out of this. I've got a division to run . . . captain . . . detective," she said, pointing at herself and then Behan.

"Sorry, guess he doesn't trust me," Behan said, attempting to look contrite.

"Alright, get him in here but tell him he's got exactly ten minutes before Detective Behan drags his retired butt back to homicide."

The desk officer retreated and returned a few seconds later followed by Buck who was wearing a dapper three-piece dark blue suit with a red tie, and carrying an expensive briefcase that looked as if it had never been used. He shook hands with everyone and sat on the couch beside Behan. He placed the briefcase on Josie's coffee table and opened it slowly. The deliberate movements made the contents appear to be more valuable than everyone knew they were.

"Did Hillary use your people or not?" Josie asked, impatiently. She was tired of waiting for the drama to play out.

"Let me get this and I'll show you," Buck said, sounding a little testy. He placed what appeared to be a kind of worksheet on the table. It showed handwritten numbers that totaled forty. "Hillary Dennis used our security on and off for about a month up to the week before she was killed . . . for special events or public stuff, but never at her residence."

"Do you have the guys' names that guarded her?" Behan asked.

"There's just one, a retired L.A. cop, Bruno Faldi."

Buck explained that Faldi had been employed by him for approximately six months. He'd left the police department to become a teacher, but claimed he needed some excitement in his life and extra income. He'd worked twenty years as a cop and could carry a concealed weapon, so he took on personal security as a lucrative second job.

"He was mostly reliable, and the clients liked him. He's a big intimidating guy. That's all I know," Buck said, stuffing the paper back into his briefcase.

"He's not with you anymore?" Behan asked.

"Nope, quit a couple a days ago."

Buck rummaged through the briefcase again and produced a company personnel folder with Faldi's home address and phone number. Faldi's references included his grammar school pastor and the principal at the girls' private high school in the San Fernando Valley where he currently taught history.

As soon as Buck left, Behan called downtown to the department's Personnel division and had them pull Faldi's LAPD file. Throughout his career, he had good rating reports from all his supervisors, no disciplinary history, and by all accounts was destined to promote much higher than the rank of sergeant. With no explanation, he retired early to become a high school teacher.

With so many active and retired police officers involved in this case, Josie decided she and Behan had to handle the bulk of the investigation. She didn't have the time to spare, and it wasn't something she wanted to do, but it was becoming increasingly difficult to know who to trust, or who had been or still was employed by Buck or Lieutenant Owens. The case could be compromised by inadvertently sharing information with one of those officers or detectives who'd worked for or felt any loyalty toward either man. Behan could do the majority of the legwork, and she would assist him the best she could. She knew it meant more work for Behan, but Marge could help, and the three of them would be the only ones involved.

Ibarra wasn't back from his short vacation, so Josie assigned a number of her upcoming meetings to the P.M. watch lieutenant. The lieutenant who worked day watch was given a stack of projects to finish, and the remainder of her work Josie intended to complete when she wasn't helping Behan.

She didn't tell her adjutant why she wouldn't be in the office, but did say she expected him to keep things organized and running smoothly and to keep her informed if anything needed her immediate attention. Sergeant Jones tried to finagle more information but finally gave up. She reasoned he was better off not knowing, and besides, she really didn't know whether he'd been involved in any of the off-duty employment. At this point, his denial wouldn't be good enough.

The most difficult dilemma for Josie was deciding how much to tell her boss. Chief Bright's close association with some of the principals in the investigation had made him an information sieve. Art Perry was involved on the periphery of the case but nevertheless involved. There wasn't much choice. Josie couldn't ignore the chain of command, but somehow she'd find a way to filter out the more sensitive information.

When she told Behan about the new working arrangement, he didn't seem surprised. He called Faldi from her office to arrange a meeting with the teacher after his last class that afternoon. Josie had expected some resistance from her homicide detective. He didn't ask questions and that wasn't like him. Behan never accepted change without knowing why, but today he seemed willing to go along almost as if he'd expected this to happen.

"Doesn't it bother you having me look over your shoulder?" She didn't think Behan intentionally cut corners, but everybody fudged just a little. She wouldn't be comfortable having her boss work with her.

"No, but if we do this we're partners, and I'm gonna treat you like a partner not a boss. If you have a problem with that, it's not gonna happen," he said.

She didn't and told him so but had to ask. "You don't seem surprised. Why not?"

"Because I knew you either had to stick your neck out and get involved or give this investigation to another division. I know how stubborn you can be. There's no way you were gonna let this case go."

BRUNO FALDI was a giant of a man as tall as Josie's son David, but he weighed at least a hundred pounds more. He was balding and had shaved his head which made him even more imposing. Josie imagined discipline wasn't an issue in his classroom. His office at the Grandview Girls Academy was cluttered with stacks of papers, books and magazines. It had one small window that looked out on a well-tended track and soccer field. The school had a small-town college appeal with two multi-story vine-covered brick buildings nestled in a cluster of mature maple trees.

"I couldn't do it anymore after she died," Bruno said in response to Behan's first question about why he quit the security job with Carlton Buck.

Josie studied the big man and thought he looked more body-guard than high school teacher. She imagined he must've been quite impressive in a police uniform when he was in better shape, but even in his best physical condition he probably wasn't the kind of guy who could buy his tailored blues off the rack. His neck and hands were huge. He was dressed informally in slacks and a sweater, but his manner was anything but casual. As he talked, he fidgeted with pens, paper clips and anything else he could touch on his desk.

"Was she your first client?" Behan asked, after making small talk for a few minutes. Josie knew he was trying to calm Bruno, who looked as nervous as anyone she'd ever interviewed.

"No, I only guarded her less than a month. I had maybe a dozen celebrity regulars in the half-year I was with Buck, but she was different . . . really vulnerable and scared. It wasn't a vanity thing with that little girl like it was for most of them."

"Scared of what?"

"Pretty much everything, but especially her crazy mother and that Goldman character."

"She thought her own mother would harm her?"

Bruno's mood changed, grew darker; his eyes narrowed. "Have you met the woman? She's a psycho . . . threatened to save her little girl by sending her back to God in a plain wooden coffin so he'd forgive her evil ways. That's nuts."

"Did Mrs. Dennis try to harm Hillary?" Josie asked, remembering the simple, grief-stricken mother she'd comforted in her office.

"Not when I was there. I never let her get close enough."

"What about the Goldman kid?" Behan asked.

"Wasn't any kid. Must've been at least in his forties."

"Cory Goldman?"

"Don't know his first name . . . oh yeah, I do, Eli, maybe."

Josie and Behan exchanged a quick glance, and she asked, "Are you talking about Councilman Eli Goldman?"

Bruno looked confused. "He's a councilman? Sorry, I don't live in the city anymore . . . guess I don't pay much attention to local politics."

Behan described Eli Goldman.

"Yeah, that sounds like the guy, kinda dorky-looking. They had a thing, but when she broke it off he pestered her all the time. The last time he knocked on her door, I answered and told him to get lost or I'd break both his arms . . . never saw him again."

"Buck told us you never guarded her at home." Josie said.

"I didn't. We were leaving to go to one of the clubs. I just picked her up there."

Bruno swore he didn't know any of the other officers who worked for Buck because he'd always worked alone. He claimed Hillary was like his daughter, and he believed mentally and emotionally she was closer to fourteen than seventeen. She'd confided in him that she didn't like the notoriety of being a movie star, enjoyed her independence but felt guilty about the wealth, and believed her mother who'd said someday she would have to pay for her freedom and extravagant lifestyle.

"Why'd she fire you?" Behan asked.

For the first time since the interview began, Bruno seemed reluctant or slow to answer. A knock on the door saved him from responding right away. A young girl, one of his students who looked to be about sixteen years old, said she wanted to talk to him about her midterm grade, and he took a few minutes to arrange another time with her. Bruno's demeanor changed. He spoke softly and smiled at her, even joked a little.

Josie watched. The chemistry between student and teacher felt all wrong to her. The girl was pretty and flirting with him, but Bruno didn't react the way an adult should have. He treated her like an equal, smiling at what Josie felt were inappropriate remarks, and the girl acted as if she were his friend rather than a student. Bruno didn't really do anything wrong, but the interaction made Josie uncomfortable.

When they were alone again, Bruno folded his arms and sat back. "The drugs," he said. "Told her to stop. She wouldn't."

"Tell us more about the drugs. How'd she get them?" Behan asked.

"Off the street, it was dangerous and stupid. Said she had better protection than me and nothing was going to happen to her . . . didn't like me nagging her all the time so she dumped me. A few days later, she's dead."

The big man rubbed his eyes as if he was going to cry, but didn't. He sat up and took several minutes to compose himself. Josie wasn't buying it. She thought he was trying hard to look upset, but his body language said he was still very much in control.

"What sort of things did she do when you were with her," she asked.

Bruno cleared his throat. "Partied, went to a club almost every night. She liked to have a good time."

"She was a minor," Josie said.

"Not really," Bruno said, defensively. "She legally lived on her own. The studio hired a tutor for her, but it was all show. I tried too, but she wasn't interested in improving her mind. She knew her success depended on her face and body."

"She was a minor."

"Of course," Bruno said, glancing at her and shrugging.

"Did she ever work?" Josie asked, wondering when the young woman found time to make all those terrible movies.

"No, not when I was with her. She checked in with her agent every day, and I'd drive her to Skylar's office or they'd meet at one of the clubs, but I never saw her on a film set and never saw Skylar offer her any kind of movie work."

"Were there other men besides Eli?" Behan asked.

"Lots, but the guys I saw the most were some geeky-looking tattooed guy and his friend. Didn't know either one of them, but

I think they both stayed with her at different times. She dumped the geek, but I had a feeling the other guy kept coming around when I wasn't there."

Josie tried not to change her expression. Maybe Cory Goldman but not David; David wouldn't lie to her about something that important.

"Anyone dating her at the time she got killed?"

"I wasn't with her those last few days," Bruno said.

"Tell me more about the tattooed geeky guy's friend," Behan said, deliberately avoiding Josie's stare. She froze until Bruno answered, afraid to take a breath, dreading and at the same time knowing who the friend was.

"Not much to tell, skinny little black guy, dressed like a Goodwill poster boy, but Hillary treated him like her best buddy."

Josie exhaled and felt as if a ton of manure had been shoveled off her back.

Bruno identified Cory Goldman's picture as the tattooed geek. The description of the black man matched the one Mouse had given them of Little Joe, but they still hadn't been able to identify the heroin dealer. Fricke and his partner claimed the dealer hadn't been seen around the Palms for several weeks, so they weren't able to snatch him.

Although Josie and Behan only talked to him another ten minutes, Bruno was able to give them some interesting tidbits about the month he'd spent with Hillary. He said she was a generous, loving girl who was overwhelmed by the money and attention she got from a number of older men who were infatuated with her. He surmised Hillary's attachment to them was compensating for the father she never knew.

Hillary considered Misty Skylar a surrogate mother figure, but one night when Hillary asked him to drive Misty home, the agent admitted to Bruno that the young girl was strictly a short-term meal ticket whose only real talent was her youthful sex appeal. Misty told him as soon as Hillary got a little older her career would be over since her acting on its own merits wouldn't be good enough to get even B-movie parts. The agent intended to drop her at the first signs of aging, but until then she'd market Hillary for every dollar she could get.

"That's cold," Behan said.

"Not in the movie business. Those young girls are used and abused, but I think Hillary was clever enough to figure out she didn't have long to make the big bucks, and she was going to live it up and get as much as she could before they kicked her out the door."

"Can you think of any reason someone would want to kill her?" Behan asked.

Bruno closed his eyes for a moment and leaned his head back. "I know she was scared. She wouldn't tell me why or what frightened her, but it was bad enough to hire me and sleep with her lights on. Now, if you'd asked about Misty that's a different story. From what I saw and heard about her she was a bitch. Probably everybody that knew her wanted to kill her at some time."

"Why?" Josie asked.

"She used people. Pushed young girls who couldn't act or weren't pretty enough into porno films or worse."

"Worse?"

"She'd get them on the payroll in those sleazy escort places. Of course, they were always eighteen on paper, and she always got her commission."

"How do you know so much about her business?" Behan asked.

"I was a cop for twenty years. I know a madam when I see one even if she's wearing designer clothes and carrying an expensive briefcase. Misty might've had some legitimate clients like Hillary, but I guarantee you she was peddling flesh on the side."

———

THERE WASN'T much conversation during the ride back to Hollywood station. Josie had tried to tell Behan why she thought Bruno was creepy, but couldn't really explain her gut feeling.

"A grown-up man doesn't behave that way with a young girl. If she were my daughter and I saw that, I'd yank her out of the school."

"What'd he do? I didn't see anything."

"I don't know. It's hard to explain. He was just too . . . familiar."

"Sorry, didn't get that feeling. He seemed accessible is all."

"That stuff about Goldman puts a whole new complicated twist on things. Keeping that information away from Bright isn't an option," she said, studying his face for some reaction.

"When do you have to tell him?" Behan asked.

"Certainly before you talk to Goldman."

"Too bad."

"Can you believe he'd let his son take all the heat when he was practically stalking that girl?" Josie asked, still relieved David's name hadn't surfaced.

"No, and I'm not buying Bruno didn't know who Eli Goldman was or that he didn't know the tattooed geek was Eli Goldman's kid, or that he just guessed what Misty was up to because he used to be a cop."

"Why would he lie about knowing the Goldmans?" Josie asked.

"I don't know, but if he was smart enough to pick up all that stuff on Misty, he should've figured out who the Goldmans were."

"But if what he says is true, Hillary was afraid of the councilman, not his son. Maybe it was the father who threatened her and not Cory. Maybe Mrs. Dennis got it wrong."

"What's somebody like Eli Goldman want with a bimbo teenager anyway?" Behan asked in a way that suggested he wasn't expecting an answer.

"No real mystery there . . . old hippie geezer with too much money trying to feel young again."

"He's not that old."

"Not that smart either."

"Some of us aren't all that clever when it comes to figuring out who we should care about." He sounded angry.

Josie dropped it. She had a feeling they weren't talking about Eli Goldman any longer, and she was probably the last person with any great insights in the personal relationship game. She told Behan she'd call Bright as soon as they got back to the station, and he could try to set up an interview with the elder Goldman that night or the next morning.

As Josie had anticipated, Chief Bright didn't take the news of Eli Goldman's possible involvement in the case very well. His immediate reaction was threatening to give the investigation back to RHD. Then he changed his mind and suggested that perhaps he should interview the councilman himself saying, "It would certainly be more appropriate."

THE CONFERENCE call lasted twenty minutes, and Josie eventually convinced Bright the Hollywood homicide supervisor was the best person to handle the inquiry. She argued that Bruno's accusation was unsupported by real evidence at this point, and it shouldn't be given additional weight by suggesting a deputy chief needed to become involved. She assured Bright that she and Behan were more than willing and able to absorb any repercussions the interview might unleash, and she didn't think the bureau needed to be exposed to unwarranted criticism. After Josie finished her rationale, she sat back and smirked at Behan. Following a lengthy pause, Bright came back on the line and agreed to allow Hollywood detectives to handle the interview.

"I'm going to get heat from city hall no matter what I do. Maybe it is better you handle this, but I expect, no, I insist you treat that man with respect," Bright said, sounding as if he were thinking out loud; and then raising his voice added, "I'm holding you personally responsible, Captain Corsino. Do you understand? Are you still listening?"

"Yes, sir," she said, shaking hands with Behan over the telephone speaker before hanging up.

"Dodged another bureaucratic snafu," Behan said, with his best W. C. Fields imitation.

"I just reminded him he'd much rather see you and me go down in flames. If Goldman makes a big deal out of this, you know

Bright's gonna deny we ever had this conversation. He'll swear he had no idea we were going to interview a city councilman."

"Don't matter, he knows you and me are still the most dangerous animals in this zoo," Behan said.

Josie sighed. She didn't feel dangerous. "Why's that, Tarzan?"

"We don't want to promote."

She agreed there was a sense of power that came with knowing you could do the right thing without worrying how it might influence your career aspirations. It made decisions a lot simpler and cleaner. But she also knew there were always ways to make life miserable for any animal as long as it lived in a zoo.

Behan called Goldman from Josie's office, and the councilman agreed to meet with them that evening. He didn't want the interview at city hall and said he'd feel more comfortable at the police station, "where there aren't as many enemy ears glued to keyholes." Goldman didn't ask what the interview was about, and said he was willing to cooperate and answer any questions they might have.

Behan had barely gone back to the detectives' squad room when Officer Fricke peeked into Josie's office.

"Got a minute, ma'am," Fricke said, stepping into the room.

"What's up?" Josie asked. She felt strange talking with him, knowing the surveillance team was probably skulking somewhere inside the station keeping tabs on everything he did and said. It was an intrusion, but a necessary one. She hoped the scrutiny would prove he wasn't doing anything wrong, and in fact, was working harder than anyone else in the building. "Where's Butler?" she asked, realizing Fricke was alone.

"Finishing reports," he said, sitting near her desk. "Can we talk?" he asked, leaning closer, almost whispering.

"Of course," she said, hearing the nervous twinge in her voice. "What's the problem?"

"I know you can't say nothing, and I'm not asking. I'm just saying me and Frankie we're pretty sure I.A.'s been following us." She didn't say anything and he continued. "I seen these guys everywhere we go . . . even when we ain't working." He stopped, and in spite of trying to be serious grinned a little. "I gotta say, ma'am, they're pretty lame. At first, I thought they might be gang-bangers setting us up for a hit, so I get all their plate numbers. When I run them they come back with no registration, and then I see some cars got two white stiffs that are for sure cops. So, I don't know why they're following us, but I wanted you to know we didn't do nothing wrong. They can follow me forever. I'll take 'em home and have my mom make dinner. They ain't never gonna see no misconduct or nothing illegal from us. I promise we wouldn't embarrass you that way." He stood, turned to leave, then came back. "It don't matter, but me and Frankie really respect you and wanted you to know," he said. She wasn't going to lie to him, but didn't tell him anything either. He nodded, shrugged and left her office.

Josie closed her eyes and rested her head on her folded hands. She had to admit she wasn't surprised. Fricke was clever. He hunted on the streets every night, outwitting human prey who had nothing to think about except new ways to commit crimes and stay out of jail. The I.A. sergeant she'd met was way out of his league.

She called the number the sergeant had given her and told him his surveillance had been burned. He couldn't understand how the policeman had figured out so quickly he was being fol-lowed and when he did, why he would tell his captain. Josie knew. Fricke was smarter than him and he trusted her, but she tried to soften the blow.

"Usually, they see some little thing that alerts them," she said. "Once a subject starts looking it's pretty much over."

"But we've never had a surveillance blown this fast," the ser-geant whined.

"This one's toast, so what're you planning to do now?" she asked.

"I'll talk to my captain in the morning. I don't know . . . maybe . . . I should get back to you," he mumbled and hung up.

She detected suspicion in his voice. It was easier to believe there was a leak, or someone had sabotaged his operation, than to admit he might've screwed up or been overmatched. The I.A. sergeant didn't appear to be a man who reflected much on his shortcomings, so Josie was fairly certain he'd try to blame her or her people for his failure. However, as soon as he interviewed Fricke and discovered how easy it was for him to identify the surveillance team, the man would be forced to face the truth. She'd like to be there when that happened. She supported her officers but resented anyone who thought she'd cut corners or do anything to prevent a thorough investigation of misconduct.

She had a couple of hours before Goldman's interview, but couldn't get motivated to look at the paperwork on her desk. Usually, she'd have it done in a few minutes and be searching for something else to do, but thinking about her conversation with the I.A. sergeant was disrupting her concentration.

David was on her mind too. He hadn't been around or called her for a day or two. There were things she needed to talk about, but had to admit she wasn't ready to confront him yet. His association with Cory Goldman and Misty Skylar had not only been a distraction for Josie, but had come dangerously close to being an embarrassment. She had always been mindful to protect her reputation, avoiding even the slightest appearance of wrongdoing. Her son's careless alliances might've altered all that. He wasn't a child and knew her position was sensitive. How could he bring those people that close to her life? Josie wanted to have that conversation with her son, but knew she wouldn't. She had other demands and ultimatums to make concerning his life and future. If she could get him back in school, he wouldn't have the time or inclination to hang around with the likes of Cory Goldman.

Wandering around the station usually cleared her head. It forced her to talk to people and stop thinking. There weren't many officers hanging around the building this evening, however; and within a few minutes, she found herself climbing upstairs and searching for her friend in the vice office. Marge was alone working on her computer. Her reading glasses were balanced on the tip of her nose as she typed and spewed a steady stream of profanity.

"I hate fucking rating reports," she shouted and slumped back when she spotted Josie.

"Have your sergeants write them," Josie said, sitting across from her.

"Great idea, then I'll have this incredibly bitching squad that walks on water and never needs another training day."

"Guess you'd better write them then."

"Did you come up here to irritate me?"

"Yes."

"What's wrong?" Marge asked. She'd stopped working and was studying Josie.

"What's new with the rodent?"

"Nothing, Mouse is a perfect law-abiding citizen . . . doesn't even jaywalk anymore . . . hasn't been anywhere near Cory Goldman since that night at Avanti's. I gave our logs to Detective Sunshine. What's wrong?"

"Has Fricke talked to you today?" Josie asked.

"Talks to me every day. Remember, he works for me now. Thank you very much."

Josie told her what had happened with Fricke. She explained the surveillance was finished and I.A. would probably be interviewing Fricke and his partner.

"Good," Marge said. "Give the damn hype car back to narcotics."

"I'll think about it, unless he doesn't get relieved from duty, then I'll still want you to keep an eye on him."

"This is bullshit, that guy's not dirty. He's hardcore cop."

"Wanna grab something to eat? I've got to get back here in about an hour," Josie asked, intentionally changing the subject. She liked Fricke too, but didn't have the luxury of ignoring serious accusations. Marge was a good cop, but too quick to defend her officers. Cops were human, so they weren't perfect. Josie found her best supervisors never closed their eyes or minds to the possibility of corruption. The way to keep the department clean was to never stop looking for that rare case where someone crossed the line. There were fallen angels. Marge acted as if it never happened, and despite all her worldliness, that trait sometimes made her seem naïve to Josie.

"I'm starving," Marge said standing and taking her jacket off the back of her chair. She seemed annoyed by the change of subject, but never turned down an opportunity to eat. "We won't talk about Fricke," she said, grinning. "You hear from Jake?"

"I'm not gonna eat with you if I lose my appetite."

"Sorry . . . so you haven't," Marge said and hesitated before adding, "I saw him at a hearing yesterday. He was defending one of the club owners we'd cited a couple of days ago."

"Great, more good news."

"Just thought you oughta know."

They walked across to Nora's and didn't talk about Fricke or Jake. Marge was in a good mood and couldn't wait to tell a story she'd heard about Chief Bright's latest escapade.

"He rolls out last night on a call about a possible bomb scare outside a synagogue in West L.A. The bomb squad's about to do a quick check of a suspicious truck parked outside the front door when 'Not So' gets there and brings everything to a grinding halt."

"Figures," Josie said.

"No wait, there's more," Marge said, giggling. "The patrol captain tries to tell him that everything he wants done has already been done, but Bright insists it's not enough and calls a citywide tactical alert, brings in officers from everywhere; and while the brass is sitting in some hardware store going through Bright's silly terrorist checklist, the driver of said truck wakes up from behind the seat where he's been napping and drives away."

"What'd Bright do?" Josie asked, laughing.

"Well, he comes out of his briefing and the truck's gone. He looks up and down Pico Boulevard and then at the West L.A. captain and the bomb squad supervisor who both shrug because they were inside the store with him. He comes unglued and demands they find the truck, but everybody's gone; barricades are down; traffic's flowing. Twenty minutes later a sergeant comes back and explains that the truck driver got sleepy and took a snooze. When he woke up he didn't realize what was happening and just drove off. It was a bakery truck, so he passes out fresh cinnamon buns and Starbucks coffee for the cops who stopped him and everybody parts friends. 'Not So' is furious, and he wants the fucking driver arrested."

"For what?" Josie asked.

"That's what the sergeant asks, and Bright says . . ." Marge stopped to compose herself then continued, "bribery . . . the sergeant had to explain that giving away cinnamon buns and coffee wasn't a criminal offense."

"You're making this up."

"Swear to God," Marge said, raising her right hand.

"The man's hopeless," Josie said and realized she felt better. Marge had a way of balancing Josie's world by reminding her that as complicated and unruly as her life might get, at least she wasn't Eric Bright.

ELEVEN

The meeting with Eli Goldman was scheduled for seven P.M., but he arrived five minutes early without an attorney. Josie and Behan had decided the best place to interview the councilman was in her office. Earlier that day, she salvaged a small round conference table from the basement and it fit nicely in the corner of her room. Behan could record the interview and have plenty of space for his computer and papers. There was ample sitting room for Goldman and his lawyer because Josie couldn't imagine he'd show up without representation. She took his solo appearance as either the absence of a guilty conscience or arrogance.

Goldman was dressed casually in a faded blue polo shirt and jeans. His complexion was still pasty white, but his long grey hair was combed and pulled back behind his ears. He looked refreshed, almost too relaxed, as if he'd gone home, taken a leisurely shower and had dinner. He immediately seized one of the bottles of water she'd set on the table and sipped while he chatted with her. She made small talk, avoiding any of the subjects Behan wanted to cover. As soon as Behan was ready, Goldman positioned his chair for some leg room, and leaned back a little.

"How can I help you, detective?" Goldman asked, grinning at Behan with a hint of smugness.

"What was your relationship with Hillary Dennis?" Behan asked.

Goldman squinted slightly as if his head hurt and said, "As I've mentioned before, I knew she was seeing my son and I disapproved."

"Did you ever have a sexual relationship with Miss Dennis?" Behan asked, almost before Goldman stopped talking.

No sense beating around the bush, Josie thought.

Goldman took a deep breath and pretended to cough. "Why would you ask such a thing, Detective Behan?"

"I have information you were seen going into her apartment late at night, and did in fact have a sexual relationship with her that ended badly."

The councilman sat up straight and put both hands on the table.

"Your information is completely wrong. I did warn her about my son. I forbid her to see him or buy him drugs, but that happened one time at Cory's apartment. My son was there. He can tell you."

"Do you deny following her, harassing her, and threatening to harm her?"

"Yes, I most certainly do. I'd like to know who would say such things," Goldman's face was flushed, but his voice remained calm, subdued. "She was a child . . . a very disturbed child . . . you can't actually believe . . ."

Behan continued the same line of questioning. He asked about times and places, made Goldman explain what he was doing on the day Bruno claimed he had gone to Hillary's apartment. When asked about the night Hillary was killed, Goldman said he was at an event in Hollywood, and he provided a list of people who saw him there. He denied knowing or even having met Bruno Faldi, and swore he'd never been in Hillary's apartment or been alone with the young woman.

When the interview was over, Josie had doubts. Either the councilman was a much better actor than Hillary, or Bruno had deliberately misled them. Goldman had almost convinced her that he'd never had any sort of relationship with Hillary Dennis, and in fact, hardly knew the woman. He appeared to be a concerned father who was totally baffled by any accusation that he could or would treat Hillary as anything other than a confused child who was harming his son.

Josie listened to Behan go through a series of inquiries. He skillfully asked the same question a number of ways attempting to confuse the man, but Goldman stuck to his story. He was candid about his broken marriage and his son's problems, but steadfastly denied any improper relationship or contact with Hillary. Josie was impressed by the way Behan kept his professional demeanor. If he was intimidated by Goldman's position and power, he didn't show it.

Finally, Behan stopped, turned off his recorder and thanked the councilman. He gave no indication that he believed or doubted Goldman's statement. Goldman's outward appearance hadn't changed much either. His jaw muscles seemed to relax, but he showed little other emotion. He stood and coolly talked for a few seconds with Josie about Hollywood business before shaking hands with both of them and leaving.

When they were alone, Josie and Behan sat without speaking. The detective sorted through his notes and eventually looked up at her.

"Well?" he asked.

"Well, what?"

"You believe him?"

"I think I might. You?" These days, Josie trusted Behan's detective instincts more than her own.

"Don't know. He's a hard read."

"He's a politician. They manipulate the truth for a living."

"Then why do you believe him?"

"Gut feeling, and I don't trust Bruno. I got nothing but bad vibes from Bruno Faldi."

Behan sighed and slumped onto the table resting his head on his arm. "Not good enough." He sat up again. "I'm gonna talk to Lieutenant Owens tonight. Can you stay?"

She looked at her watch. It was almost time for the graveyard shift's roll call. Owens should be in the locker room changing his clothes, but Josie was aching to go home. She was dead tired and becoming increasingly worried that no significant progress was being made in the investigation.

"Sure you wouldn't rather do this tomorrow when we're both fresh?" she asked.

"We're here. He's here. Let's get it over with. I got a search warrant for his car and house if we need it."

Now he had her attention. "When did you get that? Better yet, how did you get it?" From what she remembered, there wasn't anywhere near enough probable cause to search anything belonging to Owens.

"I combined the statements by Mouse, Buck and Bruno Faldi to show that Owens had a list of officers' names that might've had reason to harm Hillary Dennis."

"Really, and what reason was that?" she asked. Josie hadn't written a search warrant for a number of years, and couldn't figure out how Behan had managed to tie Owens' list to those statements.

"The short 'n' sweet version . . . according to my informants . . . officers on Owens' list worked off-duty with Hillary and might've even enabled her drug habits, and she might've threatened to expose one or more of them."

"You actually found a judge who was willing to sign that fairy tale?"

"Yes, ma'am," Behan said.

She shook her head. "I'll stay."

———

LIEUTENANT OWENS apparently hadn't heard the captain was still in the station. He conducted a ten-minute roll call, didn't give the department's mandated training, didn't do the weekly uniform inspection, and spent just enough time in the roll call room to count heads and assign cars. Josie had intended to go upstairs and talk to his officers because the graveyard shift rarely had an opportunity to voice their concerns to her directly, but before she could get there, they were on their way down. She noticed a couple of them were still buttoning their uniforms and securing gun belts as they picked up shotguns and radios in the kit room. Most of the officers who worked these bizarre hours liked the challenge of digging for crime on deserted city streets, but a few of the lazier ones had come to morning watch to escape L.A.'s crazy traffic, the busy radio calls, rigid rules, and hard-charging supervisors. The slower pace and lack of structure suited them fine, and Lieutenant Owens' laid-back, hands-off style most likely completed their dream-come-true work environment.

Behan went upstairs and escorted Owens back to Josie's office. She and Behan were hoping the lieutenant wouldn't try to hide the list until he knew he was about to be interviewed. Behan was an experienced detective and knew human behavior was surprisingly predictable. He figured Owens was arrogant enough to think he could outsmart them, and he'd wait until it was absolutely necessary before he concealed the list. Behan was also counting on the fact that the watch commander had been around long enough to believe detectives didn't stay up and interview anyone in the middle of the night.

"He wanted to stop at his locker before he came down," Behan whispered to Josie, stopping her just outside the office door as Owens sat at her conference table.

Owens didn't say anything but seemed angry. He rarely smiled, but this was different. He glared at Josie, and she almost laughed. Did this guy actually think he could intimidate her? Admittedly, there were things that frightened her, but flabby, middle-aged cops with badly styled hair and manicured nails weren't among them. His thin-lipped sneer did however tell her this wasn't going to be easy.

The interview started with Behan giving the administrative and Miranda admonishments. Owens immediately requested representation.

"Call somebody," Josie said.

"Now—it's the middle of the night. Can't we put this off until a decent hour?" Owens complained.

"No," she said. "If you want a rep, call somebody."

"Can I go up to my locker and get my phone book?"

"Detective Behan can get it for you. Give him the combination."

"Never mind, go ahead and ask your questions. I don't need anybody."

Behan started with a series of harmless inquiries before getting to the heart of his interview. Most of the answers should've been simple and straightforward but Owens was painfully slow in responding, a word miser weighing every syllable before he spoke. Finally, Behan asked him about the work permit, which at first Owen claimed he had and then admitted he might not. He denied having a list of officers that worked for him until Behan produced the search warrant.

"You'd best tell me how you operate this business," Behan said. "Right now all you're facing is working without a permit and that might cost you a couple a days' suspension. False and misleading statements are a firing offense."

Owens's gruff expression softened slightly as if a light had gone on in his lazy brain. He straightened up, rubbed his diminishing chin and leaned his elbows on the table.

"I'm helping guys get some extra spending money, that's all. There's nothing wrong in that, is there?"

"Depends," Behan said, "on what they're doing."

"Nothing illegal, that's for damn sure," Owens said, his cockiness quickly eroding.

Josie wasn't sitting at the table. She stayed at her desk watching the interview. Owens was facing her but Behan sat between them, so Owens had to look around the detective to see her. She was surprised how many times he strained to see her reaction to his answers. He'd made it clear over the years he didn't care what she thought or wanted, but this morning even he was sharp enough to realize her opinion mattered more than anything else in his world.

"Start from the beginning and tell me exactly what you're doing," Behan said.

Owens shook his head. Clearly, he didn't want to talk about his enterprise, but knew he didn't have a choice. His internal struggle was almost comical to observe. Josie thought all he needed was an angel on one shoulder and Satan on the other.

"I got a few buddies in the industry," Owens said and looked relieved after speaking those first words. He continued by describing how through his contacts in Hollywood he was able to offer bit parts in movies. "I been in this division just about my whole career. I meet people, industry people on radio calls and stuff, help them out. Producers, directors, all of them go nuts about having real cops playing police parts."

"How'd you hook up with Carlton Buck?" Behan asked.

"We worked together . . . sergeants in Hollywood before Buck made detective and got transferred to Bunco Forgery division downtown. We ran into each other about a year ago in a bar . . . some cop's retirement party. He tells me he's retired and got his P.I. ticket. He's waving lots a money at me to find cops who want to do security or protection work for celebrities. It was legitimate, all aboveboard."

"What about bit parts in the movies? Did Buck set that up too?"

"Nah, he's not connected that way. I got the studio contacts. I help them; they help me. So I keep two lists of cops that wanna work. One list is for security stuff. A few of those guys get the protection gig . . . pays better but there's a higher risk for shootings or fights. The rest do security on pricey real estate. The money's not as good but it's safer."

"What about the acting parts?"

"My other list is strictly for acting or extras."

"So, how do you make your money on this deal?"

Owens hesitated. This was the part he didn't want to talk about, so Behan asked the question again.

"I get my cut," Owens mumbled.

"What's that mean?"

Owens sighed and said, "Buck and the studios, they pay me a small percentage for every guy I bring them."

He claimed he'd never met Hillary Dennis but had arranged for officers to work on several of her films. He didn't keep records of where or when the officers worked. He went down the list and took the next available officer when there was a job. Sometimes he went out of order and picked certain officers on the list if the producer was looking for a special type. He always got paid cash so there weren't any other records.

"I wasn't doing anything wrong," Owens said. "Everybody makes money. Everybody gets what they want."

"You can't remember anyone who worked on the Hillary Dennis movies?" Behan asked.

"The studio tells me they need a cop; I send the next guy on the list. That's all I know."

"Did you know Misty Skylar?"

"That the dead woman in the alley last week?" Owens asked. "Never heard of her," he said without waiting for an answer.

Two hours later, Josie figured Behan had all he was going to get. The big redhead must've thought so too. He concluded the interview and escorted Owens to his locker where the lieutenant voluntarily opened it and gave Behan two lists of officers' names. Behan guessed they were copies because Owens didn't seem all that upset about surrendering them.

When they got back to Josie's office, she gave Owens the usual admonishment about not talking to anyone about his interview or revealing what had been asked or discussed. She told him he had a personnel complaint regarding the work permit, but didn't know if there'd be other charges, then ordered him to stop working off-duty in the movie business until the personnel complaint was finished. His demeanor reverted to nasty and disagreeable when she promised to initiate another investigation if she found out he'd conducted roll call again without providing mandatory training or failed to do a uniform inspection. He started to leave but came back and pointed at Josie.

"You think I don't know who's been snitching," Owens said. His face flushed in anger. "I know that lowlife's been out to get me for years."

"Don't know what you're talking about," Josie said, calmly. She saw Behan move a little closer to the irate lieutenant. Apparently, he thought Owens was about to do something stupid, but Josie wasn't worried. Let him try. She'd enjoy beating the crap out of the little weasel. She might've been off the streets a few years, but she could still wield a mean nightstick.

"Bruno Faldi hates my guts. I know he's the asshole telling lies about me. Fuck shoulda never been a cop," Owens shouted, stopping just short of her desk.

"Still haven't got a clue what you're talking about," Josie said again, not moving and staring at the distraught man.

Owens was so angry his face was red, and he was spitting as he talked.

"Your fucking informant," he said, grabbing Behan's search warrant and shaking it in the air. "Faldi's up to his ears in the mob. His uncle's Vince Milano. Why'd you think the asshole retired so young?" Owens looked from Josie to Behan in frustration. "I was gonna blow the whistle on him and his Uncle Vincenzo, that's why, and I got Buck to fire him, too. So this is the way he gets back at me."

Josie and Behan watched as the man dropped his verbal bomb and stomped back to the watch commander's office. Bruno wasn't the one who'd snitched on him, but it was probably better if Owens didn't know Buck had. The fact that Bruno Faldi was related to Milano was interesting, even disturbing, Josie thought, but not all that relevant since he wasn't a cop any longer. She did recall both Buck and Bruno saying Bruno had quit his security job, not that he'd been fired. It was a small detail, but she hated loose ends.

As soon as Owens left, Behan spread pages of the lists on the table, and they carefully reviewed the names, knowing they'd have to interview all of them. It wasn't a surprise that the name of almost every officer who worked on Owens' watch was there. The lieutenant took care of his people. Donnie Fricke and Frank Butler were among those requesting movie jobs, as well as Bright's adjutant Sergeant Perry and a number of the younger Hollywood vice officers. Behan hadn't expected to find so many of his Hollywood detectives working off-duty for Owens, but had to admit Lieutenant Ibarra's name on the armed security and protection list was the real shocker.

"Conflict of interest, don't you think?" Behan asked, pushing away from the table.

"He knew we were looking at the off-duty stuff . . . but never bothered to mention it," Josie said. "Did knucklehead have a work permit?"

"Don't know. Never thought to check for his name."

"Do it tomorrow . . . I'm dead tired. I gotta get some sleep," she said, yawning. "He should be back from vacation. I'll talk to him as soon as I drag myself in."

Behan didn't argue. He wanted to get home to his new wife. Although he claimed Miss Vicky didn't object to his crazy hours, Josie had noticed some telltale signs of the old stressed-out pre-marriage Behan; most notably the dark circles that had reappeared under both eyes.

During the drive up the nearly deserted Pasadena Freeway, she kept thinking about Bruno's connection to Vince Milano. It was odd the background people hadn't picked up on that significant detail before he was hired, and obviously, he didn't volunteer the information. Josie couldn't help but wonder where Bruno's real loyalties had been during his career with the LAPD. She'd found that most bad cops who slipped through the hiring cracks were predisposed toward corruption before they were sworn in. All they needed was opportunity. Bruno could've been a very valuable asset to Milano and his friends from inside the police department.

There was a web spinning slowly, linking the players in this investigation, and unfortunately it included her son. She was too tired to even begin to understand what it all meant, but every new connection seemed to trigger another level of anxiety.

She saw Jake's Porsche parked in the driveway as she turned onto her street. It was nearly dawn and she tried to clear her head to remember if he'd mentioned he was coming home for some reason. She couldn't remember. Exhaustion had wiped any relevant conversation from her brain.

The house was dark. She found him asleep in the den. He was stretched out on the recliner using his jacket as a blanket. She took one of the cotton throws from the closet shelf and covered him. He didn't stir, and she could barely hear him breathing. Her husband always slept like a mummy. The sheets and blankets were barely ruffled on his side when they shared a bed. Josie's side, on the other hand, looked as if two pissed-off bears had wrestled under the covers all night.

She watched him a few seconds. The stress lines had disappeared from his face, his shirt and suit were immaculate, and his shoes were polished. It was the old meticulous; cautious Jake again. His bulging briefcase was on the floor leaning against the lounger. He obviously had wanted to talk with her, but she didn't have the heart to wake him. Instead, she went up to their bedroom and dropped onto the bed. Whatever it was could wait until she got some sleep.

———

THERE WAS something about the combined smells of bacon frying and freshly brewed coffee that worked like smelling salts on the comatose Josie. She woke and sat up, still dressed in her pantsuit and shoes. It was only four hours later than it had been when she passed out on the bed. She waited a few seconds until her head cleared and her eyes focused. Although she wasn't completely rested she was primed to devour whatever was being cooked in her kitchen. She took a shower, got dressed in less than twenty minutes, and had nearly finished blow-drying her long hair when Jake appeared behind her in the mirror carrying two mugs of coffee. He stood there quietly for several seconds and she could feel him staring at her. Jake always said he liked watching her as she finished getting ready for work, swore he couldn't believe how good she looked without fussing. Josie pinned her hair up off her neck and turned to take one of the mugs.

"Thanks," she said. "Sleep okay?"

"Not really . . . you?"

"Like a baby."

"You look great," he said. "I got here after one. You couldn't have gotten much sleep."

"Enough," she said, pushing past him into the bedroom. "What's up, Jake?" she asked. She wasn't in the mood to play twenty questions and knew he wanted something.

"We need to talk about David," he said, following her onto the landing and down the stairs.

The kitchen smelled wonderful. He had platters with toast, bacon and scrambled eggs on the breakfast table. She glanced at the clock over the sink. It was only eight A.M., so she had plenty of time to do this. She filled their coffee mugs again, sat at the table and piled the food on her plate. Jake took a slice of toast and one strip of bacon.

"I can't believe you eat that much and stay so skinny," he said, nibbling on the toast.

"I don't want my son playing in that sleazy bar," she said, not looking up from her eggs.

Jake pushed his plate away. "He's our son and he's old enough to decide where he plays the piano."

"Why would you encourage him to work in a place like that?"

"He told me he saw you drinking at the bar . . . you and some guy."

"He saw me?" Josie picked up on the accusatory tone in Jake's voice when he said, 'you and some guy,' but she was more offended that David had seen her and didn't come over to talk to her.

"He knew you wouldn't approve, and he wasn't in the mood to argue. Besides, he didn't know if you two wanted to be alone."

Josie's first thought was 'Fuck you,' but she said, "I was working." She took a sip of coffee and glared at him. "Even if I wasn't working, what's it got to do with you anymore?"

"Nothing, I guess," he said, looking glum.

"I want David to go back to school, get his degree . . . in music or art, so he can get a real job teaching or something."

"That's not what he wants."

"What difference does that make? We've let him do what he wants all his life and if we don't step in, he's gonna end up living on the boardwalk at Venice Beach drawing charcoal caricatures for tourists."

"Don't have much faith in him do you?"

"Yes, I do, but we've lived longer. He should get the benefit of our experience. You and I both know he's chosen a path that usually ends in disappointment and poverty. At least, let's make him do something that he can fall back on if the dream falls apart."

"Like a college degree."

"Exactly," Josie said, exhaling as if she'd been trying to make an elusive point.

"He doesn't want to go to college."

"Then we stop supporting him until he does. Without our money to buy food or put a roof over his head, he won't have a choice."

"You could do that?"

"If it makes him a better man, damn right I can and will."

"No, I won't let him go hungry. He's stubborn like you, and he'll never agree to your terms. It's his life. Let him live it his way."

Now Josie pushed her plate away. She'd lost her appetite. She couldn't do this alone.

"Great, and if he never gets a break we can go visit him on some street corner and drop dollars in his hat while he plays," she said, sarcastically.

Jake laughed and held up both hands when she glowered at him. "Sorry," he said, trying to suppress a smile. "You don't see many street musicians playing the piano. The picture of his baby grand on the sidewalk at Sunset and Vine just struck me funny."

"I'm glad you think it's humorous. We'll see if you're still laughing when he's forty, hungry and playing for quarters in some downtown L.A. dive."

He stood and started to say something, but stopped himself and finally said, softly, "You can't run our kid's life like you run your police station. Not everything can be controlled and made to work the way you think it should."

"Why not?"

"Because life's messy. Let him get his hands dirty. He can fail . . . he will fail sometimes, but David's a smart guy. We brought him up to give a hundred percent to whatever he does. It might not be what you'd like him to do, but as long as he's happy, leave him alone, Josie."

Jake reached over and gently touched her cheek for a moment. His skin was warm and soft. The gesture surprised her and she was silent as he picked up his briefcase.

"I know you won't believe this," he said, stopping near the kitchen door, "but I never meant to hurt you. I'm trying to slay my demons the only way I know how. You might be done with me, but I'll never stop loving you."

The door closed and he was gone. Josie sat there staring at the empty space where he'd stood and said he loved her. Why's he talking about demons? What demons? she thought, rubbing the back of her neck. Tension was building in her shoulders again. Now, she wasn't just worried about David but about Jake, too. She wasn't angry with him any longer, or maybe she was. Her feelings were confused . . . anger, love, disappointment, all mashed together giving her a stabbing pain above her eyes.

She'd gotten out of bed that morning confident and cocky, sure about everything; she knew exactly what she wanted and how to get it. Fifteen minutes with Jake had ruined her day, sending her to the medicine cabinet for aspirin and a penetrating look into the mirror trying to rediscover the self-reliance that had vanished with what she was certain was a contrived loving touch.

TWELVE

Deputy Chief Bright was waiting in Josie's office when she arrived. He was standing with his back to the door staring at an old picture of her in uniform posing with six other officers who had worked a special robbery suppression team. The picture had been taken the day they received an honorary citation for their efforts in stopping street robberies.

"Didn't you shoot some guy when you worked this robbery thing?" Bright asked as soon as he realized she was in the room.

"Yes," she said, curtly. It wasn't something she wanted to discuss with him.

"What actually happened?" he asked, still staring at the picture. "I don't think I ever heard the whole story."

"Not much to tell. He attacked one of our decoy cops. I shot him."

Actually, she did remember the incident all too well. The decoy was Maria Solis, a two-year cop. She was barely five feet tall, but all heart and as tough as they came, man or woman. The robber stabbed Maria with a switchblade as he tore the purse strap off her shoulder. Josie was the supervisor as well as one of the covering officers and was hidden a few yards away. She fired two quick rounds killing the robber before he'd run ten feet from the injured officer. Maria lived, but had several surgeries and never worked the streets again. The robbery team was disbanded after that incident, but Josie received a lot of accolades for her quick response. She, however, saw it as a failure because it had been her job to keep Maria safe. She didn't tell Bright any of that because he hadn't spent much time on the street and wouldn't really understand.

"I remember that unit . . . good results, dangerous way to do business," Bright said, turning away from the photo. "How'd the interview with Eli Goldman go?"

"Pretty good. Sergeant Perry should've been given a copy."

"Yeah, I saw that. What'd you think?"

"About what?" Josie asked. She really didn't want to elaborate with personal insights or conclusions since everything she said to Bright would probably be shared with Goldman.

"Don't be coy with me, Captain. Did you believe him, or did you think he was lying about his relationship with that girl?"

"Truthfully, I don't know," Josie said. "He denies anything except fatherly concern for Cory as his motivation for being anywhere near Hillary, and we can't prove otherwise."

"What about the retired cop Bruno Faldi? Didn't he say Eli had a relationship with that girl?"

"Yes sir, but then he's not the most reliable source. We've got reason to believe he's related to Vince Milano."

Bright slumped onto Josie's couch. "What a mess," he said. "It would be so much easier if I gave this back to RHD. I know Fletcher wants your people to handle it, but it's getting really complicated. Maybe it's too much for you and your detectives."

"I'll let you know if we need the bureau's help," Josie said, trying to sound professional but irked at the suggestion she and her detectives weren't as good as or better than anyone in the city. "Maybe we can use extra resources at some point, but for now I think we've pretty much got it under control."

She felt nervous sweat on her hands. She hadn't told him about the off-duty jobs or the possibility one or more officers might've been involved with Hillary. She hadn't told him a lot and realized that although they'd made progress, Bright wasn't aware of it because she couldn't trust him.

Josie had to keep the investigation for a lot of reasons but primarily because she knew Behan would do it right regardless of the outcome. If it went to RHD, she feared the case would die a slow bureaucratic death. There were too many high-profile people on the periphery of these murders that might be happier if the investigation was tucked away forever in a cold case file. In those moments when she was completely honest with herself, Josie worried she might be one of them. David's proximity to the victims was troublesome, but Josie knew her son wasn't a killer, and she wasn't going to allow anyone to try to prove otherwise.

"I'm concerned you're not making much progress," he said. "I'm not comfortable everything's being done."

"Why's that?" Josie asked, not trying to hide her annoyance. She was making progress and if he could keep his mouth shut he'd know about it.

"Have you got a suspect?"

"We're working on it."

"Nobody said you're not working hard, but it's been several days. You've got to get control of this thing. Two women had their brains blown out . . . one of them practically a child. The public wants somebody held accountable," he said, rubbing his forehead with both hands. "That Dennis girl's mother keeps writing letters to the Police Commission and the mayor. If it weren't for Fletcher's interference, I'm certain I could get the chief of police to dump this whole thing on RHD."

Josie was still upset with Fletcher for her refusal to close the needle exchange, but felt pangs of gratitude that the stubborn woman was insisting Josie's detectives handle Hillary's homicide. Now that Fricke was making arrests around the exchange, she was nervous the councilwoman might retaliate and allow RHD to take it.

"Behan's a good detective. If this thing can be solved, he'll figure it out," she said.

"Just make certain Ibarra keeps me in the loop . . . and let me know before you do anything that involves Goldman or his son." He repeated that familiar refrain on his way out the door—shoulders back, chin up, showing everybody he was still in charge. Sergeant Jones stood in Josie's doorway and watched until the deputy chief was out of sight before entering.

"That I.A. sergeant sent 1.28 face sheets with misconduct complaints on Donnie Fricke and Frank Butler," the adjutant said, placing two sheets of paper on her desk. "Should be pretty simple . . . anonymous informant . . . nothing else."

"You do it," Josie said, pushing the papers back toward him.

"Shouldn't this be in Lieutenant Bailey's shop?" he asked. Josie sat back and stared at him, and he snatched the papers off her desk. "Yes, ma'am."

Before he could get out the door, she asked, "Is Ibarra back from vacation?"

"Yes, ma'am, but he called in sick this morning," he said and immediately slapped his forehead. "I forgot to tell you Lieutenant Owens pulled the pin this morning."

"Owens retired?"

"Cleaned out his locker while you were talking to the chief."

"Bright didn't mention it, so he probably hasn't been told. Does Behan know?"

"I can ask."

"Never mind, I'm going back to detectives."

Marge Bailey was coming downstairs from the vice office and called to Josie before she reached the detective squad room.

"Captain, can you come up when you get a chance?" she asked.

Josie waved at her and said she'd be there in a few minutes.

Josie figured she and Behan had either scared Owens into retiring, or he was so pissed-off after the interview he'd decided not to come back to work again. Either way was fine with her. She was happy to be rid of the dead weight, and his departure didn't protect him from the investigation. With any luck, Ibarra would do the same thing.

"I heard," Behan said as Josie approached his desk, "police work must've interfered with Owens's real job," he added.

"What was his real job, ripping off the city?"

"He had a pretty good scam while it lasted. The city pays his salary while he works every night for Buck and the studios . . . takes double-dipping to a whole new level."

"Asshole was stealing," Josie said, and saw a few of the detectives' heads turn slightly while pretending they weren't listening. She realized she shouldn't be talking about any of this in front of them. For a moment, the anger had clouded her judgment because she knew the corruption tainted all of them.

"What did Chief Bright want?" Behan asked, almost whispering.

"Curious about Eli Goldman's interview," she said, sitting closer to him with her back to the other detectives.

"Like he didn't know. . . . How much you wanna bet Goldman was on the phone to Bright before he got out of our lobby."

"You're probably right. Bright didn't seem as interested in the interview as he was in knowing what I thought about Goldman's credibility."

"What'd you tell him?"

"That I wasn't sure."

Behan nodded. "Good answer," he said and glanced around the room before adding, "let's go back to your office where we can talk."

"Come with me up to vice. We'll talk there," she said, and Behan grimaced. "Something Marge can't hear?"

"No, of course not, it's fine," he said, unconvincingly.

"I don't understand. Why's it so difficult for you two to work together?"

"We're trying, but we're different," he said, getting up.

Josie wanted to blurt out that she thought they were so much alike it was scary. Marge was a pretty, foulmouthed, female version of Behan. They both were intense and focused and had given up any semblance of a normal life to work too many hours at a job they both appeared to love more than food or sex. Josie kept her thoughts to herself. Having managed people for so many years, she knew there was more going on than they were willing to admit, but she was confident when the time was right they'd tell her . . . probably more than she wanted to know. As long as it didn't affect their work, for now anyway, the mystery could remain their business.

As usual, the vice office was empty except for Marge. She didn't allow her officers to hang around the station and kept them on the street making arrests or patrolling. She was sifting through a stack of arrest reports, and the big smile that flashed across her face when she looked up and saw Josie faded as soon as she noticed Behan.

Behan leaned against the wall until Josie told him to sit down.

"Bright's talking about giving the Dennis homicide back to RHD. You two are all I've got, so I need both your heads working on this," Josie said, pulling out a chair for Behan.

"I got the background stuff you wanted on sleazebag Milano and our hippie councilman," Marge said, taking a folder out of her center desk drawer. "I sent it as an attachment to your computer, but I thought you might want to go over some of it," she added, placing the folder in front of Josie.

"Give us the highlights. I'll fill in the rest later," Josie said, glancing at Behan who suddenly seemed interested and slid the folder closer so he could read it.

"I checked with Organized Crime and they've got Milano tagged as a low-level weasel in a wannabe crime family. His old man was a bagman for the mob and his mom made booze deliveries during Prohibition. His brother's in federal prison for murder and his brother's kid . . ." she paused for a moment. "Here's where the story gets so bitchin' good. His nephew was one of L.A.'s fucking finest."

"Bruno Faldi," Josie said.

"How the fuck did you know that?" Marge asked. Her enthusiasm had clearly been derailed.

"It's a long story. He worked for Carlton Buck's P.I. firm as personal security for Hillary Dennis. Then he either quit or got fired just before Hillary got herself killed," Josie said.

"The burning question is how he got past the background check with his daddy doing hard time," Behan said.

"Faldi is his mother's maiden name. He used it through high school and college, so apparently nobody bothered to check any further back when he applied to come on the department," Marge explained.

"It's a safe guess he wasn't completely candid when he got that teaching job either," Josie said. "Did Bruno give the department a phony birth certificate?" she asked, thinking they might be able to do something with a forged document.

"Nope, shitheads in personnel had a note in his file that he'd requested a certified copy of his birth certificate from some hospital in New York, and it would take about three weeks to get it," Marge said. "Morons never followed up and he went through the academy, his entire career, and retired from the department without anyone realizing the paperwork was missing."

"Did he really quit because Howard Owens was about to blow the whistle on him?" Josie asked.

"Don't know."

"Did he give any reason in his exit interview?"

Marge sat back, lifted her long blond hair off her neck and clasped her hands behind her head. "Bruno swore he had a fucking burning desire to bring about world peace by teaching empty-headed teenagers . . . or some such bullshit," she said, exhaling and crossing her arms.

"Maybe it was true," Josie said, playing the devil's advocate. Actually, she couldn't see Bruno Faldi as someone driven by human compassion. Especially since he'd taken a job as an armed bodyguard.

"Not likely," Marge said, snatching the folder from Behan. She found Bruno's last teaching evaluation from the girl's academy and handed it to Josie. "The school board doesn't think much of him as an educator. His students always bomb on state tests. Those pretty young girls are crazy about the handsome bald hulk, but the school administrators believe he gets way too familiar with the little mush brains. He's on probation and probably won't be asked back next term." She slid the folder back toward Behan.

"I wouldn't bet on it. Teaching's worse than civil service. It's harder to fire teachers than cops," Josie said.

"Other than being his nephew, can we connect Bruno to Vince Milano's business interests?" Behan asked.

"As a matter of fact we can," Marge said with a broad grin. "I've got a dozen field interview cards from Avanti's with Bruno Faldi's name on them. My guys have stopped him several times because he's too old to be hanging around that underage crowd. He always tells them he's a manager at the club and gets his uncle or one of the staff to vouch for him." She added with emphasis, "Bruno has never, ever identified himself as a retired cop. Do you know any cop with an ID card or badge who doesn't show it to another cop the second he's stopped?"

"No, but maybe he's smart. If you collected that many FI's on a retired cop hanging out around Avanti's it would send up red flags and get everybody's attention. If he's your average asshole who works there, it's no big deal, and he stays under the radar," Josie said.

"Wonder what he really does for Uncle Vince?" Behan said. "That teaching job's like a hobby, and if his evaluation's any indication, he doesn't seem all that interested in keeping it."

"Why did he go to work for Buck . . . just to get to Hillary Dennis? He did a few one-night gigs before her, but she's looking like his primary reason for having that job. When she dumps him he quits," Josie said, then added, "So why? Did Milano want her watched or what?"

They were quiet. Josie could feel the anxiety and understood their frustration. A criminal investigation was similar to focusing a camera. They kept adjusting the lens until the picture became clear. It was exasperating when they couldn't make out something they all knew was there.

"That teaching job gives him a couple of things—legitimacy and access to a lot of young girls. He sure didn't do it for the money," Behan said, finally. "My guess is it's the young girls he's after because his police career gave him the first one."

As Josie listened to Behan and Marge exchange ideas, she browsed through the folder containing Milano's information. It listed his businesses, arrest record, and family history. A few pages in, she found the section devoted to his nephew Bruno Faldi and replaced the teaching evaluation. The next item was Bruno's application to the police department. Josie read it and confirmed what Marge had said. There wasn't any reference to Vince Milano or Bruno's father. He used his mother's maiden name and listed his father as "unknown." Josie turned the page and was about to pick up the next item when she noticed the back of the application. It required the names of two community references. Bruno again listed his family's parish priest, but his second reference this time was LAPD Sergeant Carlton Buck.

"Small world," Josie said, showing the entry to Behan and Marge.

"I'll be damned," Marge whispered. "I never noticed that."

"I'm getting a little pissed-off that people keep lying to us or conveniently forget to mention stuff that matters," Josie said.

"No shit," Marge said, pushing the folder away.

"We'll deal with Buck later. What'd you find out about Goldman?" Josie asked.

Marge took a second folder out of the drawer and gave it to Josie. "Our hippie councilman was a Berkeley grad . . . big fucking surprise . . . practiced law up north for a few years, got involved with the scumbags at the ACLU and traveled south. He lives in Brentwood . . . ex-wife's a teacher. She left him for a dyke doctor. He's got one fucked-up son, aka Cory. Goldman hates the police department but not as much lately since the chief of police was handpicked by his buddy the mayor.

"Cory's been in and out of treatment centers for alcohol, drugs, and suicidal tendencies. Consensus is the kid's a genius who screws up by the numbers." Marge stopped and looked at Josie with a strange expression. She was clearly uncomfortable communicating the next bit of information. "The Goldman kid's got shitty social skills and according to all our sources he has one real friend . . . your son," she said, looking directly at Josie.

"What about Hillary? I thought they had some kind of relationship," Josie said, attempting to sound as if David's involvement with Cory wasn't something that worried her. But she knew the pain in her gut and sudden onset of anxiety were both related to the fact her son was associating with the drug-addicted, unstable young man, and she was certain that signs of her discomfort were plastered all over her face.

"Cory might've been friends with Hillary Dennis, but not really close from what I can find, more like a groupie or gofer," Marge mumbled.

"Look," Josie said, after a few seconds of awkward silence, and forcing herself to calm down and appear rational. "It's no secret David and Cory are acquaintances. As far as this investigation is concerned, my kid's fair game just like Goldman's kid. Do what you've got to do. If either one of you has trouble dealing with me, then take what you find to the D.A.'s office . . . I'm ordering you not to ignore evidence, don't hide anything regardless of the consequences. My son's a big boy. He made his choices." She wanted to be certain they didn't do anything stupid or out of loyalty to her, or jeopardize their jobs trying to shield her son. On the other hand, she fully intended to do whatever it took to protect David.

"You bet, boss lady," Marge said, staring at the table but obviously still uncomfortable.

Behan nodded. "Don't worry, I'd burn you and your kid to make a good case," he said, not smiling. It was her friend's typical dry sense of humor, but both he and Josie understood he wasn't really joking.

"You'd burn your grandmother to make a good case," Josie said, attempting to sound unconcerned.

Marge looked up, glancing from Josie to Behan, and when she realized they might be joking held up her middle finger. "You're both sick," she said. "This is so fucked-up. He's your kid. Make him stay away from that loser."

"He's twenty-two years old and reminds me at every opportunity I can't tell him what to do anymore."

"Then beat the crap out of him until he does what you want," Marge said with a look of disgust.

"David's six-foot-four. I'd need a ladder just to get his attention."

"Big and fucking stupid," Marge mumbled loud enough for Josie to hear. Josie winced, but wasn't certain she entirely disagreed with her friend's assessment.

"So, I'm thinking Bruno Faldi's looking more and more like my number one candidate for biggest asshole," Behan said, ignoring the two women. "Did he kill Hillary and Misty for Uncle Vince? And if he did, why would Milano want them dead?"

"That's a gigantic frigging leap into fantasyland," Marge said. "Bruno went from creep to killer in sixty seconds based on what?"

"He was Hillary's only bodyguard who conveniently got fired or quit a few days before she's killed. He hid his ties with Milano and was in the perfect place to be a lucrative source of young girls for Misty's escort and porn stable . . . yeah, actually I think the pervert's worth a second look."

Marge's left eyebrow arched and she slumped back away from the table.

"Why would a guy like Milano want to kill a seventeen-year-old girl?" Josie asked, and added, "And why shoot her in his attorney's house? That doesn't make any sense to me."

"Controlled environment . . . Lange's out of town with the perfect alibi. My guess is Hillary did something that pissed-off Milano," Behan said.

"Maybe he had to sit through one of her movies," Josie said. "That'd make me wanna kill somebody."

Behan had to smile. "Not a strong motive, boss, but I'll keep it in mind."

A uniformed lieutenant peeked cautiously around the glass partition that shielded Marge's desk from the front door of the vice office.

"Captain, you might wanna come downstairs," the lieutenant said, looking out of place in the casual vice surroundings. "Narcotics picked up some guy who claims his name is Little Joe, and he's demanding to talk to you."

THIRTEEN

E dgar Demarco, also known as Little Joe, was stashed in one
of the detectives' interview rooms when Josie finally met
him. He was a nervous little man in tight-fitting black slacks,
black boots and a polyester black shirt with a large gold cross
hanging from a hefty gold chain around his neck. Most of his
hair was stuffed under an orange and red knit cap. The few loose
braided strands she could see looked matted and badly in need of
shampoo. His right hand was behind him cuffed to his chair, but
the nails on his left hand were long and painted an ugly purple.
He crossed his legs like a woman, and with his free hand rubbed
the cross as if it were a lucky rabbit's foot as he sat staring at the
wall and jerking his head to music only he could hear.

"How can I help you?" Josie asked after introducing herself
and Behan. They sat across the table and waited for him to slowly
shift around and face them. He had an oddly curled lip that made
him look as if he were snarling. Her first impression was the guy
had the most perfect white teeth she'd ever seen. He couldn't have
been five feet tall, and she doubted he weighed even a hundred
pounds—a heroin-dealing munchkin, she thought and grinned
back at him.

"The question is how I kin assist you, Miss Corsini," Demarco
said with an affected lisp and lifted his chin, attempting an air of
importance.

"It's Captain Corsino, asshole," Behan said, calmly. "The question is what the fuck do you want?"

Demarco's little body seemed to get smaller.

"You're the ones been looking for me," he whined.

"Why would I be looking for you?" Josie asked. She and Behan worked well together. He pissed people off enough to make them want to talk to her just to spite him.

Demarco turned his shoulder away from Behan. "I'm the Little Joe," he said to Josie, emphasizing "the" as if it were a badge of honor.

"So?" she asked, shrugging. He was too smug. She was going to make him work for this.

Demarco laughed without smiling. "We gonna play games, lady. I know you been asking after me."

"And I know they just arrested you for selling heroin, and this is your third, goodbye-forever strike," Josie countered.

"No way, that ain't my shit. Can't make no case stick on me."

"Good luck in court," Josie said. She stood and walked slowly toward the door.

"Wait, I ain't saying we can't talk," Demarco said, wiggling his body to the edge of the chair and waving his free hand.

Josie sat again. "What've you got that's good enough to keep you out of jail for the next few decades?"

"I got plenty to tell, but I want that immunity shit and no jail time."

"So far you haven't said enough to get a cigarette and a cup of coffee," Behan said.

Demarco's eyes narrowed. "I gotta talk to you alone," he whispered to Josie.

"No," she said.

He lowered his head for a few seconds and stared at the floor. "Maybe I need a lawyer to protect my rights then," he mumbled without looking up.

"No," Josie said. "You talk to us now or there's no deal. You can have a lawyer when we get around to discussing the heroin."

Demarco sighed and scratched under his hat with one long purple nail. "Damn, you are one tough bi . . ."

"Watch it," Behan said interrupting.

"You wanna know about Hilly, right?"

"Everything," Josie said.

"Mouse brung her to me, vouches for the pretty lady, so I get her stuff for a while. That's all I know, and you can't never prove that."

"What kind of stuff?"

Demarco scratched his head again. "Mostly Mexican . . . black tar . . . maybe some brown. She likes tar . . . she's chipping is all."

"Did she buy it herself or have somebody else get it for her?"

"She come herself. I could see she be down already. I asked her didn't she worry about getting caught, her being famous and all. She says she got protection. Batman won't let nothing bad happen to her."

"Batman?" Behan asked.

"You know, Officer Fricke."

"Did you ever see Fricke with her?" Josie asked.

"No, but Hilly says it was Batman and that's the only Batman 'round here."

"What else did she tell you about Officer Fricke?"

"She fucked him . . . give him money so he looks the other way and nobody harasses her while she gets her taste."

"She told you that?" Behan asked, shaking his head. "Why would she tell a dirtbag like you anything?"

"Junkies talk . . . can't keep nothing to themselves. Hilly tells Mouse. Mouse tells me . . . I tell you."

"Did Mouse see them together?"

"Don't know, never asked."

"So you really don't know much of anything. You heard all this from Mouse," Behan said.

"It was me sold the shit to her. Ain't that worth something?"

"You and Cory Goldman partied with her. Tell me about that," Josie said, realizing at the same time Behan did that Little Joe was nothing more than a street dealer with secondhand information. If Fricke was involved with Hillary, the savvy policeman wouldn't be stupid enough to let this guy or Mouse see anything. Hillary might've confided in Mouse, but it was hearsay from a dead girl.

"Me an' Cory been doing clubs all the time. He tags along, digs my music . . . tries to get me to hook 'em up with Hilly. He's nothin' but a game for her . . . never means nothing 'cuz she prefers that rich, aged meat. She's got my man doing everything but wiping her ass before he figures out maybe Miss Hilly's been fucking with him." Demarco stopped, inspected his fingernails and added, "That white boy's one dumb motherfucker."

"You know Bruno Faldi?" Behan asked.

Josie saw it, the blink and quick look to the left before Demarco answered. She'd done enough interrogations to recognize the gesture that usually meant somebody was about to lie.

"No, can't say I do," he said.

Behan described Bruno, but Demarco still denied having met him.

"What if I told you he said he saw you and talked to you at Hillary's apartment?" Behan added.

Demarco seemed to be thinking about his answer. After several seconds he looked at Josie.

"I'd have to say I can't recollect ever meeting that particular gentleman," Demarco said, unconvincingly, and for the first time Josie noticed something new in his demeanor. The cocky dealer appeared to be frightened.

"You're a smart guy. Who do you think killed Hillary Dennis?" Josie asked.

Demarco didn't respond, but snorted as if he didn't think much of the question. Josie noticed his grip on the cross tighten as if he were struggling to come up with an answer. Finally, still staring at the ground he said, "I'd be thinking Officer Fricke my own self."

"Why's that?"

"Hilly, she tells Mouse about this little black book that's gonna finance her retirement. If that policeman's been doing what she says and she's been keeping notes, I'd say Miss Hilly's got him by his big white hairy balls."

They questioned Demarco for about an hour, and both Josie and Behan knew that except for selling heroin to Hillary Dennis he didn't have much firsthand information. He'd partied with Hillary, Cory and Mouse, but denied ever seeing Cory's father, knowing Bruno Faldi, or observing any interaction between Fricke and Hillary. He did slip one interesting tidbit of information into his ramblings. Demarco claimed it was common knowledge in Avanti's shortly before Hillary died that Milano would flee from his club whenever she and her entourage arrived.

It was nearly seven P.M. when they finished the interrogation and sent Demarco back to his cell with the empty promise of talking to the D.A. Josie and Behan returned to her office where they could close the door and not worry about curious officers or her eavesdropping adjutant.

"You searched her apartment. There wasn't a diary. So, what happened to it, if it ever existed?" she asked when they were alone.

"We searched Misty's apartment too; nothing there . . . no safety deposit boxes that we could find for either one of them."

"Killer's got it," Josie said.

"Maybe, but I think we should operate as if it's still out there somewhere. Did you see the look on Demarco's face when I asked about Bruno? Why would he deny knowing Bruno?"

"Bruno's connected to Milano. My guess is he's afraid to talk about Milano. You have to get home?" she asked.

"Eventually, why?"

"I need a drink. Nora's okay?" she asked, knowing it was an unnecessary question. She'd never known Red to turn down a drink, especially one she was paying for.

It was strange. She realized she was behaving like a detective again and all the old habits were kicking in. Work hard, drink hard and play hard. The first two were easy. The playing hard was on hold because her playmate was off fighting demons or some other stupid crap.

It was unheard of in the LAPD's modern era for an area captain to be involved hands-on in a homicide investigation. She knew that but it didn't matter. At the moment, Behan was the only subordinate except Marge she completely trusted. Everyone else in Hollywood had been tainted by the possibility he or she worked for Owens or Buck. Josie couldn't confide in her boss because of his adjutant, and even Bright was a problem because he was too willing to share information with Councilman Goldman. Her son further complicated the mess, and she knew the only guaranteed way of keeping him out of it was to put herself in the middle of the investigation. Her transformation back to a working detective wasn't something she desired, but for the time being it was unavoidable so she might as well enjoy it.

They hadn't been at the bar in Nora's more than ten minutes when Marge came in and sat beside Behan. She ordered a martini and Josie told her about the interview with Little Joe.

"Bullshit, that freaky midget asshole and Mouse cooked up this fucking fairy tale to get Fricke off their backs," Marge said, chewing on an olive.

"Probably right, but I can't ignore it. I'm gonna have to get him off the street," Josie said.

"Damn it, no, don't do that. It's what they want. When Fricke's gone they've got nobody messing with them."

"Settle down, girl," Behan said, looking at Marge. "It's better to get him out of the line of fire. Don't give them an opportunity to come up with worse allegations."

"I'll bet Fricke would rather take his chances on the street where he can still screw with those shitheads."

"You're probably right, but that's why they pay me the big bucks to stop guys like Donnie Fricke from committing career suicide," Josie said. She watched Marge gulp her drink and order another. Her friend wasn't happy, but Josie knew leaving Fricke on the street wasn't an option. With the new allegations, Josie also decided she'd take the personnel investigation away from her adjutant and give it to the day watch lieutenant. Marge should handle it, but she was uneasy with Marge's blind loyalty to Fricke. Josie considered him a friend, too, but if he was dirty, as far as she was concerned his police career would be over and he'd be facing criminal charges. She figured telling Marge all that could wait until morning when there wasn't alcohol involved.

The bar wasn't crowded. It was an off-payroll week and most of the detectives that frequented Nora's would be short on cash until next Wednesday when, like magic, the city deposited money in their bank accounts again. Josie took a sip of wine and glanced up just as Behan rubbed Marge's hand with the back of his wrist. It wasn't accidental. He kept it there for several seconds until he noticed Josie staring. Marge didn't look up, but didn't move her hand either.

"Jesus," Josie blurted out, not knowing if she was disgusted or angry.

"What's wrong with you?" Behan asked.

"You, that's what's wrong with me. What's wrong with you?"

He didn't respond for a moment and then said, "I gotta go." He left money on the bar, told Josie he'd see her in the morning, and left. She didn't attempt to keep him from paying. Suddenly, she wasn't feeling all that generous.

Marge didn't stay long enough for Josie to say anything. She was a few steps behind Behan, and it didn't take a genius to figure out they were leaving together. Although Josie hardly knew the current Mrs. Behan, she felt sorry for the woman. They hadn't been married a month and her redheaded screwup was already wandering. Big surprise, Josie thought, Red's fucking up again.

Before Josie could pay her tab, Peter Lange slid onto the barstool Behan had abandoned and ordered two glasses of Cabernet.

"Please don't make me drink alone," he pleaded with a warm smile.

Curiosity not thirst made Josie stuff her money back into the pocket of her jacket. She couldn't figure out why this guy kept popping up in her life like a poor relative. He wanted her attention. She wanted to know why.

"I have time for one drink," Josie said, resting an elbow on the bar and staring at him. "You spend a lot of time in this place."

He took a sip of wine and said, "Had a little business in the neighborhood. What about you?"

"What sort of business?"

"A client not happy with your accommodations."

"We arrested one of your clients . . . who?"

"Edgar Demarco, know him?"

It took a moment for Josie's brain to compute that he was talking about Little Joe the heroin dealer, because the wealthy entertainment lawyer and the street thug shouldn't be operating in the same legal circles.

"You do criminal law?" she asked.

"Only when a client's involved. Edgar's a talented musician."

"Who happens to sell heroin."

"That's a hobby. His real interest is music."

"Better book the rest of his gigs at San Quentin. The guy's a three-strike loser."

"We'll see," Lange said. "Sometimes things aren't what they appear to be."

"They caught him with a mouthful of balloons packed with heroin and a pocket full of twenty dollar bills. That pretty much seems like what it is."

Lange didn't respond, but didn't seem concerned either. He cocked his head and stared at her. Josie felt as if he were looking right through her clothes.

"How'd you ever get into this line of work? With your looks and brains you could've done anything you wanted."

"I wanted to be a cop," she said.

"Why? It's so . . . sordid."

Josie laughed and said, "And defending slimy drug dealers and guys like Vince Milano isn't."

He closed his eyes and put his hand over his heart as if he'd been wounded. "Touché," he said and added, "but it pays better."

They drank in silence for a few moments before Josie decided she'd try pushing a few buttons, see what the attorney was willing to share.

"How long have you worked for Milano?" she asked.

"A few years. How long have you been married?"

"Do you represent Bruno Faldi, too?"

"I know you and your husband aren't living together."

"Good for you."

"How about I take you to dinner tonight?"

"No."

"Are you angry with me?"

"I'm not angry; I'm married."

Lange sighed and said, "I know Bruno because of his uncle." He wasn't about to give up. "Aren't you curious how I know you're separated?"

"No," Josie lied. "But I am curious about your relationship with Eli Goldman."

"Hardly talk to the man outside city hall. Your husband's new partner and I play tennis at the same club. He told me about you and Jake."

"Small world," Josie said, trying to sound indifferent. Jake's new law partner had barely worked with him a few weeks and the jerk was already gossiping about his private life. "Why did you believe Goldman's son had something to do with Hillary Dennis's death?"

"I was told he'd threatened her."

"Who said that?"

"Don't remember. Maybe one of the policemen told me," Lange said, unconvincingly.

"At that time, nobody had the information except Behan, me and Hillary's mother. Behan didn't tell you so you talked to Mrs. Dennis." Actually, she knew one other person who'd been told—Chief Bright.

"Like I said, I don't remember."

A hint of testiness had emerged in Lange's voice. Apparently, he didn't like being interrogated while he was trying to be charming.

"What's your relationship with Goldman now?"

"What do you mean?" he asked.

"Remember, I saw you and Milano having dinner with him the other night."

"I told you outside the restaurant it was business. As I recall, we were working on the concept of public service posters for teenagers. Your deputy chief was there; ask him."

"But we both know that's bullshit, don't we," she said smiling sweetly. "What were you really talking about?"

He didn't respond, but looked at Josie as if he were trying to figure out how much she actually knew. This is one cold fish, she thought. She'd thrown out a line hoping to pull in some tidbit of information, but Lange wasn't biting. On the other hand his expression told her plenty . . . he was getting pissed-off and didn't like this game.

"If I were you, I'd be more concerned about what's going on in your own house and less about my business," Lange said in a congenial tone that didn't make his words less nasty. He waited a second or two for her clever comeback, but Josie didn't offer one. He was trying to get some emotional response from her, but she wouldn't give him that satisfaction. He finished his wine and paid the bill. "I'd still like to get together with you sometime," he said with a cold stare that made her think if it ever happened she'd bring a food tester and back-up gun. "Good night," he said holding out his hand. She ignored the gesture which prompted him to nod as if he forgave her rudeness. He patted her hand in a condescending manner and ambled away.

Josie caught the bartender grinning at her after she inspected the place Lange had touched, then wiped it on her jacket sleeve before finishing the wine.

FOURTEEN

The next morning, Josie was at her desk earlier than usual—another resurrected detective habit from her past when she'd needed to be in the office at daybreak to finish paperwork, line up witnesses, and get arrestees transported for arraignment. Today, she didn't have to do any of those things, but knew Behan wanted to go back to Buck's place as soon as he could get away and she was free. They were both eager to follow up on Bruno Faldi.

Not sleeping-in gave her an opportunity to catch up on the job she was actually getting paid to do. She spent over an hour sitting in her office going over routine matters, and gave her adjutant several pages of notes and directions until the young sergeant looked as if he'd reached his saturation point.

"You know it's strange," he said, packing up his laptop when they finished. "The bureau hasn't asked for anything the last couple of days. Even Sergeant Perry has stopped pestering me."

"Be grateful," she said, but wondered if the silence had anything to do with Eli Goldman's interview. Bright had shown an unusual interest in what the councilman had to say. Actually, he wasn't just curious; he seemed worried.

On his way out, Sergeant Jones reminded her that Lieutenant Ibarra wanted a meeting with her as soon as they finished. Josie wanted to talk with him too, and knew Ibarra probably wouldn't be all that eager if he knew what she was about to tell him.

Before anyone had an opportunity to summon him, Ibarra peeked into Josie's office.

"I saw your door open," he said. "Have you got a few minutes?"

He didn't wait for an invitation, but sat quietly at the table facing Josie until the adjutant left and pulled the door closed.

"We need to talk about your association with Howard Owens and Carlton Buck," she said as soon as they were alone. Might as well get to the point, she thought, and waste as little time as possible with this guy.

"Wish I'd known Howard Owens was retiring. I never would've agreed to leave you two lieutenants short."

"What are you talking about?" she asked.

"Chief Bright offered me the detective lieutenant job at Wilshire and I took it. It's closer to home and the captain at Wilshire and me were academy classmates. If I knew Howard retired, I would've turned it down."

Josie should've been angry because Bright hadn't consulted her about the change, but she was desperately trying to suppress a full-blown horse laugh. She'd been prepared to tell him he had to find another job. Instead she cleared her throat and managed to say, "Good for you," and suppressed the temptation to add, "don't let the door hit your incompetent ass on the way out."

"Thanks, but I can delay my transfer until you get another lieutenant if you need me . . . you know, with Howard Owens retiring and all," he said.

"Not necessary," Josie said, emphatically, and when he started to get up, she ordered, "Sit down. We're not done yet. Why didn't you tell me you were working off-duty for Owens and Buck."

"Actually, it's just Buck."

"You do protection details?" Josie asked, skeptically sizing up the scrawny man. If she were a client, she'd expect a lot more bulk for her money.

Ibarra swallowed a laugh and said, "No, he pays me to sit in a guard shack all night at the front gate of some actor's estate in Brentwood. I watch security cameras and open the gate when cars come and go."

"That's it? You never got paid to bodyguard celebrities?"

"Look at me," he said, pointing at his slender frame. "I'm not exactly the bodyguard type. I just sit in my shack and make fifty bucks an hour mostly to sleep."

Josie wrote down the address where Ibarra claimed he worked and the celebrity's name, another movie star she'd never heard of. Ibarra told Josie that unless she held up his paperwork he'd be on the next transfer to Wilshire. She assured him nothing would interfere with his departure.

"You knew Behan was looking at off-duty employment. Why didn't you tell him you worked for Buck?" she asked.

"I had a work permit on file. I guess I just figured he knew."

She didn't believe him, but there wasn't much she could do about it. Ibarra had kept that information to himself for a reason, but she figured the best way to find that reason might be through Buck.

"Ibarra," she called as he was leaving. He turned and stood by the door. "I meant to ask. Do you know Bruno Faldi?"

He hesitated, folded his arms and nervously shifted his weight before saying, "He was a sergeant who retired a few years ago, wasn't he? As I recall he retired early."

"You've never worked with him on or off-duty?"

"Not that I can remember," he said, shaking his head. "I'd have to say no."

She nodded. His nervous body language said he probably had. "Thanks, enjoy Wilshire and give my best to your new C.O.," she said, and waited until she was certain he was gone to do the YES! arm pump. She was tempted to call the captain at Wilshire who was probably gloating and thank him, but she worried he might still have time to cancel the transfer. She'd wait a few weeks. It would be more meaningful after Ibarra had worked there a while and Wilshire felt the full effect of his ineptitude.

Behan couldn't escape from the homicide table until almost eleven A.M., but before Josie could get out the back door, she got a call from Bright at the bureau. He wanted her to send Fricke's personnel complaint back to Internal Affairs.

"The chief of police's decided it's probably better if I.A. handles this particular investigation," Bright explained.

"Why's that?" Josie asked. She really wasn't concerned about who did Fricke's investigation, but knew the decision to give it back to I.A. smelled more like Bright's idea than the chief of police.

"The chief wants you to concentrate your resources on this Dennis investigation," he said.

"The allegations against Fricke are linked to her murder," Josie said, stating what she thought was obvious.

"He's being accused of some serious misconduct and it's more appropriate . . . the chief thinks it's better if an Internal Affairs sergeant handles it."

"Okay, anything else?" Josie asked. She decided deciphering Bright's convoluted reasoning was too distracting with this morning's schedule. "I'll have someone drop off the complaint after I relieve Fricke and Butler and send them home."

"Internal Affairs can do that, too," he said.

"I'll do it," Josie insisted.

She wasn't about to have anyone else order her officers out of the field. Her tone of voice must've warned Bright she wouldn't give in on that point without a fight because he didn't insist. Besides, he should've known that unpleasant task was always the commanding officer's responsibility.

Sometimes it was astounding how ignorant the man could be, Josie thought as she hung up the phone, but immediately vowed not to waste any more of her valuable time contemplating 'Not So's' shortcomings.

———

Fricke must've surmised why he'd been summoned to the captain's office several hours before the start of his shift. There was none of the usual joking and wisecracking between him and his partner. Butler closed the door and they sat quietly side by side on Josie's couch waiting for her to give them the bad news.

Josie had too much respect for the men not to tell them the truth. There was a personnel investigation with two informants alleging that Fricke had assisted Hillary Dennis in obtaining and using heroin and that he'd had an improper relationship with her. The charge against Butler was that he knew or should've known what Fricke was doing. Due to the seriousness of the charges, they would be assigned to their homes with full pay until the investigation was finished. Fricke didn't look worried, or even despondent, until she told them the investigation would be handled by Internal Affairs.

"You know how I got such a high opinion of you, ma'am, but those I.A. guys, they don't care nothing about the truth. They just want a copper's scalp to make themselves look good and get promoted."

"You both got reps?" Josie asked.

Fricke shrugged. "I guess," he said.

"What do you mean?" she asked. "Either you do or you don't."

"Protective League gave us this fat sergeant that talks a lot, but don't seem to be doing much," Fricke said. "I wanted a lawyer, but I guess they don't think I'm worth it."

Frank Butler didn't say anything. He sat next to his partner staring at his tightly clasped hands resting on his knees. His was the lesser charge, but his association with Fricke could negatively impact his career for years. They were friends but Josie had to believe Butler harbored some resentment for being in the middle of Fricke's predicament.

"What do you think, Frank?" she asked. Josie was worried about the quiet man. It wasn't good to keep anger and frustration bottled up. Sometimes, it was healthier to rant like Fricke.

"What I think is we're fucked," he said, softly, still focused on his hands.

"If you didn't do anything, you'll be alright," she said.

Now he glanced up at her. The guy was a retired marine and in his young life he'd faced tougher things than police department discipline, but they both knew what she'd just said was naïve and she really didn't believe a word of it.

"Can't Lieutenant Bailey do anything, ma'am?" Fricke asked. "She's our supervisor."

"I.A. took the complaint," Josie lied. She didn't see any point in bringing Bright into this, but was getting tired of spending so much time and effort dodging the fallout from his asinine decisions.

"Hillary Dennis was killed in Hollywood. Our complaint's tied to Hillary. Both informants are probably in Hollywood. We work Hollywood. Doesn't it seem strange to you I.A. took it outside this division?" Frank Butler asked. He sat back and waited.

"Yes," Josie answered truthfully. Butler was the kind of guy who could smell fear and bullshit better than most. Since she'd always tried to avoid both, Josie agreed with him. Besides, he was right. Everything about the Dennis case was bizarre including this personnel complaint. Butler was a smart guy so she asked him again, "What's your take on all this?"

"Somebody wanted a scapegoat and picked us. While everybody's looking at Donnie and me, the killer and the dope dealer get a pass. We get hammered—case closed."

Josie studied him as he talked. He was angry, but not the way Fricke would be. The veins in his neck were bulging slightly, but he spoke calmly, rationally, never raised his voice. His dark eyes locked on hers, daring her to be deceitful or dismissive. The man had been honored for his service in Afghanistan and had first-hand knowledge of death and dying in battle. If Fricke had done anything disreputable or illegal, Josie's instincts told her Frank Butler would not knowingly be a part of it.

She took a business card out of her desk drawer and gave it to Butler.

"Call and tell him I said he should represent both of you. He's the best lawyer I know," she said.

"Jake Corsino, he related to you?" Fricke asked, snatching the card from Butler.

"My husband," Josie said. "He used to be a supervisor in the district attorney's office, but he's in private practice now. Tell him . . ." she hesitated and then said, "Just tell him your story and give him your rep's name. He knows when something stinks." She smiled and added, "Tell him I promised he'd represent you pro bono. He doesn't need the money."

"Yes, ma'am," Fricke said, jumping up and shaking her hand.

"Thank you, Captain," Butler said. He still wasn't smiling, but at least he'd blinked.

"Get out of here, go home, and stay out of trouble until we can figure out what's really going on," she said. Josie knew Jake would represent them. He couldn't help himself. They were the underdogs. Despite all the years they lived together and his tolerance of her conservative ravings, at heart her husband was still an idealistic bleeding-heart liberal. He encouraged their son because David was everything Jake had wanted to be but couldn't because his real talent was practicing law not the piano. Although she hated to admit it, he probably did fit better in his new politically-correct law firm than he ever had as a prosecutor.

An hour later, Josie was in the passenger seat of Behan's car en route to Carlton Buck's office in West L.A. She briefly told Behan about her conversation with Ibarra, but really didn't want to talk about the meeting with Fricke and Butler, and got quiet and moody when she thought about it.

"What's the matter with you?" he asked, after twenty minutes of uncharacteristic silence on her part.

"Nothing," she mumbled.

"Right . . . what did 'Not So' do this time?"

"It's not just Bright. It's all of it," she said, not liking the whiny sound in her voice. Josie hated complainers. Her philosophy was if you didn't like something fix it or shut up, but her frustration level was higher than usual.

"All of what?"

"This Dennis thing . . . all the crap floating around the edges . . . doesn't it bother you?"

"Define floating crap," Behan said in his annoying analytical way.

"The Goldmans, Bruno Faldi, Owens, Buck . . . my own kid, for Christ sake. Mostly, it's just so damn convenient that two informants who know each other happen to identify Fricke as the fall guy. Worst part is nobody's really got a decent motive to kill Hillary."

"Fricke does."

"How do you figure that?" she shot back.

"The little black book."

Josie snorted. "Another bullshit figment of Little Joe's imagination."

"What if it's not? What if Fricke did what Little Joe said he did, and Hillary blackmailed him with her journal . . . times and places she fucked him or bought heroin with his help."

"I just don't see how Fricke could do it without Butler knowing or at least suspecting something. They're practically joined at the hip, and I can't believe Butler would allow any of it to happen. It's the Butler piece that doesn't fit," Josie insisted.

"Okay, maybe I agree with you there. They're always together and Butler's the original Captain America."

"So who's being protected while we're distracted by all those fingers pointing at Fricke?"

"Eli Goldman?" Behan asked.

"I can't see him hanging around with street scum like Little Joe."

"If Goldman dated Hillary, he might've had contact with Little Joe and Mouse, and paid them to lie about Fricke to keep the heat off himself."

Josie slumped back against the headrest and closed her eyes. It wasn't farfetched or the first time in Los Angeles that a city councilman had been involved with a young woman and things went terribly wrong; and Lange was the perfect mouthpiece to shield Goldman in legal camouflage . . . for a price, that is. The payoff for Little Joe and Mouse didn't have to be more than a few hits of their favorite drug or a couple hundred dollars.

While Behan was talking, Josie was half-listening, contemplating the tattooed image of Goldman's son that kept popping into her head. Cory Goldman, the councilman's weird progeny, was the most vulnerable link in this chain of unsavory characters. She wondered how much he actually knew. His connection to Mouse certainly put him in a position to know more than he was telling them. If the father-son relationship was bad enough, Cory might be persuaded to reveal some dirty little family secrets. The only way to find out was to drag him back into the station and have Behan bully him. She had no intention of telling Bright, and she was certain he'd come unglued when he found out; but on the positive side, Councilwoman Fletcher would love anything that embarrassed Goldman.

"What're you planning?" Behan asked.

"What do you mean?"

"Don't ever play poker, Corsino. Your face is a neon sign. The right side of your mouth goes up a little when you're about to do something sneaky."

Josie instinctively touched her lip. "I want one of your teams to bring Cory Goldman to the station."

"RHD's already questioned him," Behan said as if he were talking to a child.

"I don't wanna question him. I want you to scare him. He's an insecure mess. Terrorize him and make him tell you what he knows about his father."

"He's got a lawyer."

"So what? Forget the lawyer. We're not gonna use his statements anyway, so who cares if they're admissible. I just wanna get him nervous enough to tell the truth about his father and Hillary," Josie said.

"Great, you get the truth and I get Goldman's ACLU buddies screaming about police fascism and marching around my desk with pickets and television cameras."

"I'll take the heat."

"I know you will," he said in the way he used to when they were dope cops together and he was in charge. "All of us know you'll try to protect us, but at some point if a wall gets pounded on long enough it falls down and you won't be there for us."

"So what are you saying . . . back down?"

He groaned. "All I'm saying is we're grown-ups; let us take some of the heat so Bright doesn't destroy you and I end up working for some weenie bean counter."

"Fine, I'll tell everybody it was your idea," she said, grinning.

"Yeah, and that has about as much chance of happening as my silver wedding anniversary."

"As long as you bring it up, what the hell is going on with you and Marge?"

"Nothing," he said and dropped an icy wall of silence between them.

They arrived at Carlton Buck's office before Josie could figure out another way to approach the touchy subject. Marge was old enough to know what she was doing, but Josie had years of corroboration telling her that in the arena of stable adult emotions Red Behan was clueless.

This afternoon, the P.I.'s building was bustling with activity. It was a far different place from the uninhabited spacious office they had visited several days ago. The underground parking was nearly full, and a pretty blond receptionist greeted them inside the first set of glass doors. Behan was mesmerized by the woman's big blue eyes—and he sounded more like Dustin Hoffman's Rainman than a big city detective—so Josie interrupted and explained why they were there. The blond escorted them back to Buck's private office passing through a wave of activity—every desk occupied, phones ringing and computers lit up. A few men and women in sharp tan and green private security uniforms with cloth badges sewn above their shirt pockets wandered among the desks or drank coffee in small groups at the back of the room. It had the appearance of a very successful security business.

"Disengage," Josie whispered, as they entered Buck's outer office and Behan's stare locked onto the departing full-figured blond.

"Just a connoisseur of fine art," he whispered back.

Buck greeted them as warmly as he had on their first visit, again offering food and drink. This time Josie and Behan declined. Behan pulled out a leather chair from the conference table for Buck, and then he and Josie sat on either side of him. Buck wasn't wearing his suit jacket and had loosened his tie, but he still had the holstered semi-auto on his belt. His breathing was labored and he apologized for his appearance, explaining he'd been boxing up some old files. Josie noticed his hands were clean, and he wore a hefty gold nugget ring. His nails were manicured with a clear polish, and a Rolex watch was visible from under his starched shirtsleeve cuff when he adjusted the large-carat diamond pin stuck into his silk tie. There didn't appear to be any financial slump for this security business, Josie thought, or the former cop had another lucrative source of income.

"Why'd you lie about Bruno Faldi?" Behan asked, before Buck could settle in and get comfortable.

Buck rested his hands on his substantial beer belly and for a moment looked like a mortified, gun-toting Buddha.

"What did I lie about?" he whined, leaning toward Behan. "I told you what I knew."

"Owens said you fired Bruno. You told us he quit," Josie said.

"Don't get me wrong. I like Howard Owens, we were even partners once; but the guy's a lazy moron. He never knows what he's talking about." Buck wiggled to the edge of the chair. "Even if I did fire Bruno Faldi, why would I confide that information to somebody like Howard? Howard's a shill. He finds me cops I need for jobs." Buck waved dismissively toward Josie and slid back. "Now he's retired, he's no good to me anymore."

"Did you fire Bruno?" Josie asked.

"No, I told you he quit."

"You also told us you didn't know anything about him," Behan said.

"Yeah, that's right . . . nothing except what I already said."

"Why is it then I've got this recommendation signed by you and dated more than twenty years ago telling the department recruiter that Bruno Faldi was a great guy who'd make a dynamite cop?" Behan asked in his calm voice while handing Buck a copy of Bruno Faldi's application to the police department.

The furrows deepened in Buck's brow and his pupils mimicked combatants in a ping pong game as his gaze darted from Behan to Josie and back several times. He shook his head and it seemed as if he wanted to say something but the words wouldn't come.

Finally, he managed to blurt out, "I swear I didn't really know him. I mean I knew his family. He seemed like a good kid." Buck tugged at his shirt collar, loosened his tie a little more. "I guess

I didn't remember I did that," he said, sheepishly, staring at his signature.

"Did you fire him?"

"You don't fire Vince Milano's nephew." Buck spit the words back at her, then slumped in his chair deflated. "He quit . . . don't know why . . . just quit," he said, softly.

"You know the Milano family?" Josie asked.

"I know the Faldi family. His mom was my wife's bookkeeper. I found out later about Milano."

Josie could see Buck didn't want to talk about Bruno, but he'd been caught in a lie and cops aren't good liars. It was a strange phenomenon; guilt made them want to confess everything they've ever done wrong. She had a feeling Buck was relieved. It was as if he'd never wanted to be a party to any of it in the first place and telling them was sort of liberating.

"When did you find out about Milano's connection?" Behan asked.

"Owens told me the day he wanted me to fire Bruno. What a moron! Like I'm gonna fire Vince Milano's nephew."

"What did you do?"

"Whatever Bruno wanted me to do."

"And he wanted the Hillary Dennis job."

"Yeah, and he got it."

"Did he say why he wanted that particular job?" Josie asked.

"Nope and I didn't ask."

"Why'd he quit?" Behan asked.

Buck got up and went to the liquor cabinet behind his massive desk. He selected a bottle of whiskey and held it up. "Want some?" he asked, and both Josie and Behan shook their heads. He returned with one glass nearly three-quarters full.

"I had almost thirty years with the department working some pretty tough divisions, but this Bruno Faldi character scares the crap outta me," Buck said, taking a big swallow, nearly emptying the glass. He coughed a few times and then said, "Big bald unpredictable nut job is what he is. Who knows why he quit. He sure ain't telling me."

Josie figured Buck believed what he was saying. Even a size-able dose of whiskey couldn't keep his hands steady.

"Explain," she said, wanting more than a stupid description. "The guy teaches teenage girls for a living. He can't be all that terrifying."

"Dead eyes . . . fakes like he feels stuff. I'll give him credit, he's a good actor—makes you believe him. When he was on the job, I seen him hurt people if he thought they were in his way or he wanted to scare them. He made that Dennis girl trust him and depend on him, but I know he didn't give a fuck about her."

"How do you know that?"

"He told me. The psycho was playing with her."

"For what purpose?" Josie asked.

"He's not gonna tell me that, but one day he doesn't show up for work. Dennis girl calls me wanting to know where's her bodyguard. He won't answer my calls, doesn't even pick up his last paycheck. She's hysterical because she doesn't trust anybody else. Now that I think about it, maybe that's what he wanted. Anyhow, a couple a days later she's dead and Bruno's out of my life, forever I hope."

"Why didn't you tell us all that in the first place?" Josie asked.

"I didn't know what Bruno told you. I'm not gonna be the guy that calls Milano's nephew a liar, and then have him or his uncle's friends come after me or my business."

"You ever meet Milano?" Behan asked.

"Hell no, and I don't want to neither," Buck said, and seemed to be struggling with a thought before blurting out, "I was a good cop. If I knew what Bruno was like or that he was tied to a guy like Milano, I would've never done this." He shook the copy of the application in front of Josie and whispered, "If he hurt that girl, I'm sorry, but it wasn't my fault."

"I'm sure that'll make Hillary's mother feel much better," Behan said, sarcastically. He got up and snatched the application from Buck's hand. Buck didn't speak as they left his office. Behan was so disgusted he didn't even glance at the receptionist on the way out.

When they reached the parking garage, Josie spotted Buck's Porsche and remembered the Lexus. She asked Behan if he'd run the license plate on the silver Lexus. He had, but the number didn't come back on file, which usually meant it belonged to a cop or politician, or some other VIP who managed to keep the information out of the public database.

On the drive back to Hollywood, they agreed that Buck might've told the truth this time. Now they needed to find out why Bruno wanted to get close to Hillary and the real reason he quit just before she was killed.

"Maybe to make her think she was safe and then leave her vulnerable long enough for someone to kill her," Josie said, throwing out a possible scenario.

"If Milano wanted her dead, I'm betting he'd just kill her. So, why bother with the whole bodyguard charade?" Behan asked. "You notice there's a couple of names that keep coming up in this investigation?"

"There are a lot of names that keep coming up. Who do you mean?"

"Eli Goldman and Milano."

"And it's Milano's sleazy attorney who just happens to represent the dope dealer who's accusing Fricke."

"I'm still not convinced Fricke is completely clean," Behan said and quickly added, "You want me to pick up Cory Goldman this afternoon or wait until tomorrow to make him wet his pants?"

"Tomorrow. . . . Let's talk to Milano," she said.

"Any particular reason?" he asked.

"I can't see Bruno doing anything unless Milano gives his blessing. If we ask the right questions, maybe we'll learn something."

They got to Avanti's an hour before it opened. Behan parked near the front door where half a dozen young men in red vests leaning against a ramp railing eyed them suspiciously but didn't approach. They were parking valets, illegals who probably hadn't been in the country more than a few weeks and were living off their tips. They recognized the police car and knew enough to keep their distance. By the time Josie started up the ramp, they'd gone.

Inside the club, the lights were on but the warehouse had a drab shabby look. She knew in a few hours darkness and the glittery disco ball would transform this dreary reality into a magical place. It was all phony, but kids came here and pretended for a while it wasn't.

An elderly black security guard drinking a beer at the bar was the only one they could find inside. His uniform was wrinkled and spotted with food stains and he didn't seem interested in who they were or what they wanted. He acted pleased to have something to do and escorted them to Milano's private office.

It wasn't what Josie had expected. The room was no bigger than a large walk-in closet. Old posters of long forgotten second-rate entertainers were pasted everywhere, overlapping like tacky wallpaper. Taking up most of the space was an oak roll-top desk that had seen better days.

When the guard opened the door, Milano was sitting with his back to them. He turned quickly and at first looked surprised, then worried.

"Captain Corsino, what's wrong?" he asked, standing to greet her.

She introduced Behan and said, "Nothing, Mr. Milano, we wanted to talk with you if you have time."

"Vince," he said, clearing off two chairs for them. "I've always got time for you."

Josie explained that Behan was handling the Dennis homicide and had a few questions for him. Milano didn't seemed concerned and was more interested in getting them something to drink and eat until Behan finally convinced him to sit down so they could get started.

"How well did you know Hillary Dennis?" Behan asked when Milano settled in behind his desk again.

"Not very well, she came here with friends . . . all of them *pazzesco* . . . they acted crazy," he said, touching his forehead with both hands. "When she came, I went home. I didn't like her." He shrugged and added apologetically, "But she spent a lot of money, brought in paying customers, so what am I supposed to do."

"Did you know any of those friends?"

"Just that Goldman kid."

"Did you see or hear any of them threaten her or harm her in any way?" Josie asked.

Milano snickered. "How would I know? They don't have respect for nothing or nobody . . . always high, always mother-fucking everything. They hate the world, think they're smarter than everybody."

"Did Hillary seem scared or afraid of any of them?" she asked.

"That little tramp wasn't afraid of nothing."

Josie looked at Behan and he asked the question they were both thinking. "Then why was she paying your nephew to protect her?"

He slowly shook his head and said, "Don't know, maybe she finally pissed off the wrong guy."

Behan started to say something when the door swung open and Bruno Faldi entered as if on cue. He stopped in the middle of the room and at first seemed confused. His expression said he was trying to figure out why these particular people were here with his uncle.

"*Figlio*," Milano said, obviously pleased to see him. Bruno bent over and hugged his uncle, kissed him on the cheek.

Josie knew just enough Italian to know Milano had called him son. She figured the possibility he'd reveal anything that might implicate Bruno was diminishing quickly.

Milano didn't bother to introduce them, which also told her the two men had previously discussed Bruno's interview with her and Behan. She thought Bruno's demeanor seemed different tonight. He wasn't trying to be pleasant. He said something in Italian to Milano which she couldn't understand but it sounded angry. Milano whispered something back, attempting to calm him.

"Why are you harassing my uncle?" Bruno demanded, glaring at Josie. She figured the girls' academy must've dumped him because his Mr. Chips image was definitely a thing of the past.

His massive frame looked menacing in a black t-shirt and leather jacket. He was wearing worn Levi's and biker boots that made him look taller, and he didn't need the extra height. They were finally getting a glimpse of the real Bruno Faldi.

"Excuse my nephew," Milano said looking at Bruno and adding in a tone that left no doubt he was in charge and unhappy, "These are my guests."

Behan turned to Bruno and asked calmly, "What's your problem?"

"Nothing, I don't want you hassling Uncle Vince. How can he do business with you guys busting in here all the time?"

"You working at Avanti's full time now?" Josie asked.

"I'm helping out a while. What's it to you?"

"They want to know why you worked for that slut movie star," Milano said.

"You already asked me that and I told you. Why are you bothering him?" Bruno was becoming very agitated.

"You said she hired you because she was scared. Your uncle says Hillary wasn't afraid of anything," Josie said.

"That's what she told me."

"And there's our dilemma because we don't know what she told you, but we're pretty sure you lied to us about it," Josie said as calmly as she could with the big man pacing like a hungry lion in front of her.

"I don't know what the fuck you're talking about," he said and stopped near his uncle. "If you don't stop harassing us our lawyer's gonna make you stop. I got a badge and gun too. I'm not some schmuck off the street you can push around."

"Enough," Milano said, standing and touching Bruno's flushed face. "Is there anything else, Captain? I gotta open the club."

"No, we're done. Thank you for your time," she said, and turned to Bruno on their way out. "Too bad that teaching thing didn't work out."

He didn't respond but she could see he was seething and might've done something really stupid if his uncle hadn't been there.

"You like to live dangerously," Behan said, when they were back in the car headed toward the station.

"The guy's a time bomb. I felt it that day at the school, but I still don't think he killed Hillary," she said.

"Why not?" Behan asked. "Other than the fact nobody saw him at the house that night."

"I got the feeling he actually liked her. Milano didn't, but you're right the old man wouldn't have killed her that way."

"So we don't know anything more than we did before we talked to him."

"We know Bruno's a loose cannon with a gun and badge. Wanna stop at Nora's for a bite?"

"Can't, I forgot I promised Vicky I'd be home for dinner tonight. It's some kind of anniversary."

Smart woman, Josie thought. With Behan's track record, it was best to celebrate the days and weeks or Vicky might never get a "first" anything anniversary.

"She's a nice lady, Red." Josie wanted to say more but the right words wouldn't come.

It didn't matter. He ignored her comment and parked near the back door of the station. They walked inside together, but he peeled off into the detectives' squad room without another word. She knew she was wasting her breath. The big redhead did whatever he pleased and then fell apart when the inevitable consequences hit him like a Malibu landslide.

She wasn't going to fret about it. She was already balancing too many fragile male egos in her universe—one half-grown son, an emotional wreck of a husband, and a deputy chief who confused leadership with schoolyard bullying.

FIFTEEN

Hollywood was two different worlds at night. The west end showcased the business improvement district with private security, trendy restaurants and historic theaters with movie star footprints in cement, but on the east side of the division, the scenery changed dramatically. When the sun went down, this area around Western Avenue and beyond morphed into something mysterious and dangerous with its Mexican gangs and rampant drug dealing.

Josie occasionally drove through that part of her division to get to the Hollywood Freeway, instead of taking the closer on-ramp a few blocks north of the station. She'd found a way to gauge her officers' enforcement efforts by the amount of blatant illegal activity she could identify on any major street.

It was late and she was drained after the bout with Bruno, but for some inexplicable reason she was driving out of her way, doing something she could've easily done any other night and dragging out the process of getting home. Although she kept the police radio and computer turned on to monitor hot calls and activity in her division, she was finally alone in her steel Ford bubble and driving was a way of clearing her mind. For a few minutes, her world was static. No one could step in, steal precious seconds, ask for favors or advice or tell her what to do. Sometimes she needed this unplanned excursion down her city streets because it was therapeutic.

Tonight, she'd decided to take Fountain Avenue across to the freeway and was only a couple of blocks from the on-ramp when she passed a street sign for Sierra Way. The next light was red and as the car idled in light traffic, Josie tried to remember where and why she'd recently heard that particular street name. She had a nagging feeling it was connected to something important, and turned right and drove around the block pulling to the curb at the corner of Sierra Way. Information overload was always a problem for her. In her position, problems had to be handled quickly and sometimes superficially to keep the police machinery running twenty-four hours a day. Eventually, names, dates, times, and places started to run into and over one another.

But Josie was certain there was something significant about that street. She closed her eyes, and the memory light inevitably flickered on. Mrs. Dennis—Hillary's mother—lived on Sierra Way. Josie remembered the house numbers six-six-five, because at the time she read it she thought if the five had been a six it would've been the sign of the devil and an odd address for the God-fearing woman.

She drove a couple of blocks down Sierra and found the small two-story house with a floodlight above the front screen door. The porch was cluttered with boxes and an assortment of junk stacked up to the top of the railing. Heavy plastic tarps were draped over some of the debris. The house was dark inside except for a low light in what appeared to be the living room. A second floodlight was on the side of the house, and from across the street, Josie could make out more junk piled against the house. The garage door was open and packed with furniture. A freezer had been left between the house and the driveway.

Josie made a U-turn and parked in front of the house. It was a little after eight, but she figured as long as she was in the neighborhood, why not visit Mrs. Dennis and see how the woman was getting along—community policing, command-officer style. The truth was Josie hadn't really given much thought to Hillary's mother, but did want to talk to her again. She hoped Mrs. Dennis could give her a better picture of who the young woman really was, what she was up to. Mothers, even bad ones, knew surprising things about their kids.

The front porch was dirtier than it appeared from the street. Cobwebs clung to the security screen and hung from every corner. A chilly breeze wafted across the yard spreading the aroma of sautéed onions mixed with the stench of open garbage containers that seemed to be coming from next door. Josie peeked in the front window before ringing the doorbell. A torn shade was pulled down, but she could see Mrs. Dennis sitting near a big screen television. The woman turned and stared at the door for several seconds before getting up and coming to the window. Josie held her badge close to the glass and identified herself, speaking as loud as she could without alarming the neighbors.

Mrs. Dennis opened the door and glared at Josie through the security screen.

"Whaddaya want?" she shouted, with her hand shading her eyes as if she were blinded by bright sunlight.

"Mrs. Dennis, it's Captain Corsino."

"I know who you are. Whaddaya want?"

"I'd like to come inside and talk with you for a minute, if it's okay."

"You know what time it is? Come back at a decent hour."

"Sorry, I've had a very busy day and this is the first opportunity I . . ."

"You arrest that boy?"

"That's what I'd like to talk to you about," Josie said and tried to open the screen. It was locked.

"What's the good a talking to me?" she said.

Josie heard the latch on the screen click, and Mrs. Dennis held it open. She allowed Josie to come inside and then locked the screen and front door again. The living room was warm and clean. A three-foot-high plaster statue of the Virgin Mary sat on a cabinet in the corner with votive candles flickering in little glass holders around the base of the figure. The homemade shrine was church quality and didn't seem out of place in this particular woman's home.

The interior of the house was spotless. A sweet fruity odor saturated the air and Josie could feel her empty stomach rumbling.

Whatever was cooking wiped out the porch stench and triggered the hunger switch in her brain, and for just a moment that warm oven smell triggered memories of her mother's kitchen. Josie's love of cooking had come from the rich aromas of spicy pasta dishes and hearty stews that had always permeated her childhood home. Although the family never had much money, her mother made every meal large and special.

Mrs. Dennis turned off the television and offered Josie the chair where she'd been sitting.

"Before we talk, I just made some peach cobbler and a fresh pot a coffee. Make yourself comfortable while I get us some." She did a quick genuflect in front of the statue, but came back and said, "Better come with me in the kitchen. Not as fancy but a lot more sociable for cobbler and coffee."

Josie followed her down a dark musty hallway past the small dining room into the large country-style kitchen with a breakfast table. Mrs. Dennis was wearing a full apron over what looked like a flannel nightgown. Her thinning hair was pinned up in little ringlets around her head, and Josie could see traces of white facial cream close to her hairline. She had prepared herself for bed, but seemed resigned to entertaining unexpected company.

The table was big enough for a large family, but only four chairs were placed around it.

"Are any of your other children still at home?" Josie asked, watching her take a sizeable pan from the cooling rack and scoop out two big chunks of warm peaches covered with a thick crust. Mrs. Dennis removed a container from the freezer and put vanilla ice cream on top of the cobbler before setting it in front of Josie.

"Got their own lives," she said, placing a mug of coffee beside the mound of saturated fat. By the time Mrs. Dennis sat down to eat, Josie had nearly finished her cobbler and was scraping the last glob of ice cream off the plate.

"That was wonderful," Josie said, knowing if she were at home alone she'd be using her finger to get that last drop of peach nectar. She noticed Mrs. Dennis staring at her and realized she must've attacked the cobbler like a starving vulture. "Guess I was hungry," she said sheepishly, and put her fork down.

"Don't you ever eat? You look like skin and bones," Mrs. Dennis said, getting up and taking Josie's dish to fill it again with a bigger portion and more ice cream. Before sitting, she topped off both coffee mugs.

"Thank you," Josie said. "Guess I forgot to eat today."

"My little girl used to eat like you, never gained a pound. She coulda been a beautiful woman like you," Mrs. Dennis said, softly. She put her fork down. Her untouched cobbler sat in a pool of melting ice cream. "I pray for her every day . . . worried, you know, about her immortal soul." She made the sign of the cross.

Josie stopped eating and sat back. "Why are you worried about your daughter, Mrs. Dennis? She didn't do anything wrong. Did she?"

"Never got to repent for her sins."

"She was so young. What could she possibly have to repent that might jeopardize her soul?" Josie was gently prodding, trying to get her to start talking, to tell unguarded truths.

Mrs. Dennis tilted her head back and snorted. "My Hilly was hell-bent on damnation."

Hilly, Josie thought. The only other people she'd heard call Hillary by that name were Little Joe and Mouse. "What do you mean?" she asked.

"Got with that boy," she said, pushing the cobbler plate farther away. "He's the devil, got her whoring, taking drugs."

"Did you know any of her friends? Did she ever bring them here?"

"They weren't friends . . . led her away from God . . . got her murdered."

"What do you mean?" Josie asked, frustrated by the old woman's babbling riddles.

"She brung them here once when they got nowhere else to go. Spent every penny she'd earned. Lost her place when there weren't no more jobs."

"But she had her own apartment and lots of money when she died."

"Got money somehow, moved outta here with all her leeches."

"Who stayed here with her?"

"That boy and some foulmouthed little bleached whore . . ."

"Mouse?"

"Never knew her name . . . put ugly pictures all over her body."

"Anybody else?" Josie had to ask, but felt a cobbler earthquake rumbling in her stomach. Once again, she was struggling to keep thoughts of David out of her head, but just the possibility his name could come up ruined a great dessert.

"Negro boy dresses like a woman . . . that's all of them I ever seen."

Josie knew that had to be Little Joe and felt relief that she'd dodged embarrassment again.

"Older man ever come here to see your daughter?" she asked.

"Never saw nobody but that devil boy and the other two."

"Did they leave anything here?" Josie asked.

"Just those pictures I gave to you."

"Nothing else?"

"I looked real good after that little one come back to get some clothes she says she forgot, but I never found nothing of hers."

"Mouse came back by herself?"

"Hilly'd been dead two, maybe three days, when that woman knocks on my door, says she needs to come in and get some things she mighta forgot."

"Did you see what she took?"

"Grieving so bad didn't really notice nothing. Why, you think that little tramp whore stole from me?"

"Try to remember. Did you see her carrying anything when she left?"

"I can't say, truthfully, wasn't paying attention."

Mrs. Dennis allowed Josie to look in the three bedrooms where Hillary and her friends slept. Like the rest of the house, these rooms were tidy and clean. Josie thought Hillary's room looked as if it had been decorated by a spoiled teenage girl with terrible taste and too much money. It was a large space with a big screen television, Blu-ray player, stereo, and clashing colors of purple and green with pink lacy curtains over a big front window; there were too many stuffed animals and framed posters of all her forgettable films. There wasn't a single book in sight, but two small stacks of magazines were sitting on her desk. She'd painted the walls a dark purple and found an expensive ugly comforter to match. It struck Josie for the first time that this young woman might've in many ways remained a child until her brutal death.

When Mrs. Dennis excused herself to clean up the kitchen, Josie thoroughly searched the desk drawers, dresser and closet, under the bed and mattress . . . no diary. She looked behind furniture too, and did the same in the other two bedrooms before Mrs. Dennis called from downstairs to ask if she wanted more coffee. It was nearly ten P.M. and Josie was about ready to leave, when one more question occurred to her before she reached the bottom of the stairs.

"Did you ever talk to a lawyer named Peter Lange?" Josie asked, and then described the handsome attorney. They were standing in the living room again. Josie could see Mrs. Dennis was fighting to stay awake and looked tired, but didn't seem eager to be alone again.

"He's been here."

"What did he want?"

"Says he's the one owned that house where my little girl got killed and how sorry he was for my loss. We just talked, that's all."

"He didn't want anything or give you anything."

"That's all," she said, nervously wrapping the strap of her apron around her thumb. She wouldn't look directly at Josie.

"Are you certain he didn't take anything?" Josie said.

"I said he didn't," she snapped and glared at Josie.

"Okay, then he gave you something."

"Nothing, not a dime . . . if he did it's my business," Mrs. Dennis said weakly, studying her hands.

It always came down to money, Josie thought. Enough cash was as comforting as any words of condolence. "How much?" she asked.

"He told me not to say nothing or the deal's no good."

"Was it some kind of settlement?"

"I promised not to sue him which I wouldn't a done anyhow. I ain't mad at him, not his fault. I just want justice for my little girl."

"He didn't ask for anything else?"

"No, just not to bother him . . . he did say Hilly mighta had some book that belonged to one of his clients, but we looked same way you did and couldn't find nothing."

"Which client?"

"Don't remember or maybe he never said, but like I told him, I ain't got nothing of his and I ain't gonna sue nobody. I just want the monster that killed my little girl to be dead so he can burn alongside of her in hell. Then I can get some peace."

———

JOSIE HEARD the door and screen lock behind her as she stepped onto the cluttered porch and felt the night air cut through her light jacket. She should've been tired but felt invigorated. She'd spent three hours with a crazy old woman and ate like a pig, but she might've discovered what happened to Hillary's diary. Turned out Mouse had a little pack-rat blood and most likely snatched Hillary's diary as soon as the girl was dead. Lange had talked to Mrs. Dennis, searched the rooms and probably knew as much as Josie did. She figured the odds on Mouse's survival were better if she found her before Milano's lawyer did.

Unfortunately, her best bloodhound was sitting at home waiting for the geniuses at I.A. to figure out the allegations against Fricke were bogus. In the meantime, keeping Mouse alive and locating the diary would be really difficult without him and his partner. She needed Fricke, but even she wouldn't have the guts to put him back in the field now.

When she got into her car, Josie called the Hollywood vice office and Marge answered.

"Have a bad dream?" Marge asked, as soon as she recognized Josie's voice.

"What're you talking about?"

"Why are you calling me at this hour? All good little captains should be safely tucked in their beds by now."

"Actually, I never quite made it home."

"What's wrong? Where are you?" Now Marge sounded concerned.

"It's okay. I'm sitting outside Hillary's mother's house. I stopped by to see how she was doing."

"In the middle of the fucking night?"

"It's a long story. We'll talk about it tomorrow, but for now I need your people to pick up Mouse again. Make it your number one priority. I think she's got Hillary's diary and I'm pretty sure Lange and Milano want it as badly as I do."

They talked a few more minutes while Josie started her car and made a one-handed U-turn heading back in the direction of the freeway. She drove under a streetlight across the road from Mrs. Dennis's house and was saying goodbye to Marge when the front windshield cracked with a loud thud and then again. Josie stepped on the gas pedal and turned away as a shower of glass fragments sprayed her head and face. Her first thought was a brick had been thrown at the window until she saw the bullet-sized holes and swerved away from the light, angled her car toward the street, leaving the engine running and the headlights flooding the area where she thought the shots might've come from. She unholstered her .45 and scrambled across the seat to the passenger door, sliding out onto the ground. Her phone was nearby on the floor of the car, but she reached for the police radio.

"Commander six, officer needs help six hundred block Sierra Way, shots fired," she said as calmly as she could, directing the approaching units to what she calculated was a safe location. It took a few seconds from the shots hitting the car to the radio call, but she felt as if everything was happening in slow motion. Her hand was shaking slightly as she slipped the radio into her jacket pocket.

Using her car for cover, she crawled toward the front bumper, trying to see something, anything that would tell her where her assailant was hiding. The street was dark except for the police car's high beams, and it was quiet. One porch light came on, but no one came out. Gunshots weren't an anomaly in this neighborhood. In the distance she could hear sirens. Crouching under parked car windows, she moved further down the street. The area was deserted and eerily still. "Come on, asshole, stick that pumpkin head up and give me one clean shot," she whispered. Both her hands were on the gun and steady now—anger trumped fear.

Within thirty seconds, the street was surrounded with police cars and what seemed to be an army of shotgun-toting officers. Josie directed them and the officers with dogs to her location. The first one to reach her was that same sergeant from Rampart division who had responded to the party house the night Hillary was killed.

"We're doing a yard-by-yard search, ma'am, but we're pretty sure the shooter took off before we got here," the sergeant said, brushing some glass off her shoulder with his leather glove.

"You spend a lot of time in my division," Josie said, slowly getting up from her crouched position. "And I do appreciate that."

"You'd better let the paramedics take a look at you," he said.

"I'm fine," she said, noticing several officers standing around now, staring at her. She thought she must've gotten pretty messed up rolling out of the car and reached to straighten her hair. The sergeant clamped her wrist.

"Don't do that," he said. "Your hair's full of glass. Can't you feel the glass in your skin?"

She couldn't, but suddenly had an urge to rub her face. She stood under a dim streetlight and examined her hands. They had tiny cuts that were barely bleeding, but there wasn't any pain. The paramedics examined her face and hands and decided it was best to take her to the emergency room at Cedars-Sinai where they could more easily find and remove any tiny glass fragments and disinfect the cuts.

The sergeant took her personal items out of her car and threw them in the backseat of his black and white cruiser.

"Hop in," he said, opening the passenger door. "I'll get your car towed when they're done, but first let me take you to Cedars."

The paramedic shrugged and closed the back doors of his ambulance as Josie got into the police car.

She opened the passenger window and thanked the paramedics as the sergeant pulled away, maneuvering around several parked police cars and a couple of ambulances. "And thank you for the lift," she said, beginning to notice a little discomfort as her neck muscles tightened from tension, and feeling considerable pain in her joints.

"No problem, Captain. You just don't look like the type to lie on a stretcher and wait for somebody to take care of you."

Josie nodded, but wasn't sure she agreed. She was fighting an urge to scratch her face and thought lying on a stretcher with a shot of Demerol didn't sound like such a terrible idea right now. "Who the hell are you, anyway?" she asked, trying to keep her mind off the painful cuts and overall ache.

"Kyle Richards. I like to stay busy, and there's never too much going on in the middle of the night except in Hollywood."

"Maybe you should transfer into my division, since you spend so much time hanging around."

"Mind if I ask you a question, ma'am?"

"Probably, but go ahead."

"What were you doing in that gang-infested neighborhood by yourself in the middle of the night?"

"Community policing," she said, giving him a look that should've told him she had no intention of answering that question, at least not for him. Sergeant Richards was trim with graying brown hair. He had four hash marks on his sleeve—twenty years with the department—and judging from his salty attitude, he'd been around, probably retired military. She'd be surprised if his personnel package wasn't full of commendations.

She was always looking for competent people and this sergeant looked like a good candidate for her division.

"You feeling okay?" Sergeant Richards asked as he exited the freeway off-ramp and turned onto the surface street.

"Like a pincushion."

"Almost there. Don't scratch."

"You work any off-duty jobs?"

"No, why?"

"Curiosity."

"I'd rather spend my free time with my kid."

He negotiated the turn into the Cedars' parking structure near the emergency room door. He parked and helped her retrieve her belongings from the backseat.

"I can take it from here, Richards. Appreciate your help, but you'd better get back to Rampart so I don't get nasty calls from your watch commander," she said, gingerly shaking his hand, trying to keep her blood off him.

"No problem, he's a pretty mellow guy. Take care, Captain," he said, getting back into his patrol car. She watched him typing on his MDT computer keyboard as he left the lot. There was no downtime for this guy.

Josie was grateful she didn't have a lot of personal junk in her car and only had to carry a utility bag, shotgun and her briefcase into the emergency room. She knew a couple of captains who would've had golf bags and substantial loot from their most recent shopping spree stashed in their trunks. The area captain at Pacific division kept a packed suitcase and fishing gear in his city car for weekend getaways with his pretty senior clerk typist.

The sliding door opened, and she saw Marge standing at the nurses' station with her back to the door. Everyone in the room stopped what they were doing and stared at Josie. It must've been quite a sight because Marge's eyes widened when she turned around.

"What the fuck," Marge said, hurrying to help Josie.

"Somebody shot at me," Josie said.

"I was on the goddamn phone, remember. I get out there . . . morons say some sergeant took you . . . nobody knows shit . . . why the fuck didn't you call me back?"

"Calm down, woman," Josie said, handing her the shotgun. "Take this so I don't look like Mad Max."

Marge took the shotgun and utility bag, and gently removed the strap of the leather briefcase off Josie's shoulder. "I'd say more like Edward Scissorhands. Have you seen the side of your face?"

A nurse took Jose behind a curtain where she removed her jacket, shirt and bra, and helped her into a hospital gown. With magnifying glasses, several nurses removed tiny slivers of glass that were embedded in the left side of her face and neck. Most of the glass was on the surface of her skin and brushed off, or was washed away with the soothing disinfectant. Leaning forward, Josie combed her long hair from her neck forward and watched little pieces of glass fall onto a towel one of the nurses had placed on the floor.

An hour later, she was relatively glass-free and finally able to get a glimpse of her face in the mirror over the sink in the patients' bathroom. With her hair pulled back and her skin cleaned, she didn't look as horrible as she'd anticipated. There were lots of tiny red spots on her cheek and she could still see remnants of glass dust in her hair, but overall she felt fine. Her skin stopped itching after the disinfectant wash and her hands were hardly scratched. Marge had gathered Josie's belongings, and they were about to check out when Chief Bright arrived with Art Perry.

Marge groaned under her breath and whispered to Josie, "Just when you think things can't get more fucked-up."

"You don't look too bad," Bright said cheerfully, getting too close to her and staring at the side of her face. The bureau chief was in a tight t-shirt, sweatpants and running shoes, and looked as if he'd just finished his morning jog. He didn't seem the least bit distressed about Josie's dangerous encounter.

Perry was in a business suit and appeared ready for work although it was still only six A.M. He was uncharacteristically quiet.

"Are you okay?" Josie asked him.

He almost smiled. "That should've been my question to you. Are you done here?"

"We have some questions but they can wait if you're tired and want to get home," Bright said, talking to Josie but looking at Marge, and finally taking the utility bag from her and giving it to Perry.

"Let me grab a few hours sleep and I'll call you," Josie said. "I already gave my statement to the detectives. They recovered .45 casings but not a clue as to who did the shooting or why."

"What were you doing out there?" Bright asked, as they stood in front of the sliding glass door outside the emergency room while Perry and Marge loaded Josie's belongings onto the backseat of Marge's car. Josie explained how she'd decided to visit Mrs. Dennis, but carefully avoided any reference to Hillary's diary or Peter Lange. "Why would you go there alone at that time of night?"

"I was on my way home and saw her lights on," Josie lied. She guessed that sounded lame so she added, "I remembered you told me Mrs. Dennis was bugging you and the police commission, so I thought I'd try giving her an update on the investigation and maybe she'd give us all some breathing room." It wasn't a great explanation, but the best Josie could conjure up after nearly getting her head blown off.

"This case is too much for you. You can't be doing these things in the middle of the night. Did you get a look at the shooter?"

She didn't get the connection but answered, "Never saw anyone. Might've been some neighborhood punk who recognized the police car," Josie said. "It's the most logical explanation." She wasn't certain that was true, but then Bright didn't have as much information as she had, and any other explanation would've required filling him in on some of those facts she'd worked so hard to conceal.

———

"Wanna tell me what's going on," Marge said when they were back on the freeway headed toward Pasadena.

"You're taking me home so I can shower and sleep."

"Bullshit—why aren't you telling Bright everything?"

"Because other than you and Red, I'm not sure who I can trust anymore."

She surmised from Marge's silence that she didn't entirely buy that explanation, but Josie was surprised at how little Marge's disapproval actually mattered right now.

SIXTEEN

When they got to Pasadena, Josie invited Marge into the house to rest a while before making the long drive back across town to her apartment. Josie's body was bruised and tired, and although Marge hadn't complained, she noticed her friend could barely keep her eyes open.

Josie understood that despite her frequent expletives and disgruntled attitude, Marge became anxious when someone with authority other than herself didn't play strictly by department rules. So as soon as they were in the den reclining on loungers with glasses full of a really good Cabernet, Josie tried to reassure her that holding back information from the bureau was a necessity.

"Even Bright's not that stupid. Why do you suppose he keeps blabbing everything to Goldman?" Marge asked.

"Don't know. At the moment, I'm more concerned about someone wanting to kill me."

"Could've been a random asshole thing."

"Don't think so."

"Why not? Nobody in any way connected to this case knew you were going to be there . . . not even you from what you've said."

"I don't believe in coincidence. Besides, what if somebody was already there watching the house."

"Why and what does anybody in this investigation gain by blowing away your high-ranking ass?"

"Don't know. Maybe I was getting too close to something. Mouse went there after Hillary died and I'm guessing what she took was Hillary's diary and not some forgotten piece of clothing from her thrift store ensemble. Maybe the shooter was hoping she'd come back."

"Anything Hillary wrote isn't really evidence at this point," Marge said, placing her empty glass on the floor beside her chair.

"What do you mean? Why not?"

"Experts might ID the handwriting as Hillary's, but regardless of what she wrote, with her dead, how do you validate any of it?"

"That depends on what she wrote. We might be able to prove some of it without her," Josie said, finishing her wine. She retrieved the bottle from the coffee table and filled her glass again. Her friend's eyes were closed and she was snoring softly.

Josie sat back and sipped the wine. She should get up and take a shower, rinse the remaining bits of glass out of her hair. The warm water against her skin would feel so good, but she couldn't make herself get out of the recliner. She was very tired, but her eyes wouldn't close. Alcohol usually made her sleepy, but it wasn't working. A serious bout of frustration was the real problem. The Bright and Goldman relationship was bothering her. Was it possible Chief Bright had a reason to protect Goldman? Was her boss involved with Hillary too? She took another swallow. That was crazy, there was nothing to prove or even suggest that connection . . . too tired, too much wine.

It happened, but she couldn't remember when or how. She'd fallen asleep with the empty wine glass on her lap. When the annoying itch on the side of her face woke her, the room was dark. Several seconds passed before she could clear her head and remember why she was here and where she was supposed to be. No headache . . . that was a plus. She reached up and pulled the chain to turn on the pole lamp over her shoulder. The recliner next to hers was empty. A handwritten note was propped up by an empty wine glass on the coffee table.

It read, "I'm gone. See you at the station. Don't worry, I'll catch your little rodent. Get some sleep or you'll start doing stupid things. Oops sorry, too late. Your favorite lieutenant, MB."

"Smartass," Josie said, to the empty recliner.

The long nap had helped. Actually, she realized she'd slept most of the day. Her hands and face were a little tight from the healing cuts, but otherwise she felt pretty good. The red light was blinking on the phone. Marge must've turned down the ringer before she left. Josie hit the button and played back half a dozen messages. The last ones were from Jake and David. She called her husband and son, assured them she was fine. They told her Marge had notified them earlier that day, but she'd suggested they let Josie sleep.

A long hot shower was the best medicine. When her hair was clean, she scratched her head. Even though it really didn't itch anymore, she'd been thinking about doing that since the shooting last night. The cuts on her face were barely visible now, but she gently patted dry that side of her face and applied a cream the nurse had given her. She dressed in jogging pants and a baggy sweatshirt, letting her damp hair hang loose to dry. Food was the primary thing on her mind now. She wasn't eating right and getting too skinny. Another helping of Mrs. Dennis's cobbler would taste so good, but that wasn't going to happen.

She'd started downstairs when she heard the front door open and returned to the bedroom to retrieve her .45, but hadn't reached the nightstand before she heard Jake calling out to her.

"Don't shoot me, I'm bringing food," he shouted.

She looked over the railing on the second landing. Her husband was carrying several large bags and had a bottle of wine tucked under his arm.

Her stomach growled as soon as she got within range of the garlic and sausage smells.

"Don't you ever eat anything but Italian?" Josie asked, taking one of the bags and searching through it as they went into the kitchen.

"Not often, but I usually cook it myself. I figured if you slept all day you'd be starving, and welcome quantity and speed over quality."

She started emptying the bags while he pulled a couple of plates out of the cupboard.

Jake placed two large squares of lasagna and a couple of sausages smothered in meat sauce on a plate and grated fresh parmesan cheese over the top. She sat at the breakfast table, ate quickly and drank Chianti out of a water glass. He took a smaller portion and nibbled at the pasta, sipped his wine and watched her devour her meal.

Finally she sat back satisfied. "Thank you," she said, topping off their glasses with the wonderful wine. "How did you know I hadn't eaten?"

"We've been married over twenty years. Eating is a very low priority until you're famished. Then you eat everything in sight. That's why we've never owned a pet," he said, peering at her over his glass.

She smiled and shook her head. "I've never eaten a puppy in my life."

"I'll take your word for that. You look much better than I expected. I can hardly see the cuts."

"I was lucky I turned away fast enough. The doctor said those flying chips of glass could've done a lot of damage to my eyes, not to mention what the bullets could've done."

"Why were you out there by yourself?" he asked, and looked worried, maybe a little upset with her.

"It was stupid . . . I wanted to talk to the girl's mother again . . . and I accidentally found myself on her street."

"Why would somebody shoot at you? They couldn't have known who you were . . . could they?"

"I don't know, Jake. Don't worry; I'm not going back there."

"I do worry. I hate you being around that kind of stuff. When you got promoted I thought you'd be isolated from the guns and violence, but it never ends . . . disgusting animals doing disgusting things to one another."

"You're making a living defending those disgusting animals," she said, and then cringed a little. He was trying to be nice and she just dumped on him. "I'm sorry. I understand what you're saying."

"I only practice contract law now. You were right. I couldn't do it."

"What'd your new partner say?"

"Nothing, he needs me a lot more than I need him."

Forgetting for a second how different they were, Josie asked, "Don't you miss the excitement of the D.A.'s office?"

"I don't miss the misery and human suffering." He exhaled and put his glass on the table. "I know you don't understand. It's even difficult for me to explain, but I can't tolerate that life anymore . . . the institutional indifference, adapting to other people's pain. I'm done with all that ugliness."

"That's great, honey, but what planet do you intend to live on," she said, meaning to be a touch nasty this time.

"I'm not naïve. I know evil exists, but I'm done wallowing in it or letting it consume me so I can make a living. I can't do it anymore."

"Do you see me as somebody who wallows in human suffering to make a living?"

"Yes," he said, without hesitation.

"So, what you're really saying is you can't be around me anymore."

"I love you. I hate what you do and it's making me crazy. I'm trying to work it out."

"I'm not gonna quit."

"I know."

Josie took one last bite of pasta, but could hardly swallow. She felt like crying but didn't because she couldn't decide if she was angry or sad. How does a cop avoid ugliness? Police work usually starts with ugly. Should she come home every night and pretend she arranged flowers all day? Crime and criminals were generally repulsive with few redeeming qualities. How was she supposed to sanitize that?

"Guess you've got a problem," she said, her defense mechanism kicking in.

"Unless you're ready to retire and let me support us."

"And what am I supposed to do, start knitting?"

"Anything you want that doesn't involve killing and maiming," he said, getting a little more animated. He must've thought she was actually considering his offer.

She filled her glass about a third of the way and offered him more wine. He shook his head.

"I love you Jake and want you back in my life, but I'll retire when I'm ready or when I can't do it any longer. Since neither of those conditions exists at the moment, are you telling me our marriage is screwed?"

He got up and cleared the table. She drank and watched him. When he was finished, Jake leaned over the table and kissed her. It was warm and nice, but a long way from passionate.

"I'll call you tomorrow to see how you're doing," he said, and then he left.

Josie sat at the table until the wine bottle was empty. What he wanted wasn't fair. Do it my way or not at all. She believed he was being selfish and stubborn. So, why did she feel so miserable? Her mind said "fuck you," but her heart was broken. It hurt to think of any future without Jake, but the idea that at this stage of his life he would suddenly develop a life-changing aversion to violence almost made her laugh. He'd been a fierce, sometimes ruthless prosecutor. Maybe David was right—male menopause.

There were a lot of uncertainties in her life, but the one thing Josie knew absolutely was she had no intention of walking away from police work . . . not now, not for a very long time. So, she'd have to ride out Jake's middle-age Gandhi transformation and hope he could find his way back to her when he tuned into the real world again.

———

THE NEXT morning, she was up at sunrise. Despite consuming way too much wine the prior night, she was clearheaded and eager to work. There were tiny scratches on the side of her face and on her hands, but barely visible. It pretty much looked like a light rash.

She made a cheese omelet, hash browns and toast, ate, took a shower, called the watch commander for a black and white taxi with a uniformed driver, and was in her office at Hollywood station before any of the administrative staff arrived. The pile of paperwork on her desk and the emails on her computer had been whittled down considerably by the time her adjutant peeked around her file cabinet.

"You look great," he said, taking a big step into her office. "Sleep here last night?"

"Is Behan in yet?" she asked.

"I saw him back in detectives." He stepped closer and stared at her face. "It's hardly noticeable. You feel okay?"

"Fine, thanks. Tell Behan I need to talk to him." Last night was done and she wasn't in the mood to rehash the details. Unless the conversation involved identifying the shooter, she wasn't interested in talking about it.

A few minutes later, Behan lumbered into her office looking like how she felt yesterday. Her first impression when he sat on the couch was the guy's homeless again. His shirt was wrinkled, his hair uncombed, and he had a full-sized set of luggage under his eyes.

"Cory Goldman's gonna be here in half an hour," Behan said. "What'd the old lady tell you?" he asked, but before she could answer he added, "By the way, it was idiotic to go there alone."

"So I've been told . . . many times." She recounted everything Mrs. Dennis told her and reviewed the chain of events concluding with the shooting.

"You get any rounds off?"

"Never saw him."

"Too bad. You figure they were out to kill you or just scare you?"

"Kill, I'd say, from the location of the hits."

"The only thing she told you that's halfway interesting was Mouse coming back for something. That's probably not enough to get shot up over."

"Marge's got her people looking for Mouse. If we're lucky we'll find her first and get back what she took from the house."

"Roy Mitchell checked in. He's still breathing."

"Who?"

"Our smelly homeless witness to Misty Skylar's demise," Behan said.

"He hit you up for more money?"

Behan gave her a dirty look. He didn't think anybody knew he'd been supporting the alley dweller, but she'd seen him in the parking lot give the bum new clothes and an envelope with cash on two occasions while she was at the gas pumps. Knowing Behan, she figured there were other handouts she hadn't seen.

"We need to keep him alive," Behan said.

"Which reminds me, did you ever show him a six-pack with photos of Fricke and Butler?"

"He couldn't ID either one of them."

Good, she thought. "Is Cory coming alone?" she asked.

"What do you think?"

She knew the young man would at least bring his lawyer, but Behan told her Councilman Goldman wanted to be there, too.

"I'm surprised Bright isn't coming," she said, sarcastically.

"It's still early."

"You look like you spent the night in that alley under Roy Mitchell's box. What's going on?"

"Nothing," he said as he stood up. "Your windshield's fixed and your car's clean and parked out back. I gotta take a shower. See you in a few minutes."

Behan was gone and had managed to avoid answering her question. It wasn't necessary. Josie had seen the scenario of his crumbling marriages too many times. Last night, he'd most likely crashed somewhere other than home because either he was too drunk to drive home, or Miss Vicky'd had enough and tossed him out on his sorry ass. Josie felt bad. This had probably been his last chance to put together a decent life and have a reason and means to survive after retirement. In a lot of ways, Behan was that despondent guy standing on a ledge of a high-rise determined to jump, and she didn't have the right words to make him change his mind. She would, of course, ask him to go to the department shrink—again—but knew even with treatment a cop's self-destructive behavior wasn't easily deterred.

By the time Josie got to the interview room, Cory, his father, and Peter Lange were sitting on one side of the room with their backs to the two-way mirror. They probably figured they were being clever, but the video camera could pick them up anywhere in the room and the mirror was actually just a mirror.

She wasn't surprised to see Lange. The attorney kept popping up all over this investigation like an annoying jack-in-the-box.

"You're representing Cory Goldman?" she asked. Not too long ago he supposedly believed Cory was involved in Hillary Dennis's murder.

"Mr. Lange now knows my son had nothing to do with Miss Dennis's death and he's agreed to represent him," Councilman Goldman said.

"Really . . . I'm curious, how do you know that Mr. Lange?" Josie asked.

"I believe him, and I don't want to see the kid get railroaded for something he didn't do," Lange said.

"That's nice," Josie said, fighting a sarcastic remark. She guessed he was trying to get some sort of reaction from her. She faked a smile, and then, with her foot, pushed a chair out from under the table for Behan who'd just arrived. His hair was still damp, but he wore a clean dress shirt with a tie and khaki pants.

"You're going to have to leave," Behan told Eli Goldman as soon as the councilman stood to shake hands. The surprised man seemed frozen in place after Behan's pronouncement, and then turned stiffly toward Lange who cleared his throat and responded for him.

"His son has asked him to be here."

"I appreciate that," Behan said without altering his tone. "But he's a witness in this case, and his son's an adult, so he'll have to leave."

"What if I say there won't be an interview unless his father stays," Lange said.

"If Cory's afraid to talk to us alone, then I guess you'd better take him and go home, because I'm telling you his daddy can't be here when I talk to him. You're his lawyer. You can stay and hold his hand, but all other extraneous support has to get out." Behan wasn't backing down.

While they argued, Josie remained quiet and watched Cory. The young man was at a simmering point, clenching the arms of his chair so hard his knuckles were white. His lips were tight, and his face and shaved head were turning slightly pink. Behan was clever and had given this some thought. Cory clearly resented being treated like a child and told what to do.

"Let's go," Lange said, getting up after Behan unleashed a series of polite, albeit snide remarks about Cory's inability to think or act for himself.

"I got a better idea. Why don't the two of you get the hell out a here and let me talk to this dude," Cory said, staring at the floor.

"I don't recommend that," Lange said. Now he was upset. "Don't let this cop con you into doing something stupid."

"Fuck off," Cory said, not looking at the lawyer or his father.

Josie and the councilman watched the tense scene as spectators, and at the right moment, Behan sat down and let the young man do his work for him. After several seconds of impassioned pleas from Lange, Cory stopped arguing and glared defiantly at his attorney, refusing to speak any longer.

The elder Goldman moved hesitantly toward the door, at the same time reminding Josie that Chief Bright had agreed to let him be present for his son's interrogation. She apologized and explained this wasn't going to be an interrogation. Behan simply wanted to talk "man to man" with Cory, and the young man was free to leave anytime he wanted.

"It's up to you, Cory. You want your dad to take you home?" Josie asked as condescendingly as she could.

"Just go," Cory said, turning his back to his father. Lange was already standing outside the interview room, but before departing, he stopped and glared at Josie. She could see there was substantial hate in those handsome eyes, causing her to wonder why the pricey lawyer had worked up so much passion over a goofy kid he supposedly barely knew.

When the door closed and the three of them were alone, Cory moved closer to the table and looked directly at Josie.

"Ten minutes and I'm fuckin' outta here," Cory said.

"Good, I don't like to waste time either," Behan said. "Hillary's mother wasn't lying was she? You did threaten to kill her daughter."

"Yeah, so what? I didn't do it."

"Why'd you threaten her?"

"She pissed me off . . . wouldn't leave me alone."

"It wasn't sex, so what'd she want from you?"

Cory sat back. He seemed surprised Behan knew that much about their relationship.

"Different shit," Cory mumbled.

Behan banged his fist on the table. Cory jumped, surprised by the sudden loud noise. Josie wasn't expecting it and was startled too.

"Grow up," Behan shouted. "Stop being such a whiny baby. You knew what she was up to. It involved your father and made you mad enough to threaten her. Somebody killed her because of it, so what was she doing?"

Cory rubbed his arms under his baggy sweatshirt, and nervously pushed up the sleeves revealing numerous tattoos. Although the dark ink drawings were intended to cover them, Josie noticed scars on both his wrists—hesitation marks, unsuccessful suicide attempts done more for attention than a serious death wish. He had more tattoos around his neck, and studs in his ears and in one nostril. Her first reaction was, why does this kid hate himself? She saw all his body art, puncturing, and head-shaving as a kind of self-loathing. There was nothing scientific about her observation, but it seemed obvious to her that anyone with a modicum of self-esteem wouldn't intentionally and permanently deface his body even a little bit, and this was some major mutilation . . . graffiti to protest what?

"The bitch knew stuff about people . . . important people." Cory spit out the words, and his mouth twisted like someone had just fed him dog shit.

Josie sensed he wanted to talk about this. Every muscle in his body seemed to be struggling against the words, but they poured out. Nothing kept him in that room. He wasn't being forced to say anything. His struggle was entirely internal. She didn't say a word, afraid to change the tenuous chemistry of the interview. Behan must've felt the same way. He sat quietly watching, waiting for the young man to continue on his own.

"Misty couldn't make money in the business anymore. No major studio dude in his right mind trusted her. Her contracts were shit; all her clients were fucked-up speeders, freaks and losers."

Josie was aching to ask about David, but didn't. His name hadn't come up. She wouldn't be the one to open that door.

Cory crossed his arms and leaned on the table again, speaking directly to Behan. "Hilly and her so-called agent pissed away every dollar they made," he said and hesitated, studying Behan, sizing him up. He sighed and sat back. "They knew the movie stuff was fucked, but Hilly still got plenty a cash fucking old rich guys. So, that's it. They did all right whoring."

"Whores don't usually get their brains blown out. Who wanted them dead?" Behan asked.

Cory nervously scratched his shaved head with both hands. "The guy's a fucking psycho," he blurted out. He glanced up at Josie and then Behan. They weren't asking, just waiting. "Bruno Faldi," he said. "He works for Milano, that guy from Avanti's you were asking me about the other night," Cory said, looking at Josie. "Faldi and Misty were half-assed partners. The dude found kiddie whores and lined up a bunch a rich geezers. They made so much fucking money."

"Everybody's getting rich. What's the problem?" Josie asked. Her patience was wearing thin. She wanted the punch line.

"Nobody can know I told you this," he said, rubbing his left eye as if something was irritating it. "No fucking testifying, no signed shit, nothing. I know how you guys work and I'm not doing it."

"Okay," Behan said.

"Stupid bitches think they can go into business for themselves blackmailing rich suckers. Bruno he finds out and is fucking pissed."

"Blackmailing who?" Josie asked. This was something they didn't know.

"No way, man, I ain't going there."

"Why not . . . because your father's one of them? Is that why you threatened Hillary, to stop her from blackmailing your father?" Behan asked, but didn't wait for a response, probably knowing he wouldn't get one, and asked instead, "Anyone besides the two women and Bruno running the prostitution business? Was Milano involved?"

The remarks about his father had shaken Cory, and his brain seemed to flicker off-line for a moment. He was anxious now and had trouble sitting still.

"I told you all the shit I know. I can't do any more."

"What about Hillary's diary?" Josie asked, and Cory's face blanched. "What do you and Mouse plan to do with it?"

Cory stood. He was a little wobbly. "My dad didn't do anything. You can't tell him I said he did." The young man wasn't talking to them any longer. His words were a plea to anyone who would listen. He bumped into a chair, knocking it over as he scrambled out of the interview room.

He'd told them a lot without actually revealing much, but Josie felt a little uneasy about his agitated state when he fled. According to everything she'd heard and seen, the boy was unstable at best, but this was different. She had to admit they'd taken advantage of him and clearly he had exposed himself way beyond his comfort zone . . . but still he hadn't really been pushed that hard.

Behan told her not to worry about it, but she did.

SEVENTEEN

Josie had a healthy respect for fear. Uncontrolled, it infected the mind and altered a person's life choices. But a reasonable amount of trepidation might've saved her skin once or twice— when she hesitated before jumping with both feet into the middle of a dangerous situation.

However, when someone is consumed by fear it's different. Instead of providing an opportunity to make better decisions, it paralyzes the brain and body.

Josie recognized the unpleasant odor of a frightened man's sweat lingering in the interview room long after Cory had gone. She'd worked in crowded hallways serving search warrants with dozens of nervous detectives when they didn't know what danger waited for them on the other side of a barricaded door. They were scared, but it was a healthy fear, the kind that kept cops alive. When the moment came, most of them fought to be first through the door; but there were those who hung back a little, and when everything was over, they'd have that same stench of panicked fear on them.

She'd surmised Cory Goldman was being eaten alive by his fears. He talked to Behan to spite his father and the pushy lawyer, but at some point he was going to think about what he'd said and regret his decision. That's what guys like Cory did. They wasted their lives regretting or hiding. Josie had to admit she was feeling a bit guilty. The boy was damaged goods and she'd taken advantage of him, but she kept reminding herself it had been for an important reason.

THE EXPECTED call from Bright didn't come until the following day. The deputy chief was angry and demanded a full report on why his orders hadn't been followed. Josie calmly explained that the decision had been Cory's. The boy insisted on talking to them alone. Nevertheless, Bright's tirade continued for several minutes until he ordered her to be in his office the next morning with a better explanation. Josie didn't argue. She hoped by tomorrow his invective would lose some steam. She would pretend to be contrite, and since he was a simple man, winning the argument was usually enough for him.

There wasn't a lot of time to worry about Bright's threats. As soon as Josie hung up, Deputy City Attorney Harry Walsh was tapping on her open door. It was a pleasant surprise.

"Sorry to disturb you," Harry said, taking a few tentative steps inside the room. "Is this a bad time?"

"Actually, it's the perfect time," she said, getting up and shaking hands. Harry's sharp mind and gentle nature were exactly what she needed at the moment. The conversation with Bright had been depressing. "I've had a miserable morning."

"Sorry, I can come back."

"I need your advice," she said, and saw Harry's expression change. He looked uncomfortable.

"Don't worry, it's not a personal problem."

He immediately relaxed and smiled. "I'm not good at giving people advice, but I enjoy police predicaments. First, may I ask why I haven't had any arrest reports from Fricke for the last couple of days?"

"He's dealing with some personnel matters," she said.

"Not again," Harry said, looking disappointed. The deputy city attorney claimed every time Fricke got suspended for misconduct, there was a minor crime wave in Hollywood that persisted until he got back and restored order.

Josie closed the door and gestured for Harry to sit at the table. She'd decided to trust him because her instincts were usually pretty good about people. It probably would've been smarter to wait and see which city employee names popped up in Hillary's pay-to-play diary, but she couldn't imagine Harry involved in high-priced prostitution. She was certain now Councilman Goldman was connected, and Chief Bright's behavior was suspicious, but if other city leaders or high-ranking police personnel were involved, she was going to need someone for legal advice.

Josie carefully recounted the details of the two homicides and explained how Fricke had been implicated. She tried to cover all the complicated connections.

"So what it comes down to is, I've got a dead teenager who might've had a little black book or diary of some sort with the names of very important people who bought sex with her. She decides to blackmail a few of them for extra cash and gets herself and maybe her agent killed," Josie said without taking a breath.

"I don't believe Donnie Fricke helped that girl buy drugs or any of it," Harry said when Josie paused for a moment. He was stuck on that part of the story.

"I don't either, but the allegations are serious enough that I had to take him off the street, which I think is what they really wanted; but I didn't have much choice."

"So, you don't have any idea who's in that book."

"Cory pretty much told me his father's there, but the councilman might not be the only participant who had something to lose if word got out he was paying to have sex with a teenager. The fact that Lange wants the book tells me Milano thinks it's worth something, or Lange's got another client who's afraid he might be outed."

"Nothing Milano does surprises me, but blackmail's a little subtle for him," Harry said. "He's more the kneecap-breaking type of guy."

"Maybe there's something in there about him or his nephew he doesn't want the world to know. Problem is we'll never know if Lange finds Mouse before we do."

"You're assuming it's just you and Lange looking for her diary. What if there are other former . . . what'd you call them, participants, who want it?" Harry didn't wait for an answer. "Regardless, you're a long way from needing my kind of help. Of course, I'll do whatever I can, but I think if you find the diary you'll probably find who killed that girl. And maybe I can figure out a way to avoid publicly embarrassing a lot of weak men. With Hillary dead, most likely there won't be enough evidence to prosecute anyone anyway."

Josie wasn't going to argue with him because she respected Harry; but if embarrassing those men was all she could do, then she'd do it. They were creeps who'd taken advantage of a vulnerable, unstable young woman. Josie would've preferred throwing their sorry butts in jail for statutory rape, but ruining them would be enough if that's all she could manage.

Remembering that Harry seldom came to her office unless there was a problem, Josie asked, "Did you want to talk to me about something besides Fricke?"

"Mostly, I was curious about Fricke . . . but." He exhaled. "I probably shouldn't be telling you this, but Susan Fletcher's been sniffing around my office trying to find out what you're up to at the needle exchange."

"Really," Josie said, smirking.

"Claims she's had complaints from constituents. Although, I'm not aware of many heroin addicts who vote."

"It must be working."

"I didn't hear that. She can be very nasty, so I wouldn't poke that sleeping bear if I were you. From what you've told me, there's plenty on your plate right now without provoking her."

"With Fricke at home, the hype car's pretty much out of commission, so she should be pacified for a while."

"Somebody's arresting them. I'm getting a lot of under-the-influence reports from different cops in the vicinity of the needle exchange, not as many as Fricke, but still quite a few. Sergeant Bailey's signing as supervisor."

They chatted a few more minutes about other gossip in Hollywood. The local community leaders considered Josie their chief of police and Harry Walsh their private prosecutor. In their minds, Hollywood was a sovereign city and the captain at the Hollywood police station worked for them. From Josie's perspective that was a good thing. They were her power base. Anyone who tried to screw with her would get a big loud push back. Lately, she was counting on it.

She wasn't surprised that Marge had tried to keep the hype car busy while Fricke and Butler were assigned home, but from what Harry had told her they were making too many quality arrests for neophytes still learning the ropes. Josie had intended to transfer the unit back to the narcotics supervisor—but hadn't as yet—and was suspicious about who was training and advising them, because as far as she knew Marge had no narcotics expertise.

The vice office was empty, so Josie contacted Marge on the radio and asked if they could meet somewhere. Marge responded quickly with an address Josie recognized. It was Murray's. Big surprise, Marge was eating again.

It was too late for breakfast and too early for lunch, so the place wasn't crowded. They sat at the same table Josie and Behan had occupied about a week ago, and it started her worrying again about the unstable condition of her homicide detective's life. These days, it was complicated to talk to Marge about Behan. If that little hand-touching scene in Nora's the other night was what it appeared to be, they were involved; and Marge might've been the catalyst for what was looking like his latest marriage disaster.

Sammy took their order, came back a few minutes later to take it again, but never delivered it to the kitchen. The ex-boxer had that faraway stare reaching out to touch something only he in his world of dementia could see as he left the restaurant. They waited until his son came out of the kitchen, wiped his hands on his dirty apron, and jotted down the order a third time. He didn't even attempt to apologize for the old man's behavior. All the regulars knew about his father's condition, and he didn't seem to care much about the others.

The restaurant was nearly empty except for two men dressed in business suits sitting at a table in the corner. Dirty dishes were stacked on the counter, and the other tables hadn't been cleared. A young woman walked in and casually removed debris from the table behind Josie, placed dirty dishes on the counter, and wiped the table with a damp rag that had been left on one of the stools before she sat down. The strong smell of sautéed onions and eggs filled the small restaurant making Josie hungry again.

"Harry Walsh's telling me the hype car's been staying pretty active," Josie said, trying to keep her mind off that wonderful aroma and back on the business at hand.

They'd been friends a long time, and Josie always knew when Marge was uncomfortable and at the moment she was fidgeting. The pretty woman pulled nervously at the band around her long blond hair before saying anything.

"I've tried to keep them busy," she said, brushing some leftover crumbs off the table.

"I'm curious who's training them now that Fricke's not around?"

"The guys at narcotics have been very helpful," Marge said, and added quickly, "Donnie had given them an excellent foundation on the basics before he left."

"They must be good. It took me years to learn to do schematics and write reports that well. Frankly, just locating that many hypes is amazing for guys with their limited experience."

Marge sat back, folded her arms, and stared at Josie. "What the fuck's this about," she asked. "If you wanna ask me something, just fucking ask."

"Who's helping you?"

The omelettes oozing cheese and mushrooms were delivered to the table by Sammy's son, but neither Josie nor Marge looked at the food or moved.

"Fricke isn't the only cop in the city that knows how to do a hype schematic," Marge said, finally picking up a fork.

"The schematic can be faked if you've got a decent one to copy, but finding that many heroin addicts every night takes a lot more expertise. As far as I know, narcotics hasn't got anybody that can do what Fricke does and I know you can't."

"Well, I guess you're wrong about that because we're doing it," she said, and shoved a big chunk of juicy eggs into her mouth.

They were quiet for the five or ten minutes it took to devour their omelettes and those thick slices of wheat bread Sammy's kid brought on his next trip to their table. Sammy returned as soon as they finished eating, and cleaned up all the dirty dishes, wiped the tables and counter, and carried on a coherent conversation with the woman behind them before disappearing into the kitchen again.

"I'm going out with your talented guys tonight because I'd really like to see them work," Josie said, wiping the remnants of toast off her face. She'd suspected Fricke was working with them and Marge's reaction confirmed her suspicions. "That okay with you?"

"Why not? If you don't trust me, you can do whatever you want. It's your division. You're the boss."

"I'm also not an idiot."

Marge bent forward and her face looked pained as she tightened her mouth, scrunched her eyes nearly closed and belched, not a faint, hand-over-your-mouth, ladylike burp, but a hard-drinking, taco-eating truck driver's bellow that echoed through the small restaurant, and caused the woman behind them and the two businessmen to laugh out loud.

"Excuse me," Marge said, offering her best Miss America smile; then glancing around the room, obviously not embarrassed, she added, "My boss gives me indigestion," gesturing toward Josie.

"Be as gross as you want; it's not gonna work," Josie said. She wasn't embarrassed that easily either.

"You're like a goddamn booger stuck on my finger. Can't you give me a break and let this go. We're doing what's got to be done. What's the fucking problem?"

"Fricke is assigned to home for a reason. You can't have him out there doing police work."

"He's not actually doing anything. He's a kind of . . . technical advisor. Look, you want us to find Mouse, right? Well she's not at Cory's apartment anymore or anywhere else we've looked. I needed Fricke to do his magic."

Josie twisted in her chair. She didn't like this. Having her subordinate do the sort of crazy unconventional thing she might've done made her uneasy. She suddenly realized what a nightmare it must be trying to supervise her, and almost felt a little sorry for Bright.

"You know I wanna find her. What's that got to do with Fricke playing Russian roulette with his career?"

"He's got a snitch we arrested last night who says she'll take him to Mouse tonight in exchange for dropping her case."

Josie knew she should order Fricke to stay home, but was fairly certain she wasn't going to do that. Instead, she paid the bill, told Marge not to go without her and added, "After tonight Fricke's done moonlighting and back to his living room watching *CSI* reruns or some other crap on television that's got nothing to do with real police work."

All the way back to the station, Josie kept reminding herself how stupid it was to allow Fricke to come anywhere near Hollywood, let alone out on the street. She finally stopped worrying about it by convincing herself it would be alright because if everything turned to shit, she'd do what she always did and swear she'd told him to be there.

More and more, it was becoming difficult to shrug off her nonconformist behavior because she knew Behan was right. By always taking responsibility for well-intentioned screwups, at some juncture in the hierarchy's thinking, she was bound to become marginalized and irrelevant.

It was late afternoon by the time she drove into the station lot, and had just parked when Behan came out the back door of the building and walked directly toward her car.

"Better not go in there, boss," he said as soon as he got within a few yards of her, and then turned and got into his car.

Josie knocked on his driver's window until he opened it. She wasn't in the mood to be ordered around especially by him. "What's going on?" she asked, sounding how she felt, a little cranky.

He was quiet for a moment, then started to speak, but hesitated before saying, "Shit . . . Bright's inside waiting for you. The Goldman kid's dead." Behan reached over the console and opened the passenger door. "I'm going out to the scene. Get in."

She heard him, but didn't react for several seconds before asking, "What happened?"

"Get in. We'll talk on the way."

Josie walked around the car. Instinctively, she knew the answer to her question but wanted to be wrong. They were quiet while she buckled her seat belt, and it wasn't until he'd gone several blocks that she asked the question again.

"Ibarra's saying suicide," Behan said, not looking at her.

"Ibarra?" she asked, confused, thinking he'd taken a few days off before starting his new job at Wilshire division.

"Ibarra forgot to tell the watch commander to remove his number from the file so he got the call out. He knew you were shorthanded so he responded."

"Great, just when you think things can't get worse." Josie meant to be sarcastic, but the words left a bad taste. Seems there were worse things in life than dealing with an inept lieutenant.

"He said he'd hold down the fort until I got there."

Josie stared out the passenger window. She barely knew the boy, but the idea of him taking his own life unsettled her. The only time she'd ever felt like this was when she saw abused children or animals. She couldn't stand the thought of helpless things getting hurt or mistreated. Cory wasn't a child, but he was vulnerable in a lot of ways and she knew her uneasiness was guilt.

They had to drive across Melrose and almost into West Hollywood to reach Cory's apartment. Rush-hour traffic was just beginning, but the east-west streets were already backing up as the studios and production houses emptied and tourists began their nightly quest for the ideal restaurant or theater. Life wasn't always perfect but it could be entertaining with enough distractions, she thought, and never had understood suicide. Wasn't it like stopping a movie before you knew how it ended? It seemed to her there were enough answers or rationalizations to get a person through each day. Maybe your luck would change, or a hero would appear to confront all those impossible problems and at least make life tolerable again.

"Don't let them dump this on you," Behan said. "That kid was fucked-up long before we talked to him."

"Yeah, but I'm pretty sure we didn't help."

"Maybe not, but nothing we said or did made him kill himself."

Josie knew he was right, but it didn't make her feel any better. The sun was setting and the warming rays penetrated her window. It was going to be a beautiful evening for most people.

————

THERE WERE black and white cruisers, an ambulance, and the coroner's van parked within a block of the front entrance to Cory's apartment building on Melrose. Josie relaxed a little when she was fairly certain her son's dilapidated Jeep wasn't anywhere in the immediate neighborhood. The troublesome thought of David's negative reaction to all this had been nagging at her since she got into Behan's car. Her son had warned her about Cory's fragile psyche. In the future, he would no doubt remind her of that admonition at every opportunity. She could handle David's accusations; however, it would be better if his outburst didn't occur at this particular moment in this place. She felt bad enough right now without having to deal with him, too.

There were enough uniforms and detectives around the premises to tell Josie this must've been an unusual death. Some cops were fascinated with the macabre and had a morbid need to stop by the scene of every bizarre demise. She herded a few of them away from the building and back to their patrol duties, pulled the uniformed sergeant aside and told him to clear the street and building and to keep any unnecessary officers away. "You're not paid to be a spectator," Josie told the sergeant. She was disappointed that the guy was acting like a five-year policeman and not a supervisor. She probably overreacted but wasn't in a forgiving mood. He had to learn his new status—and bigger paychecks came with responsibilities.

The sergeant followed her and Behan into the building, and cleared the hall and the doorway to Cory's apartment. Josie got a faint whiff of putrefying flesh mixed with turpentine before they got inside and braced for the worst. One of the detectives had a small jar of Vick's VapoRub and she dabbed a little under her nose to counteract the smell.

The cramped space wasn't what she'd expected. It was relatively clean but unbearably warm and stuffy, cluttered with magazines and books stacked in piles everywhere. A large coffee can full of turpentine and a few dozen artist brushes had tipped over onto the counter between the living room and tidy kitchen. The smelly solvent was dripping onto the linoleum.

Original oil paintings covered the walls and half-finished canvasses were stacked in all the corners. Most of the pictures were dark, isolated landscapes or portraits of a man who resembled Cory's father.

The only other area was the bedroom, where she found Ibarra standing near the bed and the body of Cory Goldman. Behan had immediately pulled his detectives aside, and they were huddled in a corner of the bedroom with the medical examiner.

"How weird is this?" Ibarra said, moving closer to her.

Josie didn't answer. She was fixated on the corpse. Cory was lying naked on his back on top of an emerald green comforter. Lividity had begun leaving a blotchy, purplish discoloration on his legs, arms, and buttocks. Probably every other part of his body was covered with tattoos—only his genitals had been spared. Josie could see the ink continued around the sides of his body and most likely decorated his entire backside under the postmortem staining. It was a permanent bodysuit, his ultimate work of art.

Cory had carefully positioned himself on the bed with his arms outstretched so viewers got the full effect of the drawings. A white substance had dripped from the corner of his mouth to around his jaw and onto the pillow where it dried like milky vomit; otherwise, the boy's expression seemed more at peace than

Josie had ever seen it when he was alive and—similar to Hillary's corpse—he'd died with a faint smile.

An empty bottle of sleeping pills was on the nightstand, usually a woman's preferred method of suicide, but it fit in this case because Josie couldn't imagine the timid young man shooting himself or doing anything that might ruin his body art.

"Have you ever seen anything like this?" Ibarra asked again.

She looked at him and for the first time since entering the room realized how pale, almost grayish he was. His dark eyes were sunken in even darker circles.

"Are you sick?" she asked.

"I haven't been sleeping well."

"Wilshire not all you expected," she said.

"Actually, I haven't started yet. It's nothing. I'm just tired," he said and turned away from her. This quiet, introspective man wasn't the Ibarra she knew. He appeared lost in his thoughts and wandered a few feet from the bed before patting Behan on the back on his way out of the room. Behan turned to her and shrugged. He'd noticed it too.

The bedroom was similar to the living room with more gloomy landscapes decorating the walls, but no pictures of his father were hung in this space. There was a piano keyboard in the corner next to the bathroom door, with sheet music and composition books piled on the floor and on the windowsill. The guy wrote music too, Josie thought, picking up a half-finished page of scribbled musical notes lying on the keys.

Behan tapped her on the shoulder and she jumped at the sudden interruption. Her thoughts were consumed with not only the wasted opportunities in this young man's life, but also maybe a little apprehension about the condition of her talented son's state of mind.

"Sorry," Behan said. "You daydreaming?"

"Just thinking how sad this is."

"It's about to get worse. The bureau sent me a text the councilman's on his way."

"Probably better if he sees his kid here than in the morgue," Josie said. The gut-wrenching smells, cold, and isolation of a steel slab in the morgue made the unimaginable even more appalling.

"Okay, but I'm gonna tell them to wrap up the body and have it ready to go as soon as his father's done."

"Fine, just let the man have some time with his kid," Josie said. Her tone was testy because she hated when dead people got treated like sides of beef. She knew technically that's what they were, but she'd been brought up Catholic and couldn't help herself. She still believed people had a soul even when their blood stopped circulating and they began smelling like last week's garbage.

The medical examiner and his assistant had the body on a gurney in a few minutes, but left the boy's face uncovered for his father.

"Did your guys find a note?" Josie asked, while she and Behan stood by the bed watching the assistant carefully remove the pillow-case and put it in a manila evidence envelope for his detectives.

"My guys said Ibarra searched everywhere but couldn't find one."

"It's not usually hidden, is it? Where was he looking?"

Behan shook his head. "Everywhere . . . closets, drawers, books, but I'm told he stopped before we got here." He glanced around the room before adding, "Actually, I don't know what he was looking for, but it sure as shit wasn't any suicide note."

"I'm guessing with such a short time to look he didn't find it, so maybe your guys should do a more thorough search. There's lots of places to hide stuff in here."

She knew they weren't going to recover any suicide note, but she suspected Behan, like her, hoped Mouse had stashed Hillary's diary when she stayed here and that might've been the real reason for Ibarra's search.

"They're going through the living room now. I told them to target anything that's handwritten . . . anything." Behan's voice trailed off and he was staring past her. She turned around as Goldman entered the room with Bright and Art Perry a few steps behind him.

Goldman hurried to the gurney, put both hands on the side railings, and hovered over the remains of his dead son. He touched the boy's face, kissed his shaved head, and cried uncontrollably before unleashing a heartbreaking wail that filled the room like an ambulance siren. Nobody moved immediately to comfort him. Finally, Bright put his arm around the man's shoulder and gently steered him away from the gurney. The medical examiner finished covering the body and rolled it out of the room and into the hallway. Goldman tried to follow, but Bright stopped him, whispering something in his ear that caused the councilman to stop crying. He visibly struggled to contain his emotion and managed to recover his composure.

Josie and Behan stood quietly in the corner near the piano keyboard. She didn't want to be there and would've paid a fortune to be invisible at that particular moment. As soon as Cory's body was out of sight, Goldman turned his grieving and rancor in her direction.

"You murdered my son," he said in a throaty whisper just inches from her face. He was disheveled and his eyes were red and swollen, his long grey hair sticky from perspiration.

Behan stepped between them, but Josie gently nudged her detective aside and stood close enough to Goldman to smell the stale odor of alcohol on his breath.

"You're wrong, sir. I'm sorry for your loss, but I think we both know that," she said, not retreating when he attempted to move toward her. She felt sorry for him, but he wasn't going to intimidate her. He was distraught, but a lot of what had gone wrong with Cory was his responsibility, not hers.

"You harassed him, forced him to do this," Goldman whined, stepping back a little and finally looking to Bright for support. "You shouldn't be allowed to keep this job. I promise in my son's memory to do everything I can to fire you and make certain you never have an opportunity to do this to another father," he shouted, spewing spit and pointing his finger at her. His face was flushed and wet with perspiration and his hands were shaking.

He marched out of the bedroom with Bright following, trying to calm him.

Now that the worst possible scenario was over, Josie still felt bad but started breathing normally again. Behan gave her a consoling look as she wiped her damp palms on her uniform pants. She realized she wasn't angry at the man's words, but felt sorry for him because Goldman was wrong. He couldn't blame her for his son's death. She was only a bystander watching an out-of-control train speeding full throttle toward disaster. There were only two people who could've kept that young man on track—himself and his father.

Bright returned to the bedroom a short time later without Goldman. He didn't speak to Josie or Behan, but walked around as if he were trying to compose himself or gather the courage to say something. He stood in front of one of the paintings depicting the remains of a dreary stone farmhouse surrounded by weeds and junk cars, a depressing scene.

"I'm certain Eli didn't mean all that," he said, staring at the picture. "He knew his son was troubled." He picked up a few books, replaced them on the window ledge and moved closer to Josie. "You know you bring this negative scrutiny on yourself," he said expressionless and waited for Josie to respond. She didn't so he raised his voice and continued, "If you'd done what I told you and kept his father in the interview room no one could've criticized you."

"Sorry sir, but that's the way Cory preferred do it," Josie said, interrupting Behan before he could speak. She didn't want her detective saying anything that might make the situation worse than it already was.

Bright snickered and shook his head. "I'm certain that's what the two of you made the boy believe. I might not have your street savvy, but I'm not stupid either." He held up his hand when Josie began to protest. "Don't," he said. "It doesn't matter. It's done, and I suspect no one's really going to make an issue of it when calmer heads prevail." The deputy chief was as poised as Josie had ever seen him. He seemed resigned to accept whatever might happen.

"Was this boy's death in any way connected to the Dennis homicide?" he asked as he examined the sheet music on the keyboard.

"We don't know, but my guess is it probably was," Behan said, exchanging a quick look with Josie that seemed to say, where is this going?

Art Perry came back into the bedroom and Bright quickly dispatched him to their parked vehicle to wait for him. The arrogant sergeant's dour expression signaled his displeasure at being dismissed.

"I have some concerns," Bright said, as soon as Perry was out of sight. He sat on the piano bench and seemed hesitant to speak at first, folding, then unfolding his hands on his lap. "This is difficult, especially now, but I have to caution you not to reject the possibility Eli Goldman had a relationship with that Dennis girl."

"What are you trying to say?" Behan asked, impatiently.

"I was privy to a conversation between Vince Milano and Eli. It's possible Eli did meet with that girl . . . on several occasions."

Bright stood and said, "I wanted to share that information with you in case you still had some questions about his involvement." He looked from Josie to Behan; neither of them spoke. "Apparently, my concern was justified, so now you know and I have nothing more to say on the matter, so don't ask." He walked out to the living room lingering only briefly to examine a few more of Cory's pictures before leaving.

All of them, including Bright, knew Eli Goldman's admission of a relationship with Hillary Dennis was incriminating. But even more revealing to Josie was the fact that Bright had failed to disclose his awareness of the relationship until this moment, and that he actually thought he could make his revelation and step away without any repercussions.

EIGHTEEN

By the time Behan drove Josie back to Hollywood station, it was early evening and the busiest time of the day for police work. The darkness drew urban demons from their hiding places. Drug dealers, prostitutes, and other denizens of the night congregated and prospered in the shadows. Quiet neighborhoods morphed into deadly family disputes or gang-related drive-by shootings.

Intending to avoid getting caught up in all that again, Josie promised herself she'd drive home without setting foot inside the station. The City of Los Angeles had squeezed more than its money's worth out of her today and she didn't think she had the energy or desire to contend with another department calamity until tomorrow. At home, the inevitable confrontation with David was looming, but not tonight if she could avoid it. A light dinner, bath and bed were all she could manage.

The urgent message on her Blackberry was from the assistant watch commander. She sat in her car with the engine running, deciding whether to drive out of the station parking lot and call him from the freeway, or do the right thing—what she was expected to do—and confront the latest crisis.

"I have no life," she mumbled, turning off the ignition and getting out of the car. She'd been a captain for six years, and since the day she'd pinned those damn silver bars on her uniform collar she'd seen the last of planning or organizing her time.

The assistant watch commander was in Levi's and a sweatshirt standing at the soda machine by the back door waiting for her. He

· 241 ·

looked eager to get out of the building, and apparently, the only thing he had left to do before his shift ended was locate her.

"Captain, Lieutenant Bailey's been looking for you," he said, picking up his workout bag as soon as he saw her. "She told me not to go home until I found you." The frustration in the sergeant's voice didn't surprise Josie. He was generally unflappable, but she knew Marge Bailey was capable of making the Pope edgy. "Lieutenant says you're supposed to ride with her tonight."

Josie closed her eyes. "Shit, I forgot. Where is she?"

"Upstairs, waiting. Did you need me for anything else?" he asked, making no secret of the fact he wanted to get out of there and as far away from Marge as he could.

"Go," she said, waving him away.

Cory's death and the confrontation with his father and Bright had pushed Fricke's meeting with his informant completely out of her head. She trudged up the stairs to the vice office where Marge was waiting with Fricke and Behan.

"So, you're in on this too," Josie said to Behan.

"Nope, but I did warn her you'd figure it out and be very unhappy."

Josie didn't say anything to Fricke, and he sat quietly, looking as if he'd just finished altar boy practice. He was smart enough not to get in the middle of an argument when his opinion couldn't affect the outcome.

"I don't know how the hell you people figured you could get away with this. You think Harry Walsh wouldn't notice all those hype arrests coming in without Fricke's name anywhere on the reports?"

"I warned him to slow down," Marge said, innocently, interrupting Josie's tirade, then added quickly, "Boss, you wanted Mouse. Donnie found her, so let's go snatch the little fucker before she's in the wind again."

"Don't look so surprised," Behan said, shrugging. "She's your monster; you created her."

"I'll take credit for a lot of things, but not those two," Josie said, pointing at Fricke and Marge, "They're completely self-made."

When Josie calmed down and gave him permission to speak, Fricke recounted how he had arrested a hype that knew Mouse and was willing to show him where she stayed to keep out of jail.

"The snitch is scared shitless Mouse is gonna find out she talked to us," Fricke said. "So she'll take us there, point out the pad and split."

"Fine," Josie said, and asked, "Where's your partner?" She finally realized Fricke was without his shadow.

"Frankie, he don't wanna break curfew," Fricke said. "You told him to stay home and he ain't interested in my crazy ideas."

"He knew you'd do it anyway," Josie said. Frank Butler had done the right thing, but Josie figured he wasn't the kind of guy who'd let his partner risk something like this alone.

"Couldn't say," Fricke said, looking at Marge.

"Who gives a fuck," Marge said.

Josie did. It always bothered her when people acted out of character. Butler was more cautious than Fricke, but she was certain Marge had kept him away to protect him from possible fallout.

They loaded up in Marge's car since it looked the least like a police vehicle. Fricke met with the snitch at Hollywood and Vine at the bottom steps of the Metro station and escorted her back to the car.

Corky appeared to be in her forties, but an addict's lifestyle always made it difficult to estimate age. Her complexion was scarred by acne or lesions caused by injecting methamphetamine or some other stimulant. She wore dark glasses, a baseball cap and baggie sweater, but Josie could see both arms were covered by needle tracks and meth sores. As soon as Corky was in the backseat, the distinct odor of sweat and dirty clothes contaminated the air so badly Josie had to open the window.

At Corky's direction, Marge drove within a block of a rundown duplex on La Mirada just south of Fountain Avenue. The area was populated by poor, mostly illegal, immigrants and the MS street gang. Freshly painted patches of several different colors covered gang graffiti and recent tagging on fences and the walls of most houses. Property owners were fighting a losing battle to regain control of their neighborhood. Corky, Behan and Fricke walked to the rear of the back bungalow and out of Josie's sight. When they returned to the car, Behan told them Corky had pointed out a small shed behind the rear house. The informant stood behind Marge's car while they talked, nervously shuffling her feet and scratching at her arms. Finally, she tugged at Fricke's sleeve and begged him to let her go before Mouse or anyone else saw her with the police.

Fricke put a folded twenty-dollar bill in her sweater pocket and said, "Don't let me catch you buying your shit in Hollywood."

Corky clutched her sweater and hurried away, cutting through the side yard of one of the houses to put as much distance as fast as she could between herself and the police car.

"Does it look like Mouse's in there?" Josie asked.

"She's a junkie. If she copped tonight like Corky says and shot up, she's there," Fricke said, starting to walk back toward the shed.

"Hey," Josie said and he stopped. "Get back here and stay behind us. You make sure he does," she said, pointing at Marge. "Let's at least try not to get all of us fired."

Josie took the lead with Behan. It was a familiar scenario. They'd worked well together as detectives and she always felt comfortable with him. When they got closer, he signaled he was going around to the back. There was a small window on the side of the shed where Josie could see an electrical cord had been pulled through a tear in the screen. The other end of the cord was extended into a window of the main house. The screen and window were filthy, but she could make out most of the interior of the shed. A small blond woman who appeared to be Mouse was lying on a camping cot facing away from the window, with her hype kit on a makeshift table constructed from an old crate and a piece of plywood. The electrical cord was plugged into a mechanic's lamp hanging on the wall. The lamp was the only source of illumination in the shed, but it was enough light for what they had to do. The space was tight, maybe ten square feet, with junk cluttering the floor and stacked against the corrugated walls.

Josie tiptoed to the front door and Marge moved to the other side with Fricke hovering over her shoulder. Behan jogged back around to the front and mouthed the words, "No exit." She motioned for him to come closer and indicated she would try the door. If it didn't open, he should kick it in. There was a lock, but it was flimsy and she doubted it could be secured from the inside. She pushed down on the handle, and it opened. Josie stepped inside, drew her gun and shouted, "Police, keep your hands where I can see them."

The doorway was narrow, but Behan was in right behind her. Mouse sat up with a drowsy groan and slowly raised her hands, barely able to keep them steady above her shoulders. Her eyelids were droopy and she seemed well under the influence of her favorite opiate. She glanced over at her kit; the bloody needle and a bent spoon containing a tiny piece of damp cotton had been left next to the still-smoldering remains of a candle. The leather strap she'd used to tie off the vein in her arm lay on her lap.

Behan pulled her off the cot and made her sit on one of the larger boxes.

"How you doing, Sara Jean?" Fricke asked, using Mouse's real name as he dragged another crate closer so he could sit facing her. He lifted her left arm, palm up, and rested it on his knee. She was limp and compliant. "Don't even need my light for this one," he said, pointing at an abscess on her forearm. Josie leaned over and could see that the puncture wound at the injection site was raised slightly on the ugly red boil, and was still oozing pinkish fluid. Mouse's veins had collapsed from frequent injections, leaving long purplish scars from her wrist to her elbow. She was a classic hype—speaking slowly, scratching her face and hands, and her pupils were half the size of everyone else's in the dimly lit shed. Fricke chatted with her as he continued to examine her arms, hands, neck, and legs. The little woman had deteriorated badly since the last time Josie had seen her. Her bleached hair was tangled and dried out with her natural dark brown roots extending four inches from her scalp. Dirt was caked under her chewed brittle-looking nails.

"You're going to jail, Sara Jean," Fricke said, trying to rouse her from the heroin euphoria. When that didn't get a reaction, he added, "Not that nice clean country club the sheriff's got . . . I'm gonna book you in our city jail where we ain't got all those nice drugs that'll keep you from throwing up and shitting all over yourself when the junk stops working."

Her face-scratching accelerated and Mouse fidgeted on the box, fought the drug's effects and tried to stay conscious and alert.

"I can do something for you," she said in a hoarse whisper.

"I don't think so. We got enough junk left in that bag to file possession . . . we got your works," Fricke said, gesturing toward the table with the needle and spoon. "It'd have to be something pretty fucking fantastic."

"Wh . . . what d'you want," she stuttered, looking around at Josie, seeming confused and slowly shaking her head. But even in her stupor, Mouse knew which of them was in charge and controlled her fate.

"Hillary's book, the one you took from her mother's house," Josie said.

Mouse wrapped her arms around her body as if she felt a sudden chill. Her head nodded forward, but she jerked it up again fighting to stay awake. The heroin had attacked her central nervous system and taken control of her body, but her survival instincts were strong and she fought to find a way to stay out of jail.

"What book?" she mumbled.

"I'm not in the mood for sixty questions. Give it to me now or I'll have him take you to jail."

"Cory's got it," she said, slurring her words.

"Cory's dead."

Somewhere in the fog blanketing her mind Mouse seemed to understand. She slumped forward, rested her elbows on her knees and sighed.

"Did they kill him?" she whispered.

"Did who kill him?" Behan asked.

"You know . . ." Her voice trailed off as her eyes closed.

"Hey!" Fricke shouted, and her eyes opened again. "Did who kill him?" he repeated.

"You know," she said. "Big fucked-up dude."

"He wants the book. Give it to us; we'll protect you," Josie said, attempting another tactic.

Mouse bit the corner of her lip and grimaced. "I'm not scared of that bald motherfucker."

"Good for you; where's the fucking book so we can get the hell outta this fucking shithole?" Marge demanded, standing over her.

Mouse turned to Josie for support, but looked despondent when it was clear she wasn't going to get any.

The little woman leaned too far forward attempting to stand, and would've fallen on her face if Fricke and Behan hadn't grabbed her. They set her back on the crate.

"Just tell us. We'll get it," Josie said. She was getting tired of dealing with the heroin stupor.

Mouse pointed to her bed. "The pillow," she mumbled.

The pillow was made of worn filthy muslin with no pillowcase. Undaunted by the high probability of lice colonies, Fricke sliced the material with his pocket knife and tried to shake the contents loose. He pulled out a couple of handfuls of smelly deteriorating foam, and a black book fell onto the cot along with several used syringes and a dozen or more empty balloons that might contain just enough heroin residue for those days Mouse couldn't come up with the cash for a dime bag.

Josie took the book, thumbed through the pages crammed with names, home and email addresses, and phone numbers. Several scraps of paper and business cards were stuffed between the pages, with information hastily jotted on the backs of envelopes or torn magazine pages. Hillary Dennis's name was embossed on the cover, with her email address and cell phone number on the inside. Their search was over.

It wasn't difficult to pack up the drug evidence, so Fricke did most of it, and had Mouse handcuffed and in the backseat of the car in less than twenty minutes. He and Behan sat with Mouse between them while Marge drove, and Josie in the passenger seat went through the pages of the book using the small flashlight Fricke kept in his jacket pocket. She'd looked at most of the business cards, when she recognized the design on one of them, and had a difficult time not swearing out loud. It was Jake's. She held onto it, but kept turning over the other cards and loose pieces of paper until she'd examined every one of them. The card was the only thing that referred to her husband; and after a cursory search, she couldn't find any calendar dates or diary entries with David's name or personal information either. She checked all the places they might've been listed in the directory section but, again, didn't find anything related to her son or husband. Josie rubbed the back of her neck and pretended to stretch those muscles, while looking around to see if anyone was watching her. Everyone seemed to be concentrating on the road or the passing scenery, so she quickly slipped the card into her pants pocket.

She closed the book and sat back. She wasn't sorry about taking the card. She needed time to think and find out why Hillary had it. Jake might've screwed up, but if she could help it he wasn't going to take their whole family down. No one spoke on the ride back to Hollywood station, which suited her fine. Mouse appeared to be sleeping, but all of them knew hypes on the nod heard and remembered everything, so they weren't about to discuss the case or anything important until she was booked and out of earshot.

Aside from Jake's card, Josie also found both father and son Goldman names had been entered in the book, as well as Bright's; however, the contact information was Bright's work number and email address. She knew that could be explained away. Hillary had written down the names of two more city councilmen that Josie recognized, with their cell phone numbers and email addresses.

Josie decided they should go to her office and take as long as it took to thoroughly examine the book. Unfortunately, she'd already made one major mistake, two if she was honest with herself about confiscating Jake's business card. Seems she might've been too hasty confiding in Harry Walsh. The city attorney's name and contact information were on the last page of the book.

NINETEEN

As soon as they returned to the station, Josie admitted to Behan and Marge she'd not only talked to Harry Walsh but had given him most of the investigation. It was embarrassing and stupid because she knew better than to trust anybody in city government. Jake's business card was another matter. She intended to hold onto it, knowing it was wrong, but at the moment necessary to protect her family. She was grateful none of Jake's personal information had been written in the journal, which turned out to be more of an address book and calendar than a diary.

In the weeks before her death, Hillary had ceased making daily entries on the calendar. Before that, she'd noted work schedules and social activities. Her last filming finished two months before she was killed. She had names, sometimes two or three names, scheduled every day up to four days before the party at the Hollywood house.

"So, she stopped her entries about the same time Faldi quit protecting her," Behan said.

They had the journal on Josie's office table and the three of them were examining the contents. Josie had sent Fricke home after he finished the paperwork on Mouse's arrest and she ordered him to stay there.

"It would've been helpful if she used a few real names," Josie said. Hillary had been careful to schedule her dates with descriptions such as Blue Eyes, Baldy, Lefty, or Big Dude rather than their true identities. "Wonder how they contacted her."

"We pulled all her phone records . . . minimal activity," Behan said and added, "We're checking her computer and text messages, but that's not giving us much either."

"You're the expert," Josie said to Marge. "How'd she do it?"

"Johns probably made arrangements with somebody else who passed the info on to her . . . harder to trace . . . like an ATM pimp," Marge said, yawning. "I'm fucking beat. Let's do this tomorrow."

The energy level was nearly depleted, so everyone agreed to book the journal as evidence in both homicide investigations and finish examining the contents in the morning. Marge assured them there was always a method to connect the nicknames to real people, but she needed sleep before she'd attempt it. By the time Josie got into her car, both Marge and Behan had gone. She sat there with the engine idling and dialed Jake's cell phone number. Waiting until she got home wasn't an option.

It rang several times before he finally answered. His voice was hoarse and he sounded confused, not quite awake. She persisted in asking if he was fully conscious until she was satisfied he could understand.

"Do you know what time it is?" he asked, and when he could focus on the clock said, "It's four A.M."

"I need to talk to you."

"I'll call you in the morning . . . later in the morning."

"No, now."

"Why is everything always a crisis with you, woman?"

"I'm not gonna discuss this on the phone, so tell me where you are or come to the house. I can be home in twenty minutes."

He groaned and complained he might as well get up because he probably couldn't go back to sleep now anyway. He promised to be in Pasadena in an hour, but insisted because she'd ruined a good night's sleep and most likely his ability to work all day, she'd better have coffee and something to eat when he got there.

By the time Josie pulled into the driveway, sunlight was filtering over the San Gabriel foothills, splashing orange and grey shades of dawn over her house. She loved the valley on the rare mornings when she could actually see those mountains.

The Jeep Wrangler was parked in the driveway with dew covering the windows and hood. "Damn," she said as soon as she spotted it. Her son must've spent the night again, but she wasn't in the mood to deal with him right now. A couple of old newspapers were thrown up on the front porch. She kicked them out of the way to open the door.

The house was cold and smelled like a musty spare room desperately needing to be aired out. The place wasn't really getting lived in like a home these days. Her family had fractured, and although they occasionally spent time passing each other on the way in or out, they didn't belong there anymore. She turned on all the lights, set the thermostat higher and opened the drapes.

Dirty dishes had been left in the sink, empty takeout containers in the garbage. David had eaten and gone to bed, and as usual expected her to clean up his mess. Josie filled the dishwasher, made coffee and started chopping onions for omelettes. She usually added mushrooms and avocados, but she hadn't been to the market in a couple of weeks so the food supply was running low. The half loaf of bread had transformed into a Petri dish experiment so she unfroze a batch of biscuits, grated parmesan cheese into the omelette and put bacon on the grill.

By the time Jake arrived, the odor of sizzling bacon filled all the rooms. The kitchen was warm and cozy. He hadn't bothered to shave and wore his old jeans, tennis shoes, and a black pullover sweater Josie had given him ten years ago. His salt and pepper hair was greying more around the temples these days, but he'd lost a few pounds and despite her irritation with him, she noticed he looked handsome and better than she'd seen him in a long time.

"You look terrible," were his first words to her as he filled his coffee mug and took a piece of bacon from the greasy paper towel on the counter.

She put two plates with the omelettes, a bowl of biscuits, and the rest of the bacon on the breakfast table.

"Sit down," she ordered, and realized the frenzied cooking had been pent-up anger. First David and now Jake—were they actually scheming to ruin her career and reputation or did their asinine bumbling just come naturally?

Jake smiled faintly and gave her a sloppy salute. "Yes, ma'am," he said. "Anything you say."

"Offhand I'd say you're a moron."

He stopped smiling and said, "Okay that's a start. Did you get me out of bed in the middle of the night because you needed somebody to yell at? It's a nice breakfast but . . ."

"What's your business card doing in Hillary Dennis's date book?"

Jake shook his head, but his expression didn't change. "I don't know," he said with his mouth full of biscuit.

Josie put the card on the table in front of him. When she turned it over, there were numbers written in ink. "Looks like your private business number to me, with some kind of extension."

"You try calling the number?"

"It's disconnected."

He took a long drink of coffee, wiped his hands on his sweater and picked up the card, examining the numbers.

"Hillary Dennis had this?" he asked, looking puzzled.

"Why is your card in a dead teenage prostitute's date book?"

Jake sat back and repeatedly tapped the card on the table. He seemed to be struggling to remember something, until he glanced up and saw her expression. The insinuation in her words apparently penetrated his thought process, and he sighed.

"Give me some credit, honey. I've got higher standards than a kiddie movie star," he said, but probably read in her face she didn't believe him and slowly emphasized each word, "I did not give Hillary Dennis the damn card." He pointed at the written numbers. "You're right these first ten digits are a phone number. It was the safe line for the D.A.'s witness protection program. That particular program doesn't exist anymore, that's why it's disconnected. These last three digits are a code we used. It was the only way to identify the person. The card belonged to somebody, but not Hillary Dennis."

"Why not?"

"The program was phased out nine or ten years ago. She would've been . . . what, about six years old?"

"Is there a way to identify the person from that code?"

"We didn't have that many in the program; some stayed longer than others, but it was quite a while ago. All the files might've been destroyed by now or transferred to the feds when they took it over."

"Is there a way to ID the person who belonged to this number?" she repeated.

"Can I finish my breakfast first?"

"Eat faster," she said, relaxing a little. This might actually turn out to be a good thing. The tough part would be explaining to Behan why she "borrowed" the card without telling him. There wasn't much time to contemplate how that conversation might go because a disheveled David wearing pajama bottoms and a faded, stretched-out UCLA t-shirt quietly shuffled into the kitchen and zeroed in on the coffeepot.

Josie's stomach tightened. Her great breakfast instantly turned to indigestion at the thought of the inevitable confrontation. She and Jake sat at the table and watched him pour his coffee, drag his bare feet to the refrigerator and add cream to the mug, not speaking or acknowledging them in any way.

"You hungry?" she asked. She hated mimes, especially in her kitchen.

"No," he said, curtly.

The immediate smartass remark that came to Josie's mind was, "There's a miracle," but she caught herself.

"Is there something I should know?" Jake asked, glancing from Josie to David and sensing the tension. He'd lived through enough wife-son skirmishes to know when a battle was imminent.

"She didn't tell you?" David asked, not able to hold the coffee mug steady in his shaky hand. He was on edge and primed for this argument.

"There was no reason to tell him." Josie knew she was tense from lack of sleep, and defensive. It wouldn't take much to push her to the point of showing her son a side of herself she usually reserved for the job. He wouldn't like it. "Cory Goldman killed himself after Red Behan and I interviewed him."

"Oh," Jake said and seemed relieved, as if he were expecting something much worse and much closer to home. "Can't say I'm that surprised, David. Cory had . . . issues."

"But you'd agree badgering a . . . a fragile guy like him wouldn't be a decent thing to do . . . maybe even cruel."

"Give me a break," Josie said, immediately ignoring her vow not to be sarcastic. "Nobody badgered him, and he's the one who threw his father and lawyer out of the room." David started to say something, but she interrupted. "I don't know what this guy was to you, but I do know he was so seriously messed up, this would've happened someday even if he'd never met me."

"He tried suicide at least three times," Jake said.

David shook his head and corrected him. "No, once . . . and that was just to get his father's attention. He wasn't really trying to kill himself. Everybody knows that."

"Eli told me his son attempted suicide twice while he was in high school and once after he graduated . . . again when he studied in Italy. They pumped his stomach and had to put him in a mental facility a few years ago after he swallowed a whole bottle of sleeping pills. I used to play tennis with Eli Goldman every week. I'm positive that's what he told me," Jake said, shrugging at Josie.

"It's such a waste," David moaned, sitting at the table. "I can't believe he's dead."

Josie was quiet. She knew the wrong word now would set off another flurry of recriminations. The young man's death was sad, but she wouldn't accept blame just to make her son feel better.

David was quiet for several seconds, peering into the mug as if he were praying or expecting some message to suddenly appear in the coffee grinds. "Sorry, Mom," he mumbled without looking at her.

There should've been something she could say to make him feel better but nothing came to mind, mostly because it had become increasingly difficult to ignore the fact that not only Cory, but Hillary and Misty might've been a consequential part of his life.

"How well did you really know Hillary Dennis?" she asked, hoping that, caught up in the moment, he might let his guard down and finally tell her the truth.

He looked up but didn't speak. His expression said it all—I'm distraught and you're interrogating me.

"Honey, he's upset. Do this later," Jake said, reaching over and touching David's arm.

Disgusted, she pushed away from the table. "I'm tired. I gotta get some sleep. Clean up when you're done," she said, but only got as far as the kitchen door before returning to the table and confronting them.

"I'm done. If either of you were involved with Hillary or her whoring business, tell me now or you're on your own and don't expect me to protect you anymore. And you," she said pointing at Jake, "if you really wanna help, stop treating him like a baby."

She turned and walked away from the silence permeating the room. Suddenly, fatigue had sapped all her energy and resolve. The investigation didn't matter. If she couldn't bring order or sanity to her own house, what difference did the rest of it make?

Several bottles of wine were sitting on the dining room credenza. Without thinking or looking, Josie snatched one on her way to the stairs. Instead of going up to her bedroom, she stopped at the second floor den where she found a corkscrew on the small wet bar and opened the bottle. The cabinet above the sink had all their best glassware, so she took one of the biggest Waterford goblets and filled it with the expensive Pinot Noir she'd been saving for a special occasion. What the hell, she thought. This is special. It's the day my family officially disintegrated.

Early morning sunlight made the room unbearably bright and warm. She closed the shades, kicked off her boots, and lay on the couch with her glass and the bottle resting on her stomach. Josie intended to drink until her consciousness drowned in alcohol and she passed out. When she woke up—with any luck—the two most important and exasperating people in her life would be out of the house and she could think clearly again.

The first glassful was gone, but she lay on the couch staring at the clock on the wall and understood why people took drugs. Normally, she'd fall asleep as soon as her head touched the pillow, but for the first time in her life she couldn't rationalize or drink enough to shut down her brain.

She heard a light tapping on the open door and sat up, filled the glass again before cocking her head just enough to see David standing sheepishly outside the room, staring at his bare feet. His long hair was uncombed. When he was a boy, he'd developed the habit of twisting the ends of his hair when he was stressed. He started doing that after she made him stop biting his nails. Standing out there like that, he almost looked like her little boy again . . . a very tall, skinny version of her little boy.

"Can we talk?" he asked.

"I'm tired."

He sat on the couch beside Josie, but she wouldn't look at him. Her son's simplicity was disarming and he had a way of making her forget how angry she was with him. This time she didn't want to forget. She needed to hold onto that anger until there weren't any more secrets.

"Cory was like a little brother to me," he said, softly. "He didn't have anyone else, so I protected him."

"From what?"

"Can I have some of that?" he said, nodding at the bottle and getting up for a glass.

"Protected him from what?" she repeated, pouring a little wine in his glass.

"Himself mostly."

She felt a piercing pain building between her eyes. "No more riddles . . . if you're gonna tell me something do it, or let me get some sleep so I can go back to work."

David exhaled and sat back, took a sip of wine. "You really don't give an inch, do you? You look and talk like other mothers, but you've got the heart of a gunnery sergeant."

He'd probably intended that description to be insulting, but Josie had been called worse, and she thoroughly admired gunnery sergeants a lot more than most mothers. Nevertheless, she wasn't about to let the remark pass without countering with a dose of reality.

"Giving birth to you was the most excruciatingly painful thing I've ever done in my life, but when the nurse put you in my arms, when I smelled your hair, touched your tiny fingers, I instantly forgot the torture of labor and loved you completely. I vowed at that moment nothing would ever hurt you, and even now when I think you've been harmed in any way, it makes me angry and physically sick."

"Look, I didn't mean . . ." David said contritely, trying to interrupt her, but she wouldn't allow him to apologize. That wasn't what she wanted.

"When you were a child I treated you like one, but I can't live your life for you. You've got to skin your knees and get your heart broken. I hate it, but it's supposed to make you a better man, so stop bullshitting me and tell me what's going on before this gets to the point where I can't keep you out of it anymore."

David groaned as if he were in pain and pulled at strands of his hair. She knew he had a flair for the melodramatic so she waited.

Finally he sighed and blurted out, "Cory told me Hillary was whoring, doing drugs for years. Word got out about her heroin habit so no legitimate studio would hire her after her second or third movie . . . all her other films were soft porn crap. Cory told me his dad was her regular customer. One day she needs money and threatens to tell the media about their sex life unless he gives her a lot of cash. He refused, and a week later she's dead."

"Did Cory think his father killed her?"

"It's weird. Cory always swore he hated his father, but he was terrified when he thought something bad might happen to him."

Josie got up and stretched. She was so tired her joints were beginning to ache. "Do you know if either Goldman killed her?" she asked.

"No, I don't think so. Cory was frantic that his dad might've done it and Mr. Goldman, he asked me if I thought Cory could've done it. Misty Skylar was the only one I knew who was really pissed-off at Hillary," David said.

"Her agent, why?"

"Cory said he thought Hillary got so good at the blackmailing business she didn't need Misty anymore because they'd had a hellacious falling-out."

Josie rubbed her temples in an attempt to thwart the growing headache. "Why the hell did you get mixed up with these people?"

"I didn't. I just tried to help my friend. He told me stuff in confidence. He's dead now, so I figured it's okay to talk about it."

She put her glass on the floor and held her head with both hands. "Did he tell you who he thought killed Hillary?" she mumbled, not expecting an answer.

"He said it must've been the cop."

Josie sat up and instantly forgot the pain. "Which cop?"

"He told me Hillary's blackmail partner and lover was a cop, and they were setting up some huge score. He figured maybe they had an argument over the money, or the cop got pissed about all the guys she slept with and shot her."

For another hour, Josie scraped every bit of information she could from her son's memory. She was grateful he didn't know more, but a little disappointed too. He did know Hillary kept the journal with names, times and places, and that she got money from her more influential clients by promising not to give the media a full account of their sexual exploits—provided they coughed up enough cash. Cory had agreed to be her "gofer" to protect his father, but it was too tempting and she went after the councilman anyway.

When they finished, Josie was reasonably satisfied David was on the fringe of these people's lives, but it wasn't in her nature to wipe away all suspicion, and there was one question that still needed to be asked.

"Was your dad involved in any of this?"

David was mid-swallow and coughed, nearly choking on the wine.

"Dad?" he asked, incredulously. "Not hardly, he tried to help me find work and felt sorry for Cory . . . gave him a few bucks because he could see the guy was my friend and I worried about him."

"Your father never had any contact with Hillary?"

"Dad's not like you. He doesn't judge people. Everything's always so . . . tense with you. It's like you can't relax and just let people be themselves."

"Did your dad have contact with Hillary Dennis?" She didn't want psychoanalysis; she needed an answer before her head exploded.

"No . . . I don't think so," he said, raising his voice just enough to let her know he hadn't been intimidated.

"My head's killing me. I really need to get some sleep."

David stood and put his glass on the leather ottoman in front of the couch. "That job's gonna give you a stroke."

She rolled over onto her stomach and lay with her forehead pressed hard against the cushion. No, she thought, the job is fine. You and your father are gonna give me a stroke. After a few seconds, the room was quiet so she figured he'd gone. Josie loved her son, but it bothered her that his take on the world and hers were so different. For example, she'd never found naïveté an attractive or trustworthy quality in a man.

It was after two P.M. when Josie opened her eyes again. Apparently the headache was from lack of sleep because it had disappeared. She was still on her stomach, but her neck was stiff from tucking her head into the arm of the couch. She made two mental notes to herself. First, don't fall asleep on the couch in the den again, and second, don't drink wine for breakfast.

A shower and a pot of coffee later, she was eager to get back to Hollywood station. Jake had taped a note to the coffeepot saying he would call her as soon as he was able to link the number on the back of his business card to the subject of the witness protection program. He signed it, "Love, Jake," so apparently she hadn't pissed him off more than usual and he was still willing to help. There was no sign of David and for a lot of reasons she was relieved.

W<small>HEN</small> J<small>OSIE</small> arrived at Hollywood station, she immediately went to detectives where she found Behan in one of the interview rooms with Hillary's journal. He had piles of pages torn from a yellow legal pad full of notes he'd made that morning. He had arrived a few hours before her and had a chance to examine most of the young woman's entries and the loose paperwork. Josie explained that she'd taken Jake's business card to ask him about the number on the back, and told Behan what her husband had said and how he was looking for the person to match the witness number.

"Sorry, I should've told you," she said, when she finished the explanation.

Behan was quiet for a few seconds, taking too long to examine a page of the journal. Finally, he looked up expressionless and asked, "Would we be having this conversation if that had been Jake's personal number?"

"What do you think?" she countered stone-faced, staring into those bloodshot blue eyes.

He didn't answer, but they both knew if the card incriminated Jake, it had about as much chance of survival as he had of becoming chief of police.

Josie left him to sift through the journal, attempting to identify Hillary's customers and focus on anyone who might've had a motive to kill the young woman. She had a feeling the list would be a long one.

———

D<small>AY-TO-DAY</small> business in the station had been kept manageable by the lieutenant watch commanders. Josie put Behan in charge of detectives until the incoming lieutenant transferred. Ibarra had departed before his Wilshire assignment began, saying he needed time to get some personal matters in order before starting the new job. The fact that detectives ran smoothly without him wasn't a revelation to Josie.

She had nearly finished reviewing her calendar for the upcoming week when Jake called. He had accessed the warehoused information on the witness protection program, but wouldn't reveal how he'd managed to do it. She knew he lost his security clearance when he resigned from the district attorney's office a few weeks ago, but somehow he located and identified code number 700. The subject's real name when she lived in New York was Brenda Manuci. The new identity she'd chosen before being relocated in Los Angeles more than a decade ago was Misty Skylar.

TWENTY

In less than an hour, Jake was sitting in Josie's office with her and Behan going over the notes he'd copied from the district attorney's witness protection file. She couldn't explain how or why it happened, but her husband was exhibiting real enthusiasm for catching bad guys again.

"Luckily, they had scanned all the dead files and as usual, my old boss was out of his office sticking his pretty face in front of a news camera," Jake said smugly.

"Don't you need some special kind of password to get into those files?" Behan asked.

"The guy's a computer dummy. I set up his access code before I quit and figured he'd never change it. Of course, he didn't. Mediocrity is so predictable."

"Why'd they even let you in the building without ID?" Josie asked, still not believing this was her husband talking. What happened to that 'I'm sick of living off other people's misery' guy?

"I used my revoked identification card and nobody bothered to check it, just waved me through . . . so much for beefed-up security."

Jake told them he'd managed to scribble two pages of notes before he saw his former boss in the hall security camera returning to his office. He shut down the program and sat in the visitor's chair pretending he'd been waiting to say hello. They chatted for twenty minutes, then Jake excused himself.

"I'm sure the moron is still wondering why I came to visit, since I'd made it abundantly clear I thought he was an ivy-league buffoon when I worked for him."

Then he explained how the D.A.'s file had meticulously laid out the story of Misty Skylar aka Brenda Manuci's former life in upstate New York.

"Brenda was a second cousin of one of the least-known organized crime family bosses in the state," Jake said. Josie wouldn't have recognized the name, but she'd seen it in Marge's research on Vince Milano and knew the club owner had been associated with the Manuci family when he lived on the east coast.

"She turned federal witness on a low-level member of the family who was collecting rent from drug dealers for the privilege of occupying prime street corners in a sleazier section of downtown Rochester. She owed the guy a ton of money and wanted him out of the way, so she agreed to testify against him in exchange for immunity and a promise from the feds for a continuous flow of more cash than she'd seen in her entire life."

"She had to know the family would never let her get away with that," Behan said.

"Brenda was young and stupid and in her drugged-out little brain didn't really think her plan through," Jake said. "The guy was a lowlife but still family. The Manucis didn't take kindly to her dispatching a blood relative off to federal prison."

"Is that why they moved her out of New York?" Josie asked.

"When somebody tried to run her over with a stolen delivery van, the feds decided to move her to Southern California and change her name."

"So how did Hillary get your business card and how did she figure out Misty was really Brenda Manuci?" Josie asked.

Behan said, "If Hillary knew Misty had something that important to hide, her agent would become a perfect mark for blackmail."

"But how would Hillary know? Unless Misty made a mistake and told her." Josie said.

"That's what I'm thinking," Jake said. "But it gets better. Misty might've blabbed about working for the feds, but I know how Hillary got the whole story. Somehow she got my card with the D.A. file number and somebody figured out what it was. Any inquiries into that system are documented and there's only been one inquiry other than mine, and you'll never guess who that was."

"This isn't *Jeopardy*. Who the fuck was it?" Behan said.

"Eric Bright."

"Our deputy chief?"

"Yep, a month ago, he was allowed access for an alleged LAPD investigation."

"Him personally or somebody from his office?" Josie asked.

"Didn't say, but whoever it was probably gave that information to Hillary and she's in extortion heaven."

"If Hillary threatened to expose her to the Manucis, Misty had both motive and opportunity; she was at the party and had plenty of time to remove gunshot residue or any other evidence before we ever got to her," Behan said.

"Contact the D.A. and get any surveillance tapes or witnesses they might have for the day that information was accessed." Josie told Behan. "If it was Bright, he's got some serious explaining to do," she said.

"Who else would it be?" Jake asked.

"I don't know, but we've got no room for error on this one. We'll wait for confirmation." She wanted to drag the deputy chief into the station too, but knew she had to be right. Behan gave her a disapproving glance, but it wasn't his neck on the chopping block if they were wrong. "In the meantime, go back to Little Joe and Mouse. If Misty shot Hillary, somebody gave her that stolen gun. It was taken from the Palms and those two know everything that happens in that shithole."

Behan picked up his notes and left without another word. She knew he was upset. He didn't like her running his investigation and normally she'd agree with him, but this wasn't just another case. The fallout from this one could impact the entire city government. Chain of command had been compromised; division of labor was irrelevant until all their suspicions were tracked down and disposed of or confirmed. Red's a big boy, she thought. He'll get over it.

When they were alone, she waited while Jake collected his notes and stacked them on her desk. "You did a good job," she said, when he finished. "Maybe you should've been a detective."

"No thanks, sleuthing is way too nerve-wracking for me, but I can see why you like it so much; it's exciting." He looked at her and smiled. "You're quite a woman to do this stuff every day."

She could feel herself blushing and the only response she managed was, "Thanks." It mattered that he was proud of her.

"Guess I'll go home and get some sleep," Jake said.

"New home or old home?"

"The apartment, not really home but probably best for the time being. You don't need any more complications in your life."

"I'm a pedigreed jumper; one more hurdle's not a problem."

"Try keeping both feet on the ground for this one, honey. If it goes sideways, I'm a pretty good lawyer, call me," he said, kissing her as if nothing in their lives had ever changed; and then added on his way out of the office, "Just ask Donnie Fricke. He's about to get his complaint cleared as unfounded."

She wanted to know how he'd done that, but by the time what he said registered, he was out the door and strolling through the lobby. She always hoped the combined credibility of Mouse and Little Joe with no corroborating evidence wouldn't be enough to sustain allegations against Fricke or any other cop for that matter. Although Fricke didn't have a clean rap sheet, Butler's work history and reputation were impeccable and this time reason prevailed. Whoever got the two snitches to make the false charges had to know they wouldn't stick, but Josie suspected the allegations were a diversion to get Fricke off the street and keep her and the Hollywood detectives distracted.

If what Jake said about clearing the complaint was true, Fricke and his partner could be back on the street in a couple of days. She was tempted to call him tonight, but thought better of it. Having her most productive cops working again would be great, but it might be best for him if this case got wrapped up before he returned. Like most hard-charging cops he was an easy target, and she really didn't want him in the middle of this mess again.

By the time Jake left, it was after seven P.M. Josie was hungry and starting to fade. She hadn't had the opportunity or inclination to change her clothes and was still wearing jeans, boots, and a pullover sweater. The mirror in her wardrobe was in a dimly lit corner of the room and when she checked out the state of her hair, she discovered the appearance of tiny crow's feet at the corners of her tired-looking eyes. She had to get some sleep. There wasn't any reason for her to hang around tonight, but she could sense the case coming together and the adrenaline rush was making her antsy. Instinctively, she wanted to do what Behan was doing, be a detective again and have her hands deep into the mix, but that wasn't her job anymore. The smart thing would be to go home, get some rest and start again early the next morning.

Instead, she locked the wardrobe and went upstairs.

Marge was alone in her office, had her head down on the desk, and her face buried in her arms. Josie watched for a few seconds wondering if she was asleep.

"I'm not dead," Marge mumbled without looking up.

"Good," Josie said. "I'm already down two lieutenants."

She lifted her head just enough to peek over her arm and locate Josie standing in the middle of the room. Slowly, reluctantly she sat up and asked, "What's up, boss?"

"Nothing . . . wanna go across the street?"

"Stupid question," Marge said. She picked up the police radio lying near her arm as she pulled on her jacket.

"You okay?" Josie asked, as soon as they had settled in at the table closest to the bar. Marge was always the prettiest girl in any room, but tonight she looked the way Josie felt, weary and old. Her hair had been hastily pinned back, and makeup that might've looked good that morning needed some serious touching up.

"No."

"You gonna tell me about it?"

"Fuck, no."

"Does it have anything to do with Red?"

"No, it has everything to do with Red. That's why I'm not telling you."

"Is he leaving Miss Vicky for you?" Josie asked. She knew she was being annoying, but wanted to know.

Marge didn't answer but glared at Josie in an attempt to make her boss back down. Josie didn't blink. Scarier people than Marge had tried to bully her without any success. She'd come in here just wanting to eat, but wasn't leaving now until Marge spilled the whole story. Behan and Marge brought their personal problems into her police station and that made their relationship her business.

The menus were on the table. Marge picked one up and started reading, set it down again and looked at Josie. Her eyes were bloodshot and filled with tears, but she wouldn't cry. She took a napkin and held it over her eyes with both hands. Her lips were pressed tight as she fought her emotions. After a few minutes, she was able to sit back and take a deep breath.

"I dumped him . . . told him to go back to his wife," Marge said, attempting to sound as if she'd gotten over it. "The woman is crazy about him and she's got all that money."

"Maybe he loves you and doesn't care about the money," Josie said, immediately regretting the comment.

"Then he's a fucking moron."

"What if she won't take him back?"

"She will."

"You talked to her?"

Marge nodded. "She's willing to give him up if that's what he wants. But like I told her, Red doesn't know what the fuck he wants." She closed her eyes for a second or two and said, "If he doesn't stick it out this time, he'll just keep dragging his sorry ass from one woman to another until he dies alone and broke, just another sloppy drunk in some shit-filled gutter. She's his only shot at any kind of real life."

The woman had been her friend for years, but for the first time Josie felt some genuine admiration for Marge. This had been so difficult for her, but she did what she thought was best for somebody else.

"What did you tell Red?"

"None of your goddamn business."

"You're right, I don't want to know. Is he going back to her?"

"Yeah."

"You gonna be okay?"

"Not really, but if I drink enough I'll get better."

They sat at the table in the nearly deserted bar eating greasy fried appetizers and drinking an expensive bottle of wine until Nora's closed at two A.M. Josie felt good enough to drive, but decided to spend what was left of the night on the couch in her office. Marge found an empty cot with clean sheets in the women's locker room across from the roll call room. The female officers had three cots available when they worked late and had to be in court the next morning. All of them were empty, so Marge fell onto the closest one and immediately passed out. She was snoring before Josie threw a blanket on top of her and turned off the lights. Officers working the day watch would be arriving in a few hours, but Josie doubted even noisy locker-banging could wake her.

The assistant watch commander waved at Josie as she entered her office. She waved back and asked the sergeant if he needed anything.

"Nope, we're good, Captain," he said. "Can I do anything for you?"

She shook her head and had to smile. He'd been running the graveyard watch since Lieutenant Owens retired and was doing a great job, one headache remedied.

When she closed the door, her office was cold but quiet. Josie lay on the couch and covered herself with one of the blankets she'd taken from the cot room. It reeked of bleach and Pine-Sol, but at least it was warm.

With half a bottle of wine in her, Josie should've fallen asleep immediately, but she kept thinking about Jake and how much she missed sleeping with him, not just for the sex but his closeness. She could get through the day, but the nights had become long empty hours. Unlike Marge, she'd decided giving him up wasn't an option.

After an hour of restlessness, unable to close her eyes, she made herself think about the investigation. It didn't help . . . more frustration. If Bright was involved, it became problematic finding someone to deal with in her chain of command. The only one above Bright was an assistant chief and then the chief of police. They were both political animals whose primary focus would be damage control, and she doubted the investigation would come to a conclusion she liked. She'd decided not to go to them until all the loose ends had been tied up, the case was ready to file and beyond shelving, but she needed more horsepower in dealing with Bright. The best solution was also the worst one and painfully obvious—Councilwoman Fletcher, the woman whose support Josie had effectively managed to destroy in the last few days.

HOLLYWOOD STATION was a bunker, red brick on the outside and not a single window anywhere. Knowing when it was night or day from the interior was impossible without a clock. When the electricity went out, which it did frequently, it became pitch black inside and everyone pretty much froze in place until the lights returned.

Normally, when Josie slept on her couch the noise generated by the station coming alive for the busy day watch always woke her around six or seven, but this morning it wasn't necessary. She never really slept, but managed to close her eyes long enough to convince herself she was rested. All night her agitated thoughts bounced from Jake to the homicides. She'd pondered the different scenarios of how Hillary met her demise and what had happened to Misty and always came back to the same conclusion. Misty had killed Hillary rather than pay her extortion money, and some-how the Manuci family or one of their minions found Misty and killed her.

When Josie's adjutant opened her door to bring in the mail and deposit that day's paperwork, he was surprised to see her sitting at the conference table drinking coffee. He didn't seem to notice she was wearing the same clothes she wore yesterday, or was too polite to mention it.

"I'm hoping to have this investigation wrapped up in a day or two," she said, taking the stack of papers from him. "I want you to know you've done a good job. I really appreciate it and won't forget how hard you've worked."

"Thank you, ma'am, my pleasure," he said, too confident to fake humility. "Detective Behan said as soon as you got in to tell you he has the tapes."

She dumped the pile of papers on her desk, and without an explanation hurried back to the detective squad room where she found Behan sitting at his desk staring at the computer. He appeared to be the calm, rested, well-groomed newlywed again. She suspected all was back in order on the home front. Miss Vicky must've lured him away from the whiskey bottle last night and somehow convinced him he could survive without the home wrecker, aka the beautiful Marge Bailey.

He was concentrating on the screen and didn't seem to notice her standing behind him. The DVD of Hillary's last picture was just finishing, and Behan kept repeating the scene where the sultry star was hauled off to jail by Art Perry's handsome celluloid alter ego.

"What're you looking for?" she asked, after the third replay.

"Art Perry was the one who requested the information on Misty Skylar from the D.A.'s office."

"You saw the security tapes?"

"The D.A. still had them. Perry signed Bright's name, but it's definitely him on the tape."

"I can't believe he'd be stupid enough to risk his job and maybe jail to retrieve that information for Hillary."

"Maybe he didn't. Maybe he was doing what Bright asked him to do," Behan said, finally glancing up at her.

"Is that what you think?"

Behan yawned and stretched, followed by a long contented groan. "I don't know what I think yet," he said, ejecting the disc.

"I need to sit Perry's pompous ass down and make him tell me what he was doing and why."

"Is Perry's name in her journal at all?"

"Not as far as I can tell . . . and you can stop worrying about the city attorney. Harry Walsh was working with Hillary on a stalking case a year ago and gave her his card."

"Who was the stalker?"

"Her bizarre mother, who else. After Hillary and her groupies moved out of her mother's house, the old woman showed up at her apartment building a couple a times praying out loud in the lobby for her sinful daughter. Walsh threatened to jail her for trespassing and she stopped."

"Not crazy enough to go to jail."

"Actually, Walsh told me he found out later Hillary had given her mother a check for $25,000 and he suspects that's the real reason."

"Mrs. Dennis conned money out of Peter Lange too for a promise not to sue. Blackmail gene must run in the family."

"So it seems," Behan said.

"What's your game plan?" she asked. She needed him to take control of the investigation again. Her focus now had to be convincing Fletcher to step in and control Bright, force him to talk to Behan and not hide behind his rank. Josie feared it would be tricky business manipulating those enlarged egos.

Behan hesitated, maybe expecting to be told what to do, then regrouped and said, "Perry's our first target and then Bright. If he wasn't doing Bright's bidding, he probably did it for Hillary. If he did it for her, then the question is, 'what was Hillary to him and what was his alibi the night Misty was killed.'"

"You gonna show Perry's picture to Roy Mitchell?" Josie asked, not expecting to rely too much on the smelly bum's eyewitness account.

"I'll put a six-pack together and see if I can locate Roy."

"I thought you were keeping tabs on him."

"He's not the kind of guy that keeps regular hours."

"Take your laptop and show him Perry in Hillary's movie where he's moving and talking," Josie said. Roy Mitchell had heard a voice and saw someone that night, but his whiskey-soaked brain might need visual aides.

They decided Behan would call Art Perry first and have him come to Hollywood station, telling him it was a follow-up interview, while Josie met Fletcher in her satellite office on Sunset Boulevard. At some point, Bright would have to be confronted and the chief of police told what they had, but Josie wanted Fletcher on board before any of that happened. In order to gain the councilwoman's confidence, Josie knew she'd have to tell her everything . . . almost everything.

After a shower, Josie dressed in her uniform, felt revived, and ready to face her task. She couldn't wait until this case was over. Her uniform was getting baggier every day, which meant she wasn't eating right, was drinking too much and had lost a lot of weight, which she couldn't afford to do, since she already looked like one of those runway models on a bulimic diet. Having to reason with Fletcher probably wouldn't do much for her appetite, but it had to be done.

Before Josie arrived at the councilwoman's office, Behan called on her cell phone to say he'd contacted Art Perry. Bright's adjutant agreed to another interview and was on his way to Hollywood station.

Most of the councilwoman's staff was out of the office when Josie arrived. Fletcher had a messy desk in the corner of a room that reminded Josie of her son's bedroom when he was sixteen years old . . . tacky posters, inappropriate slogans and a casual environment taken to a juvenile extreme.

"What's going on, Captain?" were Fletcher's first words. She was cold, and obviously hadn't forgiven Josie's audacity in defying her. Josie was certain she wouldn't get out of that office without at least a lecture on trust and an apology. She intended to talk fast and crush the woman with an avalanche of facts, hoping to wipe the needle exchange arrests out of her mind.

"This is gonna take a few minutes," Josie said, and began with the two homicides, going through each of the investigations including all their connections to Milano and the Manuci crime family, and finally Hillary's journal and the possible involvement of Bright, Goldman and other city councilmen.

She explained how Art Perry had accessed information in the D.A.'s witness protection program, and why Misty Skylar had most likely been killed by associates of the Manuci family after she murdered Hillary Dennis—who was probably blackmailing her. Josie couldn't prove any of it yet, but was impressed by how convincing she sounded.

"We'll offer the snitches a deal on their felony drug charges to tell us how Misty got the stolen gun that was used to kill Hillary. The real mystery still is who killed Misty for the Manucis."

"You think Art Perry did it?" Fletcher asked.

"It might make sense," Josie said. "But why would he risk his career or worse to help Hillary unless he had a serious relationship with her?" She knew there might be a second possibility that Milano had paid Perry a lot of money to dispose of Misty as a favor to the Manuci family, but there was no proof of that.

"Maybe Hillary Dennis was blackmailing him too."

"Maybe," Josie said. That was another possibility, unlikely, but a possibility. "I've got to ask a favor," she added, finally getting to her real reason for being there. Fletcher was quiet. Josie expected her to bring up the needle exchange before agreeing to anything, but maybe being overwhelmed by so much information, she didn't. Josie quickly continued, "We need to deal with Bright without interference from the chief of police."

"You can't keep the chief of police in the dark about something like this."

"Just temporarily, until we've had a chance to confront him without the command officers' association or their lawyer protecting him. If he was having sex with an underage prostitute, he shouldn't get to walk away and pretend it never happened."

"Prove your case and he won't," Fletcher said.

"I can't prove my case if he's able to hide behind rank and department protocol. He can bully me, but if you tell him you know about the journal and you're worried he's involved somehow in Hillary's murder, he might agree to talk to us and tell the truth. Tell him you'll go to the media with the whole mess if he doesn't."

"But I don't know anything . . . not for certain."

"Who cares," Josie said, raising her voice in frustration. "The whole idea is to make him think you know more than you do. He'll talk to us about sex with a minor if he thinks he's suspected of being an accomplice to murder."

"I'm not certain I can or should do this."

"You don't have to do anything. Just tell him what I said and we'll do the rest."

Another twenty minutes of reassuring Fletcher she was doing the right thing and Josie got her promise to confront Bright, pressure him to come forward and tell the truth about his relationship with Hillary.

While Josie waited, Fletcher called West bureau and was told they expected Bright back in the office later that afternoon or early the next morning. She promised Josie she'd talk to him as soon as he arrived, and if he agreed, she'd call Josie with a time and place for the interview.

"Frankly, I can't find any real victims in this mess," Fletcher said pensively, walking with Josie out to her car. "Blackmail, prostitution, organized crime . . . it's difficult to feel sorry for any of them, even the dead ones."

She'd never liked Fletcher for a lot of reasons. The councilwoman was arrogant, oppressive and lacked scruples, but this morning Josie might've discovered the true root of her aversion. The woman was a cold, hard-hearted bitch.

TWENTY-ONE

W hen Josie returned to Hollywood station, Behan told her
Art Perry hadn't arrived and couldn't be located. She
almost expected that. He had to know any decent detective, especially one as tenacious as Behan, would eventually discover his
culpability in accessing the D.A.'s file.

Perry's car was parked at his apartment, but he wasn't there.
Not a good sign, Josie thought, and dispatched a sergeant to West
bureau to retrieve Perry's personnel package from a reluctant clerk
typist. It was only when Josie called and told the clerk she'd be
booked and charged with interfering, that she agreed to let the
sergeant have it.

The contents of Perry's personnel package were strewn over
Josie's conference table, but she and Behan were unable to find
any local addresses or contacts. His only relative was a brother
in Florida.

"He only worked a couple of divisions besides the bureau,"
Josie said, when they couldn't think of any other way to find
Perry. "But his most recent field time was in Hollywood . . . pull
the time books and see who his partners were. Maybe they can
tell us something."

"Skip Wilshire," Behan said. "He was only there as a proba-
tioner. Most of his career was here and the majority of that was
in vice."

Behan made several trips to the basement and brought back
boxes full of time books. Each watch commander kept one with
car assignments and days off. Perry had been with the department

more than twenty years, including over a year in patrol at Wilshire division after the academy. He had several years in Hollywood patrol and vice, a few months back in Wilshire patrol when he got promoted to sergeant, and then he returned to Hollywood as a vice sergeant. He worked other divisions but never left Hollywood for long. The last few years he'd been in West bureau as Bright's adjutant. Fortunately, Perry seemed to favor the graveyard shift so that simplified the search of his patrol time. The old vice logs were still in her squad room so Marge volunteered to go through those.

It was a hunch, but while Josie waited for Behan and Marge to finish their tedious search, she decided to drive to Wilshire and look at the time book for Perry's probationary year. The record clerks at that division weren't as well-organized as Hollywood's so it took nearly an hour to find the right one. Once she had it, Josie only needed a few minutes to find what she was looking for. In November 1989, Wilshire had been given two probationary officers on a transfer from the police academy. They were assigned to different watches. Perry went to the busy night watch and his classmate Bruno Faldi was on the graveyard shift.

During their time at Wilshire, Perry and Faldi took the same days off, and before they wheeled out of that division as full-fledged officers, they worked in the same basic car with a senior training officer. Shortly before the end of their probationary period on several occasions, the two young officers were allowed to work together without a training officer.

When Josie called Behan to tell him what she'd found, he informed her that he and Marge had uncovered a few interesting facts, too. After probation, Perry had transferred into Hollywood, and Faldi managed to follow him a short time later. They worked the same basic car on the graveyard shift and their watch commander was none other than Lieutenant Howard Owens. He sponsored both young men to be assigned to the prostitution enforcement detail in vice and later on assisted them in returning to Hollywood vice as sergeants.

Behan saved the most interesting information until Josie got back to Hollywood.

"Tony Ibarra was their sergeant when they first went to Hollywood vice, and when they came back as sergeants, Ibarra was in charge of the unit," Marge said. She looked miserable and avoided eye contact with Behan. Apparently, the split with the big redhead hadn't been as beneficial for her as it had been for him.

"Owens neglected to reveal that bit of trivia when he was ranting on about Faldi. What patrol car did Perry and Faldi work on mornings?" Josie asked.

"A49."

"The one bordering Rampart?" Josie asked.

"Yeah, Sunset, Western, Hollywood Boulevard over to the freeway," Marge responded. "But even more fucking coincidental is that the Plaza, Milano's club before Avanti's, was smack dab in the middle of A49's area."

"I never heard of the Plaza," Josie said, certain she knew every club and restaurant in her division.

"That's 'cuz we shut it down just before you got here," Marge said. "For prostitution, drug dealing . . . all those fabulous things that keep me employed."

"So, Faldi's patrolling all night with Perry in his uncle's backyard to do what . . . keep the police away, protect Milano's business interests?"

"Probably with Lieutenant Owens' blessing," Behan mumbled. "We'll pull Owens' bank info for any large purchases or deposits during that time and see what we can come up with, same for Ibarra. You know Owens wouldn't do it unless he was well-paid."

"When I took over the OIC spot in vice, I made Perry and Faldi find new jobs so I could bring in my own sergeants," Marge said. "A few weeks later, Faldi quits the department and Perry gets a job in the bureau," Marge said.

Nobody spoke for several minutes. Josie figured they were all thinking the same thing. Organized crime had weaseled its way into Hollywood. Milano most likely paid off Owens and Ibarra, and had Faldi and Perry on the payroll doing his bidding. His businesses could run amok all night with no police interference. Milano probably tempted guys like Goldman and Bright with huge donations and pretty underage girls, then threatened to expose them if they interfered in his enterprises.

Owens had procured lucrative movie and security jobs for his officers, assuring they'd protect him or look the other way while he operated his business on-duty. In return, Owens allowed them to do whatever they wanted and didn't hold them accountable . . . the perfect formula for police corruption. No wonder he hated me, Josie thought. During her first few months in Hollywood, she'd watched and hounded him, made him answer for his shortcomings, and interfered with his business.

"With Perry sitting in Bright's office, Milano had firsthand knowledge of practically everything that happened in West bureau, including every vice task force," Behan said.

"Anyone who was here during Owens' or Ibarra's tenure has got to be scrutinized," Josie said to no one in particular. She was making a mental checklist—off-hour and field inspections, mandatory watch rotations and much more. She knew what needed to be done to prevent corruption, but also was well aware that some serious damage had already happened.

"That's great boss," Behan said. "But for the moment, we've gotta track down Perry before Milano realizes how big a liability he is and makes him disappear forever. I don't think a guy like Milano's gonna risk Perry making a deal with us to save his own skin."

"Call the Wilshire captain," Josie said. "If Ibarra's there, have the C.O. sit on the little turd till we get there."

"Little turd?" Marge asked, grinning.

"Just do it."

———

IN AN attempt to find Perry, Behan dispatched homicide detectives to all his known hangouts, but every lead drew a blank. He understood the criminal mind better than most cops, and knew Perry had smelled danger when he was asked to show up for a second interview and was probably hiding, planning his defense or escape. At the moment, the only provable crime was accessing the D.A. file, but Josie believed he might've been involved in Misty's murder or knew something about it and that's why he'd disappeared.

"I've got a car out looking for Roy Mitchell," Behan told her when they were driving back to Wilshire. "Marge has her people searching too. If she locates him, she'll babysit till we get back."

"If he's not belly-up in a dumpster somewhere," Josie said. She knew Mitchell might be helpful, but wasn't counting on the smelly bum being found alive for a lot of reasons—his whiskey-bloated liver was probably as yellow as ripe corn and the size of a bull elephant's, and Behan had slipped him just enough cash to make him an attractive target for every scumbag on the boulevard.

"Roy's a survivor."

Josie let it pass.

———

THE WILSHIRE captain had Ibarra waiting in his office when Josie and Behan got there. The nervous lieutenant was gaunt and looked wasted.

"Good to see you, boss," Ibarra said, jumping up and offering a slightly trembling hand. Josie ignored the gesture. He glanced at Behan, then turned and watched as the Wilshire captain left the room and closed the door. "What's this about?" he said, making a pitiful attempt at bravado.

"Sit down, Tony," Behan ordered, pointing at the chair Ibarra had just vacated. She sat beside him and Behan leaned against the captain's desk.

"We know you've been working with Milano," Josie said, hoping to catch him off-guard, but expecting outrage and denial. Instead, Ibarra covered his face with both hands for a moment, and then slumped back and sighed.

"You're not going to believe me," he said, softly. "But it's such a relief to finally have this out in the open."

Cops make such lousy criminals, Josie thought. They can't help themselves. They usually have an overdeveloped conscience and can't wait to confess.

"Start at the beginning. How did you get hooked?" Behan said and looked away, giving Josie a quick wink.

"I didn't know what was going on for a long time. They fooled me into thinking they were hard-charging ass-kickers. I should've never listened to Owens."

"Who're we talking about?" Josie asked.

"Art Perry and Bruno Faldi. . . . After a while they'd tell me stuff they did on duty. It was such petty shit I never really thought much about it. I know now they were testing me. One night . . ." Ibarra's voice drifted off. He didn't want to talk about this but seemed determined to do it anyway. "We busted a massage parlor. They got me to go with them . . . one thing led to another. It went too far. I got a hand job from one of the girls and from then on they had me."

"So you looked the other way while they did what?" Behan asked.

"I didn't ask questions but they were at Milano's beck 'n' call every night. What else could I do? If I turned them in, they had pictures, dates, times. I'd be ruined, maybe go to jail."

"You did the massage thing more than once?" Josie asked. Ibarra didn't answer so she knew he had.

"I wasn't helping them; I just didn't interfere."

"With what? Don't give me that I don't know bullshit. You knew what they were doing."

"Prostitution, drugs, gambling, the Plaza was a full-service, one-stop shop. Milano bribed the right people to get them to look the other way . . . tricked the stupid ones like me."

"What about Chief Bright?" Josie asked.

Ibarra hesitated, but then shrugged and said, "He was hooked after he got involved with that Dennis girl. I figured it was Vince Milano that forced him to take Perry as his adjutant. Vince was always bragging how great it was having his nephew's buddy in the bureau."

"So when Bright told us about Goldman dating Hillary, it was just to keep us from looking at him," she said, and quickly added, "Who killed Hillary?"

"Don't know, but I'm guessing Misty, otherwise why'd they kill her?"

"Who're they?"

"I don't know."

"Guess," Behan insisted.

"Maybe Perry, he was crazy about Hillary. I think he could've done it and Bruno's just crazy. He'd do it for fun if Perry or Milano asked him."

"You tamper with either of those homicide scenes?" Behan asked.

"No, I swear to God I didn't . . . but at the Goldman kid's . . . Milano told me to look for a book, belonged to the Dennis girl. I didn't find it but I looked."

"Why'd Milano want it?" Behan asked.

"You kidding? It's worth a fortune in the right hands—names, dates, places of guys she'd been fucking."

"You willing to testify? Can't save your job, but maybe it'll keep you out of jail."

"Why not. I'm tired of lying."

"Where's Perry?"

Ibarra shook his head. He looked confused. "What do you mean?"

"He's disappeared. Where would he go if he didn't want to be found?"

"Probably be with Faldi."

"What if he didn't want Milano to find him either?" Josie asked.

Ibarra wasn't the cleverest cop, but even he figured out why Art Perry might have more to fear from the crime boss than the police.

"They'll kill him if they think he might make a deal," Ibarra said. "He knows too much."

"So, where would he hide?" she repeated.

"The only place I can think of is his older brother. He just moved out here from Florida. They aren't close, but Perry doesn't trust anybody else. I doubt Faldi even knows Perry's got a brother."

Behan got the brother's name and found his address in the San Gabriel Valley. He lived in the mountainous city of Monrovia about thirty minutes from downtown L.A. Behan tried calling but kept getting a busy signal.

A team of Behan's homicide detectives met them at Wilshire and they drove Ibarra back to Hollywood to take his formal statement. Josie called Deputy City Attorney Harry Walsh and he agreed to assist the detectives with the paperwork.

"We could call the locals, have them check the brother's house," Josie said, knowing what Behan's response would be, but dreading the rush-hour crawl on the 10 freeway, one of L.A.'s busiest highways.

"Don't think so," Behan said, getting into the driver's seat.

She didn't argue, but her instincts told her this was a waste of time. So, they'd sit in traffic for an hour just to find an empty house, or wait for the brother to get home and he'd tell them he hadn't seen Perry for a year or something like that. It was the only lead they had, but it wasn't a very promising one.

MONROVIA WAS one of those quiet little cities tucked away in the San Gabriel Mountains where bears and coyotes rummaged in garbage cans and backyards looking for snacks or edible pets.

They located the address on a cul-de-sac in a newer development with odd-looking cookie-cutter townhomes. Several cars were parked on the street but none in his driveway, and the garage door was closed and locked. Mature maple trees along the sidewalks had lifted up the cement, and walkways were covered with a thick rug of orange, red and brown leaves. The neighborhood was quiet, no signs of life—not even a barking dog.

Before knocking on the front door, Josie told Behan to go around back in case Perry was actually inside and decided to escape again. When she calculated he'd had enough time to get to the other side of the house, she rang the doorbell. She could hear the chimes inside but no one answered. She knocked, still no response. The drapes were closed, but she peeked through a narrow slit where the curtains came together. It was too dark to see anything inside.

Convinced the place was unoccupied, she'd turned to leave when the front door opened. She instinctively stepped to the side and put her hand on her weapon.

"Don't shoot. It's me," Behan said, peering around the door frame. "The back door was open."

"Say something next time," she said. "Anybody here?"

"Don't think so."

They methodically checked the bottom floor, identifying themselves before they entered each room, and then repeated the exercise on the second floor. Nobody was home. Behan tried the kitchen door leading to the attached garage and found it unlocked. He saw two cars parked inside, a white Cadillac with Florida license plates and the silver Lexus they'd seen parked at Carlton Buck's office building. They still didn't know who was driving the Lexus but Josie hoped it was Art Perry.

There was only one other place to search in the house—the basement.

"Maybe they left in another car," Behan said, as they stood near the basement door.

"Good theory, but the back door being open and that Lexus are a bit problematic," Josie said, unholstering her handgun and opening the basement door. She peeked around the door frame, but couldn't see much beyond the first few steps that led down into the darkness. The light switch was on Behan's side, so keeping as close as he could to the wall, he reached around to flip it on.

The basement was instantly flooded in a dim hazy light. Josie could see most of the spacious unfinished room, except for the far wall and some of the area to her left. She counted a dozen steps down to the floor.

"Police!" Behan shouted down the stairs, startling her. "If anyone's in the basement, come to the foot of the stairs."

"Warn me when you're gonna do that," she said, rubbing her ear.

They waited a few seconds but there was no response. She motioned to get Behan's attention and whispered, "I'll jump, give you cover." She knew she could use the retaining wall for protection down to the fourth or fifth step, and leap from there behind an alcove used to hide the washer and dryer.

"No, I'll do it," Behan said too loud.

Josie shook her head, and tapped on her chest with the knuckles of her left hand hitting the steel plate in the protective vest she wore under her uniform.

"You wearing one?" she asked.

"I don't need one," he argued.

She positioned herself to jump, but Behan grabbed her arm and said, "Wait, let me try something first." He unplugged the toaster on the counter, wrapped the cord around it and tossed it down the stairs. It crashed into the washing machine, but if anyone was down there they didn't react. He shrugged at the silence, but then Josie heard something, low and muffled but definitely a groan. She holstered her weapon again and leapt without thinking. She reached the fifth step perfectly, barely touching it before jumping to the floor of the cellar, tucking in and rolling behind the wall of the alcove where she crashed into the washing machine and banged her head on the toaster.

A gunshot hit the wall in front of the alcove and another ricocheted off the cement at the foot of the stairs. Her right uniform sleeve was torn and she rubbed her sore bruised elbow before laying flat on her stomach and taking a quick look around the wall. A man's body was lying motionless on the floor against the east wall and Art Perry was hog-tied on the floor beside it. He had duct tape across his mouth and was dirty, bloodied, and bruised but still moving. The gunshots had made a deafening noise in the small basement and her ears wouldn't stop ringing. Even worse, she couldn't pinpoint the shooter's hiding place from her location.

"Anytime, Corsino," Behan said with a whisper loud enough to be heard across the room. There were building materials, mostly wood and drywall, stored all around her. She fired two rounds in the direction of the biggest stack sitting in front of the area she couldn't see.

As soon as the shooting began, Behan attempted to mimic her jump, but stumbled like a big Howdy Doody crash dummy down the stairs and landed sitting up beside her. Another round from the other side of the basement hit the floor in front of the stairs showering them with tiny pieces of concrete.

"Now what?" she said, brushing the white dust off the front of her uniform.

"Are they alive?" Behan asked, cocking his head toward the two bodies lying near the east wall.

"I saw Perry moving, but I'm not sure about his brother, if that's the other guy."

"I called 911 after the first shots. We'll just sit tight and wait till the cavalry gets here," he said as Josie immediately started crawling on her belly toward the other end of the alcove. "What're you doing?" he asked in a strained whisper.

"Not waiting," she whispered, determined not to let some other agency rescue them and clean up their mess.

"Fucking dope cop mentality," he mumbled. "You're dangerous."

Josie didn't respond or turn around because she knew he'd be there beside her when she reached the other end, and he was. They sat with their backs to the wall as Josie looked up at a single bulb—the only source of light in the basement. She pointed at the fixture, then at Behan's gun and covered her ears. He nodded, and with another eardrum-shattering explosion shot the bulb, causing the room to go completely black. As they sat there waiting for their eyes to adjust to the darkness, Josie heard sirens wailing in the distance but getting closer.

"He's in the loft!" Art Perry's panicked shout broke the silence.

Instinctively, Josie rolled away from the wall toward the middle of the room and behind the stack of wood and drywall, pointed her .45 and flashlight toward the back of the basement near the ceiling, and for an instant in the beam caught a massive crouching figure in the makeshift loft pointing a gun in her direction. She fired twice or maybe more. She couldn't remember, but saw the muzzle flashes to her right and knew Behan was shooting as well.

A heavy object hit the ground with a sickening thud and groan. Moving several feet to her left, she turned on the flashlight again and saw Faldi lying motionless on the concrete floor. His gun had landed several feet from his hand, but Josie kicked it away and leaned over him checking for other weapons while Behan handcuffed the lifeless body. She holstered her weapon and only then did that familiar jolt of adrenaline hit her. A sudden burst of nervous energy, held in check by years of discipline, training and muscle memory, washed over her like an emotional tsunami as soon as the danger passed. She'd been in shootings before and remembered that strange sensation, as satisfying as any orgasm for adrenaline junkies.

It was as if her body had switched onto autopilot and time slowed down for those few intense seconds. She didn't hear the gunfire and couldn't tell you how many times she'd fired her weapon, but standing over the remains of Bruno Faldi, she was grateful she still practiced.

In a nearby cabinet, Behan found a battery-powered light mixed in with some stored camping gear so they were able to restore minimal light. He quickly checked the condition of the Perry brothers before examining her arm.

"I don't think it's broken," he said, bending her elbow. "We're a pretty good team. Don't you think?"

She noticed his hand shaking a little and said, "Yes I do, partner, but you jump like an old lady."

"Better code four this before the locals come in with guns blazing," Behan said, as the sirens stopped somewhere close by.

Josie intercepted the small army of officers as soon as she reached the top of the stairs, and returned a few minutes later leading a boyish-looking lieutenant and a couple of his officers.

"Ambulance is on the way," Josie said, standing over Art Perry who was untied but handcuffed now, and still had a piece of the duct tape stuck to one side of his face. His other cheek was scratched raw where he had rubbed it against the concrete floor to peel off the tape and warn them. She pulled off the rest of it. If it hurt, he didn't react. "Better?" she asked and he nodded.

His brother was lying beside him, still unconscious but breathing.

Behan was standing where she'd left him, near Faldi's body.

"Dead?" she asked.

"Very."

"What sort of operation did you people have here, ma'am?" the Monrovia lieutenant asked, looking around the basement. "And why weren't we notified?"

Josie explained they had intended to talk to Perry's brother, and how she and Behan stumbled into what looked like the attempted murder of the brothers, so naturally they were obligated to act.

"Seems to me you had time to get our help and maybe could've avoided killing this man," the lieutenant said. He might've caught Josie's disgusted expression because he added quickly, "but I guess that was your call."

All the notifications were made. Perry's brother was taken to the nearest emergency hospital but never regained consciousness. Bruno Faldi was dead as soon as he hit the basement floor. LAPD's shooting team took several hours to complete their on-site investigation and take Josie's and Behan's statements.

The shooting team determined Behan and Josie had each fired four rounds. One of Behan's rounds killed the light; two of Josie's were cover for Behan. Faldi was hit three times, but they didn't know as yet which of those did the deadly damage.

Josie was exhausted, but spent a couple of hours with the chief of police going over the chain of events that led to the shooting.

He had responded to the scene at her request, and initially wasn't happy about one of his captains putting herself in the middle of an investigation. But eventually, he had to admit the circumstances with Bright, Perry and so many other police officers being involved made it an unusual case. He agreed to allow her to continue handling the investigation, and any resources she needed. Josie suspected Fletcher might've had a hand in triggering the chief's support. She wanted to confront Bright immediately but wasn't going to get that satisfaction. She was told he had retired earlier that day.

When Behan finally got around to interviewing him, Art Perry made it clear he didn't take kindly to Milano's attempt to permanently eliminate him as a potential witness. He was especially unhappy that Milano's hitman Faldi had wiped out the only other member of his immediate family. So he willingly became a one-man flowchart, tying up loose ends on how Milano's operation worked from inside and outside the police department.

He confirmed Ibarra's story that Milano had ordered him and Faldi to compromise Ibarra, Owens and Bright to gain their cooperation and protection for his businesses. Faldi joined the police department at his uncle's direction for the sole purpose of helping the family, and he recruited Perry before they had graduated from the police academy.

Perry claimed he didn't feel any remorse for helping Faldi, but felt betrayed; he never would've talked about any of this if they hadn't tried to kill him. He bragged he'd made more money by looking the other way than he ever did as a cop.

"Who tried to kill me?" Josie asked.

"Run ballistics on that Glock semi-auto Bruno carried," Perry said.

"There's no way he could've known I was gonna be at the Dennis house that night, and why would he wanna shoot me anyway?"

"Milano told him to stake out the house on the outside chance Mouse might show again. Everybody figured she had Hillary's book. He sees you leaving and decides to kill you."

"Why?"

"He didn't like you," Perry said with a smirk. "I don't like you either."

"You know anything about Milano's connection to the Manuci family?" Behan asked before Josie had an opportunity to respond. She was grateful. It was the perfect opportunity to say something stupid, and she probably shouldn't get into a pissing contest with their most important witness.

"Yeah, that's why Faldi killed Misty. When I found out who she really was and why she was in witness protection, I told Milano and he told Manuci. Manuci says kill her because he's got no use for her."

"So you and Faldi escort her out the back door of that bar and blow her brains all over the alley," Josie said.

"Hell no, I told them I wouldn't have nothing to do with murder."

"You didn't try to stop it or warn her either."

"Why should I? I hated her guts. I knew she killed Hillary."

"Why? Because you and Hillary were blackmailing her? My guess is Misty agreed to pay you, then found out you lied to her and had already given her up to the Manucis."

"If that's true, why would Hillary go to that party expecting a big payoff and instead get her head blown off?" Perry asked, rubbing the bruise on his face before adding, "I'm not sorry Misty's dead."

At least now I know why Hillary died with a smile, Josie thought. She'd expected an envelope full of cash, not a 9-mm round through her head.

"Faldi didn't kill Misty by himself. He had an accomplice and you're looking like the best candidate for suspect number two," Behan said.

"I'm not saying Milano didn't try to get me to do it," Perry said. "That lawyer Lange had me at his house every night, told me Mouse gave Misty the gun that killed Hillary. They were hoping I'd do the Manuci family's dirty work for them; but like I told you,

I wanted Misty dead and she deserved to die, but I didn't have anything to do with it."

———

THE INTERVIEW was interrupted when Marge finally located Roy Mitchell living in a homeless shelter in downtown Los Angeles. He was broke, filthy and drunk, but after a bath and a few gallons of coffee, the bum easily identified Perry—or "Pretty Boy" as Roy referred to him—as the second man with Misty in the alley the night she was killed. Roy pointed at a picture of Bruno Faldi as the person who shot Misty, and then kicked and beat him as he lay helpless on the ground.

When Perry's interview resumed and Behan had pried all the lies and the little bit of truth he thought he could get out of him, Behan told him he was being booked as an accomplice to murder; but neither he nor Josie was surprised that Perry didn't look too worried. They had worked major cases before and knew as well as Perry did that he was a valuable witness who could easily negotiate a deal with the feds for his testimony against the crime families—and that would keep him out of jail. He'd walk away disgraced but still entitled to his police pension and lucrative benefits.

The same would be true for Bright, Ibarra, and Owens. Even if they went to jail, they did so with their considerable police pensions intact, which led Marge to complain there should be a way to wipe away all that guaranteed income.

"Not gonna happen," Behan said, in the early morning hours as they sat winding down with Josie in her office.

"They're no better than the fucking assholes. They don't deserve to get a penny of our pension money . . . city of the angels, what a fucking joke."

"Fallen angels might get to keep their wings, but they don't get a CCW," Behan said, yawning. They all knew carrying a concealed weapon was a valuable privilege given to cops who retired honorably, a privilege Perry and his buddies had forfeited. Not only their law enforcement careers and reputations, but any lucrative private security jobs were gone forever.

They all agreed that price wasn't anywhere near high enough.

TWENTY-TWO

It was late morning when the investigation reached a point where Josie felt comfortable taking a break and was thinking about getting some sleep. Harry Walsh was assisting Behan's detectives take statements and Mouse had finally signed a confession stating that Misty bought the stolen gun used to kill Hillary. Behan had attempted to contact Peter Lange, but was told by his staff the attorney had returned to New York on business and wasn't expected back anytime soon. The high-priced mob lawyer wasn't going to hang around and get tainted by his clients' business.

Harry and Behan agreed they would sit down with Perry in the next day or two and decipher Hillary's journal, making up their minds at that time if any arrest warrants could or would be issued. The one thing Josie knew for certain was that Perry, Bright, and Ibarra wouldn't be wearing LAPD uniforms again. They had resigned. It would take a week or more to do a thorough background check on every officer in her division. Anybody who'd been there too long—especially on the graveyard shift—would be fair game.

Josie was dead tired, but sleeping on her favorite couch wasn't an option. The captain's office this morning was union station minus the trains. The chief of police's office kept calling with stupid questions. The department psychiatrist insisted Josie and Behan make appointments with him to discuss the Faldi shooting so he could be certain they hadn't been psychologically damaged.

"Shooting assholes is liberating," Josie insisted, after hanging up on the doctor's second call. "Besides, you probably killed him. You're a better shot than me," she said to Behan.

"Doesn't matter, we both have to go," Behan said. "Even though you're right, I am a better shot."

"Who jumps down stairs like Raggedy Ann," she whispered to Marge.

Sometime between interviews and phone calls, Josie found a few minutes to change out of her uniform and back into comfortable civilian clothes. Now, as she watched Marge and Harry organizing the reports that covered her conference table, her eyelids felt like lead. She dug her car keys out of her jeans' pocket and slipped on a jacket.

"I'm going home to sleep. Call me at noon. If anything comes up before that, you don't know where I am."

JOSIE MANAGED to get out the back door of the station and was halfway to her car without anyone stopping her. She was contemplating the soothing comfort of her soft down pillow when Councilwoman Fletcher's black SUV drove into the parking lot and stopped by her open car door.

The heavyset woman occupied nearly the entire backseat—her young assistant was driving.

"Captain Corsino, may I speak with you a moment?" she asked in a way that wasn't really a question.

Josie slammed her car door and said under her breath, "Inches from a clean escape."

The SUV's back passenger window was open but Fletcher didn't make an effort to move her massive frame. Josie walked over to the councilwoman's car and stood by the window.

"You've had quite a night," Fletcher said. "I hope my calls to Chief Bright and the chief of police were helpful."

"What can I do for you?" Josie asked, too tired to care how ungrateful that sounded.

"I understand there might be some openings on the council in a few days as well."

Josie folded her arms and didn't speak. She'd already given the woman too much information. She was grateful for Fletcher's help but didn't feel obligated to give her more.

"All right, but if what I heard is true, I wanted to thank you."

"You're welcome," Josie said. Goldman's career was history and the whole world would know about his fate in a few hours, so Josie didn't feel bound by confidentiality.

Fletcher smiled. "I feel very sorry about what happened to Eli's son, but the father's an arrogant jackass and I'm glad he's gone." She tapped the young aide on the shoulder and the SUV started to slowly pull away, but before the window closed, Fletcher leaned over and said, "Drive down Santa Monica on your way home. I pay my debts."

What the hell does that mean, Josie wondered, but was too exhausted to try and figure it out. She was curious though and drove toward the freeway on Santa Monica Boulevard. When she reached Western the mystery was solved. The RV used for the needle exchange program was gone. The lot was empty again. To show her appreciation for eliminating her rival, the councilwoman had the RV removed—quid pro quo, L.A. style. Josie had never intended to get Goldman for Fletcher's benefit or amusement. She went after him because he'd broken the law. Josie also knew the councilwoman's gratitude was superficial and temporary. She was destined to bump heads with Fletcher as long as she commanded Hollywood station because politics and nothing else would always be Susan Fletcher's driving force.

A few of the addicts were still hanging around the lot, and Josie saw a lone uniformed officer talking to two of them as she passed it. A couple more sleazy-looking men were standing close by. She drove around the block, planning to back him up just in case he needed assistance. As she parked her car, she noticed he had a sergeant's rocker on his sleeve. She left her jacket in the car so the badge on her belt could be seen. He turned and nodded to let Josie know he saw her.

"Morning, Captain," Sergeant Richards said, facing his suspect again.

"Poaching in my orchard again?" Josie said, surprised at how pleased she was to see him.

"Not really," he said, finishing his field interview and warning the men they couldn't loiter in the empty lot. "I'm a legal resident of your division as of this morning."

It was a new deployment period and Sergeant Richards explained he had transferred into Hollywood.

"That's great," Josie said and meant it.

"You look really tired, but those cuts have healed nicely," he said, getting close enough for her to smell his aftershave and added with that broad, handsome smile, "I can't even see them. Is anybody waiting for you to get home or can I buy you breakfast?"

———

JOSIE HESITATED; home was pretty deserted and lonely these days. She was hungry for more than food and would've enjoyed his company, but she said, "I'm too tired to eat. Maybe, we can do it another time."

He looked disappointed as they chatted a few more minutes before he left to answer a radio call.

She watched him drive away and wondered what made her say no to a whole new world of possibilities. As far as she could tell he was a good person, dedicated, forthright, brave . . . everything she admired in a man.

Thoughts of her family drifting aimlessly away from a life none of them seemed to want any longer were always on her mind, but Josie had a twenty-year commitment to two people she loved and wasn't willing to abandon. Lately, David had been a pain in the ass and Jake kept finding new ways to make her crazy, but there was no denying they were irretrievably connected.

———

SHE DROVE onto her street and pulled to the curb in front of the house. She sat in the car with the engine running and couldn't help smiling. The Porsche, covered in dew, was parked in the driveway.